LOUD MUSIC

R J Coons

To Janet,
Sending some
Florida Sunshine.
Enjoy the Adventure! ☺
RJ Coons

12/14/13

ISBN 1492961205
ISBN 9781492961208

To Diane who never stopped believing.

Acknowledgements

I would like to express my appreciation to all the people who helped in the research and structure of this novel. I am deeply grateful for the police, fire, and park personnel for their insight and first-hand knowledge they brought to the story. A special thanks to Ray Harris and Theresa Foley for their computer and editing support. Most of all, to my wife, Diane, for her unqualified support and inspiration throughout the entire process.

Prologue

Hurricane Floyd exploded out of the Caribbean as a Category 4 on September the 13th, with gale force winds reaching 156 miles per hour—Floyd was a monster. Headed for the Florida coast, catastrophic damage was predicted, but Floyd veered east and barreled north along the coast gaining speed and intensity. On September 16, at two-thirty in the morning, Floyd roared ashore in North Carolina. With winds in excess of 104 mph and storm surges as high as ten feet, Floyd pounded North Carolina mercilessly. Communities in the grasp of the storm's rage were completely leveled. Two days of drenching rains flooded every river, lake and stream in the area; roads and bridges washed out, placing numerous North Carolina communities underwater and abandoned for weeks.

Floyd continued its path of destruction, barreled up the East Coast, and was predicted to slam into Long Island and batter the barrier island with 96 mph winds by nightfall.

The call from the mainland reached Park Ranger Blaine at eight o'clock in the morning instructing her to begin evacuation of Watch Hill, Fire Island; she immediately put in place the park service EEP system, the Emergency Evacuation Protocol. The National Weather Service forecasted Floyd to hit Fire Island that evening and as a precautionary measure, district office ordered all campers, boaters and day-trippers to vacate the island by five o'clock. Directed to remain on the island, Blaine was to close Watch Hill immediately and turn away all new visitors.

Blaine started work at Watch Hill, Fire Island in August after graduating from Hofstra University in June with a degree in marine biology and a minor in criminal justice. She had always wanted to work in a field that championed the environment—being a park ranger or marine biologist were her two top choices. After years of community service in high school and college with the Parks Department and numerous environmental organizations and graduating first in her class at the Ranger Academy, Blaine received her first assignment as a park ranger at Watch Hill, Fire Island.

Watch Hill, a small park compared to the other parks along the barrier island, lacked the restaurants, large marina, bars and nightlife many visitors desired. With only a tiny general store, small marina, one campground for tents only, a picnic area, a pristine white sandy beach and only a twenty-minute ferry ride across the Great South Bay, Watch Hill was Fire Island's best-kept secret and a park ranger's dream job.

By four o'clock in the afternoon, only two sailboats, looking for refuge from the storm motored into the marina only to be turned away. All the other boats had left, every campsite had packed up, and all the day-trippers had loaded on to the last ferry for the ride back to Long Island. Blaine stood on the dock, waved good-bye, and watched the ferry pull out into the channel and power up for the trip back to the mainland. Confident the park was empty, Blaine took a deep breath and for the first time looked up at the ominous gray clouds that all day raced along the horizon. Stalled over Fire Island, the gathering dark clouds blotted out the sun pushing the temperature down by the hour. There was dampness in the air, a foreboding chill that signaled a change was on its way. That change was not just meteorological, but a change so traumatic it would haunt Blaine for the rest of her life.

The park was not empty; not everyone had evacuated. Matt Purdy, a day-tripper, fell asleep drunk on the beach five miles east of Watch Hill. Purdy arrived on the 8:20 A.M. ferry from Patchogue and after buying a pack of cigarettes, a large cup of coffee, a bottle of aspirin, and a box of Entenmann's chocolate donuts at the general store, he headed down to the beach to continue his drunk fest. After a night of heavy drinking to drown the humiliation that his girlfriend of four years dumped him for some computer geek two days before the Suffolk Community College Homecoming weekend, he was pissed. Too drunk to drive home, he slept in his car parked across from the ferry depot. Still hung-over, the plan was…he had no plan, but maybe a relaxing ferry ride would help cheer him up, if not the fifth of Jack Daniels in his back pack, would help numb the pain or at least help get rid of his splitting headache.

Staggering down the stairs to the beach, Purdy's spirits immediately perked up at the sight that unfolded before him. The long expanse of pure white sand reaching down to the water was exhilarating. Tiny ripples from the clear blue water gently lapped against the shoreline as the frothy sea bubbles that marked the water's edge floated down the beach with the current. The sun poked through the white billowy clouds warming the morning as gulls flew over the beach looking for breakfast. *What a glorious day*, he thought as he trudged down the beach. Off in the distance, along the horizon, dark clouds gathered.

Exhausted, Purdy collapsed against the base of a sand dune, popped three aspirin along with a swig of Jack Daniels and looked out across the water. *Maybe, he shouldn't have hit her,* he thought. He took another swig. *Four fucking years and she dumped me.* Another quick swig. *Bitch.* A long slow drink. Purdy leaned back against the warm, dry sand, closed his eyes and fell asleep.

Hurricane Floyd slammed into Fire Island at around eight o'clock that evening. Heavy rain and punishing winds battered the Barrier Islands and Long Island relentlessly. Exhausted and without power, Blaine crawled into bed with the sound of howling wind outside her window and the rhythmic beats of the rain pounding on the tin roof. A flash of light poured into the room, off in the distance the crack of thunder sounded; she counted one, two, the storm was close. Then sleep.

Purdy woke in a panic—it was dark, rain poured down in buckets, blistering winds kicked up sand and pieces of shell bit into his body with needle-like precision, making it painful to walk and almost impossible to see. Dark, angry waves crashed onto the beach clawing away at the sand that was once an endless expanse of white powder. He was still drunk, but instinct warned him to get off the beach before the waves dragged him to the deeps. Confused and frightened, he picked up his backpack and trudged back to the park. Somehow, he managed to push through the storm, drag himself up the steps at Watch Hill and stagger to the first cottage off the boardwalk. He took his hunting knife out of the backpack and pried open the door. "Shelter at last," he groaned and walked in.

A deafening thunderclap pierced the room and shook Blaine from an uneasy sleep as a jagged flash of light raced across the ceiling. In the glow of the lightning strike, loomed the shadow of a man dripping wet holding a large silver knife.

"Do what I say and maybe you'll live...take off your clothes," Purdy growled over the thunder and wagged the knife in Blaine's face. He climbed on top of her and pushed her legs apart. All she could feel was the cold steel blade pressing against the side of her neck while the rest of her body lay numb from his assault. Only after he had finished and collapsed onto her chest did she recoil in disgust.

Time was impossible to measure in the dark, minutes and hours melted together, but sometime during the night Purdy let go of the knife and shifted most of his weight off Blaine and onto the bed. Blaine lay motionless, barely breathing as she listened to him snore. Slowly she reached over with her right hand, grabbed the knife and painstakingly brought it down to her side. Slowly, she slid her left arm free, then left leg and finally she arched her hip and carefully pulled herself free from underneath his hulk.

It was daybreak when Blaine finally stood at the side of the bed with the knife in her hand. Matt Purdy laid spread-eagle, legs and hands tied to the bedposts, and a washcloth stuffed in his mouth muffled his screams. His face, wrinkled in fear, foretold of what was to come as she brought the blade down against his skin and whispered, "I want you to understand; no one takes advantage of me!"

Chapter One

Blaine Sterling picked up the newspaper from her driveway just as she did every morning before she went to work at the Osprey State Park as a park ranger, a job she held for the past seven years. Blaine enjoyed reading the paper before work; actually, she loved reading the comics. That was the first thing she turned to. It gave her solace that the world was not going crazy, or at least she wasn't. Blaine didn't read all the comics, only her favorites: Pickles, Zits, Cathy, Baby Blues, and of course, Doonesbury. It was an addiction; she had to know what the next episode held for each character, you could say she was a comic strip junkie. Oftentimes she would toss and turn all night long trying to imagine what the next day's comic strip would detail. Jotting down ideas on a small note pad she kept on her nightstand next to the bed, Blaine feverishly scribbled words and ideas in the dark. She could not get the comics out of her head and repeatedly pictured each scene unfold until she was too tired to think or write any longer. Drained, she closed her eyes and slept.

Each morning, Blaine woke anticipating seeing her ideas in print; she grabbed her notepad and walked outside to collect the paper. Sadly, none of her ideas or drawings was there, each comic strip took on a different direction; but for Blaine, that was okay. The fun was in the challenge to create, *not everyone can be a Charles Schultz, and maybe one day my ideas will be in the newspaper*, she mused and tucked her ideas into a red binder she kept under the bed for safekeeping.

Thursday, the newspaper wasn't delivered. Scheduled to work the late shift at the park, Blaine sent Brooke off to school and went back to bed. It was well after nine-thirty in the morning when she realized her paper wasn't in the driveway. Checking the bushes, trees, and neighbors' lawns, Blaine came to the realization that no one had stolen her paper—it wasn't delivered and if she didn't act quickly she wouldn't be reading the comics. What an ordeal! First, Blaine had to call the Venice Journal Star's circulation desk; but before she could do that, she had to find the number. Of course the day before was Wednesday, recycling and garbage pick-up day, so there was no newspaper at the house to check for a phone number. Looking in the white pages under Venice or Journal Star was a big waste of time. Finally, the Yellow pages under newspaper had it. However, in this age of telecommunications, you never speak to a real person, just a recording asking for everything from your telephone number to your maiden name. The final part of the message left the caller totally confused, *'Maybe you will get the paper delivered in an hour or maybe not...depending on the situation,'* whatever that meant. In addition, if the call didn't reach the paper before ten o'clock, delivery would be the next day; bottom line—no paper before work! That meant she would have to ask her neighbor Lou Bravo for his paper.

Lou Bravo always got his paper. In fact, Lou Bravo was always getting deliveries. Fed Ex, UPS, postal service, unmarked trucks, vans, and cars dropped packages off all hours of the day or night. Neighbors joked that they could set their watches by Lou Bravo's delivery trucks. He was sure to have a paper.

"Good morning Blaine, today is your lucky day! Today everyone on Serpentine Lane is getting a free mattress; compliments of yours truly," Lou Bravo announced through the screen door as a big white truck pulled in front of her driveway. "Sadly, a business associate of mine fell into an unfortunate financial situation and had to suddenly liquidate some of his assets. So, like the Robin Hood of Sherwood Forest, you can call me Robin of Venice, I'm giving away free Sealy Posturepedic mattresses to the neighbors. How many do you want?"

"Robin of Venice that's a good one Lou Bravo, where did you say the mattresses came from? For some strange reason I don't see the name of a store or a mattress company, just the words, *Clean Sweep* on a dirty white truck." Blaine remarked with a skeptical glance towards the back of the truck where two men were unloading a mattress.

"Oh that's my friend Tony Lilly's truck; he has a cleaning business and drove to Sarasota to pick up the merchandise. That's Tony back there, the old guy; the young guy is his helper Hubba Bubba. Where should they put your mattress?"

"Thanks for the offer Robin of Venice, but I don't need a new mattress right now; what I do need is today's newspaper, mine wasn't delivered," Blaine said noticing a folded paper on the dashboard of the truck.

"Okay Blaine, it's your loss, someone else will now get two. Guys put the mattress back; the little lady isn't interested in the merchandise." The three men got back into the truck, Lou Bravo handed Blaine the paper, smiled and drove to the next house.

Chapter Two

Blaine could not believe her eyes. There on page 4E covering Zits was. . . a Christmas card:

MERRY CHRISTMAS AND A HAPPY NEW YEAR
WARM WISHES FOR A HAPPY HOLIDAY SEASON
- Earl Neigh, your newspaper guy
10 Blue Heron Ct. Englewood, FL 34224

Blaine shook her head, stared at the card, and fumed, "Brooke can you believe the nerve of this guy to put a Christmas card in everyone's newspaper? He wakes me up every day at four-thirty in the morning with his radio blasting Hip Hop music so loud my windows vibrate. I toss and turn the rest of the night until the alarm goes off. I'm exhausted all day and this man wants a Christmas bonus! Okay, Mr. Earl Neigh from Englewood, you want a Christmas present! I will give you a holiday gift, one you will remember for a very long time. Now that I know where you live, you moron, I think I will deliver it myself. It will be the holiday gift that keeps on giving."

Chapter Three

"Mom, chill, you're getting all freaked out over this paperboy thing. Just relax you know what happens when you get all hyper."

"Oh excuse me little miss psychotherapist, but he is not a boy! He's a paper man, drives a car with his radio blasting at four-thirty in the morning, and now has the nerve to ask for a holiday gift."

"Let me see." Brooke laughed as she put her book bag on the kitchen counter and reached for the card.

For a seven-year-old, Brooke Sterling was not only big for her age, the tallest in her second grade class, but she was also the smartest. Brooke seemed to learn things faster than the other students did. Learning just came naturally, a gift she inherited from her mother. Brooke could read books on a third and fourth grade level. She loved to read; she finished all the Laura Ingalls Wilder, *Little House on the Prairie* series and now was reading the *Harry Potter* books. Her first grade teacher recommended that she advance a grade, but her mother said 'No,' she wanted Brooke to stay in first grade with her peers. She felt that the move would be too disruptive.

Brooke was also a whiz at math. Last summer, at the backyard picnic table with her mother going over the multiplication tables every morning after breakfast, she memorized all the multiplication facts from one to twelve. Brooke hated the repetitious boredom, but never complained; she cherished the time spent with her mother before she left for work.

However, Brooke's favorite subject was art, she loved to draw and spent hours drawing and sketching in the special art notebook her mother bought her last year. Horses were her favorite theme; she would take out armloads of horse books from the library, open to a picture and draw. Of course, she would add her own personal touch that reflected part of her seven-year-old imagination, a colorful monarch butterfly, or a stippled ladybug perched on the ear of an Appaloosa. Brooke's drawings won awards at school and last year her drawing, *Galloping Stallion,* featured at the Venice Art Show on the island won a first place ribbon and a hundred dollar savings bond. Anything pertaining to art interested Brooke.

"I think it's a cool card—Santa in a bathing suit, carrying an inner tube and newspaper walking down to the beach. Look, mom, it even has Venice Journal Star printed on the front of the paper. It's no big deal, just give the newspaper guy $20 and wish him a Merry Christmas. Where's your Christmas spirit?" Brooke giggled as she handed the card back to her mother.

"Twenty dollars, are you crazy? That's not happening, especially after the run-around the newspaper gave me last week." Blaine closed her eyes and gently massaged her right temple.

Chapter Four

The Venice Journal Star located on the island of Venice was headquartered in a three-story, sandstone Northern Italian Renaissance-style building nestled amongst a canopy of towering Royal Palms. A sloping, terracotta tile roof, with four black, Mediterranean grated, second-floor windows and a long, winding brick walkway leading to a large, columned, doorway made an awe-inspiring statement. This style construction developed by renowned urban designer John Nolen in 1926 is, today the cornerstone of Venice's current building model.

The first thing Blaine noticed when she entered the lobby was a tall, skinny white man wearing only a bright yellow Speedo standing in front of the information counter. Some people should never wear a Speedo and this old guy was one of them. Not only was he frighteningly stick thin, but his back covered in patches of brown matted hair conjured up a disturbing thought of an ape-like creature about to swing from the light fixture over the counter. If that was not scary enough, pieces of aluminum foil that resembled a silver helmet covered his head. Blaine had an uneasy feeling about the guy so she kept her distance and let the situation unfold.

Behind the counter stood a petite, attractive African-American receptionist, probably just out of high school as she didn't seem fazed by the customer's dress or lack of clothing. As the melodrama played out, she just twirled the ends of her long black hair, blankly stared straight ahead through her red-rimmed designer glasses, and patiently listened while he waved his arms, head, legs, and other parts of the body. He ranted about his missing newspaper, two days in a row. Blaine was amazed at how calm and collected the young receptionist was. If anyone in the company should get the employee-of-the-month award, it should be her. Just give her the parking spot right next to the front door now. "I tell you aliens stole my paper again, Shaneque!"

"No, Mr. Bloomfield, aliens did not steal your paper today and they didn't steal your paper yesterday either."

"I think they did, Shaneque, and if we don't do something about it today, who knows how many papers will be stolen tomorrow?"

"Mr. Bloomfield, your newspaper carrier was out sick yesterday and is out sick today. He thinks the chilidog he ate at the Shark's Tooth Festival at the Venice Airport two nights ago was bad. He said he thinks he has food poisoning, but will try to be back to work tomorrow."

"The Shark's Tooth Festival, I was there, I didn't see Earl. What a place, I couldn't believe how many vendors were selling shark's teeth. They had two big tents just selling shark teeth merchandise. What do you think? I bought this necklace at the festival yesterday. Only cost three hundred bucks, what do you think?" Mr. Bloomfield proudly remarked and held the necklace up for the receptionist to see.

"Very handsome and big, I especially like the silver chain; it compliments your aluminum foil hat. Also, Mr. Bloomfield you should have received a newspaper yesterday and today, we have a substitute carrier delivering to your neighborhood."

"Oh, this is not a hat, Shaneque it is an Interstellar Cosmic Obstruction Ray device that protects me from deadly alien sound waves in our atmosphere. This appliance keeps the harmful beams from entering my brain and confusing me. It took me a whole day to cut and glue all the tiny pieces of foil together to conform to my head. I picked up the pattern from a web site on Alien Brain Wave Abductions. Would you like me to make one for you? You'll never know when this little beauty will kick in and save the little gray cells," Bloomfield sang out with a self-satisfied smile on his face.

"That's alright Mr. Bloomfield, it's probably working right now protecting you and everyone in this room," Shaneque smiled back.

"Well suit yourself young lady, but don't come crying to me when your thoughts get all jumbled up and you can't think straight. Moreover, to answer your question, yes I did get a newspaper today, but what happened to my morning paper? Do you see what I mean Shaneque?"

Leaning forward and looking the customer straight in the eye Shaneque, said calmly, "I do Mr. Bloomfield; I do understand and thank you for coming in today, again."

Chapter Five

Blaine stepped up to the counter and read the identification necklace the receptionist was wearing, Shaneque Cample-Receptionist, Venice Journal Star. No wonder she wasn't concerned about that nut case. He was a regular. Blaine left work early and drove directly to the paper. She remained in uniform, a forest green shirt with dark green epaulets on both shoulders pointing down to the Florida Park Service patches on the top of both sleeves. Above the right breast pocket was her gold nameplate and rank, Assistant Park Manager, a title she earned earlier in the year. Above the left breast pocket a silver badge from the Department of Environmental Protection, signified graduation from the Ranger Academy, an award she proudly wore after graduating first in her class, an honor no other female cadet had ever earned. Dark green pants, spit polished black Timberline boots, and a Bachelor of Arts degree in marine biology and a minor in criminal justice from Hofstra University on Long Island completed her resume. A subtle form of intimidation that she was a state official was the projection. Standing 5'11", with straight blonde hair tied in a ponytail, penetrating aqua blue eyes, and a slender, well-toned body, Blaine Sterling looked impressive and conveyed an air of confidence with a no-nonsense attitude. Blaine wasn't drop dead gorgeous, but she turned a head or two when she entered a room.

"Good afternoon, my name is Blaine Sterling and I'd like to see the Circulation Manager," Blaine announced.

"Do you have an appointment Mrs. Sterling?" The receptionist asked and looked down at her appointment calendar.

"No, I don't, and it's *Ms.* Sterling."

"May I ask what this is in reference to, Ms. Sterling?"

"I have a complaint about my newspaper delivery carrier!"

The receptionist walked back to her desk, picked up the phone, punched in three numbers and waited. "Mr. Dunn, there's a Ms. Sterling to see you sir. No, she does not have an appointment. Yes, I know sir, but she is, yes, I realize that today is, but she insists on seeing the manager. Blaine Sterling, yes sir." Putting her hand over the phone the secretary turned to Blaine and asked, "Excuse me, Ms. Sterling, is your address 204 Serpentine Lane, Venice?"

"Yes it is," Blaine replied perfunctorily, looked directly at the receptionist and smiled. For a young woman that just spent over twenty minutes talking to a nut case with an aluminum helmet on his head about his lost newspaper, she was having a great deal of difficulty talking to the manager. She sounded almost apologetic for calling.

"Yes it is Mr. Dunn, I will. Thank you, Mr. Dunn, sorry to...."

The receptionist looked up, instructed Blaine to take a seat in the waiting area across from the main desk, and informed Blaine that Mr. Dunn would be down shortly.

Chapter Six

Five minutes later, a short, thin man in a poorly-fitting suit, in his late sixties, a pencil thin mustache and thinning gray hair desperate for a trim, moved around the front counter, walked over to Blaine and extended his hand. "Good afternoon, Ms. Sterling, I'm Arthur Dunn, the Director of Circulation how can I help you?"

Blaine stood only to grasp a cold, limp hand that barely moved when they shook. "Pleased to meet you, Mr. Dunn I need to talk to you about one of your newspaper carriers, a Mr. Earl Neigh."

The friendly plastic smile, standard protocol for all initial corporate greetings, evaporated and suddenly took on a pained look of exasperation that spread across his sallow blank face. "I see let's take the elevator to my office where we'll have more privacy," Dunn said, pointing to the two gray doors at the far end of the lobby. As the elevator doors opened a mother and her young son stepped out. From the corner of her eye, Blaine observed Mr. Dunn ever so slightly brush against the child and smile as the two passed. *An awkward smile,* she noted.

They rode the elevator to the third floor in silence. Blaine could sense his discomfort as she watched him fiddle with his keys while he stared straight ahead at the buttons on the chrome wall panel, as if his stare could make the doors open. Even before the doors were completely open, he hurried out and walked to his office directly across from the elevator.

"Forgive the mess, Ms. Sterling, but I'm moving out today. Please take the seat in front of my desk," and pushed open the door. Mess was an understatement; the office was a disaster area. Piles of books, pictures, and plaques were scattered over the floor and on the top of every surface in the tiny room. Two open file cabinets with folders pulled half-up from every drawer blocked a tiny window at the far end of the room. Everywhere Blaine looked, there were stacks of papers, binders or folders, except his desk. The glass top was clear of all clutter; just a white business envelope resting against an old gray metal tape dispenser and a book. The tidiness of the desk juxtaposed the discord around the room; it was a disturbing contrast.

Resting his frumpy brown suit jacket on the back of his chair, Mr. Dunn sat down, and with an uncomfortable smile began, "So how can I help you Ms. Sterling?"

For the first time Blaine had an opportunity to look closely at Arthur Dunn. To her amazement, he appeared much older up close, a good ten years. The wrinkles etched across his forehead down to his chin, and punctuated with dark brown blotches from years of sun damage significantly made him look older than his age. Drawn to his eyes, a washed out pale blue, sunken and lifeless, Blaine was puzzled by their movement, they seemed to constantly dart around the room, almost purposely avoiding eye contact and invariably staring down at his watch. Dunn appeared tired, worn out from years of work; Blaine had doubts about how helpful he could be, but she needed his assistance.

"It is your delivery carrier, Mr. Earl Neigh. Every morning when he delivers the Star, at 4:30 A.M., his car radio is blasting music and it wakes me up. I cannot get back to sleep and I am exhausted all day long. I called the newspaper three times and complained about his loud music. Each time, the results were the same; the woman on the phone apologized for the inconvenience and assured me that the music would stop. Apparently, Mr. Neigh did not get the message, or if he did, it did not sink in because I still hear the music," Blaine said. "I want you to stop him from blasting his radio when he delivers the newspaper. Inform him if there is one more complaint about the loud music, he will be fired!"

Mr. Dunn leaned forward in his chair and almost in a whisper said, "Ms. Sterling, have you spoken to Mr. Neigh about the loud music?"

Blaine could not believe her ears; *was this man insane? Go outside at 4:30 in the morning, in pajamas and tell some inconsiderate asshole to turn off his radio. I'm sure that would go over well. He probably carries a gun and I'd end up with a bullet in my head. Is this man crazy!* After Blaine regained her composure, she let him have it with both barrels. "Mr. Dunn what you suggest is completely out of the question; it is your responsibility to supervise all newspaper carriers and insure that their performance is acceptable. Blasting loud music at 4:30 in the morning is not acceptable. If you cannot, or will not, rectify this situation, I will have no recourse, but to cancel my subscription and persuade my neighbors to do the same. I'm sure the other local newspaper would welcome twelve new customers."

Chapter Seven

Although Arthur Dunn dutifully looked directly into Blaine's Caribbean blue eyes and appeared to be listening, he was not. Dunn had concerns that were more important on his mind. After forty-eight years of devoted service to the newspaper, working his way up from newspaper carrier to circulation manager, Arthur Dunn had to clear out all of his personal belongings by the end of the workday. Downsizing, the new publisher Jeff Ambers said, the paper had to streamline operations, update with new technology and consolidate departments; a euphemism for the elimination of his job. The Star was his life. He wasn't married, didn't have a family, only his two Chihuahuas, Coco and Louie. His friends worked at the paper. His life was the paper. What else did he have? The only thing remaining was his five o'clock meeting with Mr. Ambers. He had to get rid of this woman in the next five minutes so that he could prepare for the meeting.

"Ms. Sterling I will meet with Mr. Neigh on Monday, inform him of your complaint and tell him if I receive another complaint from anyone, he will no longer work for the newspaper. We certainly can't lose twelve of our valued customers, can we?" Relieved, Blaine stood, shook his hand, thanked him for his time and walked to the door.

The elevator doors jerked opened and Blaine stepped in. As she turned to press the lobby level button, she spotted Mr. Dunn dashing down the hallway while attempting to button his frumpy brown jacket. She smiled, but he was too preoccupied with smoothing out the jacket to notice. Blaine was pleased with the meeting. It seemed rushed, but she was optimistic that Mr. Dunn would put an end to the loud music. The door closed and elevator began to move.

Chapter Eight

"Hello Doris, sorry I'm a little late for my meeting with Mr. Ambers, but I had an irate customer in my office complaining about the delivery carrier. You know our motto, 'the customer is always right,' it took a little longer than I expected, but I am here now. A little out of breath and somewhat wrinkled. Can I go in now?"

"Oh, I'm sorry Mr. Dunn, Mr. Ambers left for the day. He waited until five o'clock and when you didn't show up for the meeting, he left."

"But it's only 5:05, he must still be here. I have to see him," and pushed open the two large wooden doors to publisher's office. "Mr. Ambers I know you're here. Please, I have something to ask you. . .Oh *No*."

Chapter Nine

The explosion was deafening, the building shook, lights went out and the ceiling sprinklers rained down a shower of chilling water. The explosion knocked Blaine off her feet and her head struck the side of the elevator door as she fell forward into the lobby. She managed to regain her balance, but a sharp pain on her forehead began to throb as blood oozed down the side of her head. The emergency lights along the walls cast a haunting, almost surreal glow through a shower of water that was cascading down from a hole in the center of the ceiling. The beams of light silhouetted the chaos that was taking place. Panic grabbed hold of everyone, men, women, and children began screaming and crushed forward toward the front doors. A baby carriage overturned and in the rush of bodies fell forward and to the side as people pushed forward to escape. Blaine scooped up the child and handed her to the distraught mother. Standing in the center of the room, Blaine raised her arms and shouted, "Don't panic the explosion is over. Stop screaming. Walk slowly, hold hands, and move to the front doors now!"

It was magic; there was quiet, the crowd listened, held hands, and walked through the front doors into the arms of the approaching firefighters.

Battalion Chief Scott Coran could not miss the flames as he drove over the Venice Avenue Bridge. A native of Venice and veteran firefighter for over thirty years, he was familiar with the location and knew this fire was going to be a tough call. A three story building, a compacted location, surrounding buildings, minimum blacktop space, all added up to a difficult fire rescue. Chief Coran could not miss the flames as he drove over the Venice Avenue Bridge. The entire northeast corner of the third floor engulfed in flames lit up the late afternoon sky. Billowing clouds of black smoke lifted two hundred feet into the sky while crimson red and yellow flames leapt twenty feet into the air casting down glowing red ambers of fire to the ground. With a stiff westerly breeze, there was danger that adjacent buildings would catch fire. "Dispatch, this is Battalion Chief Coran, I am on route to the fire on Venice Island off of Tamiami Trail, I'm ordering a Second Alarm and request that Nokomis Fire Department be on stand-by if assistance is needed. I also need a tactical channel for communications." Coran knew right off that a First Alarm would never be able to contain the fire, let alone put it out. He hoped to hell that the extra engines, rescues, and firefighters would be enough. It had to be.

"Chief Coran, this is dispatch you're cleared for Tac 3 and Nokomis is on stand-by. Is there anything else at this time?"

"Notify the Fire Marshall, Venice PD for traffic control, and the Red Cross to assist with the injured."

Chief Coran pulled into the parking lot. Company # 2 had already arrived and positioned the trucks, emergency equipment, and firefighting apparatus around the fire perimeter. Black smoke poured out of the front doors as firefighters worked feverishly to evacuate the people from the building. A first aid station was set up behind one rescue engine where two paramedics set up a triage center for the injured and at the far end of the parking lot the Red Cross assembled a support team to comfort the remaining wet and frightened workers. Three firefighters dragging a fire hose rushed through the front doors.

In the rear of the building, two fire tankers sprayed water onto the flames that spread from the top floor down to the ground floor. The ladder engine maneuvered the bucket close to the middle of the backside of the building where a gaping hole stood where two large windows were before the explosion.

"This is Chief Coran, Lieutenant Bell, instruct your men that I don't want a Surround and Drown operation. I have a funny feeling about this fire. Limit as much water damage as possible. I want the Fire Marshal to have something to work with."

"Understood Chief, I'll get right on it," Bell shouted into the walkie and walked over to the aerial truck.

"Lieutenant, this is Harris, I'm in the bucket directly in front of the blow-out. Sir, you have to come up here and see this!" Harris could barely handle the controls that lowered the bucket, he threw up all over himself and with his helmet and face plate on had difficulty breathing.

Dizzy and unable to judge distance, images turned and spun out of focus and caused the bucket to slam down hard. Bell grabbed the bucket as it hit hard on the back platform and shouted, "Harris what the hell is wrong with you? What kind of descent was that! You look like hell and you stink. What happened up there?"

"Sir you have to see it for yourself, it's a mess up there Lieutenant, a real mess."

Bell pulled Harris out of the bucket, sat him down on the curb, and shouted into his walkie, "This is Lieutenant Bell, a firefighter is down, and I need a medic *Now*! He's back alongside the aerial." Bell pushed the lever forward as the medics hoisted Harris onto a gurney and pushed him to the triage area.

After thirty years of fire experience, you think you have seen it all, but you never do. There is always one more experience waiting to shock the living shit out of you. For Lieutenant Cary Bell, today was that day. The bucket jerked forward and stopped in front of the second floor opening. Nothing could have prepared him for the grotesque sight that lay before him. All the blood and guts was staggering. It took all of Bell's strength not to choke on the stench. He grabbed the railing to steady himself and talked into his walkie, "Chief this is Bell. I'm in the bucket outside the burnt-out office. Sir you were right when you said you had a feeling about this fire, we have a real problem up here. Blood spatter on every wall, body parts all over the room; I mean a fucking blood bath Chief. There's a bloody head on the bookcase eye balling me right now. This was no electrical fire; someone or something blew up in there. Maybe a terrorist or some wacko who didn't like to read, I don't know chief. I do know one thing; this wasn't some run of the mill office fire. The explosion was too powerful. This is definitely a crime scene now; you need to alert the Fire Marshal and police, we have a possible homicide."

"Bell, instruct your men to do a complete search of the building, evacuate everyone and cordon off the third floor until the Fire Marshal and police arrive. I don't want anyone near that office!"

Chapter Ten

Blaine turned and ran towards the stairway at the opposite side of the lobby. Taking two stairs at a time, she reached the third floor landing in seconds. She knew exactly where to go, follow Mr. Dunn. She was right. At the end of the hallway, smoke blanketed the small alcove leading to a large corner office. The water from the sprinkler cooled her face and pushed some of the smoke from her eyes. The small greeting area was a mess. The explosion blew off all of the pictures from the walls. Magazines and paper were scattered all over the floor. A small leather couch and matching chair were overturned and the office reception desk was on its side against the far wall. Blaine cupped her hands around her mouth and yelled, "Is anyone here! Does anyone need help?" Blaine turned, looked around and waited, straining to hear something over the sound of the raining water.

"Help me, please help me. I can't move my legs," a faint voice called out. Blaine scanned the room, but the smoke bit into her eyes blinding her vision. She fell to the floor to get a better view of the room and listen.

"Where are you? I can't see you," Blaine shouted again.

"I'm under the desk. Please help me," the pained voice called out again.

Blaine crawled over to the desk and there crunched up against the wall was Doris Gannon, Mr. Ambers' secretary. The force of the explosion catapulted her and the desk across the room pinning the lower half of her body under the massive double-sided mahogany desk. Writhing in pain, the old woman's face wrinkled with agony as she called out a third time, "Help me, the weight is unbearable."

Blaine reached down and touched her face, "I'm here, and everything will be alright now."

Doris slowly opened her eyes and stared directly up at Blaine. "Thank God you're here. It's terrible; I can't believe what just happened. It was Mr. Dunn; he just barged into Mr. Ambers' office and then this. I told him Mr. Ambers left for the day, but he pushed open the doors and then *Boom*. Why would he do such an awful thing? It was only a job."

Blaine tried to wipe the water from her face, but the water kept falling. "Don't talk any more. I'm going to get this desk off you." Blaine reached over, pulled out the top desk drawer when the doors to Mr. Ambers' office opened and two firefighters rushed in. Blaine stood and yelled, "Over here. Hurry a woman is trapped under a desk." Immediately the two firefighters took over. Blaine walked across the vestibule to Mr. Ambers' office. She touched the brass doorknobs: only warm, that was a good sign the fire had abated and a back draft explosion wouldn't happen when the door opened, she hoped. Slowly she pushed open the door and froze in mid-step. She was not prepared; no one could have been for the horrific sight before her. Staring down from the top of the bookcase was the bloodied head of Mr. Dunn. His twisted face screamed out in silent horror. Blood splatter covered the walls, oozing down in rivulets of red. Chunks and small pieces of flesh stuck to the walls, furniture, and floor like tiny mounds of raw hamburger meat left for the garbage. A shredded arm hung from a twisted ceiling fan, a mangled foot lay on top of an overturned table, one hand resting on the arm of a couch, the blown-out lower torso stuck out of an overturned plant and other extremities too disfigured to identify were scattered all over the room. Nails, bolts, and metal screws peppered the walls creating a Swiss cheese pock-marked pattern. The right side of the room engulfed in flames spewed out gaseous black smoke as water from the fire hoses splashed up against the side and out through a large gaping hole that was once large picture windows. The scene was something out of a classic horror film.

A hand grabbed Blaine's shoulder. "Miss, we have to evacuate the building now! Are you all right? You're bleeding. Can you walk?"

"I'm okay," Blaine choked out as she wiped the blood with her hand, "I can walk."

"Follow us; this is now officially a crime scene." The firefighters picked up Doris, walked out into the hallway and down the stairs to the lobby. Blaine followed.

Chapter Eleven

Detective Justin Beale got the call at 5:45 P.M., fire at the Venice Journal Star, civilian injuries, possible homicide. His hopes of a quiet night at the station were over. He had just punched in and started to finish the paperwork from an attempted bank robbery the day before at the Fifth Third Bank on Venice & Pinebrook. Jason Dean, age 23, address, 16 Palm Street Venice, Florida 34292. *What a dumb shit*, Beale thought, *what moron tries to hold up a bank from the drive-through window, what did he think—he was at McDonald's?* Hands the teller a note:

HAND OVER $100,000 IN SMALL BILLS. I HAVE A GUN!

Andrew Dombai, the teller, who divided his work schedule between the Island branch and the East Venice Bank, was working the drive-up window transactions at the time of the robbery. Dombai, a personable young professional with an extremely contagious smile and a mischievous sense of humor read the note, pressed the silent alarm, scribbled something down and pushed the drawer back to Dean. Dean rolled down the car window, read the note, fired two shots at the teller and drove off.

Surveillance cameras got his plate number, description of the car and twenty minutes later, picked him up at his home. The gun, robbery note, and an empty burlap sack (supposedly for the money) all stuffed under his living room couch made for an open and shut case against young Jason Dean. "Can you believe what that son of a bitch wrote," Dean spit out from the back of the patrol car. "I should've gone into that freaking bank and blown him away. Knock that big ass smile off his face. What did he think this was some kinda fucking joke?"

Beale looked down at the crumpled note:

HAND OVER $100, 000.00 IN SMALL BILLS. I HAVE A GUN!

YOU ARE A MORON!

Beale stuck his head into the patrol car and smiled, "Didn't realize the glass was bulletproof, did you asshole." Case closed.

Detective Beale had seen some dumbass criminals in his time, but Dean took the cake, a drive-through bank robbery attempt had to be the dumbest. Beale put in his twenty with the Suffolk County Police Department, worked his way up from patrol officer to homicide detective, transferred to the Venice Police Department two years ago as Detective Grade 2, and now was up for promotion, Assistant Chief. At 42, he would be the youngest Assistant Chief in the department. At six-foot-two, 185 lbs., thick wavy brown hair, big smile, brilliant hazel eyes, and a muscular physique, Justin Beale's persona was commanding. Although he looked young for his age, he was a superb detective and resolute in getting criminals off the street. He knew that the bad guys operated twenty-four seven to try and beat the system. He only had eight hours a day to stop them so he had to be at the top of his game.

On his desk a plaque read: WHERE ARE THE BAD GUYS. Beale hated unsolved crimes. Things unfinished bothered him. He would read and reread the unsolved crime folders looking for something that would break a case. Call it intuition or a sixth sense, Beale couldn't just let go. He was driven to put as many bad guys away as he could.

Chapter Twelve

Beale turned on his flashers as he approached the Venice Avenue Bridge. His white Crown Vic was given the right of way as he swerved into the left lane and accelerated south onto Tamiami Trail. A traffic cop waved him through the street barriers leading to the newspaper plant. Beale maneuvered his car through the maze of trucks, cars, fire engines, security cones, and people to a spot where he could view the total situation unfold. Position yourself where the action was taking place. This was a procedure he learned at the academy and followed religiously at every crime scene. Aerial truck, back northeast corner, pump trucks both corners of building front and back, three chief cars, five advanced life support rescues front center, a triage around the rescue trucks, and the Red Cross station at the far end of the lot. Banks of portable floodlights illuminated the front and back of the building.

Beale switched off his flashers, put down the visor with police tags, and walked straight for the triage area. That's where the action was. Two feet from the center rescue truck, Beale spotted someone who looked vaguely familiar. As he got closer it hit him, the woman on the ground resting against the truck was Blaine Sterling, his only unsolved case. Eight years ago, her husband disappeared, just vanished into thin air. Left his carpenter's job in the middle of the day and never heard from since. Beale was the lead detective and at first the police thought it was just a family quarrel, things like that happen the first year of marriage and that Mr. Sterling would return that night. That didn't happen.

Troy Sterling didn't return that night, the next day, the next week, or even the next year. No reports on his car, he was not reported seen at any bus terminals, railroad stations, or airports. No ransom note, no jealous lover arrested, no enemies, no leads; not a damn thing, it was as if the earth opened up and swallowed him and his car. Unsolved cases bothered Beale, but the Sterling disappearance ate at his core, it was the first and only unsolved case where he was the lead detective. That was a blemish on his record and privately that did not sit well

29

with him. The case became personal and still nagged at him. Troy Sterling never returned home, Beale couldn't catch a break and Blaine Sterling was left alone to raise a child.

"Blaine Sterling, is that you? I don't know if you remember me, I'm Justin Beale, the detective from your husband's case. . .What happened to you, you're bleeding!" Beale knelt down next to Blaine, moved her hand aside and pressed his handkerchief up against her head. The blood saturated the white cloth and turned crimson within minutes. "Here hold pressure on this, I need to get you a medic, I'll be right back."

Blaine looked up and barely whispered, "Thank you Detective Beale. I'll be right here, it's no big deal." The medic put two butterfly stitches on the wound and taped a large gauze pad over the cut.

"It looks a lot worse than it really is, ma'am, but I suggest that you have it checked out at the hospital." Blaine smiled and thanked him for his help.

Beale reached down and helped Blaine to her feet. Holding her steady he said, "Are you going to be okay, can you make it back to your car?"

"Sure no problem, I'll be fine."

"By the way what were you doing here? I thought you were a park ranger, what happened you make a career change? Didn't like it in the woods anymore, too many bears to worry about?"

"For your information Detective we don't have bears in Sarasota County and yes, I'm still working for the Florida Park Service, not as a ranger. I am now the Assistant Park Manager." Blaine groaned and threw the bloodied handkerchief back to Beale.

"Congratulations, but you still didn't answer my question. What were you doing at the Star?"

Blaine took a deep breath, looked into Beale's steely hazel eyes and for the first time since the explosion she felt the magnitude of the experience fall upon her. Like a shroud of darkness choking off clear vision, her mind raced through the events like pages in a book flipped faster and faster trying to reach the last page. She visualized everything, the explosion, the people, the fire, the screaming and the blood. Her lips moved, but the words would not come out, only silence. A tear fell from her eye. Slowly she murmured, "I had a meeting with Mr. Dunn."

Beale squeezed her shoulder, "Blaine are you sure you are okay? I can have an officer take you to the hospital."

"I'll be fine, thank you." Blaine turned and walked to her car.

Chapter Thirteen

Beale grabbed the first fire fighter he saw on the way to building and asked where he could find the Fire Marshal. Pointing straight ahead he shouted, "Third floor." Beale took the stairs. He knew from experience that after a fire, even though the building may have back-up generator power, taking the elevator could prove embarrassing. Ten years ago, locked in an elevator after a fire proved to be a costly mistake, one he vowed never make again.

The report came in to headquarters that a cleaning service employee spotted some guy setting a wastebasket on fire and was still in the building. When she yelled at him, he pulled out a gun and ran out of the office. The office building was on Vets Highway in Islandia, a five-story glass and aluminum complex. A large circular atrium filled with plants, chairs, couches, and small coffee tables looked more like a restaurant than an office lobby.

Beale's partner, Tony Cincotta, an old timer with bad knees said it would be quicker if they took the elevator to the fifth. "The fire was under control what could go wrong," he said. Two floors up Murphy's Law struck! Everything went dark. Power went out, the elevator jerked to a stop and they were stuck between the second and third floor. By the time back up arrived and the fire department pried open the elevator door, the arsonist was gone, and the two detectives in the elevator looked like shmucks.

The Captain reamed them out royally, placed them on desk duty, but the worst part of the punishment was they were the laughing-stock of the department for the next two weeks. Every day, there would be another bogus e-mail from Otis Elevator or a post-it note on their phones to call Larry the Locksmith. The elevator jokes were relentless, detectives would shout across the room a new one for everyone's entertainment: "Hey did anyone see Beale and Cincotta today? Yeah, I saw them getting into the elevator this morning. Should we call the fire department?"

The final humiliation came when one wiseass detective figured out how to bypass the lobby music system and dedicated songs to Beale and Cincotta when they arrived for duty. *Trapped on the Highway of Love, Baby Come Back, and Another Lonely Night* played repeatedly. Thank God, the captain ended the concert when he arrived for his seven o'clock shift. Ten hours of elevator music was more than any human being could endure.

Chapter Fourteen

Beale found the Fire Marshal, Keigin "Red" Cavanagh, at the end of the hallway photographing burn patterns along the office walls and ceiling. It was easy to spot the Fire Marshal—the carrot red hair that stuck out from underneath his helmet was a giveaway. Red, his preferred name, was a true professional. Beale worked with him before and found him to be a stickler for detail with an analytical mind. Red always dotted all the i's and crossed all t's. His work was thorough and without question, he was a perfectionist. Red loved his work and never tired of the challenges each fire presented. He worked his way up from fire fighter, to lieutenant, to captain, to Deputy Chief, to Chief and finally Fire Marshal. You could say Red Cavanagh paid his dues to climb the fire ladder to the top.

"Hey Red we have to stop meeting like this," Beale called from the end of the hallway.

"Good to see you again, detective yeah, people will start to talk," Red laughed.

Beale reached out to shake Red's hand, but before he knew it, Red gave him a bear hug that almost lifted him off his feet. The two of them made a strange pair. Beale was almost a foot taller, broad shouldered and muscular, while Red was barely 5' 6", stout and definitely out of shape.

"So where is the fire's point of origin, Fire Marshall Cavanagh? All I see out here are burn and smoke patterns along the ceiling and walls."

"That's the easy part, detective. Why the fire started is the big question, but first, have you had dinner yet?" Red asked with a smile.

Annoyed with Red's line of questioning, Beale snapped back, "What does my dinner have to do with the fire!"

Red took Beale's arm, whispered in his ear, "Because, my friend, you may be enjoying it again," and pushed open the office doors.

"Woo, what the fuck happened in here! It's a god damn blood bath," Beale shouted, and held on to the door for support while he took in the breadth of the carnage. His stomach started to churn, an acidy taste spilled over his tongue, and he swallowed to keep everything down.

Red pointed to a dark blood pool in front of a large blood-splattered mahogany desk, "My preliminary findings are that someone blew himself up right there. The explosion ignited the curtains along the back wall and then spread up all along the ceiling."

The first thing that crossed Beale's mind: a terrorist attack right here in Venice, could there be a terrorist cell right in his own backyard. What is this world coming to?

"Red, please tell me this guy wasn't a fucking terrorist!"

"Terrorist, are you kidding! This guy worked for the newspaper. He lost it and committed suicide. I talked to Doris Gannon, the publisher's secretary; she said the circulation manager, Art Dunn, stormed into the office looking for Mr. Ambers and then blew himself up."

"Why would a guy blow himself up in the publisher's office? Where is the publisher?"

"Mrs. Gannon said Dunn was late for his meeting with Mr. Ambers, so the publisher left for the day. As for the why, maybe you can shed some light on that question." Pointing to the head on the bookcase, Red said, "Let me introduce, your old friend, the Circulation Manager from the Venice Journal Star, the late Arthur Dunn."

"What! What are you talking about Red, I don't know any Arthur Dunn and he's not an old friend of mine. In fact, he's not even a new friend. I never met the guy before in my life," Beale exclaimed and took a closer look at the head.

"That's strange because he knew you detective. Let's go to Dunn's office, there's something that may answer the why you're looking for."

Arthur Dunn's office was a shoebox. The size of a small cubicle sandwiched between two corner offices. Beale couldn't believe the clutter for such a small room. The office was a disaster area, books, file folders, pictures, and papers stacked in disorderly piles all over the place.

The only clear area was his desk juxtaposed to the rest of the mess in the room its tidiness appeared staged.

"Maybe the answer to why Mr. Dunn blew himself up is on the desk, detective."

Beale walked over to the desk and there in the center resting against a gray tape dispenser was an envelope addressed Detective Justin Beale. Beale put on latex gloves and picked up the envelope. The envelope wasn't sealed, just folded in. Beale took out the letter and began to read:

Dear Detective Beale:

I first want to apologize for taking up your valuable time with my personal problems. I have followed with the highest respect your illustrious police career for the past seven years and have admired the excellent police work you have accomplished in such a short time with the Venice Police Department. In my view you are a true professional and have tempered your police work with a humane touch. For this, the citizens of Venice should be very grateful. If you are reading this letter, then unfortunately my demise has fallen on deaf ears. Today was to be my final day at the Star. Forty-eight years of devoted service snuffed out because of Ambers' new management configuration: *Streamlining* he said. Bottom line my position had been eliminated. I had become expendable and I had to be out of the building by five o'clock sharp.

The paper is my life; it is all I live for. Without my work, I have nothing. I will implore Mr. Ambers to keep me on. I would do anything for the paper. All I want is to stay with my newspaper family. If I can't, I have nothing to live for and I will take with me the man responsible for this injustice.

I have only one request, Detective Beale, would you please see that my two beautiful Chihuahuas, Louie and Choco, spend the rest of their doggie days at the loving Florida Breeze Dog Resort in Venice. I have already given them legal custody of my babies and a substantial amount of money for their boarding.

Sincerely,

Art Dunn

Beale folded the letter, placed it back in the envelope and slipped it into his pocket. He looked over at Red and just shook his head. "How is it possible someone could be so consumed with his job that he would even consider suicide, let alone carry it out," Beale added, "and to compound matters; intend to murder his boss."

"Beale, if I knew the answer, I wouldn't be up here mucking around in all this mess with you. I'd be home having dinner with my family."

"You know Red the sad part is I believe no one at the paper knew how this guy felt. Nobody took the time to see that he was way over the edge. He thought he was part of a family, but the reality was, he wasn't."

"One thing doesn't make sense, if Ambers wasn't in the office, why did Dunn detonate the bomb? Ambers was the person who started this whole thing in motion, he was the only one who could give Dunn back his job, make things right again in Dunn's mind, but he wasn't there. Why kill yourself?" Red said and walked to the door.

"That's the job for the bomb squad guys to answer. Right now, I need to go over to Dunn's house and see where he got his explosives. Oh, and see about my new friend's two Chihuahuas." Beale smiled and walked towards the stairs.

Chapter Fifteen

Lou Bravo slowly backed his banana yellow '76 El Camino down Blaine's driveway to her garage behind the house. He was careful not to scratch his truck, or drop the twenty something beach chairs stacked ten high in the bed of the truck, but his biggest fear was crushing the newly-planted yellow Allamanda bushes that lined both sides of the driveway. It wasn't that he was some kind of a plant freak or something. Actually, Lou Bravo could care less about plants, flowers, or anything else that had to be watered. He just didn't want to piss off Blaine and Brooke who spent the whole day lining the driveway in yellow. For Lou Bravo, his home, in a very basic way, was Florida friendly—no plants, no flowers, no watering; no nothing; only rocks, stones, or anything that could grow on its own. Lou Bravo wasn't into gardening.

What Lou Bravo had were connections with a capital C. He knew many people and many people knew Lou Bravo. His unofficial title was The Mayor. Never nominated, never appointed, and of course never elected, Lou Bravo loved making things happen. From time to time, he helped people solve problems and for that, people owed Lou Bravo. Just last week a large white unmarked box truck parked in front of Lou Bravo's house and unloaded, brand-new, never out of the box Sealy Posturepedic mattresses, box springs, frames, and head boards. Ten minutes later the truck rolled up to the next house, unloaded a mattress, box spring, frame and a headboard and then proceeded to deliver identical orders down the entire block until the truck was empty. What were the odds that an entire neighborhood needed to replace their bedroom set on the same day Lou Bravo replaced his?

Lou Bravo was born and grew-up in Central Islip, New York. He owned and operated Classic Touch, an auto body shop known for quality repair work at an affordable price, for Lou Bravo that meant big bucks. There were always fender benders and if you knew the right kind of people that meant work. Lou Bravo knew all the right kind of people in Suffolk County, lawyers, judges, elected officials, cops—anyone that could help him benefit he made it his business to meet.

Lou Bravo was a people person, loved to talk and shoot the breeze and at his repair shop, he had a captive audience. He could regale them with his stories when they came in to get an estimate for the repair work and when they returned to pick up their car. Moreover, Lou Bravo had the advantage; he knew potential customers weren't going to piss off the guy who is going to repair your car; if you did, maybe something would happen to your car. With that advantage, Lou Bravo had license to talk to whomever he liked, and that was everyone who walked through his door. Young, old, white, black, male, female, rich, or poor; pick a topic and he would know what to say.

It didn't matter what the topic was, Lou Bravo always had an opinion and was ready to engage in a meaningful dialogue, so he thought. Lou Bravo wasn't confrontational. No matter how heated the discussions became, they never turned into ugly shouting matches with the other person storming off in disgust. Lou Bravo had a special way of defusing tension and turning it around.

Lou Bravo's gift was his smile. That beautiful, big, bright smile would melt the meanest pit-bull disposition and in an instant, they were calm. At five-five, 190 pounds, with a shaved head and barrel chest, Lou Bravo looked like a short, stumpy, professional wrestler with muscular arms and big strong hands that always moved when he talked. He was a prominent figure throughout the political arena and donated large sums of money to the party machine that ran Suffolk County. A by-product for his support were lucrative county contracts awarded to Classic Touch. More business meant more headaches and that was what brought Lou Bravo trouble. He added another shop, hired more workers, ordered more parts, and took on a partner. Politics changed on Long Island, a new party took over, and his connections dissolved. The New York State District Attorney's Office, after a two-year investigation of illegal auto repair shops on Long Island, closed Classic Touch down. Twenty years later, he's driving a yellow pick-up.

"Lou Bravo, you better not run over my mom's flowers," Brooke yelled as she ran out the side door.

"Yah, yah what do you think I've been doing for the past five minutes." Lou Bravo grumbled. Brooke jumped up on the running board, and gave him a big kiss on the cheek. Lou loved Brooke and Blaine in a fatherly sort of way. He unofficially adopted them after Brooke's father disappeared almost eight years ago.

"Hey kiddo, don't you know it's dangerous jumping up on a moving vehicle." It was hard to get mad at a cute, little seven-year-old, especially when she was giving him a second kiss on the cheek. Lou Bravo shut the engine off, took Brooke's hand, and walked to the back of the truck. Blaine stepped outside with two large steaming cups of coffee in her hands and the newspaper tucked under her arm.

"Thought you could use a strong cup of coffee after reading about all the excitement back in New York," Blaine said with a huge grin on her face.

"What excitement? I didn't get a chance to read the paper today; I was out all morning picking up chairs for the Christmas Boat Parade tomorrow night. What happened to your head?"

"Oh this," touching her forehead, Blaine casually remarked, "It's just a little cut I got the other day, no big deal. Speaking of big deals, wait until you read about your friend, New York Governor Spitzer, it should put a smile on your face."

"My friend, that's a good one. It's because of that SOB I lost my business. What, did somebody kill the guy? I had nothing to do with it, if he is dead, but I don't know that. Is he dead?"

"Figuratively speaking yes," Blaine said and handed Lou Bravo a cup of coffee and the paper. There plastered on the front page in big bold letters: THE LOVE GUV, Eliot Spitzer paid $4,300 for romp with a 22-year-old call girl. POLITICAL CAREER OVER! Lou Bravo couldn't believe what he read. He stood there mesmerized by every word. This was the man who put the bad guys away and now he is the one getting caught breaking the law.

"Brooke would you please get the beach chairs from the garage for mommy, like a good girl."

"Oh mom, you just want me to leave so I don't hear all the bad words Lou Bravo is going to scream. He looks mad." Brooke smiled as she turned toward the garage.

"For your information young lady, he's not going to scream," Blaine called out as Brooke opened the garage door.

Lou Bravo did scream, he screamed and screamed. He ranted and raved for more than five minutes about what a *fucking hypocrite* Spitzer was. Lou Bravo waved his arms in the air and jumped around the yard like a crazy man as his face got redder and redder with each diatribe. Cookie Rosen, Blaine's eighty-five year old neighbor across the street, pushed her lace curtains to the side, peered out the window and shook her head. She lovingly cradled her orange and white tabby cat Creamsicle in her arms, whispered into his ear, and let go of the curtain. Blaine could only imagine what was going through her mind. She hoped that the gentle old woman, who loved cats with a passion, wouldn't call the police.

Bob and Mary Travers, who lived next door, were used to the drill. Close all the windows turn on the television and have another cup of coffee or glass of wine, depending on the time of day. Lou Bravo's current assault, a chorus of insults about the crime-busting governor, became merely a muffled blur like the incessant late night croaking from the frogs in the lake behind their house. Bob and Mary were from Boston, didn't much care for New York or for that matter, New Yorkers. A popular pastime of many Bostonians, especially Red Sox fans during baseball season, was to hate the New York Yankees and the Travers were die-hard Red Sox fans transplanted to Venice, Florida. This added revelation about the *"Love GUV"* and the antics of Lou Bravo only compounded their aversion toward New York. Bob would say, "Look Mary someone just took another bite out of the '*Big Apple.*' I think we should wait another year before we visit the *Great White Way.*"

Finally, Lou Bravo stopped his rant. Maybe he saw Brooke come out of the garage dragging two lawn chairs behind her or maybe he was too exhausted to speak. It was over. Brooke leaned the chairs against the truck and with a big smile said, "I think I'll go inside and rest my ears for awhile."

"Very funny missy," Blaine shouted as the screen door slammed shut. She turned and glared at Lou Bravo.

"Okay I think I'm done here. Need to stake out our usual spot - along the Intracoastal for all these chairs. So I'll see you guys Saturday night at the Boat Parade?" Strapping the two chairs to the truck, he didn't wait for an answer. A rhetorical question and Lou Bravo knew if he waited one second longer, his answer would not be from a happy camper. Or in Blaine's case from a happy ranger.

Chapter Sixteen

Earl Neigh loved cars, always did. His fascination with cars began with a bright red fire truck and its shinny chrome bell given to him on his third birthday. *This was the greatest present in the world*, Earl thought as he scooted forward to reach the pedals. It was a struggle for him to push the pedals back and forth, but he was too excited to notice the blister forming on his big toe. All morning long, he drove from room to room ringing the fire bell in an ascending order, clang, clang, clang, clang, clang. By the time Earl reached the den, six deafening clangs tolled throughout the house.

By lunchtime, Mrs. Neigh was at her wits' end. The constant ringing brought on a monster headache, so after Earl finished his peanut butter and jelly sandwich she suggested that he play with his fire truck outside. "Oh thank you Mommy, this is the best birthday ever," Earl crooned and pushed the fire engine towards the door. She reminded him to drive only on the sidewalk and driveway. If he went into the street, she would take the fire truck away.

"I promise, Mommy, I promise," he shouted as he raced out the back door with a big smile.

For the next five hours Earl peddled up and down the driveway and sidewalk, clanging the fire bell as he happily rolled along. By four o'clock Earl's little legs couldn't peddle another minute more. Exhausted he sat on the corner with his little head resting on the steering wheel.

In a blink, Susie Wilcox's white toy poodle, Cloudy, raced out of her house, across the front lawn and into the street just as a blue station wagon turned onto the block. The station wagon swerved to avoid hitting the dog, but in an instant slammed into the tiny red fire truck sitting on the corner. Earl never saw the blue station wagon. The impact was instantaneous and crushing. Catapulted ten feet into the air like an old rag doll, the little boy landed in a clump of red Hibiscus bushes.

A guardian angel was watching over Earl Neigh that day. Miraculously he only had a slight concussion, a punctured eardrum, and a cut on his forehead that required four stitches. Earl spent the remainder of his birthday in the emergency room. Unfortunately, the driver of the station wagon was not that fortunate. She crashed into a palm tree and was thrown through the windshield. With life threatening injuries, she was air lifted to Sarasota Memorial Hospital. As for Cloudy, he spent the rest of the day in the house, in his doggy cage and no doggy treats.

Earl's fascination with cars grew stronger with the years. In grade school, he started his own bicycle repair business called, "Earl Neigh, the Bicycle Repair Guy." He handed out flyers at school and nailed up posters on telephone poles throughout the neighborhood advertising his business. Earl fixed flat tires, broken spokes, bent peddles, adjusted handlebars, anything and everything to repair a bicycle. His business was an overnight success.

On Wednesdays, garbage day, Earl would ride around picking up old bicycles people threw out, take them back to his shop, repair them and later sell them. Then on the weekends, he would line up all the repaired bikes on his front lawn with a sign, "Used Bikes for Sale." By the end of fifth grade, Earl had saved $2,325.75—a nice down payment for his first car in four years, three months, two weeks and a day, his sixteenth birthday.

In junior high, he graduated from bicycles to lawn mowers, "Earl Neigh the Lawn Mower Guy." He could take apart a Briggs and Stratton engine blind-folded, clean and replace all the seals, gaskets, filters, belts, and put it back together in a day. He repaired blowers, edgers, hedge clippers and sharpened all cutting equipment. He loved working with engines; unfortunately, his repair business came to an abrupt end when he sliced off three fingers while sharpening a mower blade. Doctors reattached the digits, minus the fingernails and for six months Earl's right hand, wrapped in bandages, resembled a battered old boxing glove.

In high school, as a junior, his guidance counselor enrolled him in the Automotive Service Technology program at the Sarasota County Technical Institute. This two-year, hands-on automotive technology program was exactly the experience Earl needed. Training in transmissions, brakes, electrical systems, axles, heating/air conditioning, suspension/steering, and engine repair led to a degree in Automotive Technology.

During his senior year, Earl completed his cooperative work experience at Boxer's Chevrolet in Venice, graduated and worked at the dealership for two years. Unfortunately, the economy soured; he lost his job and ended up working nights at Wal-Mart.

Chapter Seventeen

"Shit! I can't believe this crap, that old fart in the Buick Century, driving a freaking twenty miles an hour makes the light and I'm stuck here watching the damn draw bridge gate go up; unbelievable." Earl punched the steering wheel and stared at the flashing red lights as the bridge opened. He hated waiting; it was such a waste of time.

Earl sat back and lit a cigarette. He closed his eyes, took a long drag and slowly exhaled. Earl knew smoking was bad and a nagging cough reminded him every morning when he woke up. He tried to quit, hundreds of times, but after seven years of smoking, nothing seemed to work. He bought nicotine gum, tried the patch, was hypnotized, and even had acupuncture, but nothing changed. So at twenty-two, he was still hooked.

The hot December sun beat down on his left arm; he pulled it inside and moved over in the seat. Candy, his current girlfriend, reached over and massaged the back of his neck. It felt good, but Earl knew what was coming next. It was always the same. He waited.

"Honey why do you get so upset over the little, itsy, bitsy things. What's the rush? We are just having lunch at the Le Petit Bistro on the Island. What if it takes another five minutes to get there, we don't have reservations. When we get there, we get there. There's no need to get all upset, just try and relax, honey."

"You're right baby. There's nothing I can do. So what if twenty cars are backed up on the bridge using gallons of gas, belching carbon monoxide into the atmosphere waiting for one boat to go by. So at four dollars a gallon, times twenty cars, and if each car burns one gallon on average per minute; how much is that honey?"

"Oh come on Earl, don't be upset that the car in front of you made it across the bridge and you didn't." Earl just smiled and kept his mouth shut. How could he ever be mad at her? She had the face of an angel and the body of a Victoria Secret model. Long black hair, deep green eyes, a small straight nose, pouty lips surrounded by a big bright smile and a body that filled in all the right places. How *could anyone over the age of three talk like that,* Earl thought, *well no one is perfect.*

"What's the story with the freakin' sailboat? The bridge is open, why doesn't the boat move, what's the guy blind?" At that very moment the bridge tender pushed opened the office door, walked over to the first car on her side of the bridge and said something to the driver. She turned, faced Earl's car, held up her hand as to say *Stop* and walked back into the tiny office. "What the hell is going on? What does that mean? Stop! Lady, I'm already stopped. I'm not going anywhere. Candy, can you see anything on your side?"

"Something is wrong Earl. I've never seen anyone leave the drawbridge office. . .Look, the bridge is going down again."

The instant the bridge lowered and the gates rose, deafening horn blasts from an approaching fire truck vibrated across the bridge. Three, four, five ear piercing blasts continued as the red truck barreled up the bridge behind Earl's car on the opposite side of the road. It flew past Earl like a rocket, jerked into the right hand lane and zoomed over the bridge down onto Tamiami Trail. Earl almost jumped out of his seat, "Did you fucking see that? That guy was flying sixty, seventy miles per hour maybe more, made both lights, maybe he'll make every green light, how cool would that be. Now the gates are going down, shit."

"Earl, why do you always have to curse, you know I don't like it when you talk that way. Please don't say those words any more," Candy pleaded and looked out the window.

"Okay, okay I'm sorry. But this whole thing is freakin' weird."

Attempting to change the topic Candy pointed to a small green plaque on the opposite side of the bridge, "Earl what's that little sign say over there?"

"It's a plaque with the name of this bridge, Circus Bridge. It's called Circus Bridge, because the Ringling Brothers, Barnum and Bailey Circus had its winter headquarters down there. See that big round building, the train would let the circus off on the road, all the animals and circus folk would walk over this bridge to their winter quarters, down there. It was magical looking at all the animals and circus performers in costume. I'll never forget the night I saw the famous animal trainer Gunther Gebel-Williams standing on top of a truck with a leopard draped over his shoulders, what a sight. I still have the picture. He signed it for me when we went to see him perform. I'll show it to you some day if you'd like."

"That would be fantastic; I'd love to see it. So you lived around here when you were young?"

"Yeah I lived off of Shamrock Drive; want to see it?" He said as he turned on the ignition and made a U-turn.

"Earl what are you doing! Are you crazy? You'll get us both killed!"

"Relax baby, I'm gonna show you my old house. Besides, no one's going anywhere until that sailboat passes under the bridge and that could take all day."

Chapter Eighteen

Blaine adjusted her hat so it covered the bandage that protected her twelve stitches. The spot was tender to the touch and her left shoulder was still black and blue, but she was gaining more movement with each day. *That will have to do*, she said to herself, as she took a last look in the car mirror. *I'll worry about an explanation when I get there.*

Blaine put her turn signal on, downshifted her red and white Mini-Cooper into second and turned into the entrance of the park. She glanced down at the clock, 6:30 A.M., an hour and a half before the park opened. Blaine stopped in front of the six-foot, electronic chain-link gate, lowered her window and punched 1-2-3-4 into the key pad. Every time she entered the code she shook her head and wondered, what genius thought that code up; probably Remi.

Slowly the gate rolled across the entire opening to the park; a mandate from Homeland Security after 9-11. They were concerned that a group of terrorists would be camping out in Osprey planning another attack, while roasting marshmallows over a campfire. The Washington Big Wigs were just taking precautions after determining that the terrorist group responsible for the Twin Towers, Pentagon, and Pennsylvania disaster took flying lessons at the Venice Airport six miles away. Therefore, the fence, cameras and weight sensitive alarms needed to be installed covering the entrance and gatehouse, but not without a fight. There were demonstrations in front of the park opposing the installation of the security cameras. Protesters picketed all along Tamiami Trail for months and at times blocked the entrance to the park causing major traffic back-ups.

Trucks delivering materials, pick-ups with workers, and cars filled with tourists were caught in the demonstrations. The State Police and Sheriff's Department handled crowd control and traffic. To make matters worse, on the first day of the demonstration, a State Trooper instructing a trucker to move his vehicle to the side of the road was stuck by a passing car. All lanes of Tamiami Trail were shut down so a helicopter could land and medevac the injured trooper to Sarasota General. Traffic in both directions came to a standstill. Cars backed-up south to Rosebuds in Nokomis and north to Stickney Point Road ran out of gas, engines over heated and hundreds of people with cell phones walked up and down the highway trying to figure out what the problem was. An enterprising young man walked from car to car-selling water for $2.00 a bottle. Where he came from nobody knew, but he did a hell of business that day.

To compound matters, the American Civil Liberties Union added another layer of confusion to the circus atmosphere and sued Homeland Security over the installation of cameras in a public park, which the Union argued to represent an infringement of a person's fourth amendment right against unwarranted surveillance by the government. Petitioned to the Supreme Court of Tallahassee, an injunction put a cease and desist order on all work. Construction supplies, machines, cranes, trucks, tools, and trailers dropped off and piled outside the entrance resembled a dump site for a derelict construction company; not a beautiful state park. One ranger was assigned to monitor the site on a daily basis.

Two months later, the court ruled that in a condition of national security, the government has the jurisdiction under the constitution to monitor the citizenry if they deem a threat to the nation's well-being. Therefore, the gates went up, cameras positioned, alarms installed, and the injured State Trooper was back at work.

Blaine drove up to the gatehouse and waved to Remi Cole, the ranger on duty. A ranger for ten years, Remi was an old timer by today's standards. The story goes that he saved the life of John Forrester, the current Park Manager, when they both worked at the Stub Stewart State Park in Oregon. They were checking a remote area known as Lower Table Rock when a Western Rattler bit John. Remi cut out the venom, put a tourniquet on the leg and carried him 2,000 feet down the mountain on his back. Walking down a mountain on your own was a job, but with someone on your back was quite a feat.

Sadly, the manager lost the leg, but despite the handicap, which he never recognized, was considered the one of the top Professional Land Managers in Florida. Forrester has been a champion for the protection and appreciation of the environment all his life and on a daily basis takes a "hands on approach" to promote the natural values of the park. Knowledgeable in all aspects of park management, Forrester was offered park manager positions from Hawaii to Alaska, turned them down and was content to manage idyllic Osprey State Park. However, as any good politician who unequivocally states that the rumors of leaving office were just rumors, who know what offers lie around the corner for John Forrester.

As for Remi Cole, just as in the nursery rhyme, 'Mary Had A Little Lamb,' everywhere John Forrester went, so did Remi Cole. "Good morning Remi."

"Good morning Assistant Park Manager Sterling, you're here early today. Is anything wrong?" Remi answered with a hint of agitation in his voice.

"Wrong? Why do you think something could be wrong?" She replied and handed him the attendance sheet clipboard. Blaine had a sixth sense about things and there was something in Remi's voice that didn't seem right, or was it just him. Blaine from day one had an uneasy feeling about Remington Hunter Cole. Remi, as he preferred, was named after all things, his father's favorite hunting rifle, the Remington Gamemaster 760. Remi grew up around guns and hunting all his life, so to all his friends and relatives, "Remi" made sense.

Around park campfires, Remi regaled the rangers with stories about how he would go out into the wilderness for days and live off the land. He shot rabbits, squirrels, birds, snakes, and other small game. He rambled on about how he cooked over an open fire, bathed in streams and slept in abandoned bear caves. After about the third campfire story, rangers dubbed him, "the caveman". They never called him that to his face, but when his campfire stories got gross, a ranger would get up grunting and walk around like a Neanderthal. It was an inside joke that helped break the boredom of his stories.

Remi did not look like a cave dweller, far from it, he was handsome and he knew it. He had a body builder's physique, not grotesque bulges everywhere, but well proportioned muscles from head to toe. His tight shirts also helped to accent his biceps and bulging chest. He had short black hair, military cut, squared chiseled face, small straight nose, cleft chin, beautiful white teeth, and his big broad smile could melt butter. He was good-looking and used it to his advantage.

"Oh no! Nothing is wrong, Assistant Park Manager, I just wasn't expecting you this early." A short abrupt cough ended the conversation.

"I have a school group arriving at nine o'clock and want to organize a few things before they get here. Please give the bus driver directions to the Nature Center when they arrive. Bye."

Chapter Nineteen

Blaine shifted into first gear and drove off. Maybe it was her imagination, but Remi seemed on edge and uncharacteristically nervous. She made a mental note to document the incident when she reached the office.

The main road leading into the park, lined on both sides by huge, ancient oaks that formed a lush, green canopy over the stretch of blacktop and created a dramatic entranceway to the park. Shadows of light danced between the trees, and slowly seeped down through spirals of cascading Spanish moss that hung from branches like dusty, earthen Christmas ornaments. Filtered by a profusion of greenery, the noise from the highway long silenced, the park exemplified a time when life was slower and more in touch with nature. Only the occasional squawk of a scrub jay disturbed the tranquil hush of this tropical paradise.

Midway under the canopy, the road dipped and a cool breeze blew in through the window. Blaine loved that part of the drive, especially on hot, steamy August days. Driving at eye level with the forest floor, she marveled at the profuse shades of greens and browns from nature's beauty. She took in a breath of the sweet air and smiled.

Blaine took the second left onto a narrow shell-covered road that wound down to ranger headquarters. At the end of the road, a circle of four trailers and a pole barn sat nestled among a scrub of slash pine and scrub oak trees. The first two trailers were the sleeping quarters for the rangers and AmeriCorps volunteers that resided at the park, the third building housed the local and state science/research headquarters, and the fourth trailer was the administration building. Beyond the trailers, stood the pole barn, a big open hulk of a structure, built on poles that stored all the trucks, carts, tools, and park supplies. It was also the main gathering location for the "Friends of the Park," a group of volunteers dedicated to help maintain and beautify the park.

Blaine parked in front of the fourth building and walked in. The inside was an explosion of color and excitement. Entire walls filled with posters, pictures and photographs from the Scrub-Jay 5K run, the Native American Indian Festival, Earth Day, All Trails Hike, Legacy Trails Opening Day ceremony, camping, swimming, and Scout activities represented a collage of memories for all the visitors to enjoy. Two terrariums filled with local flora and fauna accented the corners of the room. Animal and plant mobiles hung from the ceiling, swirling down so low people would have to bend their head to pass. On the left side of the room were the computer workstations for the rangers and on the right were the stations for the AmeriCorps volunteer workers. At one end of the building was the park manager's office and at the opposite end was Blaine's office and storeroom. The entire building was alive with posters and projects relating to the park and the environment. Like the room, the people who worked there were positively energized, and always trying to come up with new ideas that would make the park an exciting place to visit.

Blaine gathered up the seine nets, buckets, fishing poles, sand sifters, and a box of drawing supplies for the class and placed them outside on the road. Surprised by all the early morning activity an Indigo snake slithered across the road and into a stand of Muhly grass all the while sticking out its forked red tongue at this interloper. Blaine smiled, for she knew the black four-foot reptile was not poisonous, but instead a friend to the park who helped reduce the rodent population. Blaine continued across the circle to the pole barn to pick up an ATV.

She placed everything in the back of the ATV and returned inside to check her messages. The red light on her answering machine was blinking. Blaine pressed the play button:

"Hello Ms. Sterling this is detective Beale. I would like to stop by the park today around three o'clock and talk to you about your meeting with Mr. Dunn. If this is not convenient call me at (941) 486-2444. Thank you."

She saved the number to her cell phone, turned out the lights and left the building. She couldn't keep from thinking about that poor man and all that blood. Why would Detective Beale want to talk with her? What could she possibly tell him about Mr. Dunn?

Blaine turned onto the main road towards the Nature Center. Within minutes the landscape changed dramatically, the lush green hammock that shaded the road was replaced by the scrubby flatwoods, the habitat of the Florida Scrub Jay. The stark beauty of the low growing scrub oak, wax myrtle, slash pine, and prickly pear cactus painted a harsh tapestry of browns and grassy dry greens. To hikers, the flat open sandy terrain was unforgiving; the soft white sand caved with each step made walking difficult and the absence of shade from the punishing rays of the sun sapped what little energy was left long before they reached the shade of the Nature Center. As uninviting an environment it appeared to humans, it was the perfect habitat for the Florida Scrub Jay to bury approximately 8,000 acorns for its yearly supply of food.

Out of the corner of her eye, Blaine saw a flash of blue fly into the cover of a scrub oak tree. On cue, she pulled the ATV over and reached for her binoculars hooked to the steering column. Scanning the area from left to right Blaine finally focused on a stunted oak 30 feet from the road. There perched on a thin branch halfway from the top was a banded adult Scrub Jay. Its cerulean blue feathers and gray belly made an easy target to spot. "Fantastic!" Blaine whispered as she took out a notebook from her shirt pocket.

"Number 49, I can't believe it, what great luck." Carefully she recorded the date, red trail-center, 30 feet from road, adult, banded y-sl. "I'll check with biology this afternoon and see what family this little guy belongs to," she said to herself as she leaned over and put the binoculars back in its leather case.

Chapter Twenty

"Excuse me! I want you to get down from the ladder and walk to me," Blaine shouted squinting into the sun as a purple haze of movement scurried down the ladder. Across from Blaine's scrub jay sighting was the entrance to the park campground. In the center of the entrance was a large circular patch of grass with a 10' × 20' campground sign welcoming visitors to the campsite. Leaning up against the corner of the sign and standing on the top rung of a half, broken wooden ladder was Vardi Zammiello, fondly referred to as, *the Purple Lady*. Miss Vardi, as she liked to be called, was an aging hippie from the seventies. A retired art teacher from The Hewlett School of East Islip, a prestigious private school on Long Island, Miss Vardi, you could say was into purple. Everything pertaining to her existence revolved around the color purple. Her hair was dyed purple, her make-up when she wore any was purple, her clothes were purple, even her classroom was painted purple. She encouraged her students to have a "purple day". That was a bit of a conflict since the school had a strict dress code and all the students were required to wear a uniform. So on the first Friday of each month Miss Vardi would have "purple day" in her classroom. "Purple Haze" by Jimmy Hendrix blasted all day long, purple spotlights illuminated the ceiling in a purple glow, and all of her art classes worked on projects and activities in purple. At the end of the class, Miss Vardi would hand out a paper purple flower for each child to pin on his or her blazer. At first, the students thought she had lost her mind, but as the year progressed, every student looked forward to "purple day".

As a young girl, Vardi would cut bunches of lilac flowers from her mother's lilac bushes along the side of the house and made beautiful lilac hats. Some were round, some were square, some were tall, and some were flat, but all of them were lovingly arranged one flower at a time. At the end of every summer, Vardi would have a lilac tea party and invite all the girls in the neighborhood over. She spent days preparing for the gala event. Invitations were sent, on purple paper, in purple envelopes. Each invitation was hand written in purple ink with a small drawing of a lilac flower in the upper left hand corner of the salutation. Each table had its own unique lilac centerpiece and on the purple paper plates, a special lilac hat waited for each girl.

It was a glorious time; the girls would laugh and sing and dance, and drink purple tea all day long. When it was time to leave, the girls would gather in a circle, hug, count to three, and throw their hats into the air. Maybe it was the heat or the many days of wearing lilac hats, but after the hat toss, all the girls exploded into laughter and just stared at Vardi's head. Vardi had a purple ring across her forehead and from that day on, she was nicknamed the purple lady. With age, the infatuation with purple never withered, in fact it blossomed into a marvelous calling.

Spread out over the entire campground circle were paint cans, boxes, brushes, paint rollers, buckets, purple drop cloths and an old purple bike. "Just what do you think you're doing, Miss Vardi?" Blaine shouted as she walked across the road.

"And good morning to you, Blaine, now don't get your jets all in an uproar, all I wanted to do was add a little excitement to this boring sign of yours!" Vardi said, as she stepped off the ladder with a big smile on her face. "I was thinking maybe a big, bright purple flower here, a purple Scrub Jay over there, and a purple tortoise, rabbit and woodpecker around the boarder of the sign. How does that sound Assistant Park Manager Sterling?"

"That's not funny, Miss Vardi. You can't do whatever you like on state property just because you may think something looks boring. You must have authorization!" Blaine walked over to the sign, pointed to the State of Florida seal and then to Miss Vardi.

"Okay, okay, I was just having a little fun with you, Blaine. I spoke with the manager last week and showed him this." Miss Vardi handed Blaine a sketch of the entrance sign with the park manager's signature at the bottom. The drawing was breathtaking! Blaine was taken back at how beautifully the artist captured the spirit of the park and how the sign came alive and welcomed visitors with its deep, rich colors that vibrated off the paper. And the best part, there weren't any purple animals crawling all over the sign.

"Well I owe you an apology, Miss Vardi, it is beautiful. I can't wait to see the finished product."

Miss Vardi climbed back up the purple ladder and Blaine walked back to her ATV.

Blaine drove directly to the Nature Center, dropped off all the supplies, and continued on to the Legacy Trail gate. It was one of her responsibilities to make sure that the trailhead was secure at dusk and open for park access in the morning. As she pulled up to the gate she noticed that the sliding gate wasn't snubbed up against the support pole and the lock was open. In order to secure the trailhead gate, both procedures had to be followed or else the lock wouldn't close completely. This was the second time Blaine found the gate unlocked. She also noticed three sets of ATV tracks that originated from the trailhead entrance leading toward a remote section of the park. She jotted down the time, date, and direction of the tracks and made a notation to investigate the tracks at the end of the day.

Chapter Twenty-One

Lou Bravo's stomach began to make a grumbling sound, a low guttural noise that increased with intensity and regularity as he drove north on Tamiami Trail. He skipped breakfast to get an early start on the chairs and now he was paying for it. He had a pounding headache and felt nauseous; he couldn't decide if his condition was due to lack of nourishment, the spectacle outside Blaine's house or the heavy rain that just started to fall. *What a jerk. I can't believe I went off on her over that asshole Spitzer. What was I thinking? I guess I wasn't, that's the problem. Yeah, I'll apologize, that's what I'll do. Right after I get something to eat.*

Lou Bravo turned left on to Venice Avenue, put his right directional on and merged into the right hand lane. He eased his truck over to the curb in front of Patches, the local eatery for a great breakfast, and cut the engine. *A perfect spot to keep an eye my truck,* he thought to himself. *That's all I'd need to top off my morning if some bozo stole the chairs while I was having breakfast. I'd never live it down. I'd have to keep driving to Tampa. There's no way I could ever go back. I'd be the laughing stock of the neighborhood. Oh yeah, that's Lou Bravo the guy who lost all our chairs, but he had a nice breakfast.*

As usual the restaurant was packed. Every table and booth had customers happy to get out of the rain and have a seat. A handful of people under umbrellas lined up outside and waited to hear their names called for a table. Jackie, the new owner, stood at the counter by the door taking names. "Hi, doll face, looks like business as usual, packed. I guess the recession hasn't hurt your little corner of the world," Lou Bravo crooned as he scanned the room for a familiar face.

"Lou Bravo, good to see you, honey. Hey what can I say, we give the people what they want, good food at the right price. Couldn't be the reason why you show up here four times a week for breakfast."

"Guilty as charged doll face, you know I'm a sucker for your hash browns," Lou Bravo just raised his arms and smiled. "So Jackie, how long is the wait?"

"For you, honey, none, I got a booth by the front window right now."

"What am I the millionth customer or something? This is better than winning the lottery. What did I do to rate such service?"

"Nothing, honey, I figure if I don't seat you now, your friend in the booth who has been waving frantically since you came in will have a stroke before he pays the bill. And that's not good for business, honey."

"Not paying the bill or the stroke?" Maureen smiled and walked Lou Bravo to the booth.

Chapter Twenty-Two

"What are you blind? I've been waving to you for the past five minutes and now my arm is killing me. I think I've sprained my wrist. Yeah, look at this, I can't straighten it, it's bent. I'm crippled and it's your fault," Tony lamented and rubbed his wrist.

Tony Lilly was another transplant from New York who moved down to Florida after his business figuratively speaking went south. Tony owned Tony Lilly & Sons Trucking, which was strategically located off the Long Island Expressway in Ronkonkoma. Tony married late in life, he dated, but never had a steady girl until he met Anna Mercurio ten years ago, on Christmas Eve in the lingerie department at Macy's. Tony needed a present for his eighty-nine year old mother and as usual, everything with Tony was last minute. After a twenty-minute sortie into the depths of the robe and pajama racks without success, Anna appeared. She asked only two questions, age and favorite color, and in two minutes returned with a fluffy, blue, terry cloth robe. It was perfect, Tony's mother loved it and Tony fell in love with Anna Mercurio. Tony had a great personality and was a lot fun to be around, but he was hard on the eyes. He looked like a buzzard, tall, with a long neck that arched forward, hooked nose, bald head, and skinny as a rail. Three pairs of pajamas, two nightgowns and one robe later, Tony finally built up the courage to ask Anna out on a date. The following year they were married. Tony never had any sons, didn't have any daughters, but he thought adding "Sons" made the business sound more professional and in turn create more business. That also sums up how he ran his business—he made things up. Unfortunately, for Tony that's what brought down his house of cards. Tony had a great deal going on. He won a large bid transporting truckloads of mail for the entire Northeast corridor for the U.S. Mail. All of his trucks were delivering bags and bags of mail seven days a week, fifty-two weeks a year. The contract renewed every four years and if he didn't screw up, he had it for life. Then something did go terribly wrong, a major screw-up. Three of Tony's trucks were caught on camera at the Brooklyn Postal Dock the night the payroll for Fort Totten disappeared. The problem for Tony, his trucks only picked up/ dropped off mail out of the New Jersey Depot. Tony lost the postal contract, his business, filed for bankruptcy and he moved to Venice, Florida. Now he is in the residential and commercial cleaning business, the ice cream business, and a few other questionable ventures. With all the new OSHA restrictions on removal of contaminants, you could say Tony Lilly made a *Clean Sweep* on the name of his latest venture.

"Tony you worry too much, the wrist will be fine, when you go home rub some Ben-Gay on it and call me in the morning. Dr. Lou predicts a full recovery." Lou Bravo slapped the table and laughed so loud people stared.

"Very funny, it's not your wrist that's throbbing. Any way I have something to show you." In mid-sentence, the server arrived and placed a large plate of blueberry pancakes, hash browns and bacon in front of Tony.

"Good morning, Lou Bravo, what can I get you sweetie?" She poured steaming hot coffee into both their cups.

"I'll have what he's having and please put a rush on it Victoria, I'm starving."

With a big smile on her cherubic pink Russian face, Victoria Koklovia, a rotund, buxom waitress for more than forty years, with a no-nonsense reputation, looked Lou Bravo straight in the eyes and said, "Well I'll just drop everything and run into the kitchen and mix you up a batch of flapjacks lickety split."

Not to be out foxed, Lou Bravo replied in his most persuasive voice, "Victoria, you know how I like my bacon, extra crispy and if it's not too much trouble, a large glass of orange juice. Thank. . . ." Before he could finish his sentence, she turned and walked back to the kitchen. "This is a great table Tony, now I don't have to worry about the chairs. I have a perfect view from here. Go ahead and eat, your pancakes are getting cold. Can I have a slice of bacon? I'm starving."

"Yeah, sure take one. Anyway did you read the paper this morning?" Tony chirped in and smothered his pancakes in syrup.

"If you're talking about that Spitzer article, I read it and don't get me started on that sicko. I just finished making an ass of myself over at Blaine's house about how that asshole ruined my business. I totally lost it and now I am *persona non grata* over there. She is so pissed off at me. Now I have to figure out how to make it up to her and fast."

"No, I'm talking about the story on page 15." Tony slid the paper across the table and there in the top right hand column, in bold letters:

"Sarasota Store Robbed – One Million Dollars of Furniture Stolen"

Thieves hijacked a truck full of Ethan Allen designer furniture last night from the store parking lot. One-of-a-kind custom pieces reported the storeowner, Harvey Hielbrum. "We were preparing for our annual year-end spectacular; now we will have to re-order all new furniture." Police ask anyone with information to call 484-1234.

"Well I'll be damned; I didn't think that bastard had the balls to go through with it. One million dollars or more that fat fuck will collect on maybe, twenty grand worth of Sealy Posturepedics." Lou Bravo whispered and cleared a place for his breakfast.

"The rich get richer, Lou Bravo, and you can take that to the bank."

"You can say that again sweetie," Victoria sang out and dropped a stack of pancakes in front of Lou Bravo. "Fast enough for you sweetie, I hope you like your bacon extra, extra crispy, because they look like beef jerky to me. Anybody want more coffee?"

"Victoria, you're an angel, one more minute and I would have passed out right here on this table," Lou Bravo rejoiced and reached for the syrup.

"Well, dig in, sweetie, I don't want you passing out before you pay the bill," Victoria crowed and walked over to the next table. Lou Bravo didn't need any prompting, no sooner had Victoria placed the checks on the table, he drenched the pancakes with syrup. Lou Bravo was on a mission, to feed his face before he starved to death. Two pancakes, hash browns, three slices of bacon and a large glass of orange juice devoured in five minutes.

"Coming up for air?" Tony queried. "So now that you finished everything on your plate and my bacon, what are we going to do?"

"Do, we're not going to do a thing. The cops are looking for high-end furniture, not mattresses. Good ole Harvey gave us the perfect alibi," Lou Bravo joked and finished his coffee.

"What about the neighbors, won't they figure it out after they read the article and call the cops."

Lou Bravo leaned forward and whispered straight at Tony, "You worry too much my friend. It is bad for the heart. There is nothing to figure out. The police are looking for fine furniture, not mattresses. The only thing you need to worry about is that kid with the bubble gum, Hubba Bubba. What a name."

"Hubba Bubba, he works for me, plus he's too stupid to figure anything out. I think it's all that Hubba Bubba gum he chews, too much sugar in his system," Tony joked. "The kid can't remember what he did yesterday, let alone a few weeks ago."

"So forget about it, Tony. It's over. We made couple of grand free and clear, my neighbors got new mattresses and everybody is happy. Come on, let's get out of here, I got the check." Lou Bravo laughed and put his arm over Tony's shoulder as they walked out of the restaurant.

Lou drove under the Venice Avenue Bridge, parked and unloaded the chairs. Five days earlier, he roped off his usual spot, a grassy knoll southeast of the bridge directly above the Intracoastal, a perfect place to watch the parade. He lined up the chairs along the walkway, placed the barbeque grill, two tables and tent in the corner closest to the bridge. From experience, that corner was the best spot to grill. The wind blew in from the south, so when cooking, all the smoke would blow away from the chairs creating a smoke free zone to watch the parade. The last touch was to put the American flag on the top of the tent. It made a perfect marker for the neighbors and helped deter anyone from stealing the chairs, very unpatriotic.

Chapter Twenty-Three

Blaine finished setting up the last science activity in the Nature Center and walked outside. She sat down in one of the four rocking chairs that welcomed tired hikers to the front porch for a respite. Blaine checked her watch, 8:45 A.M., perfect timing, all that remained was to wait for Miss Maiello's fourth grade class to arrive. Blaine leaned back and closed her eyes.

It is strange how a certain event can influence a person's life and leave a profound mark deep within one's soul. Birth of a child, marriage, death of a parent are all but a few of such watershed events that have a tremendous impact that alters a person's perspective of the world. Buried within one's psyche, the significance of the event might not be immediately apparent; it may be a way the body protects itself when the person is not ready for the full realization of the message.

Blaine Sterling had one such event last Thursday night. For the past two months, she and Marybeth worked side-by-side in the Nature Center developing hands-on activities and study guides for each student. Blaine was locking up when Marybeth suggested, "Hey let's celebrate finishing the project. The Sea Basin Café is just down the road and I hear they have great wings."

"Sounds great, but I need to call the sitter and see if she can watch Brooke for another hour or two. I'll ask her to order a pizza for dinner that will be a treat for my daughter, pizza during the week." Blaine spoke with Mrs. Brecht, the sitter, and she said that she could stay and not rush home on her account.

The Sea Basin Café was right off 41, about ten minutes from the park. A quaint little place pushed back off the main road in a small unassuming strip mall. They parked on the side of the café, walked around to the front, and sat at one of the outside tables. The entire façade of the restaurant was lit up with an assortment of neon waves, palm trees, fish, parrots, and flamingos—a typical "Cheeseburger in Paradise" hangout. To complement the Caribbean ambience, Jimmy Buffett songs played creating a funky laid-back tropical feeling. The server, 'Windy,' a perky, well-endowed twenty-something in a skimpy sailor's outfit that showed more than it covered, took the order; a basket of hot wings and two draft beers. With a tip of her sailor's cap, she turned and sashayed back inside. "What's with that sailor's outfit?" Marybeth giggled. "Could she show anymore cleavage, what does she have two buttons buttoned, why bother?"

"Quiet here she comes; I think it's only one."

Devoured in record time, the wings were delicious, spicy hot, and filling. The beers were cold and refreshing, but not filling, so they ordered another round.

Blaine raised her glass, "Here's to you Ms. Maiello, to a job well done, congratulations. You created science lessons that will inspire your students."

Marybeth picked up her glass, "Here's to you, Assistant Park Manager Sterling, to a job well done. Your guidance in developing hands-on activities that go beyond the classroom will make our science lessons so much more meaningful to the students. I believe it was Socrates who said, *'I see and I forget, I read and I remember, I do and I understand!'*

"Okay Marybeth, here's to understanding." They clinked their glasses together, took a big gulp, leaned back in their Casablanca chairs and took in the moment.

A few minutes later, Marybeth leaned forward, pushed her long brown hair behind her ear and casually asked, "So, Blaine, what made you move to Florida?" Maybe it was the two beers, or the soothing night breeze, or maybe it was Marybeth's unassuming demeanor and soulful brown eyes. Whatever the catalyst, Blaine could never have predicted her reply, never in a million years; it was so out of character. The question was so innocuous, so disarming. It was as if when you ask someone how they feel; you don't expect a twenty-minute diatribe on the functioning of one's gall bladder. A simple, *okay,* would have sufficed, but Blaine let her guard down.

"I was raped!"

"Oh my God, no," Marybeth uttered and fell back in her chair numb.

"I had just graduated from college, and taken a job as a park ranger at Watch Hill, Fire Island, a barrier beach located off the south shore of Long Island. It was an amazing park, a twenty-minute ferry ride from the mainland and you were in paradise. Watch Hill didn't offer the fancy amenities that other Fire Island parks touted; it didn't have the restaurants, bars, boutiques, concession stands, or waterfront homes. What made it unique was its unspoiled natural beauty. There was a small marina, picnic area, a ranger office, general store, and small campground, a wooden boardwalk around the park, a ranger's cottage and a pristine sandy white beach. It was a park ranger's dream come true, or that's what I thought at first."

Blaine reached for her glass, but put it back down without a sip. "In September, Hurricane Floyd roared up the East Coast and slammed into Long Island like an out of control locomotive engine. I was ordered to close down the park and secure all the buildings in preparation for 90-mph winds or stronger. At four o'clock, the last ferry took off what I believed to be all of the campers and day-trippers. Unbeknownst to me, everyone didn't evacuate, Matt Purdy, a back packer, was asleep, drunk on the beach five miles east of Watch Hill. Purdy woke in a panic; dark angry six foot waves crashed onto the shoreline eating away at the beach with each pounding wave. Blistering winds kicked up sand that bit with needle-like pricks, making it almost impossible to see. Confused, drunk, and frightened, he knew he needed to get off the beach and find shelter. He turned and walked back to the park."

"By nine o'clock, the hurricane was at full strength. The pounding rain and punishing winds battered Fire Island unmercifully. Power went out. I closed my eyes and tried to sleep."

"A flash of lightning and a crack of thunder just about threw me out of bed. There standing beside me was a naked man dripping wet holding a large knife. He waved the jagged blade in front of my face and told me to take off my clothes and that he wouldn't hurt me if I cooperated. He got on top of me, pushed my legs apart and raped me. I could feel the cold blade pressing against the side of my neck, but that was nothing compared to the ripping pain from the first penetration. His moaning became louder and his thrusts more violent. Then he stopped and collapsed onto my chest. He wasn't particularly heavy, but what I do remember is his heart pounding, as I lay motionless beneath him. I didn't feel excitement, disgust, or pain. I separated myself from my body. The only thing that mattered was to come away from the nightmare alive."

Blaine stopped, reached for her glass and this time took a drink. She swallowed and waited a moment before she spoke. "Time was impossible to calculate. Minutes, hours, I couldn't tell. I just lay there not making a move. Sometime during the night, I felt the pressure of the knife relax and his hand move down and cup my breast. His breathing slowed, he shifted most of his weight off me onto the bed and fell asleep. I knew I had to get the knife. I reached over my shoulder with my right arm, grabbed the knife and slowly slid the left side of my body from underneath him. First, I wiggled my leg free, and then arched my hip to slide my lower part over and finally pulled my left arm from under his chest."

"It was daybreak when I stood at the side of the bed with the knife in my hand. As I looked down at the man who violated me, my first impulse was to cut his dick off, but the thought of going to jail didn't sound like a good plan."

"I agree, but what did you do? Did you run out of the cabin?"

"No, I tiptoed over to the desk and took out two pairs of handcuffs. His left arm was resting at the top of the bed and it was simple to cuff him to the metal bedpost. His right arm took forever to move to the top of the bed. Twice he turned and tucked it under his body. Finally, I managed to move his arm free and cuff it. I took a dock line hanging on the wall and tied his feet to the end of the bed. It was over, or so I thought."

"Oh no, don't tell me he woke up and attacked you again," Marybeth uttered as she gulped down the last of her drink.

"I called 911 on my cell phone and reported the rape. I explained how I freed myself, took away his weapon and handcuffed him to the bed. The desk sergeant explained that the devastation on the mainland was extensive, but they would send a police boat as soon as they could. I put on my uniform."

"Purdy woke up with a huge headache and shocked to find his arms and feet handcuffed to the bed. Conveniently, he had no recollection of breaking into the office or raping me at knifepoint. To refresh his memory I shoved his knife up against his neck; he screamed '*Yes*' as blood dripped down his neck. I jammed a sock into his mouth, and reminded him that now the whole world will know what a piece of garbage he was as I carved RAPIST into his stomach. His muffled screams turned to whimpering right before he passed out."

"The police arrived mid-morning and hauled his ass off to jail. I went to the hospital, had the obligatory rape test and then gave a statement to the police."

"Two months later the bastard walked out of court an innocent man. His lawyer, some hot shot from New York City, convinced the jury that it was consensual and without any witnesses, it was his word against mine. Typical 'he said she said' defense."

"I don't believe it, he went free," Marybeth gasped. "Where is the justice?"

"The weirdest thing about the trial was his attorney never mentioned the tattoo carved into Purdy's stomach. Probably it would reinforce the idea that he did rape me. I wasn't going to say anything, plus my attorney advised me not to mention it in fear of being charged with assault with a deadly weapon."

"Unbelievable, the thought of charging you with assault," Marybeth just shook her head.

"Oh, did I mention; Matthew Purdy was the grandson of the Nassau County Supervisor. Not that would have any influence on my case, but you can be the judge of that," Blaine snapped angrily and looked Marybeth straight in the eye.

"The trial took a bitter toll on my parents. The testimony, pictures and then the acquittal, my parents were devastated. A monster violated their little girl and they could not get justice. A month later, a hit-and-run driver killed my dad as he rode his bike home from school. The police never arrested the driver. Both tragedies were too much for my mother to bear and she died of a broken heart that winter. The only person not scathed from the whole ordeal was my younger brother Bobby; a senior at West Liberty State College in West Virginia, he was far enough away to not be consumed by the ordeal and smart enough to land a job in Indiana as director of operations for the Colts Stadium. So that afternoon, after the trial, I handed in my resignation,

Googled State Parks employment, found an opening in Florida and here I am."

"Well that's not your typical, I moved to Florida because of the warm climate and beautiful beaches answer I was expecting," Marybeth gasped. "I'm so sorry."

"Thank you, but speaking of justice, I received a call from my old boss on Fire Island last night. He informed me that Matt Purdy, drunk, doing 90 mph, crashed his brand new red Corvette convertible into a guardrail on the Long Island Expressway. It took firefighters, using the Jaws of Life, one hour to pry him out of the car. He'll live, but he lost his right leg and Purdy's grandfather was not re-elected, innuendos of a rape didn't make for good politics. So, what goes around, comes around, does happen," Blaine chuckled.

"I guess Mr. Purdy won't be able to see Brooke very often? After the accident," Marybeth whispered and looked over at Blaine as they left the restaurant.

"Oh no, Matt Purdy isn't the father. Brooke's father is Troy Sterling, but that's another story and there isn't enough time tonight," Blaine laughed as they both walked to their cars.

Chapter Twenty-Four

At 9:15 A.M., the school bus pulled up to the Nature Center. The doors opened and twenty-three fourth graders from Pinebrook Elementary School piled out along, with two parents and their teacher, Miss Marybeth Maiello. It was obvious by the jostling for space towards the front of the line; and their glowing faces that the students loved their teacher. Who wouldn't? Miss Maiello, only in her second year of teaching, was the most requested fourth grade teacher at Pinebrook. She was an exceptional teacher, graduated with honors from FSU, energetic, creative, and best of all she loved children. Her enthusiasm was contagious not only with children, but for adults as well.

Still a little groggy, Blaine walked down the path to the parking lot to greet the students. "Good morning and welcome to Osprey State Park, I'm Ranger Blaine and I'm glad to finally meet you. Miss Maiello has told me so much about you. Please follow me into the Nature Center." Inside the Center, the students sat at the four different workstation tables that Blaine and Marybeth set around room. Each station corresponded to a different theme pertaining to the park that the students would be working on: Life Underground, A Changing Landscape, Sights and Sounds of the Park, and Life Above Ground. "Can I have your attention please," with a big friendly smile Blaine walked up to the front of the room, "before we hike one of the trails this morning, I'd like to talk to you about the park and the job of a park ranger, but before I begin, are there any questions?"

At the last table, a hand went up. "Can I go to the bathroom?" The entire class turned and burst out laughing. Although the boy appeared big for his age, Blaine immediately noticed that he was embarrassed. His beautiful round checks turned red and his big brown eyes teared over in confusion. He bowed his head.

"Excuse me class, but I don't see anything funny about that question!" exclaimed Blaine. "What is your name young man?"

"Will."

"Will asked a perfectly good question, as a matter of fact; before we go on any hike, all the classes take a bathroom break. Some trails don't have rest room facilities and it can get very uncomfortable hiking two miles or more on a full bladder. Will, thank you for reminding me about the bathroom stop. I think this is a perfect time for a bathroom break. Will, I'd like you to be the first to line up."

"Thanks Blaine for correcting the class for making fun of Will. He tries so hard to make friends, but some of the students can be cruel," Marybeth whispered. "My heart goes out to him every time he is hurt."

"No problem, it was my pleasure. I hate bullies and the only way to stop the bullying is to confront them every time their behavior is unacceptable. Kids need to understand that bullying will not be tolerated, period. On a cheerier note, I had a great time last night. I hope I didn't bore you with my life story?"

"Are you kidding? You were anything but boring." She took Blaine's arm and walked outside, "I can't wait to hear about Brooke's father."

Blaine smiled and yelled, "Okay class; follow Will straight ahead to the bathrooms. We will meet at the fence in front of Lake Osprey to hike the Green Trail."

Five minutes later the class was looking out over the crystal blue waters of Lake Osprey and thinking how refreshing an early morning swim would be. "I bet some of you would like to jump into the lake right now and cool off. Sorry it will have to wait. The lake is manmade, it is a 'borrow pit lake.' What that means is workers borrowed the dirt from digging this lake to use somewhere else. In fact, all the dirt taken from the lake built the road in front of the park, Route 41. Lake Osprey is a freshwater lake and is only about fifteen feet at its deepest part. If you look out to the center, you can see bubbles no, it's not a sea monster; it's fresh water pumped into the lake to aerate and circulate the water. Yes, someone has a question?" Blaine asked pointing to a young man hanging over the fence.

"Are there alligators in the lake?"

"Oh, you saw the sign, very observant. What's your name?"

"Kenny La Palma." He leaned over the fence and pointed towards the corner of the lake. He was bright faced and wore a blue and white striped shirt. He had thick, straight blond hair parted neatly on the left side, high rounded cheekbones and radiant blue eyes that broadcasted his excitement. Kenny was the smartest boy in the class; actually, he was the brightest student at Pinebrook. His IQ was off the charts and his inquisitive mind was always in high gear. There were times when Miss Maiello had to look on the Internet, so she could understand what Kenny meant.

In spite of his genius he did not put on airs, he was cognizant of his gift and was very respectful of his peers and adults. A character trait instilled upon him by his mother and dutifully cultivated by both his grandparents.

"Yes and no. We had a small alligator, about four feet long, last year, but it only stayed about a week. Alligators migrate from spot to spot looking for food or a mate. I guess our alligator didn't get either, so he went off looking elsewhere. You'll notice we trucked in white sand and roped off an area for swimming, very inviting on a hot day like today."

Blaine turned and led the group down to the footbridge behind the Nature Center. "Right now we're at the beginning of the Green Trail. Straight ahead is the campground, there are 104 campsites all equipped with electricity, water and a fire pit. If you like camping, you'll love it here. Today, we are going to take the trail to the left and if we're quiet, we may spot a scrub jay or gopher tortoise."

"Ranger Blaine, why does the water look so gross; is it polluted?" A voice called out from the front of the line.

"Good question Kenny. You are right; it does look disgusting, doesn't it? Down there is South Creek, a blackwater stream that flows through the park and eventually empties into the Gulf of Mexico. The water looks dark because of tannin, a chemical from the slash pine trees that seeps into the water and makes it look black. No, it's not polluted, but I wouldn't recommend drinking from it. Okay, let's get going."

The black top trail led past two campsites and then narrowed into a sandy path only big enough for two hikers at a time. Within minutes, the area opened up into acres of low growing scrub oak, slash pine, wax myrtle, prickly pear cactus, and saw palmettos—a perfect habitat for scrub jay sightings. As luck would have it, two scrub jays flew past and lighted upon a tree directly in front of them. Blaine held her hand up, pointed to the right and immediately the entire group froze. The scrub jays, oblivious of the humans clicking away taking pictures, proceeded to pick and bury acorns in the sand directly in front of the visitors. Three minutes later, they flew off over the pine trees. The rest of the hike was hot and boring.

Back at the Nature Center, the class ate lunch, broke into their science groups and worked all afternoon. At 2:45 P.M., Miss Maiello called the groups together in the Nature Center for a sharing session. Each group had five minutes to talk about their project and answer questions. The work was outstanding. All of the topics were completed. The lake group collected enough plants, fish, frogs, and insects to fill three aquariums. The Nature Center group compiled over twenty pages of park information, twenty-three watercolor paintings of the flora and fauna, and preliminary sketches for a classroom diorama.

Will, elected spokesperson for his group, was a delight. Like a Broadway actor who found his stage, he moved from project to project, gesturing, raising his voice, and answering questions with ease. For once, he was accepted.

At three o'clock sharp, the school bus pulled up to the Nature Center, the kids got on and they pulled away. Blaine waved good-bye as a white Crown Victoria pulled into the parking lot.

Chapter Twenty-Five

Beale drove into the police parking lot and squeezed his cruiser into the third parking space along the building. A spot close to the door; a benefit ten years on the force commanded. It didn't put any more money in his wallet, but it was as good as gold during the rainy season. It beat running from the back lot to the police entrance door in the pouring rain. It's a bitch walking around wet in air conditioning all day long. Beale looked up at the swirling gray clouds forming overhead and thought to himself, *it looks like rain.* He smiled, punched in the security code and opened the door.

Headquarters was quiet. The first day shift hadn't started and the late night detail was still out. Only the hushed sound of the fax machine spitting out the night's arrest reports, or the muted beeps from an answering machine echoed down the hallway. Beale enjoyed that time of the day, he made a point to get to work early, organize his schedule, and prioritize his appointments before the rat race kicked in. A routine picked up from Tony Cincotta, his old partner from Long Island. Except for that elevator fiasco in Islandia, Cincotta had his act together as a detective. Tony believed a good detective had to have his own life together before he could clean up anything else. 'Organize your own house and then go knock on doors,' was his motto, and it worked.

Beale scheduled an early morning meeting with Stan Hordowski, his new partner. He needed to bring Hordowski up to speed on the Art Dunn bombing case before they drove out to the crime scene. Hordowski, who just made detective three months ago, was coming off a one-week suspension for unintentionally discharging his weapon, and was chomping at the bit to get back out in the field. After completing his bi-annual firearms proficiency test, he dropped his pistol, the gun fired and a bullet ricocheted off the concrete floor nicking his foot. The buzz circulating the department was that Hordowski got a raw deal; the suspension was way over the top. The punishment did not fit the crime. It was obvious that the chief wanted to send a message that sloppy police work would not be tolerated on his watch. Therefore, Hordowski became the poster boy for sloppy police work.

Beale finished organizing his paperwork when he heard a strange squishing sound coming down the hall, he looked up and there in the doorway was Hordowski, dripping wet. "Don't say a damn thing Beale, you with your privileged parking spot next to the door. I was halfway to the door when the skies opened up. I ran back to my car for an umbrella and no umbrella. I tried to wait out the storm, but it got worse. So now I'm twice as wet."

"And good morning to you, Detective Hordowski, how's the foot?" Beale replied with a big grin on his face. "I guess somebody didn't listen to the weather forecast this morning; for once the weather guy got it right."

"Yeah it's easy for you to say, you're sitting there all nice and dry and I'm standing here freezing my ass off."

All of a sudden, Hordowski began to shake his entire body around in an attempt to get some of the water off his clothes. It was hysterical: a chubby, 5'8", thirty-two-year old man with spiked brown hair gyrating around the room. Legs, arms flailing about, and his head bobbing up and down like a bobble head doll on steroids. If it weren't a police station, you'd think it was an audition for some punk rock band. "This isn't going to work, I'm freezing. Give me a minute, Beale; I have a change of clothes in my locker."

"Don't forget your sun glasses, rock star; you'll need them where we're going," Beale shouted as Hordowski squished down the hallway.

Thirty minutes later Beale and Hordowski finished their review of the Dunn case. It was seven o'clock, the second shift had arrived and everyone filed into the staff room for morning briefing. Captain McNulty was up at the podium when Beale and Hordowski took their seats. "First off I'd like to welcome Detective Hordowski back to full duty and trust he has recovered from his injury. Hordowski has been assigned to the Dunn case, so Miller, pick up Hordowski's notes on the Saw Grass robbery and add it to your caseload." If looks could kill, Hordowski would have been six feet under. He could feel the burning anger from Miller's glare on the back of his neck.

"Thanks a lot, Hordowski, maybe you should have shot yourself in the hand, then I'd get to write up your reports too."

The public denouncement took Hordowski by surprise and the rest of the briefing was kind of a blur. He vaguely remembered hearing something about a burglary on the island, a bridge tender being assaulted, and something about a naked man running around at Sharky's wearing a silver helmet. "If there aren't any more questions, let's get to work. Oh, Beale and Hordowski see me in my office."

"Oh great, what did you do now?" Beale groaned as they headed for the captain's office.

"Hey, how do you know it's something I did, maybe, just maybe you screwed up, ever think of that, Mr. Perfect?" Hordowski snarled as he opened the door. "Okay, so where are we on the Dunn case?" Captain McNulty said as he pointed to the two chairs in front of his desk. "I have the Mayor breathing down my neck and the press is screaming for answers." Both men sat.

"Well Captain we are just about finished. We have the Fire Marshal's report. The crime scene account indicated a single explosion caused the fire and the autopsy report from the coroner's office on Dunn is in. The forensics team determined that the explosives came from firework components built in Dunn's garage. Receipts from two firework companies, schematics of bomb making systems, along with a handwriting analysis, indicated they all belonged to Arthur Dunn. We have statements from the editor, his secretary, and lastly we have Dunn's suicide letter."

"So what's left? I want to put to rest any rumor that this guy was some sort of American terrorist, or worse, that he belonged to a terrorist cell right here in Sarasota County. The longer we wait to make a final statement, the harder it becomes to convince the public that this guy was a nut and just snapped when he lost his job."

"We need to collect the rest of the bomb making materials and there is one more person to interview, Blaine Sterling, she was the last person to talk to Dunn." Beale closed his folder.

"Okay, finish up at Dunn's house, find out what Sterling knows, but I want this case completed today and your report on my desk tomorrow morning. I need to schedule a press conference by the end of the week and get everybody off my back."

Beale took a deep breath, stood, and he and Hordowski left.

Chapter Twenty-Six

Beale took Venice Avenue east to River Road, turned south and a mile past Hazeltines nursery, turned left onto a small dirt road that lead to Arthur Dunn's house. The yellow caution tape was broken and wrapped around the mailbox and chain link fence. "Looks like the crime scene guys are finished, at least we don't have to worry about them getting in the way," Beale said as he reached into the mailbox and took out a handful of mail. "Hold on to these, maybe some of his bills will tell us something about this guy."

"Man, this guy really liked his privacy. It's a jungle back here, nothing but trees, palms, brush and greenery," Hordowski said. "Ten acres maybe more, I'd hate to be walking around out here at night."

"Different strokes for different folks, Hordowski. Maybe our Mr. Dunn was a nudist and liked to parade around in the buff all day, or maybe he had other reasons for living back here." Beale looked over at his partner with a skeptical glance.

"Yeah right, or maybe he was just a nut case. I don't know about you, but the thought of seeing Art Dunn walking around naked is a little creepy."

"Speaking of creepy, Hordowski, what do you think?"

Beale stopped the car at the edge of the clearing so Hordowski could take in the totality of the spectacle. In the center of a large clearing, glowing in the sunlight was a one-story ranch style house. Blinding rays of light, from the ground to its tin roof, streamed outward in all directions from hundreds of soda bottles that made up the framework of the house

"What the fuck, is that Dunn's house?" Hordowski barked and shaded his eyes from the glare with his hand to get a clearer view. "Is the house on fire?"

"Put on your sunglasses, detective, and then tell me what you see."

For more than an acre, not a single tree or flower grew; a starkness that intensified the blinding glare warning trespassers to 'KEEP OUT.' An amber glass bottled walkway led from the driveway to a massive wooden front door framed in bottles, two bay windows and more bottles. "Oh, did I forget to put in my report, Detective Hordowski, that Mr. Dunn's house was constructed from soda bottles."

"I guess you did, partner. What's the deal with all the bottles?"

"You know Dan Whitaker, the black cop in charge of the neighborhood watch unit, been on the force forever, he told me that Dunn's father, Waldo Dunn, another nut case, was a big honcho at Coca-Cola in Tampa. Well, he was getting the boot, something to do with cutbacks. Talk about déjà vu. So, to screw the company he rerouted ten tractor-trailers filled with Coke™ to Venice. Built a fake warehouse right on River Road, signed for the deliveries and hid the soda back in the woods. Mysteriously the building burnt down, all business records destroyed and the soda bottles disappeared. Coca-Cola filed hundreds of police reports, hired private detectives, but couldn't prove that Dunn's father masterminded the entire scheme. Waldo died twenty years ago and when his son went to build a home on the family property. Bingo—found the bottles—and the rest is history."

"Ten trailers. That's a hell of a lot of coke bottles." Hordowski took out his pad and started to scribble down groups of numbers.

"You can say that again, fifty cases per truck, ten trucks, twenty-four bottles to a case, that's about twelve thousand bottles and about ten thousand dollars' worth of Coke."

"I got that too, but didn't Coca-Cola want their soda back? That was a hell of a lot of money back in '82," Hordowski questioned with a puzzled look on his face.

"That's a lot of money today, but the Statue of Limitations ran out, case closed," Beale shot back with a slight grin.

"I wonder if Art Dunn had to drink it all before building the house?"

"I doubt it; would you drink twenty year old soda? Let's get to work." Beale parked the car out front and Hordowski followed the driveway back to the glass garage.

Chapter Twenty-Seven

Beale pushed open the front door and walked into the foyer. The sound of his steps echoed off the white Italian marble floor. Gradually his eyes adjusted to the dim light as he took in the pulse of the house. The only piece of furniture, if you could call it furniture, was a large Waterford crystal chandelier hanging in the center of the foyer. If first impressions were worth anything, Beale didn't like the cold antiseptic welcome he was getting. Something just didn't feel right.

To the left, double mahogany doors led to the den, then into the kitchen and the formal dining room off the kitchen. The end of the foyer opened left into the living room, lanai and pool and to the right a hallway leads toward the two bedrooms and two baths. Beale walked into the den bathed in sunlight from two large bay windows and magnified by the reflection from the bottles that created a wall on either side of a massive stone fireplace that separated the den from the living room. The room decorated with Ethan Allen furniture looked like a photo out of "Florida Living Magazine." A massive light gray leather sofa, coordinating love seat, large plasma screen television, reclining chairs, antique end tables, and matching brass table lamps filled the room. Every piece complemented one and other. Everything was too neat, too organized, too perfectly decorated. It was as if Dunn went through a designer's catalog, room by room and ordered everything on the page. The kitchen looked like an advertisement from "House Beautiful," a restaurant-size Viking stove, stainless steel appliances, a six cook top cooking island with a fluted chimney hood, and finally a country-style triple sink surrounded by granite counter tops completed the interior decorator's tour.

The living room took on a life of its own. The entire back wall was floor to ceiling Coke bottles, creating a natural diffused glow that moved with the sun as it filtered down through the bottles. The rest of the room was painted rose pink as were the majority of the furnishings in pink. A velvet bubblegum-pink sofa occupied most of the back wall with two round end tables covered in a pink peonies design fabric topped with two oriental clay lamps with pink and white striped shades. A cotton candy pink French settee with pink floral accent pillows faced the sofa, three pink high-back striped chairs, and a salmon pink coffee table completed the sitting area. Two blush wingchairs stood on opposite sides of the white marble fireplace. A pink room-sized oriental rug covered most of the wood plank floor. Paintings of dancers by Degas, brass wall sconces, a large ornate pink mirror, and an array of antiques all adorned the walls and tables in a cold systematic fashion. The room took on a sterile look, as if a cleaning company came in and swept everything about Arthur Dunn away. *Why?*

"Hello, all finished with the garage. Boxed up the last of the explosives and put them in the cruiser. Hello, where are you?" Hordowski called out from the foyer.

"I'm on the lanai, come on back."

"Wow, what a place. It's like a home tour during Christmas, but without the decorations. Did you see that Oriental rug in the living room? Has to be at least ten-thousand bucks, maybe more?" Hordowski added, "My rich aunt from Chicago has one just like it, an antique Persian Afshar, same diamond pattern."

"Do you think Dunn ever swam in this pool?"

"What, why have a pool if you're not going to swim in it? Of course he swam in the pool." Hordowski looked down at the stairs that led into water, "I think."

"I don't know everything about this house looks orchestrated. It is too clean, too neat, and too orderly. It's as if Dunn placed everything out in clear sight to hide something on purpose. Why, what was he hiding?" Beale looked outside at the two dogs playing in the dog run.

"Or maybe Dunn liked to keep things neat. Maybe he was a clean freak," bellowed Hordowski. "What's wrong with that? The last time I checked, it wasn't against the law to keep a clean house."

"Except the dog run. Dog toys, dog bowls and dog crap, now that looks used." Beale pointed out as the two dogs ran up to the fence barking like crazy.

"Can you believe it, Dunn left everything to his Chihuahuas and now little Louie and Chocó will live in the lap of luxury over at the Myakka Animal Farm. Life just isn't fair Beale."

"What's missing, Hordowski?"

"What are you talking about?"

"What is in every home nowadays? A computer, where is his computer?"

"You're right. I didn't see one."

"Check his mail; see if there is a bill from the cable company."

Hordowski pulled out the stack of Dunn's mail from his pocket, flipped through each envelope and half way through the pile found a statement from Comcast. "I found something," Hordowski called out. "It appeared Mr. Dunn just recently bundled his phone, television and internet service and this letter guaranteed a new lower fee for two years. Wow, what a great price. So where is the computer hook-up?"

"Call the cable company and ask them where they placed the cable jacks. I'm going to start in the den," Beale shouted and walked into the den.

Beale located one jack behind the television when Hordowski yelled that there were two jacks installed in the den, one on the north wall and the other alongside the fireplace. Beale crossed the room, stood in front of the fireplace and looked. There wasn't a side, only a wall of bottles butted up against the fireplace.

"Hordowski, come here. I can't find the second jack. Check all the bottles on left side of the fireplace; I'll take the right maybe the jack is hidden behind a bottle." Halfway across the wall, about four feet from the floor, Beale pulled out a loose bottle. He reached in, felt around; only dust and loose mortar filled the tiny space, no jack. Beale continued down the wall, four bottles later he pulled one out, reached in and slid a metal bolt to the left. The wall gave way. "Hordowski, give me a hand over here." Together they pulled the wall forward and to the right along a track that lined up directly behind the bottled wall. "Well, well, well, Arthur Dunn, so this is what you didn't want anyone to find. What dirty little secrets were you hiding in here?"

Hordowski stepped into the room, shined his flashlight around, pushed against walls and looked up. "It's empty Beale, not a damn thing in this cubicle. Just three glass walls, the back of the stone fireplace and the floor."

"That doesn't make sense, why would someone go to all the trouble to construct a secret room and leave it empty? Check the floor, I'll check the walls. There has to be something."

"Maybe this room isn't used anymore. Let us say, for argument's sake, Dunn stored expensive wine in here, then maybe his doctor told him to stop drinking alcohol because he had an ulcer. He had a big party and the guests consumed all the wine. End of wine, end of room, end of story." Hordowski exclaimed with a sense of pride and a resolute smile across his face.

"And maybe I'm the *Tooth Fairy*. So if it isn't being used, why isn't it dusty in here? Where are the cobwebs? This place is clean, just like the rest of the house; he's a clean fanatic. Dunn was in here recently. He used this room for something."

"Beale, over here, I found something, a ring." At the end of the room against the fireplace, embedded in the wooden floor was a small silver ring. Hordowski slipped his finger through the metal circle and pulled. A trap door opened and revealed a lighted circular glass bottled staircase that lead down to the basement.

"I knew it. I knew there had to be something here, but a basement. I'll be damned. It either takes balls or just plain stupidity to build a basement around here, with the Myakka River only a few miles away and a high water table; I'll bet during the rainy season this place is under water. Let's see what Mr. Dunn has down there."

"Wow, this is where the old man stored all the Coke. It looks like a goddamn super market down here. Check out this old time Coke machine, Beale." Rows of Coca-Cola, stacked from the floor to the ceiling filled the entire basement. A single aisle, the width of two hand trucks, ran the length of the basement with rows of soda on each side. At the front of every row, a dusty red Coke machine stood waiting for a customer to put in a coin for a cold refreshing drink. A single bare light bulb hung in the middle of each row, cast a shadowy glow out into the main aisle.

Beale walked down to the last row, stopped in front of the Coke machine, pulled the handle and looked inside. "It's filled with soda."

"So's mine down here. I wonder if you can still drink them."

"Don't even think about it Hordowski, all of this is new evidence."

"Speaking of new evidence you better get your butt over here and see this!"

Beale turned and jogged down to the opposite end of the basement and froze in front of the last row of bottles. There just beyond the entrance, a jungle exploded with life. A large oval room glowed in a deep forest green from rays of defused light that filtered through large palm fronds that covered ceiling. Plants, flowers, animals, and faces of children painted over the bottled walls jumped out in striking greens, browns, blues, reds and tans. In the center of the room was an elaborate computer station with laptops, monitors, modems, hard drives, keyboards, printer, a wireless box, and cable connections.

"This guy has some serious computer technology going on here. This isn't your everyday Joe doing word processing. There has to be over twenty grand worth of stuff here," Hordowski exclaimed and walked over to the computer station.

"You're kidding, twenty grand!"

"Yeah, the computer chair I'm sitting on is a Herman Miller, costs more than a thousand bucks and all the other stuff, easily twenty grand, maybe more," Hordowski added in a tone of awe and booted up the system.

"Why would Dunn need all this computer technology and why hide it down in the basement? There is something wrong here. Can you log on?"

"No, too many encryptions. We'll have to bring everything back to headquarters and have the I.T. guys work on it."

"Okay, I'll call the chief to send out a CSI team to pick up all this stuff. Why don't you try to log on while you wait for team to arrive? I have a meeting with the last person to see Dunn before he blew himself up."

Chapter Twenty-Eight

All morning dark gray clouds raced along the horizon gathering moisture from the Gulf. Blotting out the sun in its migration northward, damp chilly clouds foreshadowed the rains that would arrive shortly. Rain was exactly what Southwest Florida—after a three-year drought—so desperately needed and now the rainy season would provide some relief. By late afternoon, large, black cumulus clouds stalled over Sarasota County and waited to exhale. As if on cue, no sooner had Beale closed his car door and walked towards the Nature Center, the skies open up and a torrential downpour commenced. Large pelting raindrops pounded against his face as he ran towards the front porch of the Nature Center. "You better speed it up Detective Beale or you'll be drenched to the bone," Blaine called from the dry comfort of her rocking chair.

"It's too late, I'm already soaked. I can't believe I left my umbrella in the office," Beale shouted between the rains. "What's the name of that meteorologist on Channel 8?"

"Steve Jarvy," Blaine replied, and handed him a towel.

"How that guy could be so wrong and still get paid is mind-boggling. All he had to do was stick his head out the window and he'd realize it was going to rain."

"Maybe they don't have windows at Channel 8," Blaine remarked with a big smile.

"Well, Assistant Manager Sterling, I'm glad to see you have recovered from your injuries incurred at the Star and that your biting wit is still intact, which brings me to the reason for my visit."

"The biting wit or my injuries, Detective Beale?" Blaine replied as she looked at the rain cascading off the roof. Beale just rolled his eyes and bit his tongue, he knew if he uttered another word the banter would go on forever. He took out a small pad, flipped to an empty page, jotted down the date, time, place and Blaine Sterling. He underlined Blaine Sterling twice and drew a picture of a firecracker alongside her name. Call it a superstition or just habit, for every case,

Beale sketched pictures, designs or caricatures in his notepad. Most were case reminders that had a specific meaning; others were just whimsical doodles to pass time. The firecracker definitely was not a whimsical doodle. Blaine Sterling was explosive, but in a positive way.

"So, Blaine, why were you at the newspaper?"

Her eyes never left the rain. "I had a meeting with Mr. Dunn to discuss the loud music his newspaper carrier, Earl Neigh, played at four in the morning."

Beale circled *Earl Neigh.* "How did Mr. Dunn respond? Was there anything unusual about his behavior?"

Blaine turned, "You mean did I know he was going to blow himself up? No!" Blaine exclaimed. "He was very nervous, constantly checking his watch as if he was late for something."

"He was late, that was the problem and your meeting caused him to be late for his meeting with his boss." Blaine jumped to her feet and stood over Beale sitting in the rocking chair jotting down notes.

"Wait a minute, are you saying that I had something to do with Mr. Dunn's death? Is that what you are inferring Detective Beale? If so, you and I have a very big problem," Blaine snapped angrily and glowered.

Startled at her explosion, Beale looked up, "Blaine, calm down, that's not what I meant. Please sit down and let me explain." He looked into her fiery blue eyes, "You had nothing to do with Arthur Dunn's death. In fact, if you had not insisted on a meeting with Dunn, most likely his boss, Mr. Ambers would also be dead. Blaine, you saved a man's life that day." Beale drew another picture, a teardrop. "Is there anything else you can remember about your meeting with Dunn, anything unusual?"

She paused. "It may be nothing, but one thing seemed a little awkward. His office was a mess, piles of papers, folders, books and pictures scattered all over the place, which he attributed to moving out; never once did he intimate that he was let go. However, his desk was not messy at all. In fact, it was too neat and appeared cleared for a purpose. The only things on his desk were a white business envelope resting against an old gray metal tape dispenser and a book. He noticed me looking at the book and put it in the bottom drawer."

Beale drew a picture of a book with a question mark. "Blaine, tell me about the book." Blaine tried to remember what it was about the book that made her uncomfortable. It wasn't Dunn's actions, but the book itself. She tried to visualize what the cover looked like: faces, sad, forlorn faces, a jungle and small, slim figures, boys.

"*Night Boys of Thailand*, that was the title."

"That's something, because his credit card indicated a trip to Thailand last month. We'll have to take another look at that book and his trip to Thailand."

Chapter Twenty-Nine

Beale leaned back in his chair and effortlessly the chair rocked back and forth in a soothing motion. *An inspirational example of pioneer ingenuity to create such a simple piece of furniture,* he thought. The gentle motion was calming, almost hypnotic compared to the rain pounding on the tin roof. "Forget about those magic finger lounge chairs with all the rollers and heat massagers, this old rocking chair, rocks." With a sly grin Beale laughed, "Get it, rocks."

"I get it; sounds like you haven't been around rocking chairs in a while Detective Beale," Blaine remarked and rocked back in her chair.

"Quite the contrary, as a matter of fact I was on one last month and didn't fall off," he joked with a straight face. "Do you know the Cracker Barrel restaurant off Jacaranda; on their porch they have about seven rocking chairs and guess what, I took one for a test drive."

Last month Beale received a call from the manager at the Cracker Barrel, off I-75 in Venice. The manager informed Beale that he got a call from a woman who found a purse filled with money hanging in the restroom stall, but would only turn it over to the owner. She left her phone number and hung up. Beale traced the number to a home in Nokomis and arrived just as Mrs. Middleton, an eighty-six year old widow from Michigan was leaving. Beale identified himself and escorted her back into the house.

It turned out that Mrs. Middleton sold her home in Michigan for $175,000.00 and planned to relocate in Florida. Her neighbor of thirty years, Marion Minder, moved to Bay Indies, an adult community in Venice two years earlier and finally convinced her long-time friend, after an extremely harsh winter up North that the Sunshine State was for her. Mrs. Middleton didn't trust banks so she insisted on taking the entire $175,000.00 in cash, which she placed in a large pocket book that she kept with her at all times. She used the facilities at the Cracker Barrel and forgot that she left her bag hanging on the back of the restroom door. In a panic, she returned to the restaurant and the manager called the Good Samaritan. After convincing the Good

Samaritan that she was not a drug dealer and the $175,000.00 wasn't from illegal sources, Mrs. Middleton drove off to Nokomis to claim her money. The Good Samaritan, after a stern lecture from detective Beale on the virtues of turning in lost property to the police department, received a modest reward and a smiley face next to her name in Beale's notepad.

Chapter Thirty

The rain ended as suddenly as it began. The torrential downpour soaked the park, greening everything that was brown into an explosion of life to a desperately parched landscape. Milky gray puddles dotted the crushed shell parking area in front of the Nature Center and beyond the line of pine trees, the blacktop road, half covered in water, ended in a pool of water that swallowed up the entrance to the hiking trail. The welcome cool from the storm quickly evaporated as the sun beat down through the clouds. A purple blur flashed beyond the trees.

"What's that noise?" Beale stood to get a better look. "Sounds like howling from behind the trees."

"It's Purple Rain," Blaine remarked with unequivocal certainty.

"What?"

"It's a song detective, Purple Rain by Prince, a 1984 classic. It sold millions and made Prince a star. 'Don't want to cause you sorrow, don't want to cause you pain. I want to see you laughing in the purple rain.' It is an unbelievable song."

"Talk about unbelievable; what is that heading towards us?" Beale pointed to the road.

Sloshing through the water on a purple bike, pulling a beat-up purple wagon filled with purple boxes, cans, and a purple folding chair, Miss Vardi pedaled towards the Nature Center. Hunched over the handlebars, her purple rain hat that resembled a wizard's cap, nearly touched the front wheel when she pushed forward on the pedals. A large matching purple raincoat covered half of the back tire that created a rooster tail effect as water spun up from the wheel. The entire ensemble resembled a half-human, half-animal creature from a very poor sci-fi flick. Stopping in front of the Nature Center, she pulled off her hat, shook the water from her short, curly purple hair and walked over to Blaine.

"Talk about being color coordinated. The hat, coat, and purple boots, lady, you get the award hands down. I guess it's no secret that you like purple," Beale bellowed and stuck out his hand.

"Maybe you'd like to see the purple panties I'm wearing under my purple shorts," she replied and threw open her coat, revealing purple polka dot shorts.

Beale raised his hands in surrender, "No, that will not be necessary, thank you."

"Miss Zammiello, may I introduce Detective Justin Beale, Detective Beale this is our artist in residence, Vardi Zammiello. The beautiful entrance sign to the campground was painted by this very talented artist."

Extending a water-soaked hand, "Nice to meet you detective, please call me Miss Vardi. Indeed, purple is my color of choice, maybe that's why they call me *the purple lady.* " With a big smile, she grabbed Beale's hand and they shook.

"Well, Miss Vardi, the sign is a beautiful piece of art work and the ideal addition to the park. Today when I drove in, a park ranger was taking a picture of a family by the sign. What a perfect keepsake to remember their stay at the park."

"So what are you doing out in the rain?" Blaine asked and handed Miss Vardi a towel.

"I'm painting, my dear girl; until the skies opened up and turned everything into a mud swamp back there. I'm painting the old railroad bridge along the Legacy Trail, the one you showed me near the park's trailhead. Last week, I went to see the Grover Cleveland Koons' exhibit at the Triangle Inn in Venice. His photographs capturing the building of the area were remarkable. It was a photographic masterpiece of Venice and the surrounding area and sure enough, one of the photographs detailed the construction of the bridge."

"You're kidding, I didn't see that one, but I thought it was a great exhibit. My favorite picture was of a man sitting on a palm tree that was leaning out over the Myakka River. Do you think, Miss Vardi that was Koons on that tree?" Blaine asked.

"Why don't you call the Archives and ask. Well, I have to get out of these wet clothes before I catch pneumonia. Oh, by the way, I'm not sure what's going on out there, but I heard noises coming from inside the park."

"What kind of noises?" Blaine inquired.

"I think engine sounds, from a car or motorcycle, I'm not sure."

"That's weird; there shouldn't be any vehicles in that back section of the park, that entire area is off limits to the public. We haven't even surveyed the property for future hiking trails; I'll check it out when I lock the gate tonight." Blaine called out and waved good-bye.

Beale took out his note pad, wrote Miss Vardi in big bold letters and alongside, her name drew a picture of a fruitcake as she pedaled off towards the campground.

"A very colorful character if I do say so myself," Beale remarked and slipped the notepad back into his pocket.

"Yes, she is. Do you want to come with me to lock the Legacy Trail gate?"

"Good idea and we can check out those strange noises she heard in the backwoods, if in fact there were any. Your Miss Vardi looks like a person with a vivid imagination and a full palette of stories."

Chapter Thirty-One

Blaine shut off the lights, locked the front door of the Nature Center and walked over to her ATV in the parking lot. Beale continued towards his car. "Excuse me detective, where are you going?" Surprised, Beale spun around and momentum carried his left foot forward into a milky gray hole. Off balance and too late to correct his forward motion, his right foot followed into the muddy cavity. Four inches shorter, embarrassed and pissed, he stared down in disbelief. "You can't take your car, too muddy. We'll take the ATV." Shaking his feet off, Beale stepped out of the mud hole and climbed on the four-wheeler. They drove through the parking area, across the main road and onto the Blue Trail that led to the Legacy Trailhead.

Daylight was fading; the sun fell below the tree line casting shadows across the path. It would be mere minutes before dusk. Officially, at sunset, all gates leading in and out of the park are locked. The only visitors permitted inside the park after sunset were overnight campers. Blaine pulled up to the gate and despite the heavy rainfall immediately noticed several deep tire tracks leading into the park.

"Look at this Beale, three sets of tire tracks and they're not bicycle tires. No one is permitted to bring a vehicle into the park, especially off the bike trail."

Already wet and muddy, Beale knelt down and measured the tracks with his hand. "Looks like two ATVs and a larger vehicle, maybe a truck or SUV. And they all appear to be going in the same direction."

"Into the park," Blaine answered. "So right now, it appears that we have three vehicles, at least three individuals, maybe more, still inside the park. Doing who knows what, for however long, where ever they want. What I do know is that they illegally entered a State Park and that's a crime."

Pulling the gate closed, Blaine reached down to unlock the padlock hanging from the fence. To her dismay, the heavy silver padlock was unlocked and hung freely from the round metal locking ring. She noticed this twice before, one morning when she opened up and one night when she closed; thought it was just an oversight and didn't give it much mind until today. The only people with keys were park employees. Two times Blaine envisioned a forgetful mistake by a harried ranger, but three times, same location: intent. Strike three you're out. Pulling the gate shut, Blaine yelled over to Beale, "Okay detective, gate locked; no one gets into the park and nothing is getting past us. Now let's see where those tracks lead."

Twenty minutes later Blaine jerked the ATV to a stop and turned off the engine. In the darkness, the whining of a car engine and the spinning of tires cut through the night air. Blaine reached for her flashlight and motioned towards the sounds, "Let's walk the rest of the way. I think we've found what we've been looking for detective." Beale nodded and took out his gun. Ahead thirty yards away beams of light and shadows of figures moving back and forth cast a ghoulish silhouette into the sky. "I see three maybe four shadows, what do you think, Beale?"

"You're right, three or four and they seem very agitated about something. A few more feet and we'll know for sure." Suddenly a loud sound like the crack of a whip split the air, then screaming and a flurry of movement in one direction.

"Oh shit, Thor, I think the rope broke your mother's arm. Get some towels from the truck so I can wrap it and keep it stabilized. Why did you bring a fucking rope? I told you to bring a chain so we could pull the ATVs out of the mud."

"I'm sorry; Dad, but I couldn't find the chain."

Blaine and Detective Beale stepped out from behind the shadows, there were two All-Terrain Vehicles knee deep in mud, a thick-knotted horsehair rope attached to the front bumper of a black Hummer with a gold lightning bolt painted along the doors, a jeep and two people huddled around a woman on the ground. However, the most appalling sight for Blaine lay behind the vehicles. An area the size of two football fields, cut up with ruts and holes, flattened or torn up grasses, small bushes, and low growing shrubs all run over or mowed down from the All-Terrain Vehicles. Raw dirt, sand and mud covered most of the area that was once lush grassland. The landscape resembled a motor cross track after a week of competition in the rain.

"Thor, go back home and pick up a chain. If you can't find it in the garage under my workbench, ask Mr. Gruntz, he should have one. We'll never pull these bikes out of the mud with this rope."

"Don't anyone move this is the police," Beale yelled as he held out his shield and gun for everyone to see. "I am Detective Justin Beale from the Venice Police Department; I want to see everybody's hands in the air. Now!"

Blaine pointed her light in their faces, "I am the Assistant Manager of Osprey State Park Blaine Sterling. All of you are trespassing; you have illegally entered a state park and damaged public land with your motor vehicles. This is a crime and you are all under arrest."

Taking a step forward Charlie Boltier screamed out, "Wait just a minute we were given permission to four-wheel back here."

"One more step, mister, and I'll shoot you. Now, I want everyone to turn around, except you lady, you can stay down there for the time being. Put your hands behind your back. Assistant Manager Sterling will handcuff all of you."

Charlie Boltier slowly turned around and put his hands behind his back. A giant of a man at six-six, three hundred pounds and arms as thick as tree trunks, Boltier fumed. "I paid two hundred bucks a pop to off-road back here. This is the second time we rode here. I don't understand, why there's problem now?" As he spoke, the veins on his shaved head began to pop out, a clear sign he was agitated.

"What's your name, mister?" Blaine asked as she tightened the plastic straps around the big man's wrist. She noticed the enormity of the man's girth. His hands were the size of baseball gloves and the rest of his body was proportionally huge, this was an individual you did not want to upset.

"Charlie Boltier," the man growled, turned and faced Blaine.

"Well, Mr. Boltier, I don't know who gave you permission to operate your vehicles in the park, what I do know is; no one has the authority to grant permission to drive a motor vehicle on state property or damage public land."

"It was a park ranger who unlocked the gate and took my two hundred bucks, twice." Boltier spat out and glared down at Blaine.

"A park ranger, I don't believe you."

"I can prove it. He is a big guy, muscular, with short black hair, a buzz cut, a big friendly smile, and he has a cough." Boltier stopped mid-sentence, looked Blaine straight in the eye and snarled, "I bet you know him."

Blaine choked on his words. It was Remi Cole, that bastard. Trying to control her anger, Blaine took out her phone, "Park police, this is Assistant Manager Sterling; I have two adults and one teenager detained for trespassing at the Osprey State Park. They were off-roading about one mile into the park's Northeast quadrant parallel to the Legacy Trailhead. The two ATVs are stuck in the mud. I would advise four-wheel drive vehicles, the ground back here is a mud swamp. The adult female has a broken arm she will need transport to Sarasota Memorial. What's your E.T.A.?" Turning to Beale, "They'll be here in ten minutes. I have to see the Park Manager."

"I guess you do, I'll handle it from here. Good luck with the manager."

Chapter Thirty-Two

Earl pulled hard on the steering wheel, jumped the divider and raced down the bridge towards Tamiami Trail. The light on Tamiami was green as he sped through the light on Shamrock. "Shit, this is so cool, oh sorry baby about the language, but I want to see how many lights I can make before they turn red. If that fire truck can beat all the lights maybe I can do it, too." Earl punched the accelerator and the '99 candy apple red Camaro jerked forward and sped off towards Seminole Drive and the third traffic light. The speedometer held steady at 65 mph as they zoomed through the green light.

"Earl, please slow down, I'm scared. You're going too fast, please slow down, I'm really afraid we're going to get killed." No sooner had Candy screamed '*Earl*,' a yellow Volkswagen Beetle with a big pink daisy painted across the back swerved into the center lane inches in front of Earl. Earl jammed on the brakes, jerked the car to the left, squeezed into the left lane and drove on oblivious of the horns blasting and a few hand gestures to bid him farewell.

"What the fuck was with that yellow car? I'm going to kill that son-of-a-bitch. He almost got us killed, and that bastard ruined my fucking experiment. I think a steady 65 mph is the key, but I'm not a hundred percent sure now. That guy is dead meat."

"Earl, stop it. Let's just go, anyway he's a she and she's turning off the highway into McDonald's. She is going to have lunch, what about us Earl, I'm starving."

"In a few minutes, baby, here we go left on Flamingo, a right onto Crane and three houses down on the right is home sweet home. . .I am afraid to say, has seen better days."

Earl pulled to the curb, cut the engine, and looked over at the crooked FOR SALE sign that stood in the middle of the dried-out front lawn. The yellow one-story concrete block home looked weathered and rundown. Four scraggly Ixoras, too thirsty to bloom, bordered a three-paned center front window, on the right a faded green front door and at both corners two tired looking Foxtail palms completed the front façade. A sloping concrete driveway cracked and oil stained from years of traffic lead to a broken-down garage in the backyard.

"So when did you live here?"

"Twenty-two years ago. Mom passed away three years ago so my older sister, Janie, who lives in San Diego, and I sold the house to Mrs. Griffith, a widower from Indiana. She died last year, a chain smoker, smoked like a chimney. The first week she moved in she fell asleep with a lit cigarette and set her bedroom on fire. She spent a month in the hospital, and it took another two months to get the place repaired. I stopped by once a week to see if she needed anything and to check on the old homestead."

Earl opened the car door, grabbed Candy's hand and pulled her across the street towards a large Sabal Palm. "Where are we going?" Candy asked looking confused as she stared at a large gouge mark on the trunk of the palm tree.

"I want to show you something."

"A tree with a big chunk missing, I don't understand?"

"I have never been more serious in my life. When I was three years old I was sitting in my little red fire truck near the corner over there, a white Ford station wagon, lost control, hit my truck, sent me flying and then smashed into this palm tree."

"Earl, I'm sorry, I didn't mean to be insensitive," Candy whispered, reaching around his waist and hugging him. "So what happened to you?"

"Miraculously, I wasn't killed! What is even more shocking; I didn't have serious injuries, somehow the angle of the impact and the force of the collision were cushioned when I landed in a clump of bushes. I had a concussion, a punctured right eardrum and a cut on my forehead that required only four stitches. The driver of the station wagon wasn't that lucky; she didn't have her seat belt on, and when she hit the tree, she went through the windshield. Years later, my mother told me that the driver broke her neck and was confined to a wheelchair. So this tree is a reminder that life is a precious gift and that I better keep my seat belt fastened."

"Oh, Earl, what a terrible thing to happen to a three-year-old child and you still can remember that horrible accident today!" Candy sighed and squeezed Earl's hand.

"Hey, enough about the tree I have a surprise for you. Let's cross the street and go back to the garage."

As they walked up the driveway past the house, Candy looked up and over the double wooden barn garage doors was a sign in faded black letters: EARL NEIGH THE CAR REPAIR GUY. Like the sign, the garage appeared old and weathered. The wooden structure sagged to one side; most of the yellow paint had flaked off years ago, leaving patches of bare wood exposed. The four windows along the top of the doors decorated with a half-dozen BB holes appeared ready to fall apart, but the white-shingled roof looked almost new and very much out of place.

"Earl Neigh the car repair guy. So you repaired cars when you lived here?"

"Sure did, made good money and met a lot of crazy girls too. Some would drive over with their tops down and I don't mean convertible tops, just so I would work on their car."

"Did you?"

"You bet and that wasn't the only thing I worked on, but that was way back in high school, now I'm only interested in working on you baby, just you." Earl smiled, unlocked the side door, and they walked inside. It took Candy a few minutes for her eyes to adjust to the darkness, but as her eyes focused, she was amazed at the sight before her. The room was like something out of the pages of *Car and Driver* magazine. The entire building resembled a gas station garage from the sixties. Pictures of cars, motors, hubcaps, gas pumps, and drive-in movies, James Dean, poodle skirts, and Elvis covered every wall. Suspended from the ceiling was memorabilia from car shows, high school dances, football games, and old time soda fountains. There in the center of the room was a shiny, powder blue, 1957 Chevy convertible. The car looked brand-new, not a scratch or dent on the entire body. The chrome glistened in the light and the white leather upholstery was soft and subtle. Even a pair of white fuzzy dice hung from the windshield mirror.

"Oh my god, Earl," Candy screamed as she jumped into the car and slid behind the steering wheel. "I can't believe this, it's beautiful. Whose is it?"

"It's mine. I've been working on it since high school. Mrs. Griffith didn't drive, so she let me keep it in the garage, all I had to do was mow her lawn every week. Not a bad deal for the two of us, plus I got a chance to check in on her to make sure she didn't accidentally burn the house or the garage down again."

Grabbing the red steering wheel and pretending to make a turn, Candy cooed, "Jump in big boy, how about we cruise the miracle mile."

"Sorry baby, there's just one little problem with that proposition; take a look." Earl popped the hood and they both stared down at an empty shell of wires, hoses and metal tubes that once was an engine.

"Someone stole your engine Earl," Candy cried out looking for the motor.

"Nobody stole the engine, baby, I am rebuilding it. It's on a lift in the back." Earl slowly lowered the hood and clicked it shut. Just as slowly, the yellow sundress Candy wore slipped off her shoulders and fell to the floor. Dressed only in a yellow silk thong she faced Earl in all her naked beauty.

"Oh car guy, I think I have a little problem with my vehicle, do you think you could fix it?" Candy cooed as she unhooked his belt and unzipped his jeans.

"Well Miss I have to make sure I have a big enough tool for the job. I never want to disappoint a customer. Our motto is: the customer always comes first."

"I think I found your tool," as she reached into his pants. "Oh yes, this big boy will do just fine."

Earl could feel himself getting harder as Candy touched him. With one hand, he pulled off her thong and turned her around. He ripped off his pants and pushed against her warm inviting body. She let out a soft moan as their two bodies moved back and forth in a single fluid motion. An explosion of pleasure erupted and they collapsed against the hood of the car exhausted. Nibbling on Candy's ear, Earl whispered, "Well miss, I believe I fixed your problem. I hope you will come again."

"Oh yes, I'm completely satisfied. I only have one request; do you know where a girl can get lunch around here?"

"As a matter of fact I know a great place right around the corner, The Frosted Mug; they have fantastic burgers and fries. But the best part about the place is, they pour the beer into an ice-cold mug, get it Frosted Mug. So refreshing. But I thought you wanted to go to the Le Petit Bistro?"

"I did, honey, but now I'm in the mood for a hamburger and an ice-cold mug of beer."

Chapter Thirty-Three

The American flag atop the cooking tent flapped in the breeze, chairs lined the sidewalk facing the Intracoastal Waterway waiting for the boats to pass by, music from country to punk rock filled the air and there amidst the entire goings on was Lou Bravo with a floppy red-and-white Santa's hat, master BBQ extraordinaire, operating three grills. Smoke billowed up from two grills loaded with hamburgers, hot dogs, sausage, peppers, and ribs. The sweet, smoky aroma from the baked beans cooked on the third grill caught the most attention. People walking past remarked, "Man, those beans smell good, sure wish I could have a plate." Lou Bravo smiled and kept stirring the big, old bean pot; he knew if he gave away one plate, that the whole pot of baked beans would be gone before anyone from his block had a taste.

"Sorry, friend, this is a private party, I only made enough for the community people, stop by after the parade and if I have anything left, I'll fix you a plate."

"Thanks, Santa, I just might do that," replied the old man with a toothless smile, as he turned and walked towards the restrooms alongside the train depot.

Lou Bravo's three tables overflowed with salads, snacks, desserts, paper goods, and cutlery—all the necessary ingredients for a perfect Parade of Lights neighborhood party. If that wasn't enough, six coolers filled with ice, soda, wine, and beer under the tables would help take the edge off any party jitters a neighbor would feel. That included the host, Lou Bravo, who after the fiasco at Blaine's house the other day, didn't know if she would show up or not.

"Everything looks great and your baked beans smell fantastic. Is it time yet?" Shouted Ed Farrell, the first neighbor to arrive with a plate and a hungry appetite.

"You sound like a TV commercial, Ed. Everything is ready, tell all the folks to pick up a plate and help themselves. By the way, have you seen Blaine and Brooke?"

"No, they haven't arrived. I saw them back at the house Blaine was putting boxes in the car while Brooke ran around the yard looking at things through her binoculars. She spotted me drive by and waved."

"Those binoculars cost four hundred bucks, a birthday present so she could see the Sand Hill Cranes nesting in the pond behind her house. Nikon Monarch binoculars, waterproof, rubber coated, so powerful you could see a tick on a rhino's ass at four hundred yards, if that is what you wanted to. I'll have to have a talk with that girl about running with expensive things in her hands."

"Traffic was brutal; they are probably having a hard time finding a parking spot. Don't worry, they'll be here, no one misses your shindigs."

"Me, I'm not worried, just asking. Okay, go get everybody and let's start this party off with a bang."

The party start was not exactly what Lou Bravo expected. After days of preparation and hours of cooking, he envisioned his neighbors completely stuffed from all the gastronomic delights, sitting back in their lounge chairs enjoying a spectacular boat parade. Viewing boats of all sizes and shapes light up the night sky with dazzling displays of animals, cartoon characters and Santa, while listening to holiday music echo across the Intracoastal. That was Lou Bravo's intention. Unfortunately, the party did not start with a bang; instead, it started with a simple request, "Would you please turn your radio down, young man!" That request escalated into a thunderous explosion sending people running in all directions.

For the past hour, Mrs. Brecht, Brooke's babysitter, the nicest woman you could ever meet, always had a kind word, never a disparaging comment about anyone or anything had been subjected to the god-awful music from AC/DC, Kiss, Black Snake, Metallica, and a half-dozen local heavy-metal bands from Sarasota. The pounding of drums, high-pitched squeals of electric guitars, and the screaming vocals reached an unbearable level.

"What did you say lady? I can't hear you!" Stretched out on an old beat-up green-white nylon chaise lounge was a skinny, longhaired boy about nineteen, dressed in black, chewing gum and blowing bubbles. A humongous chrome-black plastic boom box rested alongside the chaise and substituted as a table to rest a beer and a bag of chips while pounding out music through its two twelve-inch speakers.

"I said, could you please turn down your music? It is giving me a headache!"

The young man took a swig of beer and no sooner had he swallowed, a big pink bubble grew and extended over his entire face, then exploded. A mask of pink-ooze and beer enveloped his face; he resembled a blue man performer, except pink. "Appears you've gotten yourself into a sticky mess," Mrs. Brecht giggled as she leaned forward on her walking stick. "Now, will you please turn down your music?"

"Forget it, lady; can't you see I have a problem here? I'm covered in gum."

The walking stick Mrs. Brecht held was a gift from her husband Ken from a trip to Ireland two years ago. On an excursion to experience a traditional Irish meal, their tour stopped for lunch in Wicklow, a sleepy, little fishing-village south of Dublin nestled beside an idyllic harbor that flowed directly out to the Irish Sea. The first stop was Molly Malone's, a quaint Irish pub that served food and drinks on the ground floor and provided room and board on the upper two. *Quite a racket, fill them up with liquor and then charge them for a room because they're too drunk to get home*, Mrs. Brecht thought to herself. The pub was alive with activity. An Irish trio was belting out, "Oh Danny Boy," on the violin, drum, and bag pipes, while a group of locals at the bar sang along and held their pints high in the air. The pub was not big, actually it was quite small, only room enough for ten or twelve tables at the most.

With pots, pans, jugs, pitchers, bowls hanging from the walls and ceiling the room felt even smaller, that created a very homey atmosphere. Maybe that was the point of an Irish pub, to make you feel welcome, like home. A long wooden bar scarred by time, spilled drinks and cigarette butts filled one side of the room, on the opposite wall, a small stone fireplace took an early chill out of the air and the entire floor of the pub covered with sawdust made for slippery walking if you weren't careful. The pub was packed. Every old wooden table over-flowed with guests, but the servers, two young girls (probably the owner's daughters), were the sweetest and most attentive girls ever. Maybe the sawdust helped them slide from table to table. They also may have had the reddest hair in all of Ireland.

After sampling *Champ,* a dish of mashed potatoes with chives, parsley, onions, shallots, peas, cabbage, and carrots, and a piece of *Barm Brack* cake, a rich fruit cake they washed down with two glasses of *Guinness* stout, the Brecht's decided to walk off the meal and do a little window shopping. Along Bath Road, one of the many narrow cobblestone streets that emptied into the harbor they came upon *The Cane and Hat est. 1756*, a small general store that appeared as weary as its sign proclaimed. A jingle from a tiny bell announced their entrance as they pushed open the old weathered door and stepped onto the wooden plank floor. Forgotten by time the *Cane and Hat* resembled a Chandlery, a general store that sold anything and everything needed to outfit a whaling ship back in the 1800s. Food, clothing, oil, tools, rope, chain, gunpowder, one-stop shopping, just like Publix's in Florida, but without the modern amenities. Like a Chandlery, every square inch of the Cane and Hat had an item standing up, either leaning against or hanging down from the ceiling. Whatever a person needed, the Cane and Hat sold it. Tucked away in the back corner of the store were an assortment of woodcarvings, sculptures, and a barrel of walking sticks. It turned out that the owner of the establishment was a woodcarver and avid walker. While on his many treks throughout the countryside, he gathered up unusual pieces of wood that he worked on back at his shop and later sold. One particular stick caught Mrs. Brecht's eye. Its shape and color resembled a girl's field hockey stick. She held it up and slowly turned the stick towards the window. "Look Ken, this walking stick looks exactly like my old field hockey stick from Leipsic High. The same light brown wood color, the rounded handle flattened on the left side and a slight hook at the bottom."

"How could I ever forget, November 1962, Ohio Field Hockey State Championship game? Leipsic vs. Columbus Grove, three minutes remaining, game tied 2-2, senior Charlene Rikard, steady girl of Ken Brecht, later to marry said field hockey sensation, scored the winning goal as the clock ran out; Leipsic Vikings 3, Columbus Bulldogs 2."

Some things you never forget, riding a bike, your birthday and winning a state championship. Grasping the shaft with both hands Charlene Brecht raised the stick and with one fluid motion the face of the handle smashed down into the right side of the boom box. An explosion of shattered plastic sent people running in all directions as broken shards of black plastic rained down on people and chrome rings from the speakers rolled along the grass. The impact sent the boom box tumbling side-over-side across the cement walkway, down the rock embankment, and into the deeps of the Intracoastal Waterway.

From the safety of the food tent Lou Bravo, took in all the excitement with delight as he flipped one last burger. *Damn, I don't believe that old gal had the balls to smash up Hubba Bubba's boom box,* he thought. There wasn't much that Lou Bravo didn't notice; he made it his business to notice things, it made life a lot simpler, not to mention safer. Plus, he didn't want some punk kid ruining his party.

He put a plate together and walked over to where all the action was. "Wow, Mrs. Brecht that is some swing you have."

"Well, thank you Lou Bravo, I was a little surprised myself."

"I imagine after all that exercise a big plate of ribs, beans and of course your own homemade potato salad is in order." Lou Bravo said.

"Please take this plate and go sit with Mr. Brecht. I need to have a word with this young man."

"Thank you, I believe I will and young man, maybe next time, you won't play your music so loud." Mrs. Brecht turned and walked back over to her husband and sat down.

Lou Bravo tightened his grip on the kid's arm, which turned a bright red, jerked him around and said, "We can do this the easy way or the hard way, it's up to you!"

"Easy way, man, but let go of my arm, you're hurting me."

Releasing his arm, Lou Bravo moved his shirt to the side exposing the steel gray butt of his Glock sticking out of his waistband holster. He reached into his pocket, took out his gold money clip and peeled off three crisp one-hundred dollar bills. Hubba Bubba froze and just stared down at the gun.

"Hey, Hubba Bubba look at me," Lou Bravo snarled and grabbed the kid's hand. Looking him straight in the eye, he shoved the bills in his hand. "I can blow your brains out right here, or you can take the money, leave now, and buy a new boom box, some CDs and a new pair of jeans. What's it gonna be?"

"Yeah, this will take care of everything," Hubba Bubba whined. "How do you know my name? Do I know you mister?"

Irritated with the boy's questions and anxious to get back to the party, Lou Bravo added, "I guess you got a short memory." Turning to walk back to his party Lou Bravo whispered, "One more thing kid, if I hear you bothered my friend, you'll be the one rolling down some hill into the Intracoastal. Now get outta here!"

Chapter Thirty-Four

Every square inch of the back seat was crammed with stuff for the parade. A cooler filled with ice, soda, water, and a bottle of Chardonnay squeezed up against the window. A box of paper goods leaned against the other side window. The rest of the supplies: two waterproof flashlights, a plastic folding table, beach blanket, two foam-padded seat cushions, a large golf umbrella, two sweat shirts, and last but not least, a tin of Blaine's famous double-fudge chocolate brownies smothered in confectionary sugar almost touched the roof leaving only a small opening for visibility.

"Brooke, it's time to go, please get in the car. Did we forget anything? It looks like we have enough stuff to camp out for a week. What do you think, sweetie?"

"I think, if Lou Bravo didn't take our chairs, we'd be sitting on that blanket all night. Just look at all that stuff. We couldn't squeeze in another thing even if we wanted to, Mom."

"Just wanted to be prepared, that's all. Okay buckle up, it's party time."

Traffic was brutal. Barely creeping along Tamiami Trail, an over-heated pick-up broke down in the left lane and backed up traffic to the Toyota dealership. People were not kind to the old man standing in the road looking down at his smoking engine. Finally, he walked across the street and waited for the police.

Blaine managed to squeeze through the Venice Avenue intersection sandwiched between a black SUV and the sidewalk.

"There Mom, a spot, right in front of that battery store," Brooke yelled, pointing out the window. "The man in the Buick can't fit in, he's leaving. Go for it, Mom, you can do it, I know you can."

"Piece of cake," Blaine added as she pulled up to the spot, shifted into reverse and parallel parked in one easy motion. "My old high school driver Ed teacher, Mr. Lenoff, would be proud of me today."

"Let's not forget that you're driving a Mini Cooper and not a humongous minivan," Brooke exclaimed with a big grin on her face.

"A minor detail, young lady what is important, we have a parking spot close to the parade, not a mile away. Okay, let's get our stuff and get going."

They scooped up their gear and joined the crowd walking down to the Boat Parade of Lights. Hundreds of people on both sides of the street pushed and jostled one another as they marched towards the waterway. People carried chairs and blankets, pulled wagons full of food, mothers and fathers held infants, while children lead or at times followed their dogs as they marched towards the Intracoastal. In spite of an occasional push or shove, everyone appeared to be in a festive mood. "How are you doing, kiddo? You look a little weighed down; want me to carry something for you?" Blaine reached over and pulled up the blanket wrapped around Brooke's neck. "Better now?"

"Thanks, Mom, I'm okay, how much further?" Brooke gasped.

"We're almost there, sweetie, our chairs are on the other side of the Train Depot, three minutes, maybe less if the people keep moving."

Parked on the opposite side of the road and pushed up against a chain link fence on a small patch of grass, was an ice cream truck. The small white box-truck decorated with bright-painted red, orange and purple balloons along the roofline and pictures of dancing clowns, playful circus animals and ice cream cones on all four sides of the truck was a delicious sight.

On the roof a sign in the shape of an elephant, in big, bright, yellow letters, read CIRCUS DAYS ICE CREAM and blinked on and off every time a customer approached. *Turkey in the Straw* played repeatedly, welcoming parents and children to stop and buy ice cream. Two blinding spot lights on the front and two on the back lit up the entire ice cream truck, sidewalk, road and the sole customer standing at the side window: a police officer.

"Let's get some ice cream, sweetie. It doesn't look like a long line." Blaine took Brooke's arm and they raced across the street. "What do you say we buy a whole bunch of ice pops and you can hand them out to all the neighborhood kids at the parade?"

"Sounds like a splendiferous idea, Mom. Can I pick out the flavors? I hope they have raspberry, I love raspberry."

"Splendiferous, that's an awful big word for someone who's only seven. Where did you hear that word?"

"In school. Miss Diane used the word the other day when we were planning our holiday party. She said Zella's suggestion about decorating the cupcakes with smiley faces was a splendiferous idea." A little embarrassed by all the attention her mother was creating, Brooke looked up at the police officer standing in front of them. "Mommy, why doesn't the policeman just buy some ice cream and leave?"

"I don't know Brooke, but it looks like we may not be buying ice cream at all today."

Flipping open his ticket book with one turn of the wrist and taking out his pen from his breast pocket, the officer repeated himself, "Sir, I'm sorry, but you cannot sell ice cream within the city limits of Venice without a permit. You only have vendor certificates for Manatee and Sarasota counties; not the City of Venice. Sir, you have to shut down and leave or I'll have to give you a ticket."

"But officer, I'm just trying to make a living. I thought people would like ice cream for the parade so I filled my truck with extra ice cream and came here. I'm way back off the road out of the way. Please, officer, I'm not hurting anybody. I'm just trying to make a buck."

"Mommy, look the policeman's face is turning all red. Is he sick?"

"I don't think so, sweetie. I think he is just a little frustrated with the ice cream man. That's all."

Tugging on Blaine's arm, Brooke asked, "What does frustrated mean, mommy?"

"Frustrated, sweetie means disappointed, unhappy. You see the ice cream man doesn't have a license to sell ice cream here. So the police officer told him he has to leave. If he doesn't, he will give him a ticket."

"Mr. Lilly, would you please turn off the music. I can't hear myself think with all that noise. Thank you, now, Mr. Lilly, for the last time, if you don't leave now, I will be forced to write you a one-hundred-sixteen dollar ticket, you will lose a day's work, plus you will have to appear in court. Is that what you want sir, because I'm very frustrated with you right now."

"Okay officer I will go. I am sorry for causing you frustration. I'll close, but what about the nice lady and young girl behind you? Can they have some ice cream?" The police officer turned and for the first time realized people were waiting and most likely overheard the entire conversation. An uncomfortable smile formed as he glanced down at Brooke and Blaine standing an arms-length away.

"Okay, but then you shut down," he repeated as he moved aside to allow Blaine and Brooke to move up.

"We would like," turning to her mother in mid-sentence, "how many ice pops should we order?"

"Ten, no fifteen, should be more than enough for all the kids."

Turning back to the window Brooke said, "We would like to order fifteen raspberry ice pops, please."

"Coming right up, young lady, since my favorite flavor is raspberry and for being so patient, I'm only going to charge for ten."

With a big bright smile and a twinkle in her eye, Blaine paid the man, placed the ice pops in the cooler and they continued towards the parade.

"How about Christmas ice cream for Earl Neigh the newspaper delivery guy," Blaine thought to herself. "I'm sure he would love a raspberry Popsicle and twenty minutes of *Turkey in the Straw* before he went to work. What is good for the goose should be just right for the gander."

Chapter Thirty-Five

"Mommy there they are. Look, Lou Bravo is waving, hurry, mommy, hurry."

"I'm hurrying sweetie, but this cooler is heavy and I don't want to drop the brownies."

With some trepidation, Lou Bravo gave the baked beans one last stir and ran over to help Blaine and Brooke. Taking the cooler and box of paper goods from Blaine, he had the feeling that the episode at the house was forgiven or, at the least forgotten. He would have to apologize to all her neighbors again for his outburst and buy the customary peace offering of a holiday bouquet of flowers or a basket of oranges from Nokomis Groves.

Never at a loss of words, Lou Bravo initiated the conversation with a non-judgmental comment to determine where he stood with Blaine, "So, the traffic was bad?"

"The worst I've seen in years, everyone in Southwest Florida must be going to the parade. Tamiami Trail was backed up to Cramer Toyota and finding a parking spot almost impossible," Blaine replied with an exhausted smile.

Brooke could not contain herself any longer and with the energy of a prancing gazelle, she shouted, "I found the parking spot for mommy. A big car couldn't squeeze into the spot and I told mommy. She parallel parked just like Mr. Lenoff taught her."

Confused, Lou Bravo took off his Santa's hat, rubbed his forehead and asked, "Who is Mr. Lenoff, Brooke?"

"He was mommy's driving teacher in high school, he showed her how to drive a car," Brooke replied proudly. "And she parked on the first try."

"Okay, now, that I know who Mr. Lenoff is, let's get something to eat. I'm starving. You guys get the drinks and I'll get the food." After putting three plates of ribs, peppers and sausage, potato salad, and an extra scoop of baked beans together, Lou Bravo led the way towards the front row of chairs. With a wave of his hand and a slight bow he announced, "Front row seats, my ladies," and handed them their plates.

"Everything looks delicious, Lou Bravo; here I brought you a diet *Coke*," Blaine said. "The baked beans have a sweet hickory flavor, no doubt your family's secret ingredient from the hills of the Great Smokey Mountains."

"Well, little lady, I hate to disappoint you all, but them beans may smell like they came from the backwoods of a Tennessee smokehouse, but this good-ole family recipe here was passed down from my grandfather, Giuseppe Bravo who grew up on the shores of Coney Island." Lou Bravo lifted his Diet Coke and the three toasted, "Salute."

Chapter Thirty-Six

There is something about eating in the great outdoors, *even though it was only alongside the Intracoastal Waterway in Venice*, for Lou Bravo, it could have been the great wilderness of Yellowstone National Park. Maybe it was the crisp night air or the warm red glow of the sunset, but for some reason, food cooked on an open grill and served on a paper plate seemed to taste better. Even the fussiest eaters left their attitude at home. Not one complaint, even Miss Fussy Eater, Brooke Sterling, devoured everything on her plate. A feather in his Santa's cap, Lou Bravo looked over at Blaine and Brooke and thought, *what a perfect night this was turning out to be.*

Blaine glanced over at Lou Bravo and whispered, "I need to talk to you." Like a punch to the gut, Lou Bravo's perfect night came crashing down like a child's sandcastle unable to withstand the constant pounding of the waves. It was too good to be true, now it was payback time for the other day. "Brooke, why don't you give out the ice pops to the kids before the parade starts? I think it would be a nice treat after dinner."

"You just want to get rid of me so you can talk to Lou Bravo." Brooke scoffed as she stood up.

"I do want to talk to Lou Bravo and yes, I don't want you to listen in on every adult conversation I have, but if you remember sweetie, you wanted raspberry ice pops!"

"Okay mommy, you win," Brooke, said, "So where are the pops?"

"They're under the dessert table and if there are any extras, give them out to the adults. Thanks, sweetie, don't forget Lou Bravo and me."

Lou Bravo looked like death warmed over. His face, the color of chalk had a painful look of despair etched in the wrinkles across his brow. His antics the other day doomed a perfect night; there was nothing he could do to prevent the tongue lashing that was about to rain down on his parade. He became quiet and listless. All that remained was to suck it up and take it.

"Lou Bravo, are you okay? You look like you're in pain. Are you sick?"

"No, I'm fine. What did you want to talk about?" Lou Bravo mumbled.

"How can I rent an ice cream truck? Complete with ice cream, candy, and ice pops." Blaine, in a cheery voice, proposed.

Lou Bravo could not believe his ears. Reprieved; it was as if someone had lifted a hundred-pound weight from his shoulders, miracles do happen, *I'll be in church Sunday, I promise.* "Ice cream, you want to know how you can rent an ice cream truck for Brooke's birthday party. What a great idea, the kids will have a ball, all the ice cream they can eat, candy and ice cream truck music, but I thought her birthday just passed?"

"I don't want it for Brooke's birthday, I want it for a Christmas present," Blaine said laughing. "Remember the newspaper carrier I told you about, who played loud music when he delivered the paper? Well, he left a Christmas card in the paper, with his name and address. So I thought I'd give him a little of his own medicine. Some loud music from the ice cream lady, Happy Holidays, hope you like your present."

Lou Bravo faintly recalled Blaine talking about the newspaper guy, the loud music every night, how she could not get back to sleep and how exhausted she was at work. How she called the paper and complained. She even went to the paper and spoke to the manager, but he ended up committing suicide. What a mess and the prick is still blasting the music. "A dose of his own medicine, payback time; I love it!" Lou Bravo bellowed.

"So, can you get an ice cream truck for me?"

"Of course, I know a guy from South Venice who has one. You met him once, the cleaning truck, the old guy with the mattresses, remember? He owes me a favor, or two, and I don't think he'd mind a little vacation, give him some quality time to buy his wife something nice for Christmas. When would you like delivery, Madame?" With a sigh of relief, Lou Bravo, inhaled deeply, and leaned back in his chair.

Blaine leaned over and gave Lou Bravo a big hug and whispered in his ear, "Next week is Brooke's winter vacation, that would be a good time. Thank you."

"Ice cream for two," Brooke yelled. Lou Bravo and Blaine turned and laughed.

Chapter Thirty-Seven

Two piercing horn blasts echoed down the Intracoastal, one long, one short and on cue; the bridge opened to welcome the arrival of the floating procession. Boats of all sizes and shapes began to move down the waterway. Sailboats, large yachts, day cruisers, dinghies, even jet skis joined in the fun. As each boat passed, the crowd exploded in applause, cheers and whistles enthusiastically welcoming their favorite. Icicle lights streamed down from the sides of boats, holiday music blasted out songs that echoed across the water all night long. Every boat took on its own character and illuminated the sky with figures of snowmen, reindeer, snowflakes, candy canes, Santa Claus, Mickey Mouse, the Grinch, Charlie Brown, trees, and marching toy soldiers. It was a magical sight.

"Here, mommy, take a look through my binoculars. It is so cool; you can see the tiniest decoration. Look at boat number ten, can you read what is written on the snowman's stomach?"

"Think snow," Blaine continued, "I don't think so Mr. Snowman, you're not in Kansas anymore, you are in Florida."

"That reminds me Brooke; Mr. Farrell told me you were running with your binoculars, not a good idea. If you fell that would have been the end of them and you could have injured yourself," Lou Bravo corrected her.

"That Mr. Farrell is a big tattletale," Brooke snapped angrily as she put the binoculars to her eyes.

"Mommy, your friend from the park is on boat thirteen, the big boat with all the red toy soldiers. He is dressed like a soldier too, but his uniform is green and brown. He also has big rifle."

"Let me see. Oh no. . . ."

The first shot struck Blaine's left shoulder and threw her back against the chairs. The second bullet tore through her lower forearm ripping the binoculars from her left hand. The third and fourth shots, by inches, missed Blaine's head as she crashed to the ground. The custom silencer and night-vision scope made the Remington 700 a very deadly weapon, especially in the hands of an experienced hunter like Remi Cole. The manufacturer's claim of accuracy up to 300 yards was right on target. The only indication of gun fire were four dull pop, pop, pop, pop sounds intentionally drowned out by the loud music from boat thirteen.

Behind the cover of the cabin door, a shadow stealthily moved down the stairs to the galley. Sitting down at the captain's table, Remi opened his gun case, took out an oil rag and began to wipe down the rifle with methodical precision. Every section of the rifle was broken down, meticulously cleaned and then put back together. Satisfied nothing linked him to the weapon; Remi placed the rifle in the box and closed the clasps. She ruined his life, took away the only job he loved, now he was going to ruin hers.

"So did you kill the bitch? I hope her fucking brains splattered all over the place. Come on up here and tell me everything Remi," Boltier crowed and handed him a beer.

"No, Charlie, she's not dead and her fucking brains are still in her head," Remi barked and grabbed the railing to the flying bridge. "That wasn't the plan, remember?"

"Okay, okay, relax. Sit down and fill me in," Boltier pleaded.

"It's not that easy to hit a target from a moving boat, especially at night and more than fifty yards away. I think I hit her twice, shoulder and arm, maybe grazed her head. Enough damage to put a real hurting on the bitch."

"That's what I wanted to hear Remi! That bitch cost me two thousand bucks, hundred hours of digging up Brazilian Pepper plants at the fucking park, and to top everything off I got served divorce papers yesterday. Fifteen years of marriage down the drain because I'm now unstable."

"Let's not forget I was fired because of her nosing around."

Charlie held up his hand. "Hold up a second, Remi, something is coming over the radio." *Parade boaters, this is John Osmolosky, Parade Chairperson, we just received a directive from the police department that a shooting has taken place at the Venice Train Depot, an apparent robbery. Three people have been injured, one seriously, and that a medevac helicopter is en route. One gunman is in custody and they are searching for an accomplice. For safety, boats thirteen through thirty-five must turn about and return to the staging area back at Osprey. Boats one through twelve should continue to the Circus Bridge and wait until we get the all clear from the police to continue the parade. I am sorry for the inconvenience, but your safety is our main concern. Thank you.*

With a big smile, Boltier turned *Off Road* about and headed back to Osprey.

"What great luck, Charlie. While the cops are looking for this other person, we can just pull away at Marker 4, head into the slip, and be gone. Now I don't need to dump the rifle under the Circus Bridge as planned. That's a savings of about a thousand bucks. I'll pawn it. I sure can use the cash since I don't have a job anymore." Remi coughed and chugged down the last of his beer.

"I don't know Remi," Charlie said as they passed under the Venice Avenue Bridge. "I think you should still get rid of the gun. Just throw it overboard and be done with it. That's what we planned."

"Well, the plan has changed. Now we have the perfect escape route all laid-out by the police. What could be easier, just follow all the boats back to the dock and walk away; I'm not throwing it away, so shut the fuck up!"

"Okay, buddy, relax. It's your ass not mine if the police find the rifle," Charlie boomed as a police helicopter flew overhead. "Here comes the medevac copter, let's just cool it and follow the parade back to the staging area." A Venice police boat pushed off from its slip at the Crow's Nest dock and headed for the train depot.

Chapter Thirty-Eight

The red traffic light at Palermo Place burned through the early morning fog as Earl pressed hard on the brakes. A damp mist rolled in off the Intracoastal at two in the morning and made for slick road conditions that caused the Camaro to pull to the right. *Got to get those brakes fixed before I'm riding on the drums,* Earl thought as he tightened his grip on the steering wheel and straightened out the car. At 65 mph, it took a while to bring the Camaro to a complete stop. "Shit, I don't believe this crap. Why can't I make all the lights?" Earl shouted as he punched the steering wheel, like that would make the light turn green. For the past week, Earl, without success, tried to make every single traffic light from the Circus Bridge to the Venice Journal Star off Miami. Ever since the incident with the fire truck on the Circus Bridge, Earl had been consumed with the notion of cruising down Tamiami Trail, wind blowing his hair and only green lights shining in his face. Unfortunately, when he went below 55 mph on Monday, and Tuesday, he got red lights at San Marco and Palermo. When he drove over 60 mph on Wednesday, he hit red lights on Turin and Miami. On Thursday, when he kept the speed at 65 mph, again he hit red lights on Turin, Milan and Miami. It rained Friday, slick roads forced Earl to slow down and endure a slow frustrating drive to the newspaper. He hit every red light that morning. With each light Earl's anger festered until he couldn't take it any longer and screamed out, as he turned down Miami into the paper's parking lot, "What else could go wrong with this fucking experiment?"

Saturday morning Earl waited for the light to turn green. It seemed like an eternity as he stared at the red light and the Circus Bridge in front of him. "Green, baby, turn green," Earl yelled and pounded on the steering wheel. "Today's the day. No stops, only green lights today." Earl's new strategy was to keep the speed at 70 mph. He needed speed to make each light and his '99 candy apple red Camaro with a 305-hp V-8 under the hood was just the ticket.

Earl punched the gas pedal and the front end leaped forward just as the light turned green. The posi-traction kicked in, the over-sized Cooper tires clawed the road, and the Camaro hit 70 mph at the top of the bridge. Darby Buick, the Pit Stop, and Avenida Del Circo were just a blurrrr at 70 mph in the dark. The Lucky Dog Diner on the corner of Tamiami and San Marco Drive was lit and ready for the breakfast crowd. Venice Regional Medical Center on Palermo Place was alive with activity; two ambulances, a Sarasota Rescue Truck and three police cars all with their lights flashing pulled into the emergency room entrance as Earl sped by. "Okay, two lights down, three to go," Earl crowed and focused on the light that just turned green on Turin Street. Unfortunately, Earl did not notice the police car parked in the front of Publix's parking lot before Turin.

Officer Warren Cox just finished the paper work on the stabbing victim he brought in to Venice Regional. The victim, Harry Potter (not the boy wizard), a 52 year-old white male, told Cox that he and his girlfriend were partying at his house and after a couple of beers got into a shouting match over the return of her DVDs. She ran into the kitchen, came out with a large bone-handle carving knife and stabbed him in the back as he tried to open the front door and escape.

Detectives took the girlfriend to the Venice Police Station for booking and Cox followed the ambulance with the victim to the hospital. Cox finished his report and was about to shut down his computer when the radar picked up a vehicle moving well over 70 mph in a 35-mph speed zone. Cox turned on his lights, jumped the curb and sped north down Tamiami. "This is Officer Cox, badge number V3452, I am in pursuit of a red, late-model Camaro, license plate number HA-HA-70 speeding north on Tamiami just past Turin. This guy is flying, just clocked him at 70 mph. Request back-up at Venice Avenue and Tamiami."

"Will send two cruisers to the area, ETA about three minutes," crackled over the speaker.

The Camaro raced past Milan Avenue just as the light changed red. Earl shot a quick glance to the left, the clock on Moody's road sign read 2:14. Looking straight ahead, he noticed that the light at Miami was red; a cold sweat ran down his spine.

"What the fuck. What do I do now; the fucking light is red! Man, do I ease up on the accelerator or keep going?"

Earl didn't have to worry about making a choice. The decision was already made with two quick blasts from Officer Cox's siren; Earl's joy ride was over. Startled, Earl glanced into the rear view mirror, a blinding glare of white from a spotlight and the pulsating red and blue police lights flashed back at him. Instinctively, Earl put his foot on the brake, turned on his right directional and eased the car to the curb. He was ten feet from Miami Avenue, the last intersection before the newspaper when he finally stopped: the light was green. Fixated on the green light, Earl did not notice Officer Cox walk up to his car.

Officer Cox leaned down to Earl's car window and said, "Sir, do you realize that you were driving seventy miles an hour in a thirty-five mile an hour zone? Was there an emergency that caused you to drive at such a high speed?"

"No officer, there wasn't. I was just trying an experiment while driving to work," Earl sheepishly replied.

"Experiment? What experiment would require you to drive seventy miles an hour?" Earl breathed deeply and began to explain how he saw a fire truck speed past all the green lights from the Circus Bridge and he was attempting to do the same thing on his way to work at the newspaper. That he attempted different speeds all week and that tonight he only had one more block to complete a perfect run.

Officer Cox could not believe his ears, he leaned through the window and sniffed, "Sir, have you been drinking tonight?"

"No, officer, I have ninety papers to deliver thirty minutes from now," Earl said with a sheepish grin.

"Sir, are you on drugs, or taking any medication that would cause you to drive seventy miles an hour?"

"I don't do drugs and I'm not taking any medicine."

"Sir, may I please have your driver's license and registration."

Officer Cox walked back to his patrol car, punched Earl's name, DOB, driver's license number into the computer and up popped everything he needed to know about Earl Haden Neigh: brown hair, brown eyes, 140 pounds, 5' 9", born 12/23/89, residence 10 Blue Heron Ct. Englewood, Florida. His driving record was an automotive disaster: three speeding tickets in the last two years, one stop sign violation this year, four unpaid parking tickets from Orlando, and a parking lot fender bender yesterday outside the Galleria Movie Theatre in Venice. Cox shook his head and wondered how high this man's insurance premiums would be with a third-moving violation added to his list of infractions.

By the time, Officer Cox finished the information on the citation, two patrol cars pulled up and two officers stood in front of their vehicles waiting. After a brief review of the incident, Cox walked back to Earl's car. "Mr. Neigh, I would like you to step out of the car and go over to those officers and complete a field sobriety check."

"Is that the test where you have to touch your nose, walk backwards, count to a million and stuff like that?"

"Something like that, sir."

"No way, I don't have to do that. I know my rights," Earl snapped angrily at the officer.

"That's correct sir, but then you will need to breathe into this breathalyzer for me or I'll have to arrest you for refusing to take a breathalyzer test."

"No problem, officer, I can do that," Earl said quickly as he opened his mouth. Officer Cox placed the breathalyzer in Earl's mouth and instructed him to breathe into the device. Cox looked at the reading and walked over to the officers. After a short discussion, the officers got back into their cars and drove off.

"Mr. Neigh, here is your driver's license, registration, and a citation for speeding. Since you were driving 70 mph, 35 miles per hour over the legal speed limit, you are scheduled for a mandatory court appearance. The date and time are on the back of the citation. If you fail to appear, we issue a warrant for your arrest and take you into custody. Do you have any questions, Mr. Neigh?"

"Two hundred eighty-six dollars for speeding! That's insane," Earl moaned, looking down at the citation.

"No, Mr. Neigh, the two hundred eighty-six dollar fee refers to someone who was speeding twenty-to-twenty-nine mph over the legal speed limit." Shining his flashlight on the new fee schedule form Earl held in his hand, Officer Cox continued. "Unfortunately for you, Mr.

Neigh, you were thirty-five mph over the legal limit and as you can see that fee is blank. I've seen fines as high as four hundred dollars; it's up to the judge!" Earl was speechless. Where was he going to get four hundred dollars? It might as well be four million dollars and forget about what the monthly car insurance bill would now be? Earl slouched back in the seat and stared at the ticket. "A word of advice, Mr. Neigh, I wouldn't tell the judge about your fire truck experiment and I'd change my license plate if I was you. Police don't appreciate drivers laughing at the state speed limit." Officer Cox smiled, "Have a nice day, Mr. Neigh," and walked back to his cruiser.

Chapter Thirty-Nine

Earl slowly backed the Camaro into his newspaper delivery spot at the far end of the parking lot. The lot took up the entire block that fronted the Venice Journal Star building, print shop, and Intracoastal. Nearly deserted, only a handful of regulars and two newbies who feverishly double-bagged their papers anticipating a big rain later that night remained. *Rookies, Earl thought to himself, it's not going to rain. You are just wasting your time.* The clock on his dash read 3:20. That was noticeably late for a carrier to arrive; by that time, most of the people were on the streets delivering papers.

"Shit, that fucking cop kept me for over an hour," Earl screamed as he slammed the car door shut. "There goes my thousand dollar bonus down the drain. There's no way I can get all these papers out by 6:00 A.M." Sarah and Farah, two gorgeous blonde co-eds attending South Florida College that Earl had been hitting on all summer, looked over and smiled. "Sorry girls, just a little police problem that's all."

"We heard, that's too bad, Earl." The girls giggled.

"Maybe the two of you beauties could come over and give me a little kiss to make the pain go away. Whataya you say girls?"

"Sorry, tiger, we're running a little late and by the looks of things, you haven't even gotten out of the starting blocks. Some other time," they cooed.

"I'll take you up on that. By the way, who told you about the cops?"

"The Star Trek Guy!" The girls pulled out of the lot singing and gyrating to the music blasting from their car radio.

Painfully, pushing a shopping cart full of papers and plastic baggies from across the parking lot was Myron Weeder, a tall, lanky, horned rimmed glasses, pocket protector geek; affectionately referred to as the "Star Trek Guy." Myron was the technology guru at Best Buy in Sarasota, a member of the Geek Squad, a computer genius. If you had a computer problem, he was the go-to guy. He knew everything about computers, it was as if he could communicate with them; the weird part was, it appeared that they communicated back.

Myron, despite his intellectual prowess, was not always living in the real world. Reality and fantasy for the *Star Trek Guy* sometime collided and the two dimensions became a messy blend that created out-of-this world problems for Myron. Consumed with the whole Star Trek phenomenon, Myron may have beamed up to the Spaceship Enterprise one too many times. His classic, pea green 1971 Volkswagen bus was for him the Spaceship Enterprise. Myron converted the interior into the bridge of the Enterprise, complete with captain chairs, workstations, lights, sliding doors, monitors, computer consoles, transporter station, and Star Trek videos that streamed on when the door opened.

At Halloween, Myron dressed up as Commander Spock; ankle-high black pants, boots, blue crew shirt with the official Star Fleet insignia, the full uniform right down to the taser gun that shot out ear piercing sound waves. He actually looked just like Spock; the pointy ears made the costume look frighteningly out of this world. However, Myron's problem was he didn't know when the party was over. He stayed in costume well past New Year's Day and overstayed his welcome back on Earth.

Delivery Manager Tanner Hatchet received a complaint that a newspaper carrier, dressed like the television character Spock, fired a gun at a customer's front yard lamppost while driving down the street. The homeowner wanted the real character to pay for the damages. A stern reprimand, a bill for $252.12 from Franklin Lighting and Myron was back to normal, well as normal could be for the *Star Trek Guy.*

"Greetings, Earthling, I bring you gifts from the far end of the galaxy."

"Man, you look like you crawled on your hands and knees from the far end of the galaxy. Don't have a heart attack on me, Myron. Here sit down and relax for a minute." Earl opened the car door and they both slid into the back seat. Myron leaned back against the cold leather and closed his eyes. He could hear his heart pound, after a minute or two the beats slowed and were back to normal. The rest and cool sensation felt good.

"I saw a cop pull you over. What happened?" Myron asked shyly.

"I got a fucking speeding ticket, could cost me over four hundred bucks," Earl snapped angrily and punched the front seat.

"Why were you speeding? What was the rush to get to work? Nobody here has to punch a clock."

"I was trying to make all the lights from the Circus Bridge to Miami. All week I tried different speeds, but just couldn't get them all," Earl sighed, "Until today I think. Then the cop pulled me over before I reached Miami."

"That is so cool," Myron enthusiastically replied, "What speeds did you try?"

"55, 60, 65 and 70 mph, but they all crapped out on me. I started at the top of Circus Bridge, but at each speed at least one green light turned red." Myron reached into his shirt pocket, took out a business card size calculator and frantically punched in numbers. Two minutes later, he looked up and nodded.

"Estimating the distance between each light, timing of the traffic light, measuring total road distance, there are more than one thousand possible speed combinations. You would be too old to drive before you lucked out and found the right speed. By then the police would have issued you so many speeding tickets, you would more than likely be taking mass transit."

"Shit. Forget about it," Earl snapped angrily.

"Don't give up the spaceship, Laddie. I'll contact Venice Public Works, retrieve all the details on their traffic lights, download the information and should have the answer for you by the end of the week."

"Forget it, Myron," Earl barked. "I called Public Works and those assholes said they didn't know what streets had traffic lights. They wait for the fire or police department to report when a light malfunctions and then they go out and make repairs. Can you believe that bullshit? The Public Works Department does not know what streets have traffic lights, bull; they just didn't want to be bothered looking it up. You're just wasting your time calling them; they'll give you the same run-a-round."

"Who said anything about calling, I'll hack into their systems, get the information I need and leave them a little surprise for giving you such a difficult time. Yeah, a cookie or two should cause a month's worth of computer headaches," Myron laughed, "Teach them a lesson in customer relations."

"You're the man. Talk to you later, I got to get these papers bagged up."

Myron held up his left hand, fingers separated in the Vulcan greeting and said, "Live long and prosper Earthling," and walked away.

Chapter Forty

Blaine slowly opened her eyes. Everything in the room appeared blurry and out of focus. She closed them again and ever so slowly, in a circular motion, rubbed her forehead and eyes with her right palm and fingers. Relief was only temporary, but welcomed. Unfortunately, everything was still a blur. Blaine could hear the tick of the round cream-colored clock on the opposite wall, but the numbers were impossible to read with clarity. Was it 6:15 or 9:15 or could it be 8:10 or maybe 5:45? With the blinds closed, she couldn't tell if it was day or night. However, that was not her main concern, the excruciating pain radiating from her left side intensified with each stroke of the clock. She turned her head to the left, reached over and lifted the sheet; her left shoulder and arm were completely bandaged. The thickness of the wrapping reminded Blaine of shoulder and arm pads professional football players wore. *Wow, a bit over the top with the bandages people,* Blaine thought. She leaned over to get a closer look at the IV sticking out of her left hand and accidentally rubbed against her shoulder. Instantly a knife-like pain cut down her left side forcing her to collapse back down on the pillow grimacing in pain. Holding her breath and trying not to move, Blaine thought, *where was the nurse's call button?*

"Hi Mommy, how do you feel?"

Blaine opened her eyes and saw Brooke standing at the foot of the bed with a big, bright smile on her angelic face holding a bouquet of flowers. For an instant, the pain was replaced by euphoria. Tears of joy rolled down her face.

"Come over here honey and give mommy a big kiss."

At that moment, Blaine noticed Lou Bravo standing behind Brooke, quiet and grim faced. She gave a faint smile, he returned a quick salute with a rolled up newspaper he held in his hand. He picked Brooke up, leaned her over the bed while she gave her mother a big kiss on the cheek.

"Mommy, do you like the flowers? They're from me and Lou Bravo," Brooke said quickly. "We bought them at the Farmers' Market this morning. Do you like them, mommy, do you?"

"They're beautiful, honey, I see you selected my favorites; yellow roses. Thank you. Lou Bravo, could you please find the nurse's call button, I need some pain medicine."

"Here it is hanging off the side of the bed." Lou Bravo pressed the bottom and then wrapped the device around the metal arm railing on the left side of the bed. "So, how do you feel?"

"For someone who's been shot twice, not bad I guess. Maybe I should be thankful he wasn't a better shot, but I could really use a pain killer, my left side is killing me," Blaine said with a faint laugh.

The door opened and a nurse in royal blue scrubs flew into the room carrying a metal tray with a green plastic water container and two plastic cups. "Good morning and how are we today?" She bellowed, surprising everyone in the room with the intensity of her greeting. She stopped at the side table, checked the computer patient file, quickly typed something and proceeded to pour water into one of the cups. "Blaine, Dr. Solinis prescribed Oxycodone for the pain and by the look on your face; I'm here just in time. Here, just what the doctor ordered. You should feel relief in a few minutes," she sang out in a cheery voice. The nametag on her shirt read Terri Butterworth and she was a real dynamo of positive energy. The other nurses nicknamed her *Miss Congeniality* because she was so friendly and upbeat all the time. Terri Butterworth's warm smile and gentle touch melted away all complaints the sourest patient uttered. She embraced each patient with compassion, as maple syrup covers a stack of steaming hot pancakes. However, the most defining characteristic nurse Terri possessed were her piercing blue eyes that took hold of you when she spoke. They reached into your very being and made you feel like you were the only thing important to her in the whole world. Moreover, at that very moment, you were and her piercing eyes conveyed that personal message. For the patient there was never a problem, Nurse Terri would protect them.

"So Nurse Terri when can I go home? I'm feeling much better," Blaine said softly, lifting her head from the pillow.

"That's the Oxycodone talking; you'll have to wait for Dr. Solinis. He is making his rounds and should be in shortly; he will give you that information. If there isn't anything else, I'll be leaving. Have a good day, Blaine." She whirled around and marched out of the room as quickly as she arrived.

"Brooke where are you? Brooke, answer me please honey."

"I'm in the bathroom, Lou Bravo told me to hide in here while the nurse was in the room." Brooke pushed open the door and jumped up onto the bed.

"Hospital rules, Brooke; no kids allowed, but you know my feelings about rules, so I snuck her up the back entrance stairs of the North Wing, a quick right turn to room 251 and here we are," Lou Bravo crowed with a mischievous twinkle in his eye. "But that's not the best part of my visit, wait until you see this!" With the skill of an experienced philatelist removing a $1,035,000.00 bright pink, 1868, 3-cent stamp depicting George Washington, from its cover, Lou Bravo unrolled the newspaper and held up the front page. There at the top, in bold print the headline read Assistant Park Manager Park Shot at Venice Boat Parade; Gunman Escapes. In the center, a large color picture of a boat in flames and below, pictures of Blaine Sterling, Remi Cole, and Charlie Boltier. Lou Bravo detailed how the police, along with the parade coordinator orchestrated an operational sting to catch the gunmen. A broadcast over marine channel 82, the parade frequency, warned all boaters that a gunman was on the loose at the Venice Train Depot and for safety concerns boats 13 and above needed to return to the staging area at Osprey. Three boats from the Venice Police Marine bureau anchored at the staging area at Marker 13 where officers waited to arrest Cole and Boltier. A SWAT team cordoned off the docks at Marker 4 Marina where Boltier kept his boat in case he left the flotilla headed back to Osprey. A medevac helicopter airlifted an elderly woman with a gunshot wound to the head, to Sarasota Memorial Hospital and Ms. Sterling with arm and shoulder injuries is recovering at Venice Hospital. As anticipated, Boltier cut the lights and slowly eased Off-Road towards the dock area where members of the SWAT team immediately surrounded the vessel. Boltier dove off the flying bridge just as the boat smashed into the dock catapulting the waiting officers into the water. Police ordered Cole to surrender, but were answered with gunfire from inside the cabin. The SWAT team returned fire and minutes later, the boat exploded in a fireball of flames. Police extracted Boltier hiding under a floating dock at the far end of the marina, but the body of Remi Cole was not located.

"Unfortunately, Mrs. Cummings, a seventy-six year old snowbird from Michigan, died this morning at Sarasota Memorial." Startled, everyone looked up to see Detective Beale standing in the doorway. "Now we can add murder to the charges facing Boltier and Cole. Ballistics confirmed it was Cole's rifle used to shoot you and kill Mrs. Cummings. By the way how do you feel, Blaine?" Beale asked as he walked over to her bed.

"Detective Beale what a surprise," Blaine said softly with a faint smile. "I feel a little better now, thank you. The medication has numbed most of the pain in my shoulder, but I am heartsick to hear about Mrs. Cummings."

"I just happened to be in the neighborhood so I thought I'd stop in to see how you were. I also wanted to thank Brooke for identifying the boat and Remi Cole as the shooter. With her information we were able to set up the sting, apprehend Charlie Boltier and retrieve the murder weapon."

"Oh, where are my manners! Detective Beale, this is Lou Bravo, a friend of mine, Lou Bravo, this is Detective Justin Beale from the Venice Police Department." The two men shook hands.

"We met the night you were shot," Lou Bravo exclaimed and gave Blaine a quizzical glance, "I guess you weren't in any condition to remember much of anything after being shot twice." He turned to Beale and asked, "Remi Cole, any idea where that bastard is? Dead I hope, blown into a million little pieces, small enough for the tiniest baitfish to devour in one bite. That's where I hope he is, on the bottom of the harbor being chewed up right now."

"Brooke is here. A little too graphic, please stop," Blaine protested and gave Lou Bravo one of her looks.

"Sorry."

Beale's cell phone rang and Hordowski's name and number illuminated the screen. Hordowski explained that police divers completed the search along the entire marina, and came up empty. They hauled wreckage from the boat out of the water and the CSI team was still sifting through the debris in the parking lot. So far, no body, or body parts, nothing. The marine division dragged the harbor and a fleet of boats searched the shoreline up and down the Intracoastal. The Canine Unit had dogs on both sides of the harbor, but no trace of Cole yet. Beale thanked him for the update and mentioned he'd be at the marina shortly.

"Nothing yet, the CSI team is examining all the debris from the wreckage and should give us an answer soon. We have people in the water and teams searching both sides of the Intracoastal."

"You don't think he survived the explosion, do you Detective Beale?" Blaine asked.

"Nothing is being ruled out. Right now, we are investigating every possibility. We'll find him or what's left of him. You can count on that! On another note, Blaine, I need to talk to you about Arthur Dunn. His personal computer, after our IT guys finally broke through the fire walls, contained disturbing sites on child pornography and trafficking. When you leave the hospital and are stronger, I'll call and arrange a time."

Beale's phone rang again, on the read out Hordowski's number appeared. "Beale, what's up?"

Hordowski said there was a break in the case. The dogs found scuba gear on a dock at the mobile home park across the harbor from the explosion. The homeowner, Julie Hargus, was Cole's girlfriend. She has a restraining order against him. Seems Cole likes to play rough with his girlfriends, so after two beatings she kicked him out. "No sign of Cole and she denied knowing anything about the scuba gear, said she hasn't seen him in over a month."

"Hold on a minute; Blaine do you know if Cole scuba dives?"

"Yes, and he has all his own gear. Last summer he came back to the park with a big shark's tooth, as big as my hand. He volunteered to help clean-up garbage under the fishing pier at Sharky's restaurant.

They collected over two hundred pounds of debris, plus a half dozen shark's teeth."

"Hordowski," Beale shouted into the phone, "put out an APB for Cole's car and alert TSA at the Sarasota, Fort Meyers, and Tampa Airports to be on the lookout for Cole. I'll be down there in a few minutes."

"Does that mean he's still alive," Blaine muttered as she pulled the blanket up to her face to help cover her fear.

"Not necessarily, we just have to cover all bases. I'll put an officer out front for security. Don't worry, you will be fine. I'll call when you return home." Beale turned and rushed out the door.

Lou Bravo, who for the past five minutes couldn't get a word in edgewise while Beale was holding court, finally lost patience and blurted out, "Talking about leaving, when are you getting out of this nut house Blaine?"

Startled by his outburst and knowing his history of theatrics, Blaine leaned forward and as calm as possible whispered, "Why don't you ask the doctor yourself, he's standing right behind you."

Chapter Forty-One

Lou Bravo spun around and came face to face with Blaine's doctor. Like a child caught with his hand in the cookie jar, Lou Bravo was trapped by his own doing. Nothing he could say or do would erase the embarrassment of the moment. He turned and waited for the next shoe to drop.

"Dr. Solinis, this is Lou Bravo and my daughter Brooke. Everyone, this is Dr. Solinis, my doctor," Blaine whispered still embarrassed by Lou Bravo's comment.

"So Blaine, this is the infamous Lou Bravo. I am Dr. Joseph Solinis, pleased to meet you." Solinis reached out and grabbed Lou Bravo's hand with such force, the handshake almost knocked him off his feet.

Startled by the viselike grip from a man half his weight and a good ten years older, Lou Bravo's face changed from embarrassment to shock. Dr. Solinis grinned, satisfied that he had Lou Bravo's attention.

As a young boy, growing up in Sicily, Dr. Solinis worked every morning in his parents' bakery preparing the dough for baking before he walked the two miles to school. Years of constant kneading, pounding, and rolling dough built up muscles in his arms and hands to a point where his handshake could be painful if not controlled. However, control came at a price. At an early age, Dr. Solinis observed customers come and go at his parents' bakery in Sicily and he became acutely aware of how people for any number of reasons: ethnicity, religion, appearance, language, or status—treated one another. The old adage, "Don't judge a book by its cover," clearly was not adhered to, a practice upsetting to the young Solinis. By the time Dr. Solinis graduated from college, he resolved if only for a moment, for every greeting he would engage both parties on an equal footing of respect. Before Lou Bravo could reply, Dr. Solinis side stepped him, moved along the bed, and reviewed Blaine's computer medical file.

"Ms. Sterling, you are a very lucky young lady. The bullet penetrated the Coracohumeral ligament, the fleshy part of your shoulder, one inch either way, your injuries would have been much worse. Your rotator cuff could have been shattered, which would have meant replacement/surgery and months of rehabilitation. Your forearm looks good, the bullet made a clean exit through the Flexor Pollicis Longus, the large meaty muscle on the lower forearm. Fortunately, the bullet did not sever the artery, thus, you had very little blood loss. X-rays report no permanent damage, no broken bones, and no arterial deterioration. Your wounds are clean, no infection. You will be sore for two weeks. So I don't see why you can't be released tomorrow morning."

"Oh, that's wonderful news doctor, thank you." Blaine gave her daughter a big hug.

"No work for the next three weeks and call the office to schedule to have your sutures removed." Dr. Solinis turned and put his hand out to Lou Bravo. Still sore and anticipating another excruciating assault on his manhood, he timidly held out his hand. To his relief, the handshake was courteous. "Nice to have had your attention, Lou Bravo," Dr. Solinis remarked in a cheery voice and walked from the room.

"I'll pick you up tomorrow if you like, Blaine, and I promise not to embarrass you, well not too much. Just kidding, in fact, I have a big surprise for you as a going away present," Lou Bravo said as a peace offering.

"Going away present? Where are you going Mommy?" Brooke asked in a confused tone. "Am I going, too?"

"Oh sweetie, Lou Bravo meant going away from the hospital, leaving the hospital, Brooke." Blaine added and gave him a look. "Isn't that right, Lou Bravo?"

"Yes, of course, Brooke, leaving the hospital; that's what I meant. Now give your mother a kiss, I have to meet a man about a vacation. Bye, Blaine, see you tomorrow morning." Brooke hugged her mother, gave her a big kiss and they both waved as they stepped into the hallway.

Blaine leaned back against the pillow, closed her eyes and savored the morning quiet now that everyone had gone. She was comfortable knowing that she would be home in her own house by this time tomorrow. Nagging at her conscience was something Lou Bravo said earlier, about *a surprise and seeing a man about a vacation.* Blaine could only imagine what he had up his sleeve; she only could hope the surprise and vacation did not involve her.

Chapter Forty-Two

WHY CAN'T VENICE UTILITIES MANAGER TURN OFF THE LIGHTS?

The headline jumped off the page. The stack of twenty papers dropped from Earl Neigh's hands and almost landed on his foot. "That crazy Geek, he did it, he hacked into their computers. Unbelievable, he said he was going to leave them a little present. How ironic is that, 'the lights are on, all day, but nobody's fucking home'." Earl laughed out loud.

The front-page editorial was a scathing diatribe on why Izzy Brella, the utilities manager, has not been able to turn off the lights at Hecksher Park. As a result, for the past week the lights over the six tennis courts, eight basketball courts, fourteen shuffleboard courts, two handball courts, and a children's playground were on twenty-four hours a day. The newspaper contacted Florida Power and Light and learned that the cost to operate forty-nine 1,000-watt halogen spotlights, five 1,000-watt incandescent spotlights, and nine 60-watt spotlights for a week was $1,016.40.

Dragged in front of City Council to explain the lighting problem at Hecksher Park, Mr. Brella reported that the situation was quite unusual and that nothing like this had ever happened in his five years as utilities manager. He described how his department worked on the malfunction to his computer that automatically operated the Park's lights, but could not remove the virus or reprogram the automatic light sequence. The City Council asked why the lights were not turned on/off manually? Mr. Brella informed the members that the cost to pay an employee to turn the lights on at dusk and then to return at 11:00 P.M. to turn them off was more expensive than to leave them on.

Midway through the inquisition, a council member asked why the lights weren't turned off and the park locked at night? Cries of outrage from the audience almost cleared the chamber, but the mayor brought order to the meeting by reassuring everyone that the council would not approve closing the park. After a five-minute recess, the remaining four members voiced their disapproval of removing any facility from the residents and a relative calm prevailed. After an exhaustive in-house attempt to repair the computer, Mr. Brella stated that IT Associates, the software company responsible for the lighting program, promised to have the computer program restored in two days.

At the bottom of the article was a remark from a city council member that stated he was going to bring up the matter of the park's lights again at the next council meeting. He intended to make a motion, which because of his ineptitude, Mr. Brella, should be required to pay the $1,016.40 Hecksher Park utility bill. Earl could hardly contain himself, "The Star Trek Guy did it," Earl yelled. "There is justice in this world. Maybe that asshole will think twice before he blows-off another taxpayer."

Slowly the pea green VW bus loaded with six strategically placed bundles of newspapers, two stacks on the left seat, two on the right and two bundles on either end of the back seat, all of which covered exactly half of every window, moved across the parking lot. Every few feet, the vehicle jerked back and forth as the driver attempted to shift into second gear. The piercing sound of gears grinding was a nightly serenade carriers endured until the Star Trek Guy eventually drove out onto Tamiami Trail and over the bridge. However, this night the grinding lasted longer than usual, it continued for another five minutes as the bus angled towards the opposite corner of the lot and came to an abrupt stop in front of Earl Neigh. Sticking his head out the window and leaning forward to get a better look, Myron boldly called out, "Greetings Earthling, your earth spirit shines bright this night. Your good fortune is for all to see now and to see in a future time."

"Star Trek Guy, you're the best. I can't believe you hacked into their computers and turned on the lights. How did you do it?"

"People are so lazy when it comes to their password. For something so important, I can't understand why so little effort was taken to protect their identity. This moron's password was so obvious any hacker with an ounce of creativity could have figured it out. It took me all of three minutes to figure out that self-absorbed utilities manager's password. Take a guess what it is."

Earl picked up the paper and stared at the article. His eyes scanned each sentence picking up important words or phrases that could incorporate a password: Hecksher, Park, utilities, manager, lights, basketball, tennis, shuffle board, Venice, Izzy Brella, five years, power hungry and a prick.

Nothing jumped off the page, only a jumble of words and phrases about Izzy Brella and his job. "I don't know, Myron, nothing fits, but if I had to guess, I think the password has something to do with his job and name. The guy is an egomaniac so it has to be about him."

"Very good, space traveler. Yes, it is all about Mr. Brella and how he perceives his role as Utilities Manager."

"Okay, so what's the password?"

"Umbrella, if you think about it, umbrella covers it all. Um for utilities manager and brella, he covered the job. He was the job; every decision had to go through him. He controlled everything, even the lighting system at Hecksher Park had to be on his personal computer. The rest was easy."

"Now the poor bastard will have to pay a $1,016.40 light bill," Earl laughed, "couldn't have happened to a nicer guy."

"That's the least of Izzy Brella's problem. When the IT guys open his hard drive and erase the virus I left behind; they will find a half dozen gambling web sites along with times, dates and transactions all from Mr. Brella's work station. I don't think city council will look favorably upon their utilities manager gambling on their dime."

"So Myron, what's the deal with the traffic lights? Did you figure out the whole speed thing?"

"Patience, young space jockey, I've saved the best for last, step aboard my vessel and become enlightened." Earl pulled back the van's side door and immediately two silver doors with the dark blue Federation symbol painted in the center slid apart. Earl stepped inside and the silver doors closed behind him. The interior of the van was awash in bright lights, it took a few seconds for Earl's eyes to adjust to the images pulsating from the monitors and screens. The room was an exact replica of the Starship Enterprise. It was as if Myron transported the entire TV set of Star Trek and beamed it down to his van. The bridge with two captain chairs, monitors all along the walls, transporter station complete with mannequins of Captain Kirk and Mr. Scott stood ready to beam them down, workstations and sounds of commands and futuristic music piped in from grey metal speakers along the ceiling filled the room. Seated at a workstation along the back wall, Myron smiled and waved Earl to a seat. Myron hit a key and all the monitors around the room reprogrammed and came alive with data on the City of Venice. Everything was there: maps, pictures, names of streets, location of lights, street distances, timing of lights, intersections, numbers, figures, and formulas.

Directly above their workstation an early map of Venice that John Nolan developed outlined the neighborhood sections along with the streets. A powerpoint presentation outlined the construction process, times, distances, labor costs, work force needed, construction equipment and details of the parks and open space for the residents.

"Wow you really did your homework."

"No big deal, it was all there on Brella's computer neatly laid out for the taking. All I needed to do was to download it and put it all together in one little neat formula. Take a look." Pointing to the screen directly in front of him, computations of numbers, letters, and equations covered the entire screen. Resembling a page out of a high school algebra book, a class Earl had to repeat in summer school; formulas and equations crisscrossed, overlapped and intersected each other making absolutely no sense at all to Earl. The entire page could have been in Russian for all Earl knew.

"What the fuck is that?" Earl blurted out. "Do you think I'm some kind of math nerd or something? The only math class I didn't fail was General Math Twelve and all we did all semester was balance a fucking checkbook. I have no idea what you have up on the screen."

"Oh ye of little patience cast your gaze on the final chapter to the equation and achieve total nirvana."

Staring at the last equation, Earl had an uneasy feeling Myron had gone off on another Star Trek adventure and unfortunately for him, had not totally rejoined the real world. At the bottom of the page, in bold print, **'get your kicks on Route 66.'** *What did get your kicks on Route 66 have to do with driving down Route 41?* What a waste of time Earl thought.

"Look Myron, I have to get these papers delivered. I don't have a clue what all your writing means. So either explain it to me in English or we're done here Star Trek guy."

"My dear Earl, sorry for all the confusion, but it was my way of adding a little levity into the mix of all the boring numbers. I guess you are too young to remember the television show from the 60s, 'Route 66'? It was about two guys in a Corvette, driving around the country on Route 66. *Get your kicks on Route 66* was the show's theme song. It was a pretty cool show back then."

"I still don't get what that show has to do with me driving down Tamiami Trail?" Earl snapped angrily and turned to leave.

"Sixty-six miles per hour impatient one," Myron blurted out. "That's the acceleration you were looking for; Route 66 and 66 mph, comprehend the analogy, young traveler?"

"Shit I get it now, sorry for the blow-up. That's really cool; I'll be getting my kicks tomorrow on Tamiami Trail, doing 66 mph. Thanks Star Trek Guy, gotta go, my papers won't deliver themselves."

Earl walked to the silver doors, they slid apart and he stepped back into the night. With a big grin on his face, he imagined, *the cool wind blowing on his face as he cruised down US 41.* Earl packed the last of his papers and drove out of the parking lot.

Chapter Forty-Three

Morning brought rain, not the gentle spring rain that ushered in May flowers, but a pounding December thunderstorm. Like most Floridians, Lou Bravo welcomed the rain and the relief from the heat it brought. For the past four weeks, the sun relentlessly beat down cooking the Sunshine State and not a drop of rain. Clear blue skies and temperatures in the high eighties everyday, a tourist's dream vacation, but the daily building heat was a precursor for change. However, one needed to be careful for what one wished for in Florida. The furiousness of the storm and the massive amount of water over a short period caused major flooding throughout the state, a fact Lou Bravo experienced first-hand.

Many a night after a rainstorm, the drive home from Bogey's Sports Bar invariably ended with his El Camino stuck in knee-high water at the corner of Venice Avenue and Grove Street. An expensive ride home in a tow truck brought back many sour memories from Venice and Grove.

Lou Bravo turned the windshield wipers on high as he approached the dreaded Grove Street flood zone, not a puddle in sight. After years of community complaints about the flooding, a public sit-in at a city council meeting, led of course by Lou Bravo and friends, last April, Venice Public Works put in a new sewer system to alleviate the flooding. For a month, Venice Avenue was like a combat zone, with dump trucks, bulldozers, cars, and dirt flying everywhere. Large slabs of broken concrete littered the road, city workers attempted to divert traffic into a single lane, traffic backed up, and throw in the eighty-five year old drivers, who on the best of days could barely make it over the Venice Avenue Bridge, and it was a driver's worst nightmare. Finished ahead of schedule, the flood problem was resolved and Lou Bravo's forays to Bogey's resumed flood free.

Maybe I'll send City Manager Brella a congratulatory letter on the sewer project; he could use a little good press considering the predicament he's in with the city council, Lou Bravo thought as he pulled into Patches' parking lot.

As usual during tourist season, the lot was nearly full; a positive sign the restaurant serves good food at a reasonable price, a bad sign if you are looking for a booth without a wait. All the coveted parking spots near the entrance door or on the opposite side shaded by the Car Doc building were taken. Lou Bravo had to settle for a spot at the far end of the lot along the alley. "If it ever stops raining and the sun comes out, this spot is primo," Lou Bravo laughed out loud and flipped open his umbrella.

"Good to see you this beautiful rainy morning, Jackie," Lou Bravo said as he closed his umbrella at the counter.

"And a good morning to you, Lou Bravo, we sure do need the rain."

"Has Tony Lilly arrived yet? I'm supposed to meet him for breakfast," Lou Bravo said, scanning the room.

"Yes, he and his side-kick just gave Victoria their orders. Tell me what you want and I'll give it to the kitchen."

"I'll have the blueberry pancakes, hash browns, whole wheat toast, and bacon. Tell the cook crispy, I like the bacon crisp, Victoria knows how I like it. Oh, I see them, thanks Jackie."

Lou Bravo walked back towards the booth where Tony and Hubba Bubba were enjoying their morning coffee. First to spot Lou Bravo, Hubba Bubba jumped to his feet, shouting obscenities. Pointing his finger at Lou Bravo he screamed, "This is the crazy man who pointed a gun in my face and tried to kill me at the Boat Parade. I thought he was going to blow my brains out. He is a menace to society and needs to be in jail. We can't have this mad man going around waving guns at people. How would you like it, mister, if I shoved a gun in your face? I bet you'd shit in your pants too."

Tony grabbed Hubba Bubba's arm and yanked him back down into the booth, "Calm down kid, you're frightening all the costumers."

"And good morning to you fellas," Lou Bravo said as he slid into the booth across from Tony. "Listen, kid, you better shut your mouth or next time I will shoot you and I'm certain you won't like where the bullet ends up. Take a look under the table."

Hubba Bubba leaned over and looked under the table, saw the gun pointing straight at his privates and gasped, "Okay I'll shut up, but please put the gun away."

"Well, this is a lively little group this morning. Who ordered the blueberry pancakes and crispy bacon?"

"That would be me, darling. Good to see you Victoria," Lou Bravo said and gave her a big smile.

"And the two egg specials for you both. Anyone need more coffee?" Everyone at the table raised their hand. "I'll be back in a minute with the coffee, enjoy your meal." She hurried off to the coffee station.

A few minutes later Jackie appeared, "So how's everything at this table? All settled down and quiet like we like it here at Patches. Anyone need more of anything?" Jackie poured hot coffee into all three cups.

"Everything is fine Jackie," answered Tony in a very conciliatory tone. "Sorry for the outburst, it will never happen again, right, Hubba Bubba?"

"Yeah, it will never happen again, I promise. The last thing I'd want to do is piss off the owner."

"Hey, watch your mouth," Tony blurted out and smacked him on the back of the head.

"That's good, I'd hate to cancel your eating privileges here, but you know I can't afford to have any problems. You remember what happened to Ken Sternfeld, he was a regular, just like you boys; well he came in drunk one morning, tried to line dance on the tables and almost broke his neck. What I hear his dancing days are over after he fell off a table one night at the Gold Rush and broke his kneecap. He's no longer welcome here and I'm pretty sure he's persona non grata at the Gold Rush also." Jackie smiled and walked back to the cash register.

They finished breakfast, sat back enjoying their second cup of coffee when Lou Bravo leaned forward, "Tony, I need to borrow your ice cream truck this week."

Tony jerked back in the seat and coughed out his last sip of coffee into his napkin. Embarrassed more than anything else he tried to catch his breath and regain his composure. He just stocked the truck with a fresh supply of ice cream, candy and snacks anticipating a profitable week now that schools were on Winter break, plus add in all the families from up north visiting grandma and grandpa in Sarasota County. This week would make the entire season for Tony.

"No way; it's the busiest week all year. How about next week?"

"Oh come on. You owe me a favor, or two. Anyway, it's for Blaine, she wants teach her newscarrier a lesson."

"A lesson, in what, eating ice cream, you're kidding, right." Tony scoffed and took another sip of coffee, this time without coughing like a fool.

"Listen, Tony, every night when Blaine's newscarrier delivers the paper he blasts his radio. It wakes her up and she can't get back to sleep. She wants him to feel what it's like not to get enough rest."

"So what do you need my truck for? Why don't we just go a pay this newspaper guy a little visit, smash out his radio, tell him not to play loud music anymore or we'll come back and break both his knee caps. How does that sound?"

Lou Bravo thought for a moment, took a drink of coffee, and slowly nodded. "That sounds like a plan, but you know Blaine. She wants to do it her way. Listen, she doesn't want any of the money. She'll give you all the money they collect and to sweeten the deal here, this is from me." Lou Bravo took out an envelope from his shirt pocket and slid it across the table towards Tony.

"They, is someone else going to be in the truck with Blaine?" Tony asked and tore open the envelope.

"Brooke, she'll be off from school, plus the doctor told Blaine to take some time off from work until her shoulder heals. So this week would be a perfect time to teach Earl Neigh a lesson in manners."

"I can't take this; it's a ten day cruise to the Caribbean. It's too much Lou Bravo, too much." Tony pushed the envelope across the table.

"Hey man, I'll take the cruise, I love the water, let me take a look at those tickets." Hubba Bubba reached across the table. No sooner had his fingers touched the envelope a knife smashed down on the white envelope in-between Hubba Bubba's index and middle fingers. The silver blade nicked a piece of skin from his middle finger and a crimson red circle oozed across the envelope. No one moved; no one spoke as Lou Bravo pulled the knife out of the table, wiped the blade with his napkin and put it back into his pocket.

"The tickets belong to Tony. Let us say, an anniversary gift. I know how much Anna loves cruises. Look at the brochure, the ship leaves from Tampa for a ten-day, nine-night cruise to the Cayman Islands, Cozumel and Belize. You will have a balcony suite; the ship has a casino, shows, spa, three pools, and gourmet meals all day long. You'll have a ball, go enjoy yourself, you owe it to Anna. I won't take no for an answer." Lou Bravo pushed the envelope back across the table.

"The keys are in the glove box. Thank you."

Chapter Forty-Four

Lou Bravo pulled up to the hospital entrance music blasting and lights flashing. Dressed in a clown costume, with Brooke all dressed up as a cat, they jumped out of the ice cream truck and walked towards the entrance doors. Lou Bravo's large white clown shoes made it difficult to walk, as a result, the parking valet, a skinny; red haired, pimply-faced teen ran over and blocked their path to the hospital. Hands held up like a traffic cop, he shouted, "Sir, you can't leave your vehicle in the entrance driveway. Here is your validated parking ticket. I'll park your vehicle for you."

Lou Bravo reached over, grabbed the boy by the shirt and growled, "Listen, kid, don't let the clown outfit fool you, if I wanted my truck parked I would have parked it myself. Leave it where it is, I have to pick up an injured friend. I'll only be ten minutes at the most. Here's twenty bucks and if you sell any ice cream, keep the money."

"But, sir, it's against hospital policy."

"What is. . .parking in the entrance or taking a bribe? Oh, look another customer just pulled up; now get out of my way."

"You win. The ice cream truck can stay," the valet yelled as he ran over to the approaching car.

"I always do, son, I always do." The front doors opened automatically, welcoming the clown and the pussycat into the lobby.

Shuffling across the lobby, the duo caused quite a commotion. All heads turned, volunteer greeters sat down and caught their breath, attendants shook their heads and smiled, two elderly women took out their cameras and snapped off three shots before the clown and pussycat disappeared into the elevator.

Seated in a wheelchair, a bouquet of flowers in her lap and an envelope containing discharge papers, Blaine was ready to leave.

"Mommy, you're ready to go," Brooke screamed as she ran into the room. They hugged and then the entourage paraded down the hallway to the elevator. All the nurses, attendants and volunteers pushed into the hallway to say good-bye and gawk at the clown and pussycat. It's not every day the circus comes to Venice, but it brought back joyous memories for some of the elderly patients.

"So, what's new, pussycat? Sweetie, why are you wearing a cat costume?"

"Oh, it's a big surprise, Mommy. You'll love it," Brooke purred.

"So Lou Bravo, this is the going away present you promised wouldn't embarrass me? I guess you consider clown and cat outfits normal attire people wear when they leave the hospital these days. By any stretch of the imagination, would there be an elephant in the parking lot to take us home?"

"An elephant in the parking lot," said Lou Bravo. "What a vivid imagination you have, Blaine. Sure you didn't bruise your sense of humor and for your information where would someone get an elephant anyway?" Lou Bravo laughed as they all pushed out of the elevator. Everyone in the lobby jumped up, clapped and cheered as the parade left the building.

Outside Blaine was overwhelmed from the deafening blare of "Turkey in the Straw" that vibrated off the emergency entrance walls from two large speakers attached to the roof of an ice cream truck. Lights flashed red, orange and purple; painted balloons hug along the roof; drawings of circus animals covered three sides, and on the back in big, bright yellow letter the words, CIRCUS DAYS ICE CREAM, were printed for all to see.

"Now I get it, circus costumes, circus ice cream. Thank you Lou Bravo, what a wonderful surprise; now I can visit Mr. Earl Neigh and give him a scoop of his own medicine. I wonder if he likes pistachio."

"That's his problem, jump in my lady, your carriage waits," Lou Bravo added, bowing and giving a sweep of his hand. He closed the door behind Blaine and Brooke and off they drove.

Blaine's cell phone rang as they crossed the Circus Bridge.

"Hello. Yes, John, I'm out of the hospital. I feel fine. Yes, I know today is the opening of the Lake Osprey trail. Of course, I'm planning to attend. Hold on a minute. It's the park manager; do you guys want to go to the park today? They're celebrating the completion of the new lake trail. It will be like a big party, food, music and an inaugural walk around the Lake Osprey trail. What do you guys say?"

"Like this?" Lou Bravo asked with an outstretched arm and his big clown smile.

"Why not, I could use some practice selling ice cream. It will be fun," Blaine replied.

"Please, Lou Bravo, I love the park please." Brooke pleaded.

Without a word, Lou Bravo turned north onto Tamiami Trail, leaned over and slapped Brooke a high five.

"We'll see you in a few minutes, John, save us a couple of hot dogs."

The truck bounced along the highway towards Osprey, all the while Lou Bravo explained what freezers held the ice cream and ice pops, the variety and prices of everything, where the candy and snacks were kept and most importantly, that all the money collected needed to be turned over to Tony at the end of the week. As the truck turned into the park, Lou Bravo switched on the music and the lights. At full volume, *Farmer in the Dell*, echoed down the road scattering two Mourning Doves searching for food under a picnic table across from the ranger station. The loud music also caught the attention of the park ranger in the entrance booth. No sooner had the truck reached the entrance window, Park Ranger Linda, rushed out with her arms in the air. A small, thin, thirty-something woman with short black hair and an almond complexion yelled, "You cannot sell ice cream in the park, you'll have to. . . ." Stopped mid-sentence, Ranger Linda was speechless when she realized that a clown was driving the truck. Her expression, a cross between fear and amusement appeared awkward and alerted Blaine to step in.

Blaine slid open the door, walked around the front of the truck and stuck out her hand. "Hi Linda, I'm sorry for the confusion, this is my friend Lou Bravo and my daughter Brooke. They just picked me up from the hospital and thought the costumes and ice cream truck would cheer me up." Blaine added, "We are here for the dedication."

"Oh, sorry for the delay Assistant Park Manager, but I did not quite know what to make of the clown. It's not everyday we get a clown driving into the park. Do we?"

"This could be the first and hopefully the last. Again, my apologies, but my friend has a flare for the theatrics."

Linda regained her composure and quickly returned to a business-like persona. "I'd like to report that there are over one hundred visitors and an unusual number of police. Enjoy the dedication and Mr. Clown, don't sell any ice cream," Ranger Linda ordered and saluted as they drove off.

"Wow, what a little firecracker," said Lou Bravo. "I'd hate to get on her wrong side."

"You're already on her wrong side, Mr. Clown, and she is exactly what I need after putting up with Remi Cole's shenanigans. I welcome a ranger who will put in a full day's work and not put up with any nonsense. Park the truck in front of the picnic tables past the Nature Center."

Chapter Forty-Five

Beyond the last hiking trail, in the northwest corridor of Osprey State Park, a small section of untouched land rested for over fifty years. Left in its natural state, slash pines, scrub oaks, saw palmetto and native grasses formed an impenetrable thicket that blocked public access. However, for an experienced camper, an individual able to live off the land and a fugitive from the law, this section of the park provided the ideal refuge for a murderer on the run. It was perfect for Remi Cole.

Last summer while hiking, Cole stumbled upon the old clearing in the forest. Outlines of a building foundation, rotted footings, and fence postholes were still visible. A handful of scraggly orange trees were alive and bearing fruit, but most important was an artisan spring that poured clear, fresh water into a stream that meandered along the perimeter of the property. Remi pulled out his compass, checked the coordinates, "Shit this must be the old South Creek Ranch the Friends' workers spoke about at the planning meeting last week." Remi recalled the men saying that in the 1930s there was a working farm back in the original section of the park. That Waters and Elsa Burrows planted an orange grove, grew vegetables, and raised chickens. They eked out a meager living selling produce to the locals and at her death in 1955, Elsa Scherer Burrows willed the property to the State of Florida for a public park. The original tract of land remained untouched; however, a worker suggested construction of a new hiking trail from the Nature Center to the South Creek Ranch. Fortunately, for Remi Cole, the park manager stepped in and convinced everyone to construct a new accessible-to-all trail around the lake.

After he was fired, Remi put in motion his plan to punish Blaine Sterling for ruining his life. He constructed a small lean-to for shelter, cleared an area for cooking, split wood, channeled the stream with rocks to form a separate spot for bathing, stockpiled canned goods, dried food, and built a latrine. The camp melted into the woods, every addition became an extension of the original landscape and to the untrained eye, didn't exist.

A small fire glowed in the night sky, not large flames that would draw attention—rather a small campfire with little smoke—but hot enough to cook an evening's meal of squirrel. On one side of the fire-pit, a can of baked beans sat on a rock and bubbled. A thick brown liquid oozed down the side of the can and spilled onto the fire, spitting thin white clouds of smoke into the air. On the other side, a pot of coffee perked in its blackened metal container burnt from the heat of fires and years of use.

The night's entrée was the second squirrel snared in a week along the stream that ran behind the compound. Fresh water was a necessity in the harsh Florida climate. The artisan spring that fed the stream made it possible to have an abundant supply of fresh water for drinking, washing, and cooling off. A fresh supply of water meant fewer trips outside the park, which meant fewer chances the police would have to notice a fugitive.

The outline of a big man cast a shadow against a line of trees behind the fire pit as he bent over and turned the squirrel cooking on a simple wooden spit suspended over the fire. His shaved head and scruffy black beard made him look like a werewolf. His wrinkled red-and-blue checkered shirt hung below his waist and his jeans had a few small dirt marks from sleeping on a mat of dried reeds for two weeks. Remi Cole was in his element. The remote section of the park was the perfect location to hide from the police, but close enough to put his plan to teach Blaine Sterling a lesson into action.

During the day, Remi worked side by side with volunteers to build the Lake Osprey Trail, but at night, he worked on his personal project: a tunnel alongside the trail to imprison Blaine Sterling. On the trail's second turn, a large stand of Scrub Oak and Saw Palmetto pushed up against both sides of the trail and obscured the path ahead. High above, the canopy allowed only rays of dappled light to shine down through its thick canvas of leaves. Thin shadows of light danced along the path and the bright light before the turn darkened into a late afternoon glow. It would be at that juncture, during a time of confusion, two people would melt into the undergrowth undetected.

Five feet from the trail, a thick clump of Saw Palmetto concealed the opening to the tunnel. On the third night, with only four feet of the tunnel completed, Remi hit rock. He panicked and banged away with such force his shovel broke. On his hands and knees, he feverishly brushed away the dirt from the slab of stone. To his surprise, the rock was not just a rock that impeded his progress, rather a three-foot long stair cut into the ground. Over the next two nights he unearthed twelve, three foot long stairs that lead to a subterranean cave. The discovery was breathtaking, but for Remi it ended the arduous task of digging and discarding the dirt along the trail. Moreover, the cave offered a natural jail to house his prey: *poetic justice for a park ranger,* he thought.

Sandwiched between two hulking chunks of rock, separated from the walls thousands of years ago, the cave entrance was barely wide enough for one person to squeeze through. The main passage was 20 feet high and 40 feet wide, followed a dried-up riverbed of sand, and pebbles that carved out a meandering passageway deep into the bowels of the cave. Kerosene lamps, placed along the pathway, illuminated hundreds of rock inclusions, ledges and a natural bridge that protruded from the cave walls. Light reflected off stalactites, stalagmites that fell from ceiling and rose from the floor, so numerous at times, to maneuver between the columns took time and patience. After twenty minutes, the passage abruptly opened into a main gallery the length of a football field with a cathedral ceiling so high it disappeared beyond the light of the lanterns into darkness. Large massive blocks of stone, that broke off from the ceiling, during the long course of the cave's development strangely only littered half the cave floor.

On the west side of the streambed, all of the rocks were cleared and arranged in a two-tier platform along the entire back wall. In the center of the top platform was a clay sculpture of a giant headless animal, about twenty feet tall, standing on its rear two legs with its front two legs kicking out at an invisible attacker. Arranged in a circle around the sculpture were twelve square, stone block seats and on each seat rested a distinct carved palm frond human facemask. On the floor, alongside the statue, laid a perfectly preserved skull of a twelve-point deer. Ancient puncture marks over the body of the statue, from numerous spear points, revealed some type of ceremony may have taken place before a big hunt.

Chapter Forty-Six

It's not every day a clown and a pussycat stop by a park to celebrate the grand opening of a new hiking trail, but then again, it's not every day a new hiking trail is opened. Everyone assumed Lou Bravo and Brooke were part of the entertainment, an extra attraction to the festive mood of the day. "Mommy, come over here and get a hot dog," Brooke yelled from the food line that snaked along the path behind the Nature Center to a tent where hot dogs on two grills cooked away. A volunteer in a red-and-blue checkered shirt passed out soda and water, while two other volunteers handed out bags of potato chips and homemade cookies.

"I'll be over in a minute, sweetie. I need to talk to the park manager about something." Blaine replied and walked over to John Forrester, the park manager who was seated at the first table with members of the Friends of Osprey Park. "Everything looks great; I can't wait to hike the trail."

"Thanks for the compliment, but it was all done by the Friends of the Park, they deserve the credit; the band, the food, the speakers, and the construction. We are very fortunate to have them, especially, Russ Delaney, their president. Now Blaine, are you sure you're up to it?"

"No problem. The doctor said the sling comes off in two days and after three weeks I should be as good as new. What's this I hear about the police being here?"

"Why don't you turn around and ask him yourself," John answered. There dressed in a bright yellow, palm tree design Tommy Bahama shirt, khaki shorts, a wide brim Panama hat, and Polo wrap-around sunglasses was Detective Justin Beale.

"Hello, Blaine, how are you feeling?"

"Detective Beale, is that really you? Nice outfit, not the standard attire for a police detective, would you say? Are you moonlighting for the beach patrol?"

"Something like that," Beale removed his glasses, "we had a report Cole was seen in the area and thought he might turn up for the ceremony today. Had to dress the part, a Florida tourist visiting the park, what do you think?"

"Well you had me fooled, but I can't keep worrying about Remi Cole. Right now I'm going to get a hot dog and then hike the new trail everyone came to see." Blaine turned and joined her daughter in line.

Lou Bravo was already on his fifth hot dog when Blaine and Brooke sat down at the picnic table.

"Brought you a cookie for dessert, I know how much you like sweets, but I see you already have three. Didn't you see the little sign that said one cookie per customer?" Blaine scoffed, but reluctantly added another cookie to the pile.

"I wasn't aware of the cookie limit. Somehow the cookie box covered the warning when I was in line." Clutching four cookies to his chest and with a sad clown face Lou Bravo added, "Don't you think it would freak everyone out if a grown man, dressed in a clown costume, walked up to the cookie table and dropped three cookies back into the box?"

"Okay, you win. Just keep them," Blaine said.

"Mommy, does that mean Lou Bravo can get six more hot dogs?"

"Brooke, how many hot dogs has he already eaten?"

"Five, he told the man he was a hot dog-eating champion from New York and could eat twelve hot dogs in ten minutes. The man laughed and told him he could have six more if he finished the ones on his plate in five."

"Oh, no you don't Lou Bravo, I know all about the famous 1973 Nathan's Fourth of July Hot Dog-Eating Contest at Coney Island. The weigh-in with the Mayor of New York, the *Hot Dog Time* song, the pictures and the mustard yellow Hot Dog Belt of Champions, I've heard it all. I have to work with these people and you are not going to turn today's ceremony into some kind of circus act! No pun intended. Do you understand no more hotdogs!"

Lou Bravo shuffled over to the hot dog man and explained how upset Assistant Park Manager Blaine Sterling was about him making a spectacle of himself if he consumed another six more dogs. The volunteer smiled and handed him a plate.

Lou Bravo turned and walked back to the table. On the plate was one hot dog.

"Blaine, do you see that big guy over by the band, the one who looks like Wolfman Jack, the late night disc jockey from WABC radio station who howled every time he played a new record? The man in the red-and-blue checkered shirt, dancing some line dance with two rangers."

"It's the Texas Two Step," Brooke, blurted out. "They're pretty good; we just learned that dance in gym class. It's easy, want to join them?"

"No, thank you, Brooke. Anyway, every time I look around, he is staring at me. It creeps me out."

"You think someone dressed in a clown suit doesn't stick out? Remember the movie, *My Cousin Vinny*, when Joe Pesci and Marisa Tomei first get into the Alabama town, dressed in black leather, big sunglasses; Joe Pesci is looking at his front tire and says to Marisa Tomei, 'You stick out like a sore thumb.'"

"Marisa Tomei answers, 'Me what about you?'"

"Pesci replied, 'At least I'm wearing cowboy boots.'"

"Do I think you stand out, without a doubt, people are staring at you right now. It's not Halloween for another ten months. Be glad he's just staring, do you see the size of the knife on his belt?"

"You're right. Isn't there a park rule about the size knife a person can carry around? What's this guy think, he's Jim Bowie?"

"I think he's over the four inch blade regulation. I'll mention it to the park manager after the ceremony." Blaine picked up a cookie and in a cheery voice said, "Forget about it. Eat your seventh hot dog and enjoy the music."

"Excuse me, Blaine," John Forrester injected, "but we're about to the start the ceremony. I'd like you to join me and the other guests on the podium."

"Mommy, Lou Bravo promised I could have some ice cream before I hiked the trail. I'll meet up with you as soon as I finish. Please, Mom."

"Okay, honey," Blaine added, "but only one cone. I'll meet you on the trail."

Chapter Forty-Seven

Four metal chairs stood on the grass alongside the entrance to the Lake Osprey Trail. Strung across the path, a bright red ribbon with a large elaborate bow in the middle flapped in the wind. Over 100 visitors crowded around the trailhead while photographers snapped pictures of the speakers and anyone close to the platform. Every one quieted as the park manager walked up to the microphone.

"Welcome to the opening of the Lake Osprey Trail. We are very proud of this new addition to the park, a barrier-free trail that offers superb hiking opportunities for our visitors, including those with disabilities that come to the park." The Park Manager detailed the steps the park followed to complete the half-mile path that circled the lake and then introduced people who brought the trail to fruition.

First, Russ Delany, President of the Friends of Osprey State Park, spoke about the many volunteer work hours it took to complete the trail; next, District 4 Park Manager, Valinda Subic, outlined the process of securing the $10,000.00 engineering study necessary before work could commence. Sarasota County Commissioner Jon Thaxton, long time supporter of the park and advocate for the Florida Scrub Jay whose habitat was the park, read a proclamation to Lee Weetherington a local developer who made a generous donation to fund the construction of the Lake Osprey Trail.

Blaine looked down at her watch; thirty minutes of speeches took its toll on everyone. Some of the visitors moved back under the palm trees to escape the unbearable heat and search out a small patch of shade. Blaine scanned the crowd, but couldn't spot the man with the knife. *"Maybe he went back to the campground to cool off. I need to remember to tell John about the knife,"* she thought. Blaine gave John a friendly elbow, pointed to her watch and smiled.

"Ladies and gentlemen, I have been informed that the heat is chasing away some of our visitors, so would our distinguished speakers please join me and two of our local students, PJ Minder, who is wheelchair bound, and Julia Greenwood, who is blind, with the ribbon cutting ceremony," Forrester announced and gave Blaine a wink. The crowd pressed forward and a thunderous applaud erupted when the ribbon fell to the ground. "I declare, that the Lake Osprey Trail is officially opened, would PJ and Julia please lead the first of many walks. Thank you all for participating in today's ceremony and enjoy the rest of the day."

Chapter Forty-Eight

In high spirits, everyone pushed forward along the trail bumping and jostling each other, in a good-humored way, eager to gain a position close to the front where photographers feverishly snapped away. As the parade neared the first turn, three billowy white cumulus clouds stalled in front of the sun. Suddenly the skies darkened and only dull shadows illuminated the path. In front of Blaine, an elderly woman in a pink flowered sundress and large purple hat called out, "What a relief, my poor arms were baking."

"It feels ten degrees cooler," a voice from the back called out. "Does anyone have a sweater; I feel a chill coming on." Everyone burst into laughter and picked up the pace. Like a magic potion, the clouds offered a reprieve from the sun's oppressive heat and burning glare, everyone's spirits lifted as they approached the first turn. However, their merriment was cut short as they walked beneath the lush green canopy of palms and oaks that formed a natural roof above the path.

The hikers with sunglasses were the first surprised by the sudden plunge into darkness. A moment of confusion, turned into panic. Unable to judge distance, the first row abruptly stopped to remove their glasses. That innocuous action put into motion a disastrous chain of events.

The second group of hikers marched forward unaware of the impending danger that blocked their path. It all happened so fast, a combination of natural and human malice created what some would call *the perfect storm*. An anomaly of events, harmless by themselves, but arranged in tandem produced a recipe for disaster. From behind the bushes, a small log thrown under the front right wheel of the wheelchair, jammed its movement and jerked the chair forward catapulting PJ into the air. Instinctively, PJ reached out and grabbed the first thing he saw, Julia, who in turn also fell forward to the ground. The sudden stop created a chain reaction like a line of dominoes cascading in syncopation one right after the other. The first row of walkers fell over the wheelchair, the next group of hikers followed suit until piles of fallen hikers littered the path. People screamed as they fell and cried out when fallen upon. Others turned and ran back towards the Nature Center, which only compounded the collisions; piles of bodies were now strewn about in all directions making it impossible to move and difficult for help to arrive.

That was exactly what Remi Cole envisioned for the *Opening Day Hike*; a pleasant afternoon in the park turned upside down and a diversion of perverse proportion to camouflage the abduction of Assistant Park Manager Blaine Sterling. Attention focused on the injured hikers fallen along the pathway, their painful cries for help. While everyone was busy helping the injured back to the Nature Center, Cole created a chaotic diversion. He turned fear into mayhem and mayhem to his advantage. No one noticed the real tragedy about to unfold, except one.

Blaine pulled out her cell and punched in the number for the main gate, "Linda, this is Blaine Sterling; there's been an accident along the Lake Osprey Trail. About sixty hikers fell over each other and need medical treatment. Broken ankles, wrists, arms, a few head and neck injuries, a lot of cuts and bruises; nothing life threatening, but we have elderly hikers that need immediate attention before their injuries turn into something more serious. Call the Park and County police, the Nokomis and Venice fire departments and have them set up a medical team at the Nature Center, ASAP. Call me back when they arrive. I have to go."

In all the confusion, Blaine kept her focus, part training and part instinct. Automatically her brain sequenced steps that would lead her to control the situation and bring order. Strategies her academy instructor, Knut Chestnut, drilled into his students with countless socially incorrect anachronisms in his Basic Survival Techniques class. Captain Knut Chestnut, retired Tampa City detective, nicknamed *"the nutcracker,"* a by-the-book ball buster, who had a thing for drill and memorization.

It did not matter who complained, or how many negative evaluations went into his file he did not change. He had an acronym for every topic, each more offensive than the previous: dicks, piss, balls. . . . "Remember *dick*s, Miss Blaine when organizing the five strategies of Basic Survival Techniques," he would say with a big grin on his face. "Develop a plan, Identify the problem, Control the problem, Keep focus on the problem, and finally Secure the problem."

Blaine began to develop a plan when a hand grabbed her right arm. "Don't say a word or this here knife against your side will gut you in a country minute Assistant Park Manager," a voice growled and then a low quick cough. "Do what I say and maybe you'll live," another quick cough; Blaine recognized the cough.

Jerked off the path towards the bushes Blaine knew she had heard that cough before, a short nervous cough the body manifests when under stress. It was Remi Cole. It was the same guttural sound she heard when she questioned him at the ranger station a few weeks back. She was sure of it. The beard, shaved head and camper's clothes, a perfect disguise for a man on the run who wanted to blend in with the surroundings. His nondescript costume enabled him to move freely about the park undetected for weeks, while the police scoured Florida; Remi Cole was right under their nose, what a devilishly simple plan. Who expected a fugitive to be so close to home? He fooled everyone for a time.

Blaine knew she was at a disadvantage. Her surprise gave Remi the advantage, but her training told her she had to act quickly or she would be dead. She needed to create a diversion, something that would break his routine, take his mind off the plan and cause him to make a mistake. One mistake, one wrong step, was all she needed, she knew it would come, it always did, bad guys always made mistakes.

"I guess I won't have to report your knife to the Park Manager. By now everyone in the park knows."

"Shut up, I told you not to talk." He jabbed the knife into her side. The blade cut through her shirt and nicked a rib. Blaine winced and felt blood ooze down her side. The wound was not deep, but a dull pain along her rib cage reminded her that this guy meant business.

"I know it's you, Remi, your little disguise didn't fool anyone. If I figured it out, I bet the police did also. Nice plan to hide in the park, too bad it didn't work."

"Police, the freaking cops are here?" Remi coughed. "Shit, I don't believe it," and then another cough.

"News flash bad guy, someone spotted you in the park, you've been under surveillance for the past week, looks like your perfect plan wasn't so perfect after all," Blaine scoffed.

"Shut up or I'll cut you again," Remi growled and yanked her closer.

"Okay, Remi, but tell me, why me, what did I do to you?"

"It's over Cole," a voice bellowed from behind, "drop the knife and release her!" Standing in the middle of the path with his gun pointed straight at Cole was Detective Beale. Behind him stood a cadre of park, state, and local police all with guns drawn, all aimed at Remi Cole. Inside the woods, just beyond the path, sounds of movement and broken branches got louder and louder. Cole spun around and using Blaine as a shield brought the knife up to her neck.

"Come any closer and I'll slit her fucking throat," he barked and yanked her head back with his free hand exposing Blaine's long slender neck.

"It doesn't have to come to that, Remi, you don't want to hurt her, just drop the knife and let Ms. Sterling go," Beale pleaded. "You have my word, no one will harm you, put the knife down and we can walk out of here together. What do you say, Remi? Do we have a deal?"

"She ruined my life! I got nothing because of this bitch. She got me fired. I don't have a place to live. I don't have any money. I'll never be a ranger. I got nothing to live for. All because of her!" Cole yelled and pressed the knife against Blaine's neck. The bite from the blade burned as the knife tore the skin. The wound was superficial, but a thin red line of blood formed along the slit across the left side of her neck.

Blaine did not fight back. She remained calm and waited for the mistake. She planted the seed and knew from experience, doubt would eat away at any best-laid plan.

Remi, for the first time, did not seem sure of himself, surrounded by a phalanx of heavily armed police, his actions were tentative and clumsy; indicators Blaine knew marked a change in the balance of power. It was just a matter of time before she would act.

It is strange how the body protects itself under the worst of circumstances. Somehow, the brain has the capacity to transfer messages to various parts of the body to mask pain. Crazy as it sounded, all Blaine could think about, during the ordeal, was how to take control. Somehow, her body blocked out the pain, the weakness from loss of blood and channeled all energy in one direction, survival.

Never once did she dwell on her injuries, rather her focus was on not remaining a victim.

"Remi, Blaine didn't fire you, I did!" John Forrester shouted as he pushed to the front of the crowd that stood mesmerized during the standoff. "I knew you were making money from the off-roaders for years, but no one ever got hurt, so I didn't say anything. After the last incident, I could not protect you, the investigation reached District 4, and it was out of my hands. I had no choice, district instructed me to fire you. Blaine Sterling had nothing to do with you losing your job. Please, let her go, Remi."

An uncomfortable silence choked the air. No one spoke, no one moved; only the squawk of a scrub jay calling off in the distance interrupted the tension. Blaine sensed her moment was at hand, when she felt Remi tremble. The rock solid façade was cracking as doubt chipped away at his plan. It was the end for Remi Cole. Blaine felt it and Remi Cole knew it.

Blaine's cell phone rang.

Detective Beale stepped forward, lowered his gun and broke the silence.

"Remi, drop the knife, she had nothing to do with you losing your job. Let her go."

Remi raised his arms over his head and let out a mournful scream, "Nooooo!" Instantaneously, Blaine broke free and sprinted forward as he brought the blade across his throat. A river of red exploded from Cole's neck spraying everyone and everything within a six-foot circumference.

For what seemed an eternity, Remi stood motionless in a pool of dark red blood; his eyes transfixed upon the crowd no longer appeared menacing or controlling, they reflected only the image of a defeated warrior. Slowly his arms dropped to his side and the bloody knife slipped from his fingers and fell to the ground. He collapsed to his knees and then fell face forward to the ground.

Lou Bravo and Brooke caught Blaine in their arms.

"It's over, you're safe now," Lou Bravo whispered while the three hugged.

Brooke, tears flowing down her cat face, cried, "Mommy your neck is bleeding. Hurry Mommy we have to fix you."

"It's just a little cut, honey, I'll be fine." She said softly and kissed her daughter's cheek.

Chapter Forty-Nine

The park came alive with activity. Detective Beale, undercover officers, the SWAT team, and the park police surrounded Cole as firefighters ferried people from the trail to the medical recovery area in front of the Nature Center. The injured on stretchers or in wheel chairs were directed to the right side of the Nature Center; everyone else with minor injuries was sent to the picnic area on the left to be examined and then released. Rows of cots, tables and boxes of medical supplies filled both triage areas.

Park rangers removed the split beam posts allowing the fire rescue trucks to back up along the fence in front of both picnic areas to administer aid and be ready to transport patients to the hospital if necessary. The police kept everything running smoothly while the fire departments emergency medical teams coordinated the treatment.

"Assistant Manager Sterling, please take the third cot on the right," the fire chief instructed. Lou Bravo and Brooke guided Blaine to the cot where a paramedic waited to examine Blaine. She smiled and reached out to help her sit. Carefully she turned down Blaine's blood-soaked collar, opened two buttons on her shirt and examined the cut along the left side of her neck.

"Good news; no real damage was done, a couple of inches deeper your carotid artery would have been severed and we wouldn't be having this conversation. The wound is only superficial; I'll clean the wound and bandage it up. I would suggest you see your family doctor to get a tetanus shot, who knows how clean that knife was. More than likely you won't even have a scar."

"She also has a wound on her side." Brooke pointed to the red stain on her right side. "See the blood." The medic pulled up Blaine's shirt and gently touched the bloody area.

"You must have a guardian angel looking over you Ms. Sterling. This is also a superficial wound and it appears the blood is already coagulating nicely around the wound. I don't think you'll need stitches, but have your doctor look at it all the same."

The medic finished bandaging Blaine's wounds when Detective Beale walked over. "He's dead. You won't have to worry about him any more," Beale informed the group. Blaine didn't respond she just stared out across the park and watched a fire rescue truck drive away, its flashing red and yellow lights reflecting through the palm fronds as it disappeared.

"That son-of-a bitch deserved to die," Lou Bravo, barked. "He put Blaine through hell, good riddance."

"That could have been me in that ambulance headed for the hospital or worse, the morgue. What did he think he would accomplish? It doesn't make sense."

"That's something the police will have to solve. I know this is not a good time, but I need to ask you a few more questions about Arthur Dunn."

"You are right, Beale, this is not a good time, can't you see Blaine is in pain. She's been through a lot today, and your questions will have to wait!" Lou Bravo moved in front of Blaine blocking access to her.

"It's alright, I'm fine, surely a few questions won't be a problem," Blaine added, "let's move over to the picnic tables beyond the swings, we will have more privacy there. Brooke, why don't you go back to the truck with Lou Bravo, I'll join you in a few minutes, okay honey."

Detective Beale sat down and reviewed the events that preceded the search of Dunn's house. He outlined the discovery of a sophisticated computer network with numerous firewalls, encryption protocols, passwords and the subsequent retrieval of very damaging files and websites incriminating Arthur Dunn as a conspirator in a child trafficking syndicate. He mentioned that this office was cooperating with the FBI, the Child Abduction Task Force and Florida's Child Predator Cyber Crime Unit in penetrating the leaders of the consortium. That Dunn was only a small clog in the total operation, but his computer revealed that one of the major players was in the Sarasota area. To date the task force did not have anything substantive. Since she was the last person to talk to him, and in light of this new information about Dunn, Beale was instructed to interview her again and see if there was anything more, she could remember about Dunn.

"It's been awhile. I remember telling you about the book, the one about boys in Thailand, and how uncomfortable he was when he noticed me looking at it," Blaine remarked.

"Yes, we found the book and checked all of Dunn's credit card records and now have a travel agent from Sarasota under surveillance. But is there anything else you can remember, anything unusual about the man, anything he did or said that was out of the ordinary?"

"Wait a minute, his watch was on backwards, well not exactly backwards, the face was turned towards the underside of his wrist. I thought it's peculiar; usually the face was on top of the wrist so not to scratch the crystal." Blaine pointed out. "He was constantly looking at it."

"Can you describe the watch," Beale inquired as he scribbled down everything she said.

"The clock face was squarish, probably white gold with diamonds on the two sides, it only had roman numerals twelve and six, the rest of the numbers were diamonds, and a metal band, most likely white gold also. It looked expensive. He said it was a Patek Phillippe whatever that meant."

"That's the name of a very expensive watch maker. What was a newspaper manager doing with a $20,000.00 wrist watch?" Beale answered and wrote PATEK PHILIPPE $$$$ in bold letters followed by dollar signs. He then drew an arrow from the last dollar sign and wrote; where did Dunn get the money for the watch!

"He said his benefactor gave it to him."

Beale almost dropped his pen when he heard Blaine say *benefactor;* the explanation caught him off guard, *someone gave Arthur Dunn the watch, but why? What did he do to deserve such an expensive gift?* For the first time in the investigation, Beale had a solid lead that could link another person, the benefactor, to Dunn and eventually to the child trafficking ring.

"Benefactor!" Beale exclaimed. "Dunn said someone gave him the watch. Did he say who gave it to him, or why, or when he got it?"

"No, he just said his benefactor gave it to him, but it looked new."

Beale took out his cell and called Hordowski back at the station, "I want you to check online what jewelers from Venice to Sarasota carry Patek Philippe watches. There can't be that many; it's a pretty high end watch for a store to carry in its inventory. Find out who purchased the watch for Mr. Dunn and when. Also do a background check on the store, the owner and its employees; let's see if there's a connection to this child trafficking ring. Gotta go. I have another call on the line."

Beale's screen read *Cyber Crime Unit*, "Beale, that's great news Cal, it may be the break we needed. Did you say Englewood? Listen we just received a tip. I'll have Detective Hordowski give you a call right after he checks out a few things and Johnson, thanks for the heads-up."

Beale called Hordowski to relay what Cal Johnson, Chief Detective from the Sarasota County Sheriff's Cyber crime Unit said about disabling one of Dunn's encrypted programs. It appeared that Dunn made contact with a person of interest from Englewood and the Sheriff's Department now has his Blue Heron residence under surveillance. "Maybe you better expand the search to include jewelers in Englewood."

"Blaine, thank you, you have been very helpful. I hope you feel. . .What is that noise coming from the parking lot?"

"That's *Turkey in the Straw*, music from my ice cream truck and my cue to leave. I have a very busy day tomorrow; you remember the movie 'Ground Hog Day,' 6:00 in the morning the clock alarm blasts Sonny and Cher *"I Got You Babe,"* and then the same day happened over and over to the weatherman, Bill Murray. Well tomorrow is 'Ice Cream Day' for one special customer, but instead of Sonny and Cher, I have "Turkey in the Straw," over and over again. See ya around the neighborhood, detective."

"Ice cream truck, things getting a little slow at the park, now you have to moonlight as an ice cream man?"

"Excuse me, ice cream delivery person Detective Beale," Blaine said as she walked away, "or have you forgotten women have the right to be in the work place."

"Remember, *ice cream person*, you need a permit from Venice to sell ice cream within the city limits. I'd hate to be the one to give you a ticket," Beale added with a slight smile.

"Don't worry detective I'm only making one stop and that's in Englewood, so I guess I won't need that permit. If doctors can offer boutique medicine, make house calls to only premium paying patients, why can't I offer door-to-door ice cream for a very special customer? It's a new marketing strategy in the ice cream business, delicious concept, don't you think?" Blaine called out as she stepped inside the truck and waved good-bye.

Beale stood and watched the truck drive away while *Turkey in the Straw* assaulted the eardrums and musical palate of everyone in the park. It didn't make sense. No vendor in his or her right mind would sell ice cream to one person? Strategy, that wasn't a strategy; she was up to something. Beale took out his note pad, made a note to call over to Englewood and ask them to keep an eye on her; it would not be too difficult to observe a white ice cream truck decorated with animals with the propensity to play Turkey in the Straw in front of one house. Next to the note, he drew an ice cream cone and a big question mark. Beale planned to be part of the stakeout operation in Englewood; maybe he would surprise her and buy a tootie fruity double nut scoop cone, couldn't be any nuttier than Blaine Sterling's idea to sell ice cream.

Chapter Fifty

It took Earl six nights to get it right, well maybe only four since two nights were blown fooling around with outside distractions. His dilemma was to synchronize the car's speed with the green lights, starting times with acceleration and most important the initial location, that Star Trek Guy conveniently neglected to mention, to launch the *route sixty-six experiment.* That revelation ultimately raced up to him serendipitously. Saturday night after Earl attempted two unsuccessful runs to cruise the Trail, the first began at Tamiami and Business 41 By-pass, the second on the middle of the Circus Bridge, his car flew through red lights at Avenida Del Circo, and then at Palermo Place, both attempts ended miserably.

Stopped at the light on Center and Business 41, Earl stared out across the bridge, oblivious to the light change and everything else around him. Earl Neigh, the newspaper guy, was consumed with the notion of cruising Tamiami Trail without stopping for a single red light. "Shit, why isn't this working? All I had to do was to keep the speed at 66 to make all the lights, so what the fuck am I doing wrong?" He yelled. "If that Star Trek weirdo is fucking with me, I'll kill him," and squeezed the steering wheel until his knuckles turned white. Exhausted, he leaned back in the seat and closed his eyes.

Call it kismet or just dumb luck, but the answer to Earl's dilemma pulled up along side him in a white convertible.

"Hello, dream boy, hello, the light's green, where we come from that means you can go. Hello, please don't be dead." Jolted from his stupor Earl bounced up in the seat and stuck his head out the window. Still groggy and half awake, to his shock along side him in a white BMW Z4 convertible were two gorgeous Asian girls laughing and gyrating to Cindi Lauper's record, *Girls Just Want To Have Fun.* Their long, silky, black hair swishing from side to side, accented their creamy white faces and big bright smiles, but what grabbed Earl's attention were their breasts that poked out from skintight yellow T-shirts that clung to their slender bodies.

"Excuse me, and where exactly is it you two beauties come from?" Earl drooled with a stupid grin on his face and a warm bulge in his pants.

"My mother said I was a gift from heaven, but my driver's license reads Peoria, what do you think?" The driver sang out. "I'm Yumia Chen, but my friends call me Yumi and this is my BFF Zoë Wang."

"Well, Yumi, I think I've died and gone to take-out heaven."

"Funny, very funny, so what are you doing stopped on the bridge at 2:15 in the morning, you're not going to commit suicide are you?" Zoë called out with a playful laugh.

"Suicide, what are you fucking crazy. I must have fallen asleep. That damn ice cream truck wakes me up every day, blasting the same fucking song over and over again. Then it leaves and just as I'm about to fall asleep, the god damn ice cream truck is back blasting the same fucking music."

"What kind of ice cream truck drives around neighborhoods selling ice cream at night? What's the guy, a drug dealer?"

"It wasn't at night; it was at 11:00 every fucking morning. I work at Wal-Mart from 4:00 to 12:00 at night and then the papers until 5:00 in the morning, so I sleep during the day. It's not a guy, but a lady and her kid selling the ice cream. She's kinda hot, blonde, nice body, cute face and all that, but for the past week I couldn't get any sleep. I'm falling asleep at work and now I'm nodding off in my car. Anyway, to answer your first question; I'm playing a game, a driving game," Earl barked out, "and by the way what are you two babes doing out so late?"

"We're heading back to our hotel on the beach in Venice," Yumi yelled over the music. "We were bar-hopping along Dearborn St. in Englewood; someone told us that a local band was rock'n the house down there so we decided to check it out. They were right; ever hear of the Steve Tevens Band? They were hot and the margaritas they poured at the bar were ice cold delicious."

"Yeah, we'd still be at the Elbow Room sipping margaritas and having a blast if *little miss pick-up* here didn't try to steal away some townie's boyfriend," snorted Zoë still visually annoyed with Yumi.

"He was cute; how could I know he had a date from hell, anyway that *blonde bimbo* girlfriend of his was psycho. That crazy bitch picked up a pitcher of beer and threw it at me. Not only did she soak me, she also drenched everyone standing at the bar; including the lady bartender who called the cops right after a fight broke out. We decided the party was over and left as the police pulled up. Look at us we're soaking wet and smell of beer," Yumi carped.

"I'm looking; yeah I can see that your T-shirts are all wet. I thought maybe the two of you went for a late night swim or something?"

"A swim at 2:00 in the morning, not likely," Yumi called out as she switched off the CD. "So you like to play games dream boy, so do we!"

"Hey stop calling me dream boy, my name is Earl."

"Okay, Earl, feeling lucky tonight? We have a game you will like, it also involves cars and we know how much you like car games. The best part of the game is it only has one rule, so it is very easy to play even if a player is sleepy. If you can catch us by the first traffic light, you can have us," Yumi cooed.

As if on cue, Zoë stood up, flipped her hair back and pulled off her top.

"What do you think Earl, nice set of tits and if you like hers wait until you see mine. I promise you won't be disappointed. So what do you say—are you up for the game big boy?"

Earl sat up speechless as his wildest fantasies spun and churned around in his perverted little mind. Propositions from two sexy vixens only happened in movies, never on a bridge in Venice, Florida and certainly not to a newspaper delivery guy sitting in a shiny, candy apple red, 1999 Camaro at 2:00 in the morning. *It had to be a dream; he'd wake up and find himself at Wal-Mart, asleep, sprawled out on top of a pile of men's underwear that he had to straighten up before his dinner break at seven o'clock*, he thought. Slowly, with both hands, Earl rubbed his face, massaging his forehead, temples and ears with the tips of his fingers. Once composed, he opened his eyes and to his twisted gratification, Zoë was still standing, tits and all. A lecherous grin spread across his face.

"Let me get this straight. I beat you to the first light and the two of you are mine for the night," he crowed, as the big boy in his pants painfully grew bigger by the minute.

"That's right."

"What happens if you reach the light first?" Earl moaned as if in pain.

"You'll never know, will you," Yumi said with a devilish smile.

Earl looked down at the fancy little sports car next to him with its supple ivory white leather seats that enveloped its passengers, the rich natural wood grain trim that accented every line and corner of the platinum dashboard, doors and console and the premium sound package with concert hall tonality and grimaced. There is a fine line between infatuation and disgust; both points of view have their champions. The problem arises when the lines cross, combine and jumble. It is at that juncture, confusion leads to indecision.

There were no blurred lines about foreign cars with Earl Neigh: he was a Chevy Guy. Earl came from a family that only drove Chevrolets. Earl drove a Camaro, his father drove a Chevrolet, and his father was a Chevy man. Even his Uncle Ron from Tampa drove a classic *1964* banana yellow Stingray Corvette. Earl never forgot the first and last time he rode in the Stingray, they were returning from Nokomis Beach just as the drawbridge started to open, Uncle Ron veered around the flashing gate, floored the Stingray and flew over the opening bridge to the opposite side and raced away down Albee Farm Road. Earl's mother and father sat in their car paralyzed as the Corvette disappeared down the road. That was the last time Earl rode in Uncle Ron's Corvette, or any other of his cars.

Earl grew up around Chevys. Blindfolded he could change a Chevy's oil, plugs, even tune-up the engine until it purred like a kitten, but with foreign cars he hadn't a clue. That is all the Neigh family knew, Chevys. Earl didn't know anything about nor did he care much for all the foreign cars now driving around Florida. Earl remembered his daddy say, *those damn foreign cars taking American jobs away from us; we ought to send them back to Japan, every last one of them.* Yup *that's what should be done and the sooner the better.*

Earl's father would be turning in his grave if he saw all the little foreign cars driving all over Florida. Today not only do cars come from Japan, but from Korea, China, Italy, Germany, England, and Sweden and now right beside him was as Candy would say, *one of those little itsy bitsy foreign cars*. Pressing down on the accelerator the Camaro roared, feeling its 305 hp V8 jump forward, Earl was confident he could destroy that little bug of a car. How could he possibly lose?

"You have to be kidding. You think you can beat me in that little Tonka toy of a car. Where do you wind it up?" Earl laughed with a pompous smirk on his face. "Bring it on ladies, I'm game! This is one bet I'll enjoy collecting."

Unfortunately, for Earl his knowledge about cars revolved around oil changes, tune-ups and brake jobs for American automobiles, exclusively Chevrolet's. Lacking any knowledge of European automotive technology, Earl's cocky attitude based upon size and size alone, *that bigger is better*, was fraught with potholes. Unbeknownst to Earl, the car Yumi was driving, although only a two-seater, was a custom edition Z4 35i Roadster from Germany. The 335 hp twin turbo charged 6-cylinder engine was capable of turning 0-60 in less than 4.6 seconds. It solved the mystery that *good things do come in small packages.*

Che-Wei Chen, Yumi's father, as a reward for his daughter's good grades and for the second year was named to the Dean's list at Bradley University, completed all the arrangements for her one-week trip to Venice, Florida. He called the BMW dealership in Sarasota and reserved the only convertible available, a white special edition Z4 Roadster. The rental agreement was costly, a $10,000 security deposit, and $1,000 a week car rental, but Mr. Kim could afford it, his chain of Chen All You Can Eat Chinese Buffet Restaurants, even in a depressed economy, were turning a hefty profit. People had to eat and Mr. Kim's restaurants were full every night.

"在鸡未孵出之前数只数是无意义的。Earl Neigh," Yumi said quickly and giggled.

"What did you say darling?" Earl yelled.

"It's an old Chinese proverb: Don't count your chickens before they hatch," Zoë explained. "You say you will win the race, but no one knows until the race is completed. Maybe you will win, maybe not."

"Chinese saying, bullshit! We have that saying in the United States too."

"It doesn't matter Earl, it's just a saying. Anyway if we had the car we drove last year, we would definitely win," Zoë snapped and turned to Yumi.

"Yeah, what kinda car was that," Earl barked out.

Zoë smiled and said, "A SLK 350 Mercedes Benz, a cool two-seater, with the top that folds down into the trunk, but Yumi drove it on top of some trees and now they won't rent her a Mercedes."

"It was a stupid accident. It was raining hard, the road was slippery and the car slid off the exit ramp. How was I supposed to know the car would fly off the road and land on a bunch of palm trees?" Yumi cried out and gave Zoë a dirty look.

"Well maybe if you weren't on your cell phone blabbing away to some Billy-Bob or Bobby-Ray we wouldn't have been twenty feet up a tree for three hours waiting for the fire trucks to get us down. How embarrassing, just sitting in the car while the newspapers and television cameras took our picture."

"Oh Zoë it wasn't that bad, so they *blacklisted* me from ever renting a Mercedes in Sarasota County, for life, after all we did get to meet some pretty cute fireman, right," Yumi giggled and they both hugged each other hysterically.

"Well ladies I hate to break up your party, but don't we have a race to start?" Earl yelled over the roar of his engine as he stomped down on the accelerator. "Get ready to eat some Chevy exhaust."

Chapter Fifty-One

Disaster slammed the hood down on team Chevy from the get-go. At 2:30 A.M., the light turned green and both cars peeled out in a cloud of burning rubber. Side by side to the bridge gate, Earl's engine screamed as he redlined first gear to over 6,000 rpm before shifting into second. He pushed second gear to 60 mph and from the corner of his eye; he saw the BMW inch forward. That loss of concentration, a mere split second of distraction, spelled impending disaster. In a panic, he jerked forward the gearshift, missed third gear and jammed the shift into fifth. The Camaro choked down and bucked backward as the BMW disappeared over the bridge. Instinct kicked in, Earl immediately shifted into second and punched the accelerator to the floor, but it was too late. The race was over and he knew it as he sunk back in the seat and watched the BMW zoom past Darby Buick and head for the green light at Avenida Del Circo and the prize.

Sometimes an individual loses a battle, but not the war, and serendipitously that scenario was about to drive Earl straight into the winners' circle. No sooner had the Camaro passed the last bridge railing and the front tires touched down on the pavement the cruise control kicked in. Earl eased his foot off the accelerator, sat back and looked down the road at the first red light as he passed Darby Buick. Off in the distance, he saw the two girls jumping around topless, giving each other *high fives* and shaking their tits up and down for the whole world to see, or maybe just for Earl to notice what else he lost.

Deflated in many ways, all Earl could think about was not getting laid. One missed shift and the opportunity of a lifetime flushed down the fucking drain. About twenty feet before Avenida Del Circo and the gyrating disco twins, the traffic light turned green and the Camaro cruised through the intersection as Earl waved to the screaming girls, who seemed surprised that he didn't stop.

"Shit, this may be it, the combination I've been looking for all fucking week," Earl screamed. "Thank you, Yumi and Zoë, you crazy chicks, thanks for the wild ride. Okay let's see if it happens; turn baby, turn, turn green. . .Yes!"

The light turned green at San Marco Drive as Earl barreled past the Gold Rush BBQ Restaurant, through the intersection and up to the Lucky Dog, an eclectic little eatery that welcomed two and four legged patrons equally with open plates. Its bright blue roof with blue striped awnings, pea green building and a hand painted orange Lucky Dog sign caught his eye. Earl smiled and thought, what a great advertising strategy, throw together a wacky color combination, offer great food at a reasonable price and customers will keep coming back, just like in the movie "Field of Dreams," '*If you build it, they will come.*' They do, packed for breakfast and lunch every day customers show up to the Lucky Dog hungry and leave full.

The traffic light past the Venice Regional Hospital at Palermo Place remained red. Earl's eyes burned as he focused on the fast approaching red circle glowing above the intersection. Beads of sweat formed on his forehead and slowly rolled down his face while a pounding along both temples sounded the onset of a splitting headache. A queasy sensation churned away in his stomach with each dreaded second as he sped closer to the light and the fear that his cruising days, like the television series *Route 66*, were about to run out of gas. However, when the nose of the Camaro passed the hospital's emergency room entrance, the light at Palermo turned green and Earl breezed under the light with a cocky grin on his face and a sigh of relief. He stuck his head out the window and screamed, "Oh yeah, three lights down, three to go, keep it coming baby, keep it coming. Watch out Venice, Earl Neigh the Cruising Guy, is back in town." Joyously, Earl relaxed and breathed in the damp sweet air that pushed in off the Gulf savoring its early morning freshness as the Camaro raced down Tamiami Trail.

A few yards away Earl saw that the light was green at Turin Street or Indian depending on the turn. Earl didn't give a shit what they named the road, he was going straight and only cared about making the light. He scooted past Turin as the lights at Milan and Miami in concert turned green. At the corner of Milan, the clock on Moody's Insurance billboard read 2:34 as the Camaro passed the intersection and sped towards the last light at Miami Avenue and the checkered flag. *"Four minutes, from the Circus Bridge to here; that's all, how is that possible?"* Earl thought and jerked his head around for a second look.

"Shit the clock still reads 2:34 only four minutes, it feels more like four hours, and I feel like crap, I'm exhausted. The pressure to make all the lights is unbearable. Ready or not, Miami Avenue, here I come," Earl howled as the car sped towards the light. Twenty feet before the light Earl eased the Camaro left beyond the double yellow lines preparing to make a wide arching right turn onto Miami and into the paper's parking lot. Two seconds later the Camaro exploded through the final green light, past Pineapples Restaurant and Tiki Bar and down Miami Avenue. Across from Babes Hardware, Earl tapped on the brakes, disengaged the cruise control and rolled into the parking lot.

Intoxicated by the sweet taste of victory, Earl was so distracted by pounding on the steering wheel and stomping on the floorboards that he almost ran over the Star Trek guy who stood frozen next to his newspaper loading spot. Caught in the glare of his headlights, Earl jammed on the brakes and jerked to a complete stop inches from a terrified Mr. Spock.

"Shit, what the hell are you doing here? I almost killed you." Earl shouted as he turned the engine off and jumped out of the car.

"And greetings to you, Earth traveler, I have come to congratulate you on a successful journey."

"Thanks, but why the fuck didn't you just tell me to start at the Center Road light. You might have saved me a lot of time screwing around trying to find out the right combination," Earl snarled. "Listen I haven't been able to get any sleep all week, I'm exhausted and I have to get these papers bagged."

"My dear Earl, that was the quest, for you to solve the puzzle, for that, not only would you get to cruise the Trail, but you would have the satisfaction of knowing that you solved the mystery," said Star Trek Guy, "and I have one more surprise."

Star Trek Guy reached into his pocket and pulled out a round, shiny, black disc the size of a cell phone, but much thinner, the thickness of a silver dollar. Recessed on one side of the device were three tiny silver buttons placed in a triangle in the center of the object. The other side was smooth, devoid of any buttons. He pointed the device at his van, pressed the top button and from the center of the roof, a silver antenna rose about a foot. Star Trek Guy turned the device and the round ball on the top of the antenna followed in the similar direction.

"Look to the skies, young traveler; it is time for your reward to be celebrated by all." With a sweep of his arm in a majestic gesture, he pointed the device at the Star's Building and pressed the left button. An ice blue light burst from the antenna and illuminated the entire facade of the building with a picture of Earl; head out the window of his Camaro super-imposed over a backdrop picture of a long dusty highway in the middle of nowhere and off in the distance a rusted white and black Route 66 road sign. At the top of the picture in big, bold, red, white and blue letters: EARL NEIGH THE CRUISING GUY.

"Wow that is so cool. The picture is humongous. How did you do that," gasped Earl, shaking his head in amazement.

"I guess you could say it is out of this world. It's just a little program I put together, something like a projection TV, but 1,000 times faster based upon Nano electronic technology. But enough of the technical jargon; do you like it?"

"I love it. Thanks Myron, but when did you get the picture?"

"Last week during one of your unsuccessful attempts to run the green lights, I think it was at Turin. I've been charting your progress and calculated that you'd unravel the puzzle last night, but for some unknown reason you blew past the newspaper and turned into the Hamilton Square Shopping Center. I wanted to congratulate you on your conquest, why the sudden departure young traveler?"

"Oh yeah, last night, well Candy was with me and she wanted to give me a surprise for such a fantastic ride. She wasn't quite finished with my present when we hit Miami, so I drove over to Hamilton Square for the climax, if you know what I mean, dude."

"I totally comprehend, zealous traveler, but at this moment I believe you have a more pressing problem; delivery manager Hatchet is marching across the lot in your direction and by the expression on her face, she's not happy. I wish you good fortune and I bid you farewell." With a crisp Federation salute, Star Trek Guy smiled and hustled back to his van.

Chapter Fifty-Two

"Earl, I need to talk to you, but first what is the meaning of your picture covering up the entire building?" Hatchet shouted, pointing to the exposition that lit up the night sky. Tanner Hatchet, as her name signified, had the reputation as a no-nonsense manager. She did not like problems, hated when her delivery chain of command was interrupted and didn't tolerate change. Procedure was by the book, her book or not at all. Anything out of the ordinary, different or not from the way she ordered it was a concern and dealt with punishing consequences. A short, stout woman in her forties, Tanner's closely cropped black hair and muscular build gave her the appearance of a Marine drill instructor. Known to push people around, Earl clearly remembered how last summer she destroyed poor Simon Blister, a college student who played Elvis music all the time.

Hatchet received a complaint from the local neighborhood association that the music from the paper's parking lot was loud and if the music continued they would notify the police. Hatchet immediately sent a memo to all the carriers, informed them of the complaint and subsequently banned the playing of all music in the parking lot. Unfortunately, Simon either didn't receive or read the memo or cruised into the lot that evening with Elvis belting out *You Ain't Nothing But A Hound Dog* from his car stereo. From that day on the word 'BLISTERED' became a euphuism for being 'attacked'. Leaning into Simon's car, one swift blow from her claw hammer, used to snap the plastic ties that held the paper bundles, silenced Simon's CD player for good. Plastic and metal fragments splintered into hundreds of tiny pieces; the only thing left was a gaping hole in his dashboard that once occupied a premium sound system. That was Simon's last day and the last night music played in the parking lot.

"It's only a joke, something the guys put up, Ms. Hatchet," Earl mumbled staring down at the claw hammer in her hand.

Pointing the hammer straight at Earl's face, Hatchet yelled, "You know I don't like jokes, take it down, immediately!"

"No problem, Ms. Hatchet. Myron shut down the show," Earl shouted across the lot. Immediately Earl's picture vanished and only the pale yellow glow from the lampposts illuminated the busy circles of newspaper activity throughout the parking lot.

"Now Earl, you know I don't like problems and right now you have two very irritating ones that need to be fixed. Unfortunately, when you create problems, I have to clean them up and that creates a problem for me and that's not good, understand?"

"Yes, Ms. Hatchet, I understand, but what's my problem?" Earl asked almost in a whisper, his eyes still glued to the hammer that Hatchet raised to eye level.

"Problems, Earl, you have two problems, two separate complaints from your customers stating that their papers were not delivered properly," Hatchet wagged the hammer in front of his nose. "For the past three days, Mrs. Pickett from Valencia Lakes complained that she had to dig out her paper from under her Bougainvillea bush along the front of the house, not on her driveway as usual. In addition, Mr. Brickmeyer, another account of yours, from Summer Green Condominiums, right off Capri Isles Boulevard, an eighty-eight-year-old retired veteran stated that he had to march down to the first floor and retrieve his paper, which is normally placed on his second floor doorstep. Why is this happening Earl?"

Mesmerized by the twirling motion of the hammer in Hatchet's hand, Earl could not respond. Frozen in a daze, Earl's eyes focused only on the hammer's two silver metal claws that spun menacingly inches from his face. With each turn, Earl's heart pounded faster and harder, a glaring reminder that a *blistering* could occur at any minute.

"Well, answer me! Why are your papers thrown all over the place?" Hatchet spat out and shoved the hammer inches from his face.

"I can't get any sleep," Earl answered with a painful cry. "For the last two weeks, an ice cream truck parks in front of my house selling ice cream and blasting nursery rhyme music all morning long. *Farmer in the Dell, London Bridge is Falling Down, Turkey in the Straw,* and *Here We Go Round the Mulberry Bush* are chiseled into my brain, I know them all by heart, would you like me to sing one?"

"Of course not," Hatchet snapped.

"Every day, more and more kids showed up, I had no idea there were that many children in the neighborhood, but there they were, hanging out, waiting to buy ice cream. They yelled and screamed from the moment they arrived until the time they left, the boys even had wrestling matches on my front lawn, which destroyed what little grass I had to begin with. It was impossible to fall back to sleep; if I'm lucky maybe I get three hours of sleep a day. I would fall asleep at work; a few times, I dozed off at the wheel and almost smashed into a yellow blinking construction sign along the Round-A-Bout off Jacaranda Boulevard. I don't have any energy and find it impossible to concentrate on my deliveries; I'm a wreck, Ms. Hatchet."

Conveniently, amnesia must have set in, for Earl neglected to mention that the card games, two nights a week, could have contributed to his lack of sleep. Earl lowered his head and waited.

"Earl, I don't give a crap about your ice cream problem, all I care about is correcting the newspaper delivery problem today, understand?" With a final spin of the hammer, Hatchet turned and marched back towards the office. She reached the first lamppost, stopped, turned around, pointed the hammer straight at Earl and screamed out for everyone in the parking lot to hear, "Earl, one more complaint and you know what that means!"

Humiliated, Earl gasped for air and mumbled, "A blistering?"

"That's right, mister, and you can kiss off your $1,000.00 bonus. You know the policy, three strikes and you're out, no bonus money." With a final shake of her hammer, Ms. Hatchet turned and walked towards the news building shaking the hammer with each stride.

The thought of losing one thousand dollars in bonus money provided a huge incentive not to make mistakes, not to mention, incurring the wrath of Ms. Hatchet, was another inducement for Earl to get his act together. For the next three days, Earl mustered up enough strength to become a model newspaper carrier. Ms. Hatchet even complimented him on the change after she received a call from Mrs. Pickett regaling the joys of getting a newspaper delivered properly.

However, on day four, like a house of cards, the world came tumbling down on Earl Neigh, the newspaper delivery guy. After nine sleepless days, exhaustion finally took its toll. After making the turn

Chapter Fifty-Three

The normal drive from Venice to Englewood, calculating traffic, lights, time of month, and the number of *snowbirds* on the road was approximately twenty-five minutes. However, driving around town in a brightly colored ice cream truck, lights flashing, and music blasting from two outdoor speakers didn't come close to normal. The ice cream drive to Earl's house, because of the number of unexpected interruptions that occurred along the way, was ten to fifteen minutes longer. At least three times a week, while stopped at a light, drivers would call out, run up, or just throw money in through the window to purchase ice cream.

On the first day, a UPS driver pulled alongside Blaine shouted that she had a flat tire and should pull over. After looking at the tire, the driver apologized, said he thought it looked low, but since she stopped, could he buy a strawberry shortcake ice cream bar. Blaine realized it was just a ruse, but acquiesced and handed him his prize with a smile.

Another time while driving off from a red light, a man on a bicycle raced out from a side street, grabbed onto the passenger window and road alongside the ice cream truck. He yelled out to Brooke that it was a matter of life or death. His wife was pregnant and had an insatiable craving for an ice cream sundae. He stopped at two convenience stores, but they only carried popsicles and ice cream bars, when he spotted the ice cream truck stopped at the light he knew he had to act fast. In desperation, he crumpled up a five-dollar bill, threw it into the truck and told her to keep the change. Brooke reached into the freezer, pulled out a sundae and handed over the coveted prize. With an appreciative smile, he let go and coasted back onto the sidewalk.

The most memorable ice cream sale took place while driving back home from Englewood. A minor fender bender involving two cars in front of the Dome, a year-round mega flea & farmers' market off SR776 in Venice, turned into an ice cream frenzy. Traffic backed up past MTR nursery adjacent to the Dome when Blaine heard a loud banging on her side of the truck. She looked out her window and saw a line of young girls waving dollar bills and shouting, "Ice cream, ice cream, we all scream for ice cream" over and over again. It appeared that the local, under-14 girls traveling basketball team, had just won the Hoops for The Heart Tournament in Englewood and were headed back to Venice when their bus was caught in the traffic jam. Excited to see an ice cream truck stopped in front of them, the girls, along with their coaches and parents, piled out of the bus to purchase a celebratory ice cream treat. Brooke passed out twenty ice cream bars, ten cones, eight ice pops, five smoothies, four waters, and thirteen bags of chips, pretzels and nuts. Meanwhile, ten MTR landscaping trucks returning from their lawn jobs attempted to cross in-between the line of stalled cars and drive onto their lot adjacent to the highway. Unfortunately, the lead truck became wedged between two cars. While attempting to back up, it hooked its front bumper to the first car locking the two vehicles where they stood. Unable to move, the truck, car and nine other landscaping trucks brought traffic south of MTR for almost a mile to a standstill. Frustrated, hot and tired, drivers lined up behind the ice cream truck to purchase anything cold and refreshing. After twenty minutes of nonstop sales, Blaine and Brooke sold out. Disgusted, the few empty-handed customers turned and walked back to their cars cursing along the way.

Suddenly, the back door on a green Toyota in front of the ice cream truck flew open and a man jumped out screaming, "My wife is having a baby. Please, somebody help." Blaine grabbed a handful of clean aprons and towels, a pair of latex gloves and rushed to the car. She shouted to Brooke, "Call 911, and tell them we have a woman about to have a baby, boil some water and bring it to me as soon as possible."

Blaine slid into the back seat and saw a young woman, no more than twenty, writhing in pain. Her curly black hair wet with perspiration clung to her face; while her dark eyes swollen with tears mirrored the agony her labored body was experiencing. Her small, thin frame, pale by comparison to her protruding stomach, shook uncontrollably as she cried out. Blaine reached over, tenderly stroked her face and said, "Everything is going to be all right."

Blaine slapped on the latex gloves, placed towels under her and all along the seat, and reached under her pink dress.

Overhead a Channel 6 News traffic helicopter circled sending pictures of the accident, the long line of cars and a report of commotion around an ice cream truck and car back to the television station. Two minutes later, a call from the main office to Bryce Faceman, Channel 6 investigative news reporter, also caught in the traffic jam, instructed him and his film crew to *"go live"* and get *a "juicy human-interest"* story for the six o'clock news. Faceman's adrenalin, already pounding after viewing the Englewood footage on his exposé: Child Abduction and Trafficking, the Florida Connection, eagerly accepted the front office request to ferret out a story. *Another opportunity to see my face on television,* Bryce thought, *thank you Channel 6 for making me a household name.*

Last week, an anonymous tip from a person identified only as IC, alerted Faceman that one, possibly two boys, ages 14 and 12, held in a house in Englewood, could very well be a boy from the Amber Alert abducted several days ago from Punta Gorda. IC also reported that the Blue Heron Court residence had all the earmarks to be an exchange location for abducted boys and could be a distribution point for child pornography. The address, detailed description of the boy, kidnapper, house and the license plate number of a green pick-up truck police believed used in the abduction, appeared credible. Finished viewing the footage, Faceman could not believe his good fortune; there beyond the weathered, locked stockade fence that barricaded the entire property, in a second floor window peering out from behind a dirty lace curtain was a veiled face of a frightened young boy.

"Unbelievable Tommy, you caught a picture of the kid. Take a look, second floor, center window, directly above where I'm speaking." Faceman pointed to the window and grinned. "If I play my cards right, this story is going to get me a Pulitzer. You can count on it Tommy Boy, it is like money in the bank. Thank you IC, whoever you are."

"You're right, Bryce, I see him. Man, he looks sad, like he is grieving and his eyes are haunting, a lifeless pale blue, they look so mournful. When we get back to the studio I'll enhance the image and see if he is one of the abducted boys."

"If the pictures match up we have to come back tomorrow with the police. I must be on camera when they arrest that son-of-a-bitch," Faceman quipped as he ran a comb through his thick black hair, "but first I have to interview people about a traffic accident. Oh, and Tommy, don't forget the close-ups of *The Face*."

True to his nickname, "*The Face*," because he insisted the camera focus on his face, Bryce and his cameraman packed up their gear and marched off towards the accident. The line of cars extended almost a mile back towards Englewood. A handful of cars jumped the median, drove on the opposite side of the highway north towards Jacaranda Boulevard; however, police re-routing vehicles off 776 stopped and ticketed each wrong-way driver, unfortunately creating another problem. Not a single car moved in both directions.

Hearing talk of a woman giving birth, Faceman waded into the crowd, pushed his way past the ice cream truck and up to the green Toyota. A baby's cry came from inside the car and the crowd erupted in cheers and shouts. Blaine stepped out of the car and announced, "It's a girl, a beautiful, healthy little girl." The crowd exploded with joy, grabbed hands and danced around the car singing.

Microphone in hand, Faceman elbowed his way past the dancers into the back seat of the Toyota. The camera panned the crowd, the car and a close-up of Faceman, the mother and baby. Wrapped in a white towel the mother cradled her baby and gave a faint smile when Faceman asked her how she felt. Leaning over the front seat, the husband gushed with pride thanking everyone for his or her help. He reached over and lovingly touched the baby's face.

"What will you name the baby?" Faceman asked the father, as the camera slowly moved from a close-up of *The Face,* to the father and back to Faceman.

With tears of joy rolling down his face that was not on camera he replied, "Destiny. It was destined that our precious little girl be born here today. I want to thank everyone who helped, especially the *IC lady* for delivering our baby, thank God she was here."

"IC lady," a stunned Faceman replied!

"Yes, the ice cream lady over there," he pointed to Blaine leaning against the back of the Toyota, "she delivered our Destiny."

Midway through his interview with the father, the police and paramedics arrived. The police cleared the crowd aside, escorted the father, Faceman and the cameraman out of the car while the medics examined the mother and baby. Satisfied the two were in stable condition; medics placed the mother and baby on a stretcher and carried them to the fire rescue truck.

With the camera rolling, Faceman not ready to give up the spotlight, turned to Blaine and Brooke, "So, you're the hero that delivered the baby. What is your name?" Faceman shoved the microphone up to Blaine's face.

"Blaine Sterling and I'm not a hero. I did what anyone in my position would do. I helped a person in need, that's all."

Still distracted by the mention of IC, Faceman regained his composure and interjected with his usual condescending sneer, "And what exactly is your position Blaine Sterling, how does an ice cream vendor come to deliver a baby?"

"For your information Mr. Smarty Pants, my mother is the greatest park ranger in the world and this is not the first baby she delivered," Brooke snapped angrily.

Last March, a month after Blaine completed the Florida First Aid re-certification training at the Ranger Academy in Tallahassee, a family from Indiana just checked in at the Ranger Station when the wife went into labor. With his three girls, wife and camper, the husband drove straight to the Nature Center for assistance. The Thursday Pancake Breakfast was in full swing and Blaine, two rangers, a dozen volunteers, and thirty campers were enjoying blueberry pancakes when the husband burst through the Center's door in a panic that his wife was about to give birth. Blaine and the two rangers raced outside and into the camper. There in the back salon, propped up against an array of multicolored pillows, a menagerie of stuffed animals and calmly reading one of the many celebrity gossip magazines strewn all over the queen-sized bed was Mrs. Boxler.

"We were told you were having a baby," Laura Magner, a first year ranger, called

"Oh, that husband of mine, such a worry wart, he gets everyone all worked up and look no baby," Jane Boxler blurted out, waving her magazine in the air as if she was attempting to shoo away an annoying fly. "I already have three kids, all girls; you'd think he'd realize by now that I can tell when the baby is ready. His problem is he wants a boy and does not want anything to go wrong. So what does the genius do; plans a camping trip to Florida, go figure."

With emergency training procedures fresh in her mind, Blaine knew exactly what to do: take control and establish a stress-free environment for the mother and baby. "I'll stay with Mrs. Boxler, Laura, you and Brooke collect some clean linen, a pair of latex gloves, boil some water and bring them back here in an hour. The rest of you go back and enjoy your pancakes." Two hours later, Brian Boxler, a beautiful baby boy was born. Blaine cleaned the baby, wrapped him in a sheet, and handed him to his mother. The mother smiled and hugged her child for the first time. The proud father ran around the park handing out cigars and announcing he had a son, Blaine and Brooke returned to the Nature Center to finish their pancakes.

"Well young lady, thank you for the information and what is your name," Faceman asked, looking down at a fiery seven-year-old.

"Brooke Sterling and I also helped my mother deliver both babies."

Faceman turned to Blaine and remarked, "You're a park ranger? Why are you driving an ice cream truck?"

"Actually, I'm the Assistant Park Manager and the ice cream truck adventure was a Christmas present to my daughter," Blaine added in an authoritative voice.

"Well viewers, it appears that the police cleared the accident scene and are instructing everyone to return to their vehicles. This is Bryce Faceman for Channel 6 News reporting to you live from the traffic jam along Route 776 in Venice. I am glad to report that there were no fatalities here today, only the birth of a baby girl, Destiny Childs. Thanks to the heroic actions by Blaine Sterling, ice cream vendor/ park ranger and her daughter Brooke, a beautiful baby girl is now sleeping peacefully in her mother's arms." The camera close-up slowly faded from Faceman, panned the line of cars, ice cream truck, the green Toyota, back to Faceman and finally the picture went black.

Chapter Fifty-Four

The next day Blaine turned onto Blue Heron Court. The forest of Australian pines that crowded both sides of the road swayed gently in the late morning breeze. A familiar low, soft whistle played through the long spindly gray/green needles of the pines as the ice cream truck passed under its umbrella of thick leaves that swayed above the road. Blaine pulled over to the side of the road and turned off the engine.

"Do you hear the whistles, Brooke?" Blaine mused, "The sounds remind me of the summers when I was about your age spent with my grandparents in South Carolina. They lived on a small farm in the country; they grew vegetables, had chickens, pigs, cows, and a gentle brown and white plow horse named Daisy. Daisy was too old for farm work, so everyday I would ride her, bareback, what fun. What I remember most about the farm, was those hot summer nights watching fireflies dance outside my bedroom window. Finally, I'd fall asleep listening to a faraway whistle from a freight train as its cars slowly rambled along the tracks past a railroad crossing. Listen, it's the same quiet, faraway whistle we hear now through the pines."

"I hear it and it does sound like a faraway whistle, like someone wants to tell you a secret, but what happened to Daisy?"

"When my grandpa died, the farm was sold and my father got a job in New York."

"Do you think another little girl rode Daisy?" Brooke asked and stared out the window at the pines.

"I don't know honey, maybe, but ten years ago I went back to visit the old farm and the place looked abandoned. The farmhouse and barn were boarded up, there weren't any animals in the pens and the property was overgrown with weeds and wild flowers. It was a very sad day, just like today, Brooke. Today is our last day to enjoy the music; Mr. Lilly returns from his trip tomorrow and wants his ice cream truck back. So let's sit here awhile longer and enjoy the music."

Several minutes later and still staring at the line of trees along the road that crowded back into the woods, Brooke turned to her mother and in a soft, faraway whisper said, "It looks scary in there Mommy, is it always so dark?"

"That's the problem with Australian pines sweetie, because they grow fast, they crowd out the other trees, their branches with long spindly needles are so numerous they block out the sunlight and all the vegetation below dies."

"Why do people plant them if they're so bad?"

"They were brought to Florida from Australia around 1800 to help control beach erosion and provide people with fast growing shade trees," Blaine answered, "but something went terribly wrong, the trees grew so fast that they killed the native plants around them and as you can see nothing survives under the pines."

"So why don't people cut them all down?"

"They do, we remove them all the time at the park. Last week, our Friends volunteer work group removed a large section of Australian pines along the South Creek Trail and next week they will clear a large forested area of pines behind the Youth Camp," Blaine explained in her best ranger information speech.

"I don't mean park people, Mommy, regular people, why don't people in this neighborhood cut them down?" Brooke snorted in disgust.

"Oh now, I'm not a regular person, thanks a lot," Blaine shot back with a big smile on her face.

"You know what I mean, Mommy."

"I know, sweetie, I'm just being silly, I guess you didn't hear the funny story Mr. Boomer told yesterday when we pulled up to Earl Neigh's house? It was about his pine tree, he told it right after he bought ice cream for his daughter Jillian." Blaine asked, unable to contain her giggling.

"What story?"

Max Boomer, a big, overweight, balding man in his fifties was a loud, fast-talking boat sales representative from Kansas. He was always telling stories. If a person was breathing, Max was telling a story. His credo, 'If you can sell boats in Kansas, you can sell boats anywhere, Toto,' was his signature greeting, guaranteed the conversation would revolve around him and that was exactly what the storyteller from Kansas craved.

Max Boomer, for the past six years, was Intracoastal Yacht Brokers' number one sales representative, bringing in more revenue than all the other sales people combined. Max had the gift of gab and customers loved when he put on a show, it was as if the circus was back in town, and Max was the master of ceremonies. Max was always ready to deliver, a boat, a yacht, a joke, or a story. He never ran out of material and most of all, never needed coaxing as long as a customer plucked down cash, which they invariably did. Six 'Salesperson of the Year' plaques were prominently displayed behind his desk for the world to see. They extolled Max Boomer's sales genius and always a convenient topic for Mr. Boomer; they bolstered his ego daily and verified his narcissism.

All his life, Max pushed the envelope to the "Max." His jokes were brash, his pranks outrageous, his laugh contagious, but his antics were never malicious. Max just wanted to have fun with people; it didn't matter who you were rich, poor, white, black, or green, Max was an equal opportunity offender. He didn't care who he pranked as long as he could be the center of attraction and weave his stories.

Max's crowning moment in storytelling was ten years ago when he called his friend, David Crane, a wild and crazy DJ from radio station 107 in Florida and convinced him to pull an Elvis Presley birthday prank on his wife Belinda-Jo.

Belinda-Jo was an Elvis Presley fanatic. All her life she collected Elvis memorabilia, records, posters, movies, commemorative stamps, magazines, statues, jewelry. Anything remotely associated with Elvis Presley, she purchased. Belinda-Jo transformed an entire bedroom into a shrine to "The King," all of her Elvis possessions hung from or filled every wall, table, shelf and every inch of floor space available. Two narrow paths wound along the sides of the room, permitted visitors to view her Elvis exhibit. Standing in the center of the room was a life-size, cardboard mannequin of The King, Belinda-Jo purchased at the 2002 Elvis convention and swap meet held at the Municipal Auditorium in Sarasota. Dressed in a powder blue jumpsuit, covered in glittering rhinestones that Belinda-Jo glued on herself, guitar slung down below his hips, the poster directed visitors to the main attraction and Belinda-Jo's most cherished possession, a silk, cherry-red scarf hanging from *The King's* neck she purchased on E-bay for $3,000.00. She even convinced Max to marry her in the Elvis Presley Chapel in Las Vegas. Not the proudest moment in Max Boomer's life, on a scale of one to ten, maybe a four, but if it made Belinda-Jo Boomer happy, it made Max very happy.

For Belinda-Jo's thirtieth birthday, Max bought two round-trip first-class plane tickets, two-night accommodations at the Heartbreak Hotel, three VIP day passes to Graceland that included tours of the mansion, grave site, stables, automobile museum and a private tour of Elvis' two jet airplanes, for Belinda-Jo and her girlfriend Marlee, another Elvis Presley maniac.

The trip was an experience of a lifetime for Belinda-Jo and her girlfriend, but quickly turned into an unbearable nightmare for Max. From the moment Belinda-Jo's feet touched the ground at Sarasota's International Airport and for the next three days, Max endured hours of Elvis Presley minutia. Pictures, personal videos of Belinda-Jo and Marlee on the airplane, on the ground, in the terminal, getting their luggage, in the hotel, at Graceland, the jungle room, the bedrooms, the cemetery, the cars, and of course the famous room of Elvis' Show Costumes, all catalogued with particulars, enumerations and narratives only an Elvis fanatic could appreciate, let alone understand.

On the third day, the day of her return and a day before Belinda-Jo's actual birthday, Max reached his saturation point of Elvis Presley trivia. She had finally worn him down. With his car keys in hand, Max was ready to drive to Tampa, park at the top of the Skyway Bridge and jump, but as fate would have it, a last minute reprieve altered Max's appreciation for Elvis Presley.

"I have a surprise for you Max," Belinda-Jo cooed and held out her hand. Belinda-Jo's final surprise was a small leather pouch filled with white, stone pebbles. "I took these from a path behind a Graceland walkway, I'm sure Elvis walked on them, aren't they beautiful?" This revelation set in motion his greatest prank of all times, an Elvis birthday phone prank for Belinda-Jo.

Taking Max by the hand, Belinda-Jo dragged him into her beloved Elvis Presley room. There in the center of the room stood a large, wooden crate that for the past two days, Belinda-Jo meticulously decorated in red, white, and blue crepe paper strips. The Elvis poster stood on the crate's glass top where Belinda-Jo carefully poured out the pebbles around the King's white patent leather boots. After painstakingly arranging every single pebble, she reached along the side of the crate, flipped a switch and a blinding white light burst through the glass illuminating the pebbles and the Elvis poster.

"Awesome, I think the patriotic stand, the light and of course the Graceland pebbles complete the room. What do you think, honey?"

"Well Belinda-Jo, I don't know what to say, it's beyond belief." Max was speechless for when Belinda-Jo switched on the Elvis light, instantaneously, a switch turned on in Max's mind; an epiphany moment of monumental proportion, the hours of Elvis minutia finally became substantive. The stolen pebbles would act as the catalyst for his greatest prank of all time, an Elvis Presley birthday prank, and the birthday girl recipient would be his beloved Belinda-Jo.

That night Max phoned DJ David Crane and persuaded his friend to call Belinda-Jo at work tomorrow during his morning radio show with an outrageous birthday prank his listeners would never forget.

Initially, David identified himself as Chief of Security from Graceland and informed Belinda-Jo that his department had her on camera stealing stones from Graceland. That the police matched their photo of her stealing the stones to the picture of her taken at the gift shop, when she purchased a poster of Elvis Presley in the 1958 King Creole film, a Graceland Christmas ornament and an Elvis bobble head doll with her credit card. That the theft of the stones, petit larceny, violated Tennessee criminal code # 45621, removal of property from a historic location, and if convicted, was punishable by up to six months in jail and /or a fine of $1,000.00. David ended the charade with a passionate plea:

"My department would be willing to drop all charges, if you mail back the stones today; if you refuse, this office would have no choice but to issue a warrant for your arrest and extradite you back to Tennessee for trial."

Belinda-Jo's initial reaction was that it had to be an office prank, but after glancing around the room and not seeing anyone on the phone, her demeanor rapidly deteriorated into panic. Sobbing uncontrollably, she promised to go home during her lunch hour, collect all the stones and mail them back immediately. Crane, a master at weaving the unexpected into a story, wasn't ready to let Belinda-Jo off the hook, so to add additional credence to the prank he instructed her to call her friend Marlee and inform her, she too needed to mail back her stolen stones. A task, in-between dabbing her tear-soaked eyes and blowing her nose, Belinda-Jo woefully accepted.

The entire prank aired for approximately five minutes and after David gave her the address of Graceland, he said, "Belinda-Jo before I hang up, there's one more thing; Max wanted me to wish you a happy birthday, I'm not really Chief of Security at Graceland, but David Crane morning DJ from radio station 107. I want to thank you for being such a good sport and happy birthday from all of us at 107 and your friends at the office."

There was a moment of radio silence, then earsplitting screams of profanity, which Crane frantically blocked, and then a chorus of happy birthday orchestrated by a smiling Max Boomer waving a dozen red roses in the air as he directed the office choir. Belinda-Jo could not believe how easily they suckered her into the prank, but her reward for being such a good sport and to celebrate her birthday, the radio station emailed her two tickets to see a play at the Venice Theatre and dinner at Luna's Ristorante.

"The story Mr. Boomer told happened last week. Do you remember the big windstorm we had, the one that blew our hats across the parking lot while we were enjoying our vanilla and orange ice cream cones at Nokomis Groves? That same day, a big Australian pine that stood along Mr. Boomer's driveway blew down and blocked the entrance to his property. The tree was gigantic, over forty feet tall."

"What did Mr. Boomer do?" Brooke asked.

"He had to cut it up and remove it from his driveway because that evening, Mrs. Boomer invited all of her friends from school for a Christmas party, about thirty teachers. But that wasn't the problem." In mid-sentence, a white Crown Victoria raced down the road past the ice cream truck and disappeared around the bend in a blinding cloud of gray-white dust. "What's that guy's problem? Where's the fire, mister?" Blaine screamed out the window only to choke on a mouthful of road dust that enveloped the ice cream truck.

"So what was Mr. Boomer's problem, Mommy?" Brooke questioned with a skeptical glance, "Didn't he have a saw?"

"He had a saw, but he didn't have a place on his property to store all the cut up logs, plus it would take days to drive to the landfill with all that wood," Blaine answered with a short laugh.

"Okay, I give up," snapped Brooke with an irritated smirk on her face.

"Well, honey, first you have to know Mr. Boomer likes to play jokes on people, not mean jokes, funny ones. So he decided to play a prank on Mrs. Boomer's friends that came to the party and get rid of the logs at the same time."

"So, what did he do?" Brooke blurted out now eager for the answer.

"Remember last week, you brought home from Sunday school a beautiful drawing of a Yule log you colored in class. You told me how people, long ago in England, during the Christmas season burned the Yule log in their fireplace and that it brought families good luck. So on his computer, Mr. Boomer printed out a Yule log holiday card from the Boomer family. Unlike your picture of a big log burning brightly in a fireplace, and a beautifully decorated Christmas tree, Mr. Boomer had Santa in a bathing suit, at the beach sitting in a chaise lounge next to a beach fire that had an enormous log sticking out of a fire pit. Over the picture he printed in big, bold green and red letters:

THE ENGLEWOOD YULE LOG
SEASON'S GREETINGS FROM THE BOOMERS

"So how did he get rid of the logs," Brooke snapped angrily just as a police car sped past them kicking up clouds of dust from the sand and shell road as it skidded around the corner.

"First, Mr. Boomer cut off all the branches from the Australian pine leaving a perfectly straight tree-trunk, then he cut twenty-eight 24-inch logs, sandpapered both ends of the log smooth, tied a red ribbon bow in the center of each log, stapled the Englewood Yule card to the bow, and placed one log in each of the guests' trunk."

"What a nice way to get rid of all the logs, don't you think Mommy?"

"I think I would say, creative, my dear Brooke. Incredibly only one teacher complained, made Mr. Boomer drive to her condominium at Summer Green, clean out her trunk and take back the log. She informed Mr. Boomer that she didn't have a fireplace to burn his holiday log and the aroma of pine nauseated her. Only one log returned, not bad considering he gave away twenty-six in one night." Blaine laughed and gave Brooke a big hug.

"I thought he cut twenty-eight logs?

Blaine took a deep breath, "He did, but not to have her feel left out, Mr. Boomer put a log in Mrs. Boomer's car, so when she drove to Publix the next morning and opened her trunk, *voila~* the Englewood Yule Log. That's why only twenty-six logs were given away. Not to be outdone, Mrs. Boomer put the log in a box, wrapped it in red Christmas paper with green pine trees, tied a big red bow in the middle, attached an Elvis Christmas sticker addressed to Max and placed the present under the tree. Christmas morning they both had a good laugh when Max opened his Yule log."

"Well, Brooke, story hour is over, time to sell some ice cream," Blaine added as she flipped on the lights and music. No sooner had the truck touched the pavement than a Sarasota Sherriff's patrol car raced past them, narrowly missing the blinking caution sign that automatically flipped opened when the lights went on.

"What on earth is going on, has everyone gone mad?" Blaine shouted as she slammed on the brakes jerking the truck to an abrupt stop. All of the items Brooke neatly organized that morning, paper products, bags of potato chips, pretzels, peanuts, boxes of candy, ice cream cones, anything not nailed down, tumbled to the floor.

"Good thing we had our seat belts on Mommy or we'd be on the floor rolling around with the gum balls and lollipops." They both laughed as Blaine eased the truck, now on the cracked shell and dirt road, slowly left into the curve. Their joy was short-lived. Four deafening explosions boomed beyond the bend in the road.

Chapter Fifty-Five

Blue Heron Court was a relatively short block with only six homes on one side of the road and a larger, much older, run-down house at the end of the cul-de-sac. On the left side, a state preserve bordered the neighborhood providing a safe habitat for the gopher tortoise, Florida mouse, indigo snake and other threatened species and acres of undeveloped privacy for its residents. After the two newly-constructed Courtyard Homes, the black-top pavement on Blue Heron Court ended and the original cracked shell and dirt road curved left and continued to the end of the cul-de-sac.

Unlike the other well-maintained homes on the block, Earl Neigh's house, like the dirt road, appeared dusty and worn-out. The small patch of lawn out front, brown and in dire need of water only added to the home's depressed appearance. The original royal blue paint had long since faded to a chalky pale blue hue. The white-tiled roof that once proudly glistened in the scorching Florida sun was now chipped, broken and covered in dark stains. Each day Blaine parked in front of the fifth house and sold ice cream.

Midway into the turn four deafening explosions, one right after the other, pierced the air. Startled, Blaine eased up on the gas, brought the truck to a crawl and cautiously completed the turn. Staring down the road what Blaine feared most was occurring right before her eyes.

Yellow caution tape flapped and twisted in the wind. Blaine no longer heard the whispering of the pines, only the constant snap of the police tape that blocked access to the cul-de-sac and the old house. An armada of Sheriff's cars, Venice police cars, SWAT trucks, CSI vans and unmarked police vehicles parked in a jig saw arrangement around the last house.

Gray smoke rose from the collapsed stockade fence that lay on the ground in pieces as an army of SWAT personnel dressed in black riot gear charged up the weather-beaten wooden stairs carrying riot shields, rifles and a battering ram. In one swift movement, they shattered the front door, stormed through the splintered entrance and eight SWAT officers disappeared into the house. Throughout the action, tucked strategically between a stand of Australian pines, Bryce Faceman from Channel 6 News broadcasted.

Slowly, Blaine eased the truck to the curb in front of Earl's house, where most of the neighbors gathered to watch the police operation unfold. She turned off the engine, switched off the music and outside lights and stepped out of the truck, she had a feeling not many people would be in the mood for ice cream.

"Blaine, you're not going to believe what happened," Max Boomer shouted. Exhausted he collapsed against the truck out of breath after running over so he would be the first to give her the news. "All morning the police hostage negotiation team talked to the guy in the house at the end of the cul-de-sac, but he wouldn't come out."

"What were the four explosions I just heard?" Blaine asked keeping her eyes glued to the old house.

"I guess negotiations stalled, so the cops blew down the fence and rushed the house. It appeared the police received a tip that a person on Blue Heron Court abducted two boys. When detectives arrived to investigate the allegations, they noticed a green pick-up truck in the back garage that matched the description of a vehicle seen speeding away from the scene of the kidnapping. They ran the truck's plates, which confirmed it belonged to the owner of the house and here they are."

"So what are the police doing now?" Blaine asked still staring at the house.

Catching his breath, Max looked down the block and replied, "The SWAT team is still in the house." Turning back to Blaine in a muted voice, he continued, "I thought he only had one kid all these years, a son Bobby, three years and no one had a clue Bobby was kidnapped. He played with my daughter, rode his bike around the neighborhood, not one word about the abduction. . .If only I noticed something, anything, that might have saved Bobby sooner."

"Don't blame yourself Max, that's how kidnappers operate; they terrorize their victim to such a degree that it would be unthinkable for a child to confide in anyone. I would suspect no one on Blue Heron Court knew what was going on in that house either. He picked this block, quiet, small, secluded, and best of all, very little interaction amongst the neighbors and their children, that is, until I arrived with my ice cream truck." Blaine added with a faint smile.

"And Bobby's supposed father, Devin Kirkland, if that's his real name, never caused any trouble. He was polite, minded his own business, and went to work every day leaving his son home alone. I assumed Bobby was home-schooled." Max stared down at the ground and kicked at the shells until a small hole formed. Still staring down he asked in a whisper, "Why didn't the kid leave? He wasn't locked in a closet, or chained to a wall. You saw him; he bought ice cream almost every day, so why didn't he just leave? It doesn't make sense."

Blaine turned to Max, "You answered your own question, Max, he is a child and like the small hole you dug, Bobby's fear of retribution was so overwhelming it made it impossible for him to climb out of his hole, the fear of the unknown was too frightening. I had an uneasy feeling about Bobby, something in his eyes cried out for help; so I notified the police and the television station."

"What are you saying, Blaine, you brought the cops here, you sell ice cream on this block for two weeks and figure out that Bobby had been kidnapped? How was that possible? Are you some kind of psychic?" Max growled and reverted to his old pushy self.

"I'm not a psychic, Max and clearly not a very good ice cream vendor; I'm a park ranger and trained to identify signs of child abuse and required by law to report any such abuse. At the academy, I completed programs to identify manifestations of child abuse. It became second nature to analyze visual signs and subtle nuances and then create a profile. Something else that triggered my concern for Bobby's safety, something your daughter told Brooke. Honey, tell Mr. Boomer what Jillian told you the other day."

"She said Bobby told her that he was getting a new brother, maybe next week."

"That didn't make sense; you don't maybe get a sibling next week and when the Amber Alert broadcasted information about a green pick up and another abduction, it all made sense." Blaine added and gave Brooke a hug. "That's when I called the police and local television station."

"I can just imagine what my profile looks like," Max mumbled and looked down.

Chapter Fifty-Six

Blaine did not answer; she did indeed develop a profile of Max Boomer and was certain he would not enjoy hearing what she had to say, but that wasn't the image flooding back in her mind. It was what she said about interpreting certain nuances, *'words not spoken compared to the phrases uttered.'* Why she was still haunted after all these years? As much as she tried to push them out of her mind, the terrifying memories remained.

It was a sweltering August morning. By eight o'clock, the thermometer on the side of the ranger station registered 87 degrees and climbing, an unmistakable sign that the day was going to be a scorcher. The humidity was almost at saturation level and moisture from the night air still clung to the leaves of the old oaks that shaded the road and gate office. The sky was clear, not a single cloud to block the sun's bright glare or oppressive heat and the usual morning breeze was nowhere in sight, making for a painfully hot start to the day.

Blaine had morning gate duty and was first to welcome Mr. and Mrs. Owen Cornfield and their ten-year-old daughter Lizzie to the park. They didn't have a campsite reservation, but that wasn't a problem, because during the summer, the park was never full; except for the Fourth of July when all the crazies arrived with box loads of fireworks and booze.

The first red flag Blaine observed was the Cornfield's old beat-up truck with a torn blue tarp that partially covered four metal drums, boxes marked farm and bags of plastic 2-liter soda bottles crammed into the open back bed, pulling a brand new Airstream camper. Why spend all that money on a new camper only to drive an old rusted out truck ready to break down before they reached the campsite? It did not make sense and if it didn't make sense, then there must be a problem, Blaine thought.

The second alarm on Blaine's list, a boa constrictor curled up on the dashboard. In her three years at the park, Blaine had never seen, nor had she heard from any of the rangers, of a visitor that drove around with a snake in his vehicle. Blaine attempted to make light of the situation and remarked, "All pets needed to be leashed or confined, sir, and well behaved at all times." Mr. Cornfield didn't grasp or acknowledge the humor; he said it was a pet and continued to complete the registration form.

The third and most disturbing warning was his tattoo: a black dotted line around his neck with the words 'CUT HERE' printed below the line on the left side of his neck. Blaine cringed at the macabre message the two words proclaimed and questioned what would possess a rational human being to tattoo something like that on his body. There was only one answer and Blaine already filled in the dotted lines.

Mr. Cornfield spent an unusually long time looking at the campground map and finally selected a remote site at the far end of the campground. As they pulled away, Blaine wrote down the truck and camper's license plate numbers placed them in the campground folder along with Cornfield's registration form, photocopy of his driver's license, the 14-day campsite receipt (paid in cash) and a note to call DMV to check on the vehicles; not standard procedure, just a feeling. She also made a mental note to check on the family after they set up their campsite: standard park courtesy protocol.

The next morning during her rounds, Blaine spotted Lizzie building a sand castle along the edge of the lake behind the Nature Center. Her straight brown hair, uncombed and messy, fell to a dirty white collar on the same blue flowered dress she wore the previous day. Hunched over the half-completed structure, her pale, thin arms and tiny hands painstakingly sculpted one of the four minarets that rose from the wall that surrounded the castle. However pitiful her appearance, it was Lizzie's eyes that tore at your heart and pulled you to her. The sadness stared not at you but beyond, somewhere distant, maybe to a far off place safe and nurturing.

"What a nice sand castle," Blaine called out and sat down next to the little girl. They talked about the castle for a while; Blaine complimented her on a job well done, all along staring painfully into those sad wounded eyes. Blaine mentioned that she was on her way to enjoy a pancake breakfast at the Nature Center and asked if she would like to join her. Lizzie said that Owen and her mother were still asleep and that Owen warned her never to talk to strangers or he would beat her. Blaine controlled her anger and reminded her that she wasn't a stranger that they met yesterday when they checked in to the park. Lizzie smiled and they walked hand in hand up to the Nature Center.

Lizzie devoured two blueberry pancakes, two link sausages, and was about to finish a second glass of orange juice when Owen Cornfield stormed into the building screaming about obeying his rules. Startled, Lizzie's glass slipped from her hand, hit the edge of the table and splattered juice across her face and all over her dress. Paralyzed by fear, she was unable to wipe off the pulpy mess dripping down her face, or the puddles of juice that soaked her dress. Lizzie sat motionless, frozen to her chair, as Cornfield slammed his fist on the table and shouted into her face that she was never to leave the campsite. Blaine attempted to explain, but Cornfield would not listen, he grabbed the little girl by the arm and yanked her out of the chair. Instantaneously, Blaine stood, seized Cornfield's hand and bent it back to his wrist. Grimacing in pain, he released Lizzie and fell to his knees screaming that she broke his wrist. Blaine bent down and told him if he ever laid a finger on Lizzie, she would call the police and have him arrested for child abuse. He nodded and she released her grip.

The next day Blaine drove past Cornfield's campsite. The truck was gone and Blaine noticed Lizzie peering out a small side window. Her sad eyes stared beyond the thick, high plants that imprisoned the campsite; the same look of vulnerability cried out. Blaine made a quick U-turn, pulled the club car into the parking spot in front of the camper and knocked on the door.

The door slowly opened part way, Lizzie stuck her head out and in a frightened little voice muttered, "I'm not allowed to talk to you."

"Hi Lizzie I was driving by and just wanted to see how you were doing," Blaine answered in her cheery ranger voice, while attempting to look inside the camper. What little Blaine could see the place was a mess. Plastic soda bottles and containers littered the floor. The kitchen counter was filled with open boxes, plastic tubs and ripped packages of Sudafed and other cold medicine packages and a nauseating smell of sour milk permeated the camper.

"Why can't you talk to me, sweetie, did I do something wrong?" Blaine asked calmly, knowing the answer and trying very hard not to stare at the red bruise over her left eye.

"Because I have to stay inside and open all the boxes on the kitchen counter before Owen gets back," Lizzie answered shyly and closed the door part way.

"Okay sweetie I don't want to get you in trouble, but see the small, white sandy path along side the palm tree behind your fire pit. That path winds around the campsite to a large clearing filled with hundreds of blueberry bushes planted years ago when the park was a farm. Almost all of the blueberries are ripe just waiting for a little girl to pick some. Remember the delicious blueberries on our pancakes yesterday, well, all of the berries were from the same field. I bet your mother would love a small basket of fresh blueberries, they go great with vanilla ice cream," Blaine said cheerily as she reached into her knapsack and handed Lizzie a small wicker basket. Blaine walked to her club car and drove straight to her office.

Something was terribly wrong; Blaine's training told her that this little girl was in trouble; too many nuances of abuse or at the least neglect presented itself. A call to DMV confirmed her suspicion; the Airstream did not belong to Owen Cornfield, but to Mr. Ronald Elliot of 5 Narwood Court, Merrick, Florida. Elliot's home answering machine had a recording that the family was vacationing for two weeks, in their new camper, at the Myakka State Park Campgrounds. Blaine phoned the Myakka's park manager, Dawn Woods, a close friend, to confirm that the Elliot's were camping at the park. Woods confirmed that the Elliots were camping at the Big Flats Campground; however, yesterday the Park Police arrested Mr. Elliot for running up and down the canopy walkway like a crazy man naked. Mr. Elliot underwent drug testing and tested positive for methamphetamine, but the weird part was his wife, ten-year-old daughter, and their Airstream camper were missing from the campsite, vanished!

Blaine almost exploded! "They're here," she shouted into the phone. "I knew something was terribly wrong when Cornfield registered at our park two days ago. I have to call the Park Police; I'll get back to you later. Thanks for your help, Dawn."

Blaine and the Park Police arrived back at the campsite just as Cornfield and Lizzie's mother drove onto the site. Cornfield, carrying two bags of groceries, acted agitated and was in a big hurry to get inside the camper. The officer drew his gun, ordered Cornfield to stop, get down on the ground and put his hands behind his back. Handcuffed, informed of his rights and placed in a police car, Cornfield sat arrested for stealing the Elliot's camper. Suddenly, Lizzie's mother shouted that Cornfield drugged her husband and forced the two of them to help him make drugs in her camper.

Earlier that morning, after Blaine left the campsite, Lizzie's long hair gray cat Romeo, while chasing a small gecko around the kitchen and out the screen door Lizzie left ajar, tipped over a can of Coleman lantern fluid that set in motion a chain of events of catastrophic proportion. The fluid spilled out along the kitchen counter soaking a bag of drain cleaner which dripped into an open plastic tray of battery acid; that deadly combination and four portable propane burners sitting on the counter, ignited a firestorm of toxic chemicals Cornfield assembled to produce methamphetamine. The explosion blew out all the windows, doors and the sunroof above the kitchen stove, within minutes the walls and ceiling inside the camper were completely engulfed in flames. Angry red and orange flames clawed their way out every opening and raced up the sides onto the roof until the silver camper was a massive red ball of fire.

Thick sooty black smoke poured out of the Airstream's sunroof and blanketed the campsite with a sickening aroma of sour milk. Shrouded in black smoke, faint shadows of trees, shrubs, and plants beyond the perimeter created an almost surrealistic snapshot of the campsite against the rest of the park. However, with each labored breath a choking sensation and a burning in the eyes brought every one back to the reality that a raging fire raced out of control before them.

"Oh my god, Lizzie is in the camper," Mrs. Elliot screamed and raced towards the fire. Instinctively, Blaine reached out and pulled her back, even at twenty feet, the intense heat from the fire burned at the skin making it impossible for anyone to get any closer. Shaking hysterically, she cried in Blaine's arms until the fire department arrived and placed her in one of their trucks.

Standing just beyond the reaches of smoke was the outline of a tiny figure surrounded by palmetto and scrub oak. With Romeo rubbing against her legs and holding a small wicker basket of blueberries, a terrified little girl stepped out from the chalky gray haze of the fire and walked onto the campsite. Flames from the burnt out camper smoldered and grayish black smoke spiraled up through the canopy as firefighters and park rangers tirelessly dug a trench around the perimeter to contain the last of the burning ambers.

Blaine was the first to recognize the frightened little girl tentatively moving through the curtain of smoke, she raced over, scooped her up and sprinted back to the fire truck.

"You picked the blueberries, Lizzie," Blaine cried out as tears of joy rolled down her checks. "Let's show Mommy how many blueberries you picked."

On that hot August day, Blaine reflected, *a mother and child were reunited; tragedy thwarted, they embraced and held tight a treasured moment, but the stark realization that a much different outcome could have easily transpired, frightened her. The same haunting ache that pushed against her at the campsite reappeared and she questioned whether the scenario playing out on this sleepy little cul-de-sac in Englewood would conclude with a joyful reunion of two boys and their mothers or would tragedy trump a cheerful culmination for Bobby and his new brother?*

Blaine was pulled back to reality when Max shouted, "Look, something is going on at the house, I see a lot of movement!"

A crush of black-helmeted SWAT officers streamed out of the splintered doorway and marched down the stairs in perfect unison. Two officers carrying gray crowd control shields led the precession, followed by two officers holding AK-47 assault rifles. Sandwiched between two burly officers, two blond heads bobbed from side to side as the formation advanced down the stairs and finally one SWAT officer carrying a shotgun protected their backs as the entourage disappeared through the open doors of the first SWAT vehicle.

It wasn't planned or orchestrated by any one person, only a spontaneous outburst of raw emotion that took hold of an entire community. Max and his daughter were first to clap, then Blaine and

Brooke, next a group of teenagers, followed by the twins Julia and Melissa, Mr. and Mrs. Peterson, then finally the doctor, and his wife. The crowd erupted in jubilant applause; the boys were finally safe. The rejoicing echoed down the block, everyone was in high spirits, clapping, yelling, and giving each other high-fives, but the celebration was short lived; a single shotgun blast blew out the middle, second floor window and sent everyone scrambling for safety. Blaine pulled Brooke into the truck and slammed the door shut as people raced back towards their homes. Shards of glass rained down onto the porch roof sparkling like ice crystals in the morning sun. Suddenly, a SWAT officer and Kirkland burst through the splintered window and crashed down onto the roof. A second shotgun blast rang out and shattered the communications antenna on top of the SWAT truck as the two grappled for control of the weapon. The men rolled off the roof and fell to the ground where a troop of black clad officers subdued Kirkland and dragged him to the nearest patrol car. It was over.

Chapter Fifty-Seven

Blaine leaned against her seat, peeled back the paper on two ice cream sandwiches, handed one to Brooke, and took a big bite of hers. A cold, creamy ice cream sandwich was exactly what they needed, a piece of comfort food to soothe all the troubles of the day away. They smiled and watched the parade of law enforcement personnel remove boxes of evidence from the house while a CSI technician photographed the exterior, surrounding properties and garage oblivious to Bryce Faceman who broadcasted from his perch between the pines. Blaine grinned and thought, *Faceman finally got his big story and two boys are now safe.*

"Mommy, what are those policemen doing?" Brooke asked wiping vanilla ice cream from the corner of her mouth.

Blaine turned to Brooke and answered slowly, "They're collecting evidence that will put the man who kidnapped Bobby and the other boy in jail."

"Will he get out of jail and try to kidnap me, Mommy?"

Blaine reached over, held Brooke in her arms and whispered, "No sweetie, that man will never hurt another child again, I promise."

From the corner of her eye, Blaine noticed Earl Neigh's side door open and a skinny, brown haired man in his early twenties, with a small goatee sprouting from his chin and an eagle tattoo on his right forearm move down the metal handicapped ramp on a motorized wheel chair and turn towards the ice cream truck. A cast up to his thigh on his right leg rested on the stirrup and extended forward, his left arm in a cast above the elbow rested in an American flag sling across his chest and a thick, white, surgical collar around his neck supported his head in what appeared to be a very uncomfortable fit.

"Mommy, a man in a wheelchair is banging on the truck. He looks angry, his face is all red," Brooke shouted looking out the serving window.

"Maybe he wants some ice cream," Blaine replied and moved towards the window. "How can I help you sir?"

"How can you help me? Don't you think you fucking helped me enough lady," Earl shouted up at Blaine. "Just look at me, my leg is broken, my arm is fractured in five places and I can't turn my neck, all because of you and your fucking music. Every day your loud music woke me up, I could not get any sleep, I was fucking exhausted and two nights ago, I fell asleep at the wheel and drove my car into the fucking Intracoastal. No barricades, not even a fence at the end of the road; just a fucking curb and then water. The next thing I remembered; I woke up in the fucking hospital like this. I lost my job, my car and today I lost my girlfriend because she didn't want to care for an invalid, all because of you and your fucking ice cream music."

So this was Earl Neigh, *the newspaper guy*, who wanted a Christmas present, doesn't he know anything about making a good first impression, Blaine thought.

"I beg your pardon sir, but I have my daughter in here and don't appreciate the type of language you're using," Blaine snapped angrily and shut the window.

"You don't appreciate my language, well fuck you lady, you destroyed my life and I don't give a fuck what you think," Earl screamed up at the closed window and pounded on the truck.

"I think that's about enough Mr. Neigh, maybe you'll care about what I think," Justin Beale shouted as he walked up behind the wheelchair.

Surprised someone called him by name, Earl spun the wheelchair around to face his accuser and teach him a lesson in minding one's own business and as a bonus, maybe vent some of his anger upon this interloper. Unfortunately for Earl, standing in front of him wearing a police SWAT vest and holding out his detective's gold shield was Justin Beale and at six foot two, muscular and a police officer, Earl Neigh wasn't going to teach any one a lesson; in fact he was about to receive one himself.

"If you continue to scream profanities, I'll have one of my police officers issue you a summons for disorderly conduct, have you arrested and hauled off to jail, wheel chair and all. Understand."

Meekly, Earl answered, "Yes sir, I understand."

"Apologize to the lady and her daughter and then return to your house before I change my mind and call over an officer right now," Beale demanded reaching for his cell phone.

Earl sheepishly uttered, "I'm sorry," turned and hastily motored back home.

"Hi Blaine, Brooke, you two alright," Beale called out and tapped on the closed window. "Just happened to be in the neighborhood and thought I'd stop by and buy a pistachio ice cream cone with chocolate sprinkles."

Blaine slid the window open, "We're fine, thank you Detective Beale, I'll be right out. Just in the neighborhood, I don't think so detective; no doubt you were involved with the kidnapping operation at the end of cul-de-sac."

"Guilty on both counts, Madame," Beale answered and raised his hands in surrender. "Actually, Bobby. . .Tyler Corrigan asked me if I would pick up two ice cream sundaes for him and Shawn so they would at least have a little something to eat before they left for Sarasota. They're starving."

"So his name wasn't Bobby after all, it was Tyler. All this time the poor boy wasn't even allowed to hear his own name, how depraved," Blaine sighed as a wave of emotions swelled up inside and washed over her in a cold sweat. She looked away as a single tear feel to the ground.

Beale was not just in the neighborhood, he was part of a special operation, code name "Round-up," a year-long investigation into human trafficking, child abduction, and the distribution of child pornography in Southwest Florida. A combined task force of federal, state, and local law enforcement agents under the alliance with the National Center for Missing and Exploited Children and the Attorney General's Cyber Crime Unit, finally obtained the evidence necessary to arrest "Mister Big," the head and the higher echelon operatives within the organization. All the phone and credit card records, personal surveillance photos, emails between Arthur Dunn, Devin Kirkland, and the Thailand travel agency connections weren't enough evidence to close down the operation. The final piece to the puzzle and the evidence authorities desperately needed, that ultimately led straight to the doorstep of "Mister Big" on Longboat Key, was the Patek Philippe watch he purchased for Arthur Dunn with a credit card at a St. Armand's Circle store. And who did Beale have to thank, Blaine Sterling.

"That's right," Beale said, "Bobby's real name is Tyler Corrigan from Punta Gorda and Shawn Dean is from Ocala, both twelve with similar physical characteristics, size, hair, blue eyes, complexion, and at first glance, placed side by side there was a striking resemblance, they could have been mistaken for brothers. Maybe that is what Kirkland needed, a pair to deliver. All I can say is that they are safe and shortly will be reunited with their families."

Blaine smiled and was comforted to hear that the frightened little boy that hid behind lace curtains those first days and loved ice cream sundaes with extra chocolate syrup was out of danger. That the monster who robbed innocence, Devin Kirkland, handcuffed and soon to be incarcerated for a very long time, would never hurt another child again. However, Blaine's joy was tempered by the memory of the night eight years ago when her innocence was stolen; she trembled at the thought that after three years of torment, what nightmares Bobby would relive. Her only solace rested in her promise to be in control of her own destiny and to challenge abuse on every level.

"Oh, I have one other thing," Beale added, but before he could finish the sentence his phone rang, "Excuse me Blaine, but I have to take this. . .Beale." He stepped away from the truck, all the while shaking his head in agreement or responding with yes or *that was great news*.

Beale closed his phone and walked back to Blaine, "That was my partner, they just arrested the head honcho of the child trafficking organization at his mansion on Longboat Key and he is singing like a caged canary. He admitted running the enterprise, identified all the people involved, including the Thailand cartel and finally turned over the location and numbers of all the offshore accounts. No doubt, the feds made a deal for his cooperation, but if it was not for your information about the Patek Philippe watch, we would still be looking for *Mr. Big*. Thank you."

"You mean to tell me the CSI guys couldn't find a trace of Dunn's watch, not even a small piece," scoffed Blaine.

"That's right, nothing was recovered, maybe one day the cleaning service will turn up something, but right now because of your information, case closed." Beale took out his notepad, wrote case closed and underlined closed, twice.

"Oh, one last thing, Hordowski said, I'll be on the six o'clock news tonight. The entire task force, along with the Attorney General will announce, from the steps of the Federal Courthouse in Tallahassee, the arrests and shutdown of a major child trafficking organization in Southwest Florida. Maybe, you should tune it in? Plus, the feds have a plane at the Sarasota Airport to fly everyone to the news conference, so I have to run."

"Maybe I will, good luck, Detective Beale."

Brooke leaned out the window with two large, double scoop, with extra chocolate fudge syrup ice cream sundaes and shouted, "Here's your ice cream Detective Beale, please say good-bye to the boys for me."

"I guess that's my call to leave, thanks again, Blaine." Beale walked over to the window, slapped a ten-dollar bill on the counter, took the ice cream, and walked away.

"Hey what about your pistachio ice cream cone," Brooke yelled out holding a green dripping mess in her right hand and hand full of bills in the left. "Detective Beale, your change, you forgot your change?"

"I only have two hands, keep the change. I have to run, the ice cream is melting, bye," and disappeared behind the Channel 6 van that pulled onto the road. As the van approached the ice cream truck, Faceman leaned out the window and shouted, "Thanks for the tip IC lady. Call me if you need a favor, you have my number: 322-3626."

"Well sweetie I think it's time for us to leave, I need to return the truck to Mr. Lilly and we have to get ready for our day at the beach tomorrow. Did I mention Miss Maiello and her niece, Morgan, she's about your age, will meet us at the beach?" Blaine said and stopped in mid-sentence as a caravan of police cars, vans and trucks rolled down the street and disappeared beyond the pines. In the last unmarked police car, Bobby pressed his face against the window, ice cream all over his face, he smiled and waved good-bye. His eyes were bright and alive. Tyler Corrigan was going home.

"Mommy, this has been the best winter vacation ever," Brooke chirped and buckled her seat belt. "Can I turn the music on one last time?"

"It's not over yet honey, don't forget our beach picnic tomorrow," Blaine sang out and whistled as they passed under the Australian pines, with *Turkey in the Straw* blasting away.

Chapter Fifty-Eight

It stormed all night; a pounding, heavy rain mercilessly beat against the bedroom windows and woke Blaine from an uneasy sleep. Shadows from a darker time crept along the ceiling after each crack of thunder and flash of lightning, as their veiled outlines unlocked the wounds hidden deep within her. It was during the rains that scars from the rape reopened and exposed how fragile life was, but at the same time, the rains strengthened her resolve to be in control of her own fate. Unable to sleep Blaine turned on the side lamp, took out her notepad and jotted down what she needed for the picnic. Turkey sandwiches, peanut butter jelly sandwiches, pickles, chips, fruit, chocolate chip cookies, juice boxes, water, napkins, cups, plates, ice, chairs, umbrella, towels, sunscreen, camera, sand toys, Florida snow shovels, Kindle, and finally in capital letters, HAVE A GOOD TIME, filled four pages. The only pleasure she could embrace from the night was the hope that the storm would rain itself out and morning would bring a bright, sunny day for a perfect beach picnic. With that thought, she turned off the light, lay back on her pillow and closed her eyes.

Chapter Fifty-Nine

"Don't forget a hat sweetie and can you get the beach umbrella from the garage, I think we're ready to go, let me check my list." Blaine quickly glanced down at all the check marks, only HAVE A GOOD TIME remained; she underlined it twice and smiled. At last, she pushed the umbrella through the back window and secured it to a bungee cord hanging from the back seat. "11:30 A.M. right on schedule, hop in."

Once over the bridge Blaine crept along Venice Avenue in second gear, mindful of tourist season, she stopped at all three crosswalks as pedestrians loaded down with packages scurried to the other side. At the light Blaine turned south onto Harbor Drive, a picture postcard roadway, with ancient oaks in the median, their huge limbs covered with long strands of Spanish moss. Grand Mediterranean style homes constructed in late 1920s by the Brotherhood of Locomotive Engineers lined one side of the road. Beach and cottage style homes, all attractive and meticulously kept, on the other side added a unique pleasure to the drive.

"Here we are, Mommy, Brohard Beach, look that white van up front is leaving, go for it," Brooke screamed. Two women pushing baby strollers turned and gave Brooke 'the children should be seen and not heard' look. Brooke, of course, did what any other seven year old would do; she stuck her tongue out at them.

"Our lucky day, Sweetie," Blaine said as she cruised into the empty parking spot and jammed on the brakes. The two women, just a few feet from the Mini Cooper, shook their heads and stomped up the boardwalk to the pavilion while Blaine and Brooke laughed hysterically. Together they unloaded all the beach stuff from the back seat, locked the car, and trudged off to the beach.

From the pavilion deck, Blaine and Brooke rested against the wooden railing and gazed down at the magnificent white sandy beach and aqua blue waters that quietly lapped at the shoreline leaving only a thin border of foam that bubbled down the beach for miles. A few feet from shore, small waves broke over a sand bar where swimmers walked in ankle-deep water searching for sharks teeth and colorful shells. A gentle breeze off the water helped cool Blaine and Brooke as they plodded along the hot sand loaded down with all their beach gear. Straight down from the pavilion, about three feet from the water's edge, Blaine spotted Marybeth and Morgan under a big red and green beach umbrella, relaxing in sand chairs, wearing matching yellow bikinis.

Marybeth looked stunning, straight brown hair that spilled over her shoulders revealed a slender figure of an athlete, well-toned, and healthy. Her yellow bikini, stretched perfectly against a golden tan that accented all the right parts and Blaine was convinced that in ten short years, Morgan would also look as lissome.

"Hello Marybeth and Morgan, we finally made it," Blaine called out just before they dropped all their belongings all over the blanket. "Good to see you both. I had no idea how heavy all this stuff was."

Marybeth stood, gave Blaine a big hug, introduced Morgan and then the four unloaded all of the new beach paraphernalia.

"Brooke let's make a sand castle!" Morgan called out, as she picked up the bag of shovels and pails, linked arms with Brooke and together they raced down to the water.

"Well they seem to be hitting it off," Blaine laughed and waved to the two of them digging furiously in the sand.

"The way they play together, someone would have thought they had known each other for years," Marybeth remarked. "I wanted them so much to like each other. I guess I don't have to worry about their friendship any longer."

"I love your bikini, where did you get it?" Blaine inquired with a tinge of envy in her quiet tone.

"Splash in Venice, I was driving by the store and a big sign in the window said, '70% OFF SALE,' I wanted to buy Morgan a new bathing suit; so I figured what the heck, 70%, I'll get one too. It's her first bikini, that's why we match," Marybeth added with an impish smile. "So how was your Christmas, what did you guys do over the vacation?"

"It's been the best vacation ever, if you omit the part when I was shot and delete the part where I was almost stabbed. A fantastic two week respite from work," giggled Blaine. "First we had an unbelievable Christmas Eve dinner at Lou Bravo's house, a gastronomic experience of never ending seafood—calamari, shrimp, lobster, pasta with clam sauce, stuffed clams, clams on the half-shell, bacon wrapped scallops, and stuffed flounder. Then as if anyone could eat another thing; there was dessert, a chocolate lover's delight, or a weight-watcher's nightmare, chocolate cakes, chocolate pies, chocolate pudding, chocolate brownies, chocolate ice cream, hot fudge sundaes, chocolate mousse and of course hot chocolate for the young at heart."

"After dessert we exchanged presents; Lou Bravo bought Brooke a pink MP3 player so she could listen to her own music, instead of the Country/Western I play constantly. He bought me a beautiful Tiffany sterling silver necklace with a fancy script letter 'b' charm that came in an elegant powder blue leather pouch; excessively expensive, I love it! Brooke gave him a cool, twisty clip-on book light she bought at her school's holiday fair. I gave him an autographed copy of *The Gatehouse* by Nelson DeMille; I bought it when the author had a book signing in Sarasota. Lou Bravo loves to read books that have a New York theme; I guess it reminds him of home. I told him he had better enjoy the book as I stood in line for two hours to get him a signed copy. We saw The *Christmas Carol* at the Venice Theatre, third year in a row and each year we enjoy the performance more and more. I guess you could say *The Christmas Carol* is now a family tradition. After the play, we walked across the street to Luna's, a charming Italian restaurant to end the evening with a sumptuous dinner. The food was out of this world, it was like eating a home cooked meal and the portions were huge, we had leftovers the next day. During dessert, which is on the house, if you tell your server that you attended the play, Brooke casually mentioned that maybe she would like to be in a play. I think I will enroll her in the summer acting program for children at the Venice theatre, let her get a taste of the acting bug and who knows maybe next year we can all go see the *Christmas Carol* and watch Brooke perform? We sold ice cream, from an ice cream truck everyday in Englewood, but that is another story for another day. What about you, how was your vacation?"

"It was amazing; I can't believe it's just about over, where does the time go? I had Christmas Eve dinner at my dad's house in Punta Gorda. Rocco has a great place right on a canal and at Christmas, the Maiello house turns into a winter wonderland. I don't know if the decorations were for the grandchildren to enjoy or my father, but every tree, shrub and square inch of lawn had inflatable, animated, or musical Christmas figures welcoming visitors. He even had a snow machine, blowing out fluffy white flakes of confetti as children walked up the path to the house. Snow in Florida, how cool was that for children to experience. Every year he added one new attraction, this year he placed a life-sized Santa Claus climbing down the chimney, with colorful lights twinkling around the presents in his bulging pack. Everything looked magical and for a moment, I was a child again standing in front of our Christmas tree in the early morning shadows, breathlessly waiting for my parents to wake so I could open my presents."

"We also had a seafood dinner, not as elaborate as yours, but delicious. My sister Allison brought shrimp scampi; Dawn, angel hair pasta with marinara sauce; Rocco prepared his famous antipasto salad; and I brought dessert, a homemade cheesecake from Publix. They have an awesome bakery. Everything was perfect."

Marybeth explained that Dawn started a new job as nurse practitioner for three hospitals and was only eligible for one week's vacation, so Morgan spent the last week of her vacation with her. They had a blast; went to the movies, bowling, miniature golf, and Marybeth's favorite attraction, the Crowley Estate Christmas Festival of Trees. The mansion was breathtaking it was an education on how the rich lived. First, the three of them had tea and scones in a beautiful wood paneled dining room that overlooked the well-manicured grounds and then a leisurely tour of the mansion. For Christmas, every room was decorated with a different Christmas theme, welcoming guests to enjoy the elaborate decorations and cast a vote on their favorite room. Marybeth and Madison voted for the Christmas room from the fifties. A majestic live twelve-foot tree decorated with big red, green, blue, yellow, and white old fashion light bulbs, bubble lights and strands and strands of silver tinsel that dripped down from all the branches stood in the center of the room. An old black Lionel train with four passenger cars and a red caboose circled the tree passing beautifully wrapped presents for some good little boy or girl. A Howdy Doody puppet rested on top of an old black and white television set that played *A White Christmas*, a small blue bicycle, red wagon, and a Flexible Flyer sled rested in front a crackling fire.

Marybeth leaned back in her chair, took a long, slow drink from her water bottle and in an exasperated voice said, "I'm exhausted; raising a child is hard work."

With a sympathetic grin, Blaine answered, "You're preaching to the choir girl, I know it's hard, I live it every day, but the love you receive in return is priceless. But anyway, all this talk about food is making me hungry, let's eat, I'm starving."

Chapter Sixty

Together they set out lunch and then walked down to the water where the girls were putting the final additions on their castle. Almost completed, the castle needed a moat, so the four of them dug a trench around the castle to protect the structure from the pounding waves, well *the ripples* that barely reached the front door of the castle.

"Smile, let me take a picture of you two next to your first sandcastle," Marybeth called pulling out her camera. "Say cheese, one more for good luck. Okay, now let's have lunch."

Lunch was fantastic. Everyone talked and laughed and both girls ate everything in record time and didn't complain once. Marybeth took plenty of pictures and after lunch, the girls raced down to the water with their Florida snow shovels to look for sharks' teeth. It was turning out to be a perfect day.

Blaine was putting away the leftover food when Brooke ran up to the blanket shouting that she found something in water. Out of breath, she knelt down on the blanket, reached into the metal basket of the Florida snow shovel, pulled out a handful of sand and what appeared to be a weathered silver coin.

"What is it Mommy? It looks an old coin. Is it valuable?" Brooke cried out and handed it to her mother.

"I don't know, sweetie. It looks like a quarter, but I don't see any monetary markings that say how much it's worth, just letters and a drawing on one side. I'll hold on to it, why don't you go back with Morgan and try to find some sharks teeth." Blaine ordered and feverishly began to remove the sand from the coin.

"What's wrong? Blaine, you look like you've just seen a ghost?"

"I have! This medallion belonged to my husband. He threw it off the Venice Fishing Pier for good luck the night we met eight years ago. I'm sure it's the same one, he scratched a line under the 'WE OUR ONE,' before he kissed me and threw it into the water," Blaine uttered and dropped the silver medallion into Marybeth's hand.

About the size and weight of a quarter and worn smooth in places from years of pounding by the surf and sand, the coin felt like a seasoned piece of sea glass. Around the circumference of one side, Marybeth made out the name Trace Foundation and in the center she traced with her finger the outline of two hands, one small, and one large locked together at the fingertips, both inscriptions were barely visible. On the reverse side, in the center of the medallion, inscribed in block letters: **'WE OUR ONE'** and a scratch mark. Marybeth had never heard of the Trace Foundation or the grammatical significance of *our* in the inscription '**WE OUR ONE**.' She took out her smartphone and Googled Trace Foundation.

A watershed of emotions flowed from Blaine's lips, not as the hysterical babbling of a grieving wife, but in a rational tone of years of pain and unbelievable sorrow. It was startling how one object could unlock old wounds of sorrow and loneliness hidden away, too agonizing to voice out, but now flooded back as if it were yesterday. For eight long years Blaine kept busy with work, raising Brooke, attending school functions, volunteering, hurrying from place to place. She never slowed down; afraid that somewhere waiting in the shadows the paralyzing fright from the past would rear its ugly head and devour her. Exhausted, Blaine once more relaxed her defenses and exposed her grief to the world.

"My husband's name is Troy, Troy Sterling. We met right over there, eight years ago at Sharky's. They sponsored a fundraiser for the owners of the Bavarian Inn Restaurant that burned down; I'm not sure why I went. I never ate at the Bavarian Inn, didn't really care much for German food, but it was a beautiful December day, so I went." Blaine began with a far away look on her face.

"The Bavarian Inn, I ate there a few times; the restaurant was on Tamiami Trail in Venice, near the ABC store. It looked like a cute little German chalet, even had fake snow on the roof and inside hundreds of ornate German beer steins lined the bar and dining room. I was too young to drink, but my father loved their beer and Wiener schnitzel. The only thing I enjoyed was their strudel covered in powdered sugar that would fall down like snow over my dress upsetting my mother with every bite," Marybeth cooed.

"Sharky's restaurant was packed, hundreds of people danced to a calypso band, the tiki bar was three deep, grills cooked burgers, hot dogs, and chicken, raffles every fifteen minutes, and crazy team games; the place was rocking. I won a beach blanket, that's how I met Troy, he also won a blanket and his pick-up line was: 'Nice beach blanket.' How lame, I couldn't stop laughing, but it was love at first sight, we just connected. In front of me was a tall, good looking man with a linebacker's physique, piercing brown eyes, and long wavy blonde hair all packaged with a disarming personality, he had me hooked."

"Wow, you are the first person I ever met who fell in love like that, maybe there's hope for me yet," Marybeth interrupted with an impish laugh and a mischievous glint in her eye.

"I don't think you have anything to worry about Marybeth, *your prince in shining armor* is right around the corner. Anyway, we hung out together the whole day, that night we walked to the end of the fishing pier, watched the sun melt into the Gulf and paint the horizon a brilliant red and orange glow, that's where Troy threw the coin into the Gulf. As if standing in front of a gigantic fountain we made a wish, watched the coin soar into the air, fall and then disappear under the water. I wished that the feelings I had that day would never end; little did I know eight years later I would be holding the same coin and reliving that day once again."

"Afterwards we strolled down the beach and made love, those two beach blankets came in handy. It just happened; one minute we were holding hands looking out at the sunset and then we flew into each other's arms and then. . .For the first time since the rape, I felt alive and safe. Finally, we collapsed and I fell asleep in his arms. We moved in together and three months later we were married on the beach next to Sharky's."

"A beach wedding, I know how romantic! Last year, my girlfriend Mercedes had her wedding on the beach at Siesta Key; I was her maid of honor. Her father is loaded, owns a car dealership, Mercedes, wouldn't you know it. He rented out an entire floor of rooms at the Ritz-Carlton and had all three hundred of the guests ride in horse drawn carriages over to the hotel's private beach for his daughter's wedding ceremony. What an extravaganza, Mercedes' dress was designed by Vera Wang, she had six bridesmaids and ten groomsmen, and they all arrived at the beach by helicopter. Her father had a large Chickee hut built for the ceremony, rented the red and white circus tent from Circus Sarasota, and hired Grandma and Friends to perform during the reception. A twelve piece band, cocktail hour, white gloved, three course sit-down dinner, a four tiered wedding cake by cake artist Buddy Valastro, and at the end a candle lit limousine ride back to the hotel. The Venice Journal Star touted it as the *Wedding of the Year*, too bad it only lasted six months." Marybeth reached into her bag, sprayed sunscreen on her legs and laughed, "Her father was so pissed, sold her Mercedes SL and made her drive a Jetta. Only for one year, embarrassed by the innuendos about Mercedes *new* car, he bought her a new Mercedes convertible."

"Some punishment, I'd like to drive a new Jetta for a year and then get a Mercedes," Blaine snapped. "Anyway, my beach wedding was romantic, nothing like your friend's," Blaine said, "but your friend and I have one thing in common, my husband also didn't last a year, he disappeared two months before Brooke was born. Seven months pregnant, he vanished. He was a carpenter, about to finish a custom fireplace in a house at Valencia Lakes, a man stopped by, they talked and then Troy left work."

"The police investigated the disappearance, could not locate the stranger, could not find my husband, his car, or a reason for his disappearance, he's still classified as a *Missing Person*. He never hugged his daughter, Brooke never saw her father, and we never celebrated a holiday as a family. It's been eight agonizing years." With tears in her eyes, Marybeth reached over and the two hugged.

Chapter Sixty-One

Marybeth looked down at her smartphone, highlighted the information on the screen and handed it to Blaine. "I'm not sure, but the medallion may be the key to your husband's disappearance, take a look at what's highlighted."

In bold print, Blaine read:

"Trace Foundation, Portland, Oregon. Find your biological parents. Unable to break through all the red tape, tired of the bureaucratic run around. Let our experts get the answers. We will locate your birth parents. Call 1877 MY TRACE or www.tracefoundation@yahoo.org."

Locate your birth parents exploded off the screen like a heavy weight boxer's punch to the gut in the twelfth round. Breathless, Blaine's body throbbed; dizzying questions flooded over her as tears of joy rolled down her face. Dare she hope that a direction to answer the questions that for eight agonizing years paralyzed her very existence was in sight? Would the nightmares finally end and bring closure to her broken heart, or would there be further questions on the next page? Where did Troy go and what happened to him? Unable to take her eyes off the words, *find your biological parents*, Blaine could not help but think that Troy left work to meet his biological parents, but why didn't he return home with the good news, what happened to him? Finally a scintilla of information, a direction, but where would it lead?

"I have to call," Blaine reached for her phone and pressed "1 877 my trace." The phone rang.

"It's Sunday, Blaine, and isn't Portland three hours earlier?" Marybeth added, "that would be about nine in the morning their time."

"I don't care, I have to try, hold on, they're answering, I'll put it on speaker phone." *'You have reached The Trace Foundation. Our business hours are Monday through Friday 9:00 A.M. to 5:00 P.M. Pacific Standard Time. Please call back during regular business hours, thank you.'*

"That wasn't very friendly," Marybeth reacted as she turned off her smartphone, "I'm not sure I'd use Trace Foundation to find my birth parents that is if I had a need to, which I don't."

"The advertisement didn't say anything about amiable, only results. That is what adoptive children want, Marybeth, results. I'll call tomorrow and see what information they can provide. It would be a miracle if Brooke could walk in the park with her grandparents and father. I have such a good feeling about this."

"Blaine, I don't want to rain on your parade, but there are laws and legal procedures regarding adoption and access to information, I'm no expert, but I don't think this Trace Foundation or the State of Florida or any state will just open its records to anyone. Anything related to government business is a nightmare; look how long it takes to mail a package at the Post Office." Marybeth laughed, noticed a slight smile on Blaine's face and added, "You know what I'm talking about, you've been in line waiting and waiting and waiting." They both laughed uncontrollably.

Halfway through cleaning up Marybeth mentioned that she belonged to a computer club and had a friend, a little weird, but a genius with computers. Head Geek Squad guy over at Best Buy in Sarasota, he was the technician they called on to diagnose and repair the most troublesome computer problems that came to the store and he also designed a software program to hack into any computer system out there.

"Remember the newspaper article about the Venice Utilities manager fired because he couldn't turn off the lights and then they found gambling sites on his computer?" Marybeth asked. "My friend put the sites on his computer because he was rude to a friend of his who called the manager's office. If you want, I could ask him to hack into Trace Foundation and see what they have on your husband."

"Thanks, but let's see what happens Monday."

They finished cleaning up and walked down to the water and the girls. The crystal blue water was cold at first, but after the first dunk and a lot of splashing, everyone found the water refreshing. The girls found four small shark's teeth, a handful of colored shells and two pieces of greenish-blue sea glass, a perfect collection to remember a special vacation. Blaine found hope.

Chapter Sixty-Two

Good morning, Trace Foundation, how I may direct your call? Blaine knew precisely the direction her call should take, because she understood a battle was about to play out and she was prepared for the assault. Preparation was the key and being organized was half the battle. To orchestrate a coherent, well thought out argument, Blaine collected all her husband's personal and business papers from their home safe. Business receipts, phone records, pay stubs, tax records, insurance policies, Social Security card, marriage license, Brooke's birth certificate, her birth certificate, and Troy's birth certificate filled two large folders she placed in her attaché case. A three-hour window between Oregon and Florida afforded an entire morning to prepare before her call at noon to Trace Foundation. Armed with a leather case full of information and an attitude of confidence, Blaine left for work.

The drive to the park was a blur. Questions about adoption, birth parents, and Trace Foundation bounced around in her head throughout the trip. Blaine's imagination abounded and jumped from joyous intoxication to deep melancholy. Haunting images of the birth parents and the pain they must have endured flashed before her. 'Were they still alive?' 'Were there siblings?' And most frightening the determining question that tugged at Blaine's very essence, 'Would the birth parents want to be a part of Brooke's life?'

Still in a slight funk, Blaine shifted into first, jerked the car down to a slow roll alongside the ranger station, and then braked. Immediately, the office window opened and ranger Linda Ash's smiling face popped out and dragged Blaine back to reality. The two had not seen each other since the park dedication and Blaine privately hoped that Linda had forgotten the ice cream truck fiasco along with Lou Bravo's embarrassing clown incident.

"Welcome, back Assistant Manager Sterling, how are you feeling?" Ranger Ash said as she handed her the sign-in clipboard. "It's good to see you back at the park again."

"Thank you, Linda, it's good to be back, the only thing I dread is the mountain of paperwork waiting for me after a two-week hiatus." Blaine answered and handed her the clipboard.

"If there's anything I can do, please let me know."

"Thanks! I just may take you up on the offer. How many camp sites are filled as of today?"

"We're full up, all one hundred and four sites occupied," Linda proudly announced, "with five RVs in the parking lot and twenty people on the waiting list. I really think we need to add more camping sites."

"I agree. Is the Park Manager in today?"

"No, he's in Orlando this week with his family, a little R&R time. He deserves it, the man never stops." Linda blurted out in her usual quick snappy tone.

"I agree he is dedicated and with the new policy on vacation time Tallahassee just implemented, '*Use it or lose it,*' John would be foolish not to take a well-deserved vacation. My two-week recuperative stint obliterated all of my accumulated vacation time, but I'm thankful I had a bank of time, I can't fathom two weeks without pay. If you see Jay please tell him to see me. I need to speak with him about books. Bye."

"What? Do the two of them belong to a book club?" Linda wondered aloud. Befuddled, she stood there and watched the Mini Cooper drive away.

Blaine took in a deep breath as her car passed under a great hammock of ancient oaks, the cool crisp morning air, dry and sweet filled her lungs and invigorated her spirit. Two bicyclists waved as she reached the top of the incline and out into the glare of the morning sun. The fields on both sides of the road, part of a prescribed burn seven months ago lay open, big and flat. A smile of satisfaction lit up Blaine's face as she looked out at the fields of new growth where acres of blackened trees and scorched brush once stood, now the beginnings of a balanced habitat for the park's wildlife. As a certified prescribed burner and a member of the park's *burn team*, she understood the importance of fire to restore the original landscape and insure the survival of the native plants and wildlife. Pleased with the results of the latest burn, she glanced in the rear-view mirror just as the pair on a bicycle-built-for-two sped down the road and disappeared into the shadows of the oaks. Blaine was excited to be back in the park, so when she said to Linda, "Glad to be back," it wasn't just a hollow euphemism about returning to work, but a statement of fact. She loved her job, loved working with nature, and loved surrounding herself with people passionate about preserving the environment. Her commitment to nature and wildlife, ingrained in her at an early age was the foundation of her work ethic and the force behind her desire to protect nature for future generations.

Chapter Sixty-Three

Blaine's enthusiasm imploded seconds after she pushed open her office door and observed the disaster area in front of her. Her desk was covered with piles of letters, flyers, brochures and pamphlets that resembled a Halloween prank gone wild. Her in-box basket overflowed into a heap of jumble that completely buried Blaine's laptop. Handwritten phone messages held together with a large yellow paperclip sat under the phone, and there amongst the jumble of paper, in a tiny carved out circle; stood a small white porcelain clown holding three colored balloons. A sheet of pink colored paper, signed by all the rangers said, *Welcome Back, with a big green smiley face on the bottom.* Blaine smiled and said to herself, "I guess they remembered," and began to wade through the paperwork.

Blaine's cellphone rang. "Hi, how's it going the first day back, Assistant Park Manager Sterling?"

"Well Marybeth, if you get your kicks sorting through tons of mail, than I would say, fabulous. You should see my office; it's a postman's worst nightmare. I have no idea where anything is or how long it will take to sort through all this correspondence. What I'd like to do is toss everything in the garbage, claim it was lost in the mail and start fresh."

There was an uncomfortable moment of silence and then Marybeth added, "I hate to add to your nightmare, but I just e-mailed you something about the Trace Foundation. Last night I told my friend about your situation and this morning, Star Trek guy sent me a newspaper article that you must read before you call the Trace Foundation."

"Star Trek guy, Marybeth you have to be kidding."

"I know, he's a little weird, but trust me, he's a genius with computers. Without a doubt, he could hack into the Trace Foundation's computer network; retrieve user names and passwords and download every bit of data you would need to find your husband. You have to read his e-mail. It's frightening. I have to get back to class. Call me after you speak to the foundation."

"Okay, I'll read it if I can find my laptop under this landfill of paper, bye."

Five minutes and an exhaustive search later, Blaine booted up her laptop, downloaded Marybeth's e-mail and gasped at the headline:

TRACE FOUNDATION ACCUSED OF CYBER SPYING
Trade secrets stolen in seconds
Portland Gazette, November 4, 2009

The news article began with a brief exposé on multimillionaire Conrad Tracefeld, CEO of the Trace Foundation and coffee kiosk czar of Portland, Oregon and then segued into a poignant account on how the man carved out a monopoly in the coffee kiosk industry. Allegations of strong-arm tactics, business improprieties, pay-offs, and political connections painted a very sordid picture of Conrad Tracefeld. In five short years, competitors were bought out, closed down, or under questionable circumstances, disappeared, leaving Tracefeld's coffee kiosk empire license to blanket all of the most lucrative street corners in Portland and make millions.

An enlightening section on the birth of the Trace Foundation detailed how Tracefeld, frustrated with the state's adoption system in locating his birth parents and stymied by bureaucratic red tape formed the Trace Foundation. He assembled a group of computer experts with Ph.D.s in mathematics, engineering, and science, designed and built a state of the art computer system and housed the entire enterprise in a windowless low-rise building in the old Flat Iron industrial district alongside the Willamette River. The only indication that a business occupied the building was a small, pitted brass plate with the name TRACE FOUNDATION affixed to the concrete wall along side the gray metal door. There under the guise of an advocacy group for adoptees, the Trace Foundation was born.

However, the most damaging accusation, highlighted in the last paragraph of the article, inferred that the Trace Foundation was not just an unassuming adoptee search company, but also a rogue organization dealing in cyber-economic espionage. A broad array of private companies holding large volumes of sensitive technology reported hackers broke into their corporations' database, installed a sophisticated computer virus program that infected their classified network and sent back propriety technology to its creator. Dates, specific breaches of security, along with phone records and financial statements alluded to a shadowy connection to Russia and China. Nothing conclusive linked the Trace Foundation to the Russian or Chinese cyber attacks; however, the National Security Agency has assembled an elite team to investigate a possible association.

At the end, a note scrawled in italics, *reporter died in a fiery auto accident, all of her research destroyed, mw.*

Chapter Sixty-Four

Two hours later with a cleared desk, personal papers in hand and the resolve of a woman on a quest, Blaine picked up the phone.

"May I speak with Conrad Tracefeld, this is Mrs. Troy Sterling, and my husband is a client."

"One moment please."

It is never a moment; once on hold, music plays bombarding the captive listener with a cornucopia of tunes from Mozart to Manilow, Yanni to Neil Young, and even Elvis to elevator music depending on the area of the country one is calling. For some unexplained reason the longer the wait, the softer the music, possibly a ploy to lull the listener to sleep or better yet into complacency. Unfortunately, the opposite occurs, the listener becomes annoyed, then irritated, offended and finally reaching his or her breaking point either slams down the phone in disgust or remains on the line, numb and in a state of total frustration. After what feels like a lifetime, the music stops, an ominous cracking/clicking static sound breaks in, no music, no human voice, an unmistakable prescription for disaster.

"This is Jackson Palmeter, Director of Client Services, how may I help you, Mrs. Sterling?" A short abrupt tone vibrated across the line. Blaine waited.

"I was hoping to speak with the owner, Mr. Tracefeld," Blaine answered holding in check the desire to reach into the phone and ring his neck, a deep-seated resentment for the long wait, but she took a deep breath and regained her composure.

"Mr. Tracefeld is out of the country, in his absence I am in charge of all client information. What can I do for you, Mrs. Sterling," Palmeter replied again in a curt tone.

"I would like to request all information you collected for my husband, specifically the names and addresses of his birth parents," Blaine insisted with an air of authority.

"What proof do you have Mr. Sterling employed our company to search for his birth parents?"

"Mr. Palmeter, I did not call to play a game of twenty questions, I have a silver medallion with the name of Trace Foundation that my husband possessed, so I assume he contracted with the Foundation to locate his natural parents, now I am trying to locate my husband," Blaine retorted. "If his birth parents are alive I want our daughter to be a part of their life, can you understand that desire, Mr. Palmeter?"

"We haven't given out consummation medallions in seven years. You mentioned that you are attempting to locate your husband. Why has it taken so long to contact us?" Palmeter condescended.

"It's a long story, but I only found the medallion yesterday. Will you send me the information my husband contracted you to uncover!"

"I'm sorry Mrs. Sterling, but it is company policy not to divulge any client data, other than a comprehensive report directly to the client."

"Where is the report?"

In a cursory tone, Palmeter added, "Mr. Sterling has not requested we turn over the final report yet."

"Are you telling me Mr. Palmeter, that for eight years or more you have held on to Mr. Sterling's report and now his wife contacts you and you say you can't turn it over, it's company policy?"

"That's correct, Mrs. Sterling."

"That's absurd, by the way how much does Mr. Sterling still owe for your services?"

Silence again, no music this time, only the sound of a keyboard in the background and the flipping of pages.

"A final payment of five thousand dollars is still outstanding on Mr. Sterling's account."

"If I pay the remaining balance will you send me the portfolio?"

Silence, then….

"Yes."

"Send a bill to, BlaineSterling@verizon.net and I'll send you a certified check."

"I will have the necessary forms drawn up by the end of the day. Thank you for contacting Trace Foundation. Have a nice day." The phone went dead.

Blaine closed her cell phone, rubbed her forehead and wondered *where she would get five thousand dollars.* The answer was about to walk through the door dressed in a red Santa Claus costume.

Chapter Sixty-Five

His black patent leather boots glistened in the sunlight, a big silver belt buckle radiated wide beams of light from his waist and his snowy white beard and long hair flowed freely down to his frumpy red suit as he, and two elves rushed across the parking lot towards the library's service entrance door. Lou Bravo dressed as Santa, along with his two elves Tony Lilly and Hubba Bubba waved to an astonished crowd standing outside the Woodmere Library's main entrance waiting for the ten o'clock opening and the After Christmas Books in a Bag Sale. "Ho, Ho, Ho, enjoy the book sale," Lou Bravo bellowed as the trio disappeared into the building.

Assuming it was some kind of publicity stunt for the Books in a Bag Sale everyone cheered and shouted back, "Thank you, Santa, thank you." Little did they suspect, Santa and his two helpers were about to have their own private book sale fifteen minutes before anyone walked through the door.

For Lou Bravo that was not his concern, he was on a mission, operation *Snow Job* was about to commence and he was the fat man holding the shovel. At his holiday party, after unwrapping an autographed copy of *Gatehouse*, by Nelson DeMille, his favorite author, Blaine revealed that the library at the park was in desperate need of books. Operating on the honor system for the past twenty-five years, their library of over three hundred titles, at last count, had only a paltry fifty books on the shelves and most of them were in poor condition. *Honor system that is the problem people,* Lou Bravo thought to himself. *Forget the honor system, you need a sign-out form and fine schedule for every lost or stolen book, then you will not have a book shortage,* but first they needed books.

Two weeks later, after reading in the paper a notice about the Woodmere Library Two Dollar, Books in a Bag Sale, Lou Bravo put his plan into operation. A quick call to Elsie Donnelly, a spry eighty-something from West Hempstead, Long Island and longtime volunteer at the Woodmere Library started the ball rolling. A second call brought

Tony Lilly and Hubba Bubba on board and finally a trip down to Babe's Hardware to purchase a construction grade wheelbarrow to haul fifty bags of books to his El Camino, operation *Snow Job* was about to explode through Woodmere Library like an out of control snow plow. Call it a belated Christmas gift or a welcome back to work present for Assistant Park Manager Sterling, but fifty bags of books for her beleaguered library certainly would cheer her up. Hopefully, the shock of seeing Santa Claus and two elves standing outside her office in the middle of January holding plastic bags of books wouldn't send her back to Venice Hospital again.

"Thank you Elsie," Lou Bravo called out as the four hurried down the service corridor and out into the library in front of the bookstore. Decorated with twinkling lights, holiday pictures and brightly colored balloons, the bookstore overflowed with literary celebration. Every bookcase lined from top to bottom with books; many with multiple copies that jutted out from the tops of the original books into the aisles made for easy access and quick acquisition, truly a book lover's paradise. Along both sides of the hallway, stacks and stacks of books covered the tables that ran the entire length of the hallway to the computer area. Hundreds and hundreds of books were for sale.

"Here are your fifty bags, I'll take your donation now, you have fifteen minutes to fill your bags and then you must leave before I unlock the front door. Is that understood?" Elsie stated in a perfunctory tone and placed the crisp one hundred dollar bill in the moneybox marked, *Friends of Woodmere Library*.

"Perfectly clear, thank you Elsie," Lou Bravo whispered in her ear as he smothered her with a big bear hug that lifted her off her feet. "Okay, boys, let's rock and roll. You both have your lists, Hubba Bubba you collect authors A thru M, Tony, you bag authors N thru Z and I'll concentrate on the local authors and current titles, any questions?"

"Do I look by the first name or last name on this list," Hubba Bubba called out.

"Last name numbnuts," Lou Bravo groaned and pushed him towards the A shelf. "Here start with Auel, take these three books, remember take only the authors with an asterisk next to the last name and if you see a double asterisk scoop up all the books. Now get going, we only have twelve minutes."

"Tony, change of plans, start with Patterson then go straight to Woods and then back to N, we don't have much time and you should fill at least four bags just between the two authors. Let's fly."

A blizzard of disorganized activity plowed through the aisles as hard-covered, soft-covered, thick, thin, new and old books flew into the trio's bags. Arms, hands, feet running, grabbing, seizing one book after another. After filling four bags, they would run down the corridor, drop their booty into the wheelbarrow and then race back to pillage the remaining bookcases. After ten minutes, the wheelbarrow overflowed and a hulking mass of books piled up around the space that was once a wheelbarrow. Eventually, all three just threw their weighty bags into the corridor and closed the door.

Three minutes remained, when disaster struck Operation Snow Job, Hubba Bubba in a rush to fill his fourth and final bag slipped on *Charm School*, by Nelson DeMille, a book he dropped earlier. Momentarily, blinded by a bubble gum explosion and weighted down with four bags of books, he catapulted head-first into a bookcase with the impact of a three-hundred-pound linebacker from the Tampa Bay Buccaneers. A disastrous chain reaction unfolded, like a child's orderly row of dominos, one, two, three the bookcases toppled one right after the other. An avalanche of books flew in every direction, hundreds of titles littered the floor and in the center of the mayhem, Hubba Bubba laid spread-eagled under a fallen bookcase. Time was counting down and Lou Bravo knew he didn't have the time or manpower to right the bookcases or straighten up the mess.

"Shit, what a disaster, I am so screwed," Lou Bravo groaned and yanked Hubba Bubba to his feet. "What is wrong with you? Look at this place. I should shoot you right here and let you deal with Elsie and all the people out there."

"I don't know what happened, last thing I remember was blowing a big bubble and crashing into something. My head is killing me."

"I guess they'll be taking your library card privileges away after today. No more free DVDs for Lou Bravo," Tony laughed and put *Charm School* into his bag.

"That's not the only thing they'll take away, more than likely I'll have to pay for a new wing to the library before this is all over! Let's get out of here," Lou Bravo said quickly and pushed the two elves into the corridor. The last thing Lou Bravo heard as the door closed:

"One minute remaining Santa," Elsie announced as she grabbed the entrance door key from her pocket and walked towards the main door.

Chapter Sixty-Six

The yellow El Camino with Santa at the wheel, Tony the good elf riding shotgun and Hubba Bubba, the bad elf in the back of the truck sandwiched between forty-six bags of books and a wheelbarrow pulled up to the ranger station. With a big smile on his face jolly ole Saint Nick handed the ranger a five-dollar bill and bellowed, "Keep the change young lady, a present from Santa."

"Oh no, it's you again, don't you ever dress like a normal human being? Last month a clown outfit now, you show up in a Santa suit. I think it's time to call the Park Police." On duty was ranger Linda Ash, she worked the main gate the day Lou Bravo drove to the park in an ice cream truck dressed as a circus clown, along with a costumed Brooke Sterling dressed as a cat. Their initial meeting was confrontational at best and Ranger Linda was in the process of contacting the Park Police when Blaine interceded. Today's encounter appeared to be moving in the same direction.

"No wait, I can explain," Lou Bravo quickly said, realizing the alarmed expression on her face, "I just wanted to give Assistant Park Manager Sterling a present; books for the park's library. She told me that the park desperately needed books, so here I am."

"And you thought dressing up as Santa Claus would do what?"

"Let's say a belated Christmas present, I thought it would help cheer her up on her first day back to work, get a big laugh, and also help out the park," Lou Bravo added with an uneasy smile and a faint laugh.

"Okay, crazy as it sounds, I believe you, take the second left to her office and for your information, Santa, admission to the park has gone up, it's now five dollars. Have a nice day."

Lou Bravo flawlessly backed the El Camino up against the office handicapped ramp and front door, a skill he honed as a young man when he drove an eighteen wheeler on Long Island. Hubba Bubba jumped down from the back, pulled the wheelbarrow out and filled the metal hopper with books. Together the merry group marched up the ramp to the office. Tony pulled open the door and the trio rushed in. "Ho, ho, ho, good tidings to all," Lou Bravo shouted and waved his arms in the air as a friendly greeting to the stunned rangers working in the outer office. "Don't be alarmed, good people; we are here only to wish Assistant Park Manager Sterling a merry, merry homecoming. Is she here?"

"She is in her office," Bailey Rivers, a petite, quiet first year ranger from Colorado said in a hushed voice and pointed to the door at the end of the room. Simultaneously, the three marched down the corridor in single file and burst into Blaine's office. The impact threw open the door, flipped over the wheelbarrow, and spilled out hundreds of books in every direction. The forward momentum and layers of books sent the three merry men tumbling to the floor in a heap of total confusion. Blaine jumped up from behind her desk, a phone in her left hand, and her first place trophy from last year's Sarasota 5 K Run in her right.

"Get up, who are you, and what are you doing in my office?" Blaine shouted at the pile of bodies rolling around on the floor. "Marybeth, I have to call the Park Police, some weirdos broke into my office and. . .oh wait, it's Lou Bravo. I'll get back to you later, thanks for that update on Trace. Bye."

"Blaine, it's me Lou Bravo, please put the trophy down, I only wanted to surprise you on your first day back and give you some books for your library. You know like Santa Claus, presents, cheer people up, that was the plan," Lou Bravo pleaded as he pulled off the white beard and wig.

"Surprise, you bet I was surprised and for this practical joke you almost got your head bashed in. For your information, Santa, it's January, Christmas was last month, I'd say a little late with the presents old fella," Blaine scoffed as she placed the trophy back down on the desk.

After a fifteen-minute dissertation about the book fair, a hundred dollar donation, the Woodmere mishap, costumes, missing park library books, and the latest unfortunate encounter with Ranger Linda Ash, Lou Bravo finally convinced Blaine that his heart was in the right direction even though his mind was on vacation. It was at that conciliatory moment Jay Appelle, a long time park volunteer, walked into the office. He was a formidable man, six-foot-two with a linebacker's physique, weathered from years of manual labor on a cattle ranch in Montana. Not much shocked Jay, but the surprised expression that enveloped his round puffy face was cause for concern. Immediately Blaine interceded and performed the awkward, but necessary introductions and a delicate explanation for the costumes and wheelbarrow full of books. To everyone's astonishment, Jay burst out in laughter and gave Hubba Bubba a powerful slap on the back that sent him tumbling to the floor. Everyone joined in the laughter, lessening the tension allowing Blaine to introduce park business, "Jay, originally I needed you to canvas the campground and collect any outstanding library books from the campers, however due to Lou Bravo's generosity that will not be necessary. Mr. Bravo has graciously donated over three hundred books to add to our sadly depleted collection of titles. The wheelbarrow full of books is only a small portion of the donation; the greater part of the collection is in his truck. Would you please go with the two elves and fill the park library's shelves with all the new books. Oh, and starting today all campers need to sign-out each book, *no more honor system lending.*" She gave Lou Bravo a quick wink and smiled. Blaine closed the door as the yellow El Camino drove down the road to the park library.

Chapter Sixty-Seven

Blaine picked up the antique cane high-back chair resting in the far corner of the room, a gift from her late grandmother, set it alongside her desk and motioned for Lou Bravo to take a seat. She reached into the attaché case, pulled out the Trace medallion and handed it to him. Confused, Lou Bravo repeatedly turned the coin-sized medallion over, examining the writings, inscriptions and pictures etched into the object. Unable to decipher a thing, a perplexed expression glazed over his face.

"I need your help," Blaine said in a faraway voice, "last Sunday while searching for sharks' teeth, Brooke found the medallion you are holding. Eight years ago, my husband and I made a wish and threw that medallion off the Venice Fishing Pier."

"How do you know this is the same medallion?" Lou Bravo replied staring down at the silver coin in his hand.

"I'm positive, do you see a line under WE OUR ONE, Troy scratched it in with his car key right before he threw it into the Gulf. Take a look." Slowly Lou Bravo moved his thumb along the bottom of the WE OUR and ONE and felt an uneven edge under the three words. A closer inspection revealed a crude scratch mark.

"The medallion is from an organization that among other things locates birth parents. Yesterday I received information that my husband was attempting to locate his birthparents and contacted the Trace Foundation in Portland, Oregon. You can see their name printed along the top of the medallion. I called them and they refused to release any information until they were paid five thousand dollars, the remaining balance on Troy's contract. I do not have that kind of money," Blaine declared in an exhausted sigh.

"What guarantee do you have that this Trace Foundation has one shred of credible information to help you find your husband, let alone his birth parents? The whole operation sounds like a scam. They collect money from your husband, now they want another five thousand dollars from his wife, doesn't sound legit to me." He bit down on the coin.

"I just have a feeling, call it a woman's intuition, but I believe the Trace Foundation is the key. A stranger shows up at Troy's job, they speak; Troy leaves work early and then disappears. Something the man told Troy made him leave work abruptly. I know it."

"The guy could have been a bookie, gave your husband a hot tip on a horse at Tampa Bay Downs and tells him to place his bet right away. Your husband leaves work, gets involved with some undesirables and disappears. What are you going to do? Fly to Portland, flash your pretty blue eyes, and hope to get some answers?" Lou Bravo mocked.

"For your information, my husband didn't gamble, he was an honest man," Blaine snapped back, "and no I don't plan on flying to Portland. Right before you and your two elves burst into my office, I was on the phone with a friend who informed me that the Trace Foundation has a satellite office in Venice at the Brickyard Plaza off Tamiami Trail. I plan to go there tomorrow, flash my Florida Department of Environmental Protection badge, and demand some answers."

Lou Bravo could feel the resolve in Blaine's voice. The tenor of her words cut into the very fabric of her being, while the plea, *I need to know,* echoed the most urgent message she so desperately needed answered. For eight empty years, Lou Bravo watched her agonize over the mystery surrounding her husband's disappearance and his good name. There were no answers, no evidence, no closure, only hurtful rumors and innuendoes for Blaine and her daughter to endure. Now, for the first time Blaine believed she possessed the evidence that would lead her to her husband. How could he possibly destroy her dream?

Lou Bravo could not muster the courage to look at her. For what seemed an eternity, he stared down at the silver object in his hand and then flipped it into the air. Startled by its simplicity, Lou Bravo almost dropped it. There in his hand he held the answer, the medallion. Uncovered, the coin screamed out the combination that would unlock all of Blaine's questions.

Finally, he looked up and said, "I don't think the people at the Brickyard office will give you any information and flashing your badge in their face will only get you into hot water, maybe fired."

"Do you have a better idea?" Blaine snapped and stood glaring down at him.

"Yes," Lou Bravo said with a wild grin across his face as he sprang to his feet and danced around the room like a crazy man. For two intoxicated minutes, he spun around in dizzying circles, his red costume flared out like burning wings spiraling out of control until he plopped into to the chair totally exhausted.

"Do I have a plan, you bet I have a plan lucky lady," Lou Bravo sang out and wiped his forehead with a big red handkerchief. "Please sit down and inhale the good news." Blaine sat, folded her hands, and stared intently at the disheveled man slouched down in front of her and waited.

"Forgive my French, but this Trace Foundation doesn't give a shit about your husband or your little problem. I don't even think they care about the paltry five thousand dollars. They're into bigger deals, more likely, shady or illegal arrangements, so forget about getting an honest answer from those bozos. We deal with them exactly how they deal with others, we steal the file."

"What just walk in and take it?" Blaine scoffed and shook her head in disbelief.

"Exactly, in broad daylight, in front of everyone; we walk in and take it. Simple as that," Lou Bravo exclaimed with a wave of his hand and a tip of his head.

"You are insane, Lou Bravo; they won't let you take the file. It can't be done."

"Oh, my dear naive Blaine, it can and we will, but first I have a little story to tell." Lou Bravo sat forward in his chair and in his characteristic style, for the next half an hour, lectured on the commercial dynamics of his friend Tony Lilly, the key to the entire operation.

Chapter Sixty-Eight

Tony Lilly, like Lou Bravo, had many entrepreneurial enterprises bubbling in his business action pot, some above reproach and others questionable; that mindset was why the two of them got along so well. Opportunists, their success more often than not, boiled down to one attribute, being in the right place at the right time. Both of them possessed the uncanny ability of not being in the wrong place at the wrong time. This inborn trait on numerous occasions put them one-step ahead of disaster.

Six years ago, Tony bought Circus Days Ice Cream from his neighbor Denny Circus, who after a hunting accident became an amputee and couldn't stand for long periods of time. Denny fancied himself a big hunter, every November he and a group of old high school friends went deer hunting in upstate New York. One night while the boys sat around the campfire drinking beer and bullshitting about their hunting prowess, out of nowhere a deer jumped out of the dark, leapt over their fire pit and ran towards the tree line. Scared shitless, everyone scattered, and Tony's best friend Lou Moribeto, a retired cop, pulled out his pistol and fired five shots at the fleeing apparition that sailed over the low rock wall along the tree line. One shot ricocheted off a rock, and hit Denny in the right leg. The bullet severed an artery and bled like shit; Sam Belliva, a retired gym teacher and wrestling coach, put a tourniquet on and the four friends drove down the mountain to the nearest hospital, a thirty-minute drive. Denny lost the leg that night and his hunting ticket. Unable to stand for long hours in the ice cream truck he offered the business to Tony. A 3,000-square foot concrete block building in Seaborne Industrial Park, a five-year-old white box truck, three commercial freezers, and one freshly painted ice cream truck; a steal for twenty thousand dollars. He and Hubba Bubba switched off peddling ice cream on the weekends, holidays, and the occasional art/craft festivals in and around Sarasota County. Tony wasn't making big bucks, but the ice cream business paid the bills and for an occasional weekend trip to the casino.

Last summer, Bruno *The Bone Crusher* Toughs, who owned Clean Sweep Cleaning Service, the business adjacent to Circus Ice Cream, died. A retired professional wrestler, *Bone Crusher*, a giant of a man, was fishing a mile off Venice Beach for Sheepshead when his beer line (lowered net of beer off the starboard side to keep drinks cool), wrapped around the prop. *Bone Crusher* jumped into the water to untangle the line, unfortunately, the engine was in gear and when the line loosened, the propeller lurched backward and severed both his arms. The Coast Guard found his boat circling in reverse that night and three days later what was left of his body washed up on shore off Siesta Key Beach.

Bone Crusher's wife detested the stigmatism attributed to owning a cleaning business, and a week later sold the entire enterprise to Tony for a pittance. The grieving Mrs. Toughs moved to Boca consoled by her newfound wealth, a five million life insurance payout on her late husband and the never-ending attention from a new twenty-five-year old toy boy Carlos.

Bone Crusher, despite his womanizing, heavy drinking, and volatile temper, over the past twelve years built up the business and for the past three, Venice Monthly named Clean Sweep the number one cleaning company in Venice. His most recent acquisition, a five-year cleaning contract with the Osborne Group, owners of the Bellagio Center and the Brickyard Plaza was *Bone Crushers'* most ambitious business transaction, a fifteen-office cleaning guarantee that would impress even the likes of billionaire investment mogul Warren Buffett.

"Once a week Clean Sweep cleaned fifteen office suites on the second floor of the Brickyard Plaza, the largest suite, number 223, is the Trace Foundation. I know because I helped Tony clean that monstrosity for an entire month last summer after Hubba Bubba broke his arm skateboarding behind the Venice Train Depot. A task I don't relish repeated anytime soon, but for you, Blaine I'll make an exception."

Blaine sat up with a jerk; she could not believe what she heard. "That is unbelievable. Talk about being in the right place at the right time and Tony has keys to the entire Brickyard complex. I told you I had a good feeling about the Trace Foundation, but how do you know Mr. Lilly will risk his business to help me?"

"Tony Lilly will do anything for a buck," Lou Bravo snapped nonchalantly. "Put a dollar sign next to a scheme and Tony is in. I'll talk to him when they get back from filling your bookshelves and arrange everything."

The next four days, Blaine busied herself with work and doted over Brooke incessantly, but nothing freed her mind of the impending engagement on Friday. The days were endless and her nights sleepless. To compound matters Marybeth called Wednesday and reported that Star Trek Guy was unable to penetrate the numerous firewalls at the Trace Foundation. However, there was one piece of news: Tuesday he hacked into a conference call between the Portland office and Venice, and learned that the Trace Foundation warehoused all paper files to the Venice office, which they intend to shutter after they complete the digitalization of all records, that will begin next Monday.

Troubled by that new revelation, Blaine confided in Marybeth that the Trace Foundation wanted five thousand dollars for her husband's file, a sum unattainable on an assistant manager's salary. She also revealed that Tony Lilly's cleaning business serviced all the offices at the Brickyard Plaza and on Friday, she and Lou Bravo planned to break into the Trace office and remove Troy's file. Blaine expressed concern for the risk and possible legal ramifications that surrounded the break-in and theft, but the overwhelming desire to find her husband took precedence over her safety.

"Oh no, you can't!" Marybeth cried out. "Think about Brooke, what if you're arrested? If you take the file, the Trace Foundation will know who stole it. Who contacted them, who told them about the coin, who lives in Venice and whose last name is Sterling? It is so obvious, you! Take the file and you will be arrested Monday morning."

"I have no other choice. You said they start work on the files Monday, Friday is my only chance."

"Don't remove the file, take pictures. Use your cell phone, e-mail the pictures to StarTrekGuy@verizon.net, delete everything from your phone and throw it into the Intracoastal when you cross the Venice Bridge. Star Trek Guy will contact you."

"Why all the cloak and dagger stuff, Marybeth? Why can't I just download everything to my computer and print it out?"

"You read the bio on Conrad Tracefeld and the allegations of cybercrime. I wouldn't be surprised if the Trace Foundation had their dirty little hands in the celebrity cell phone hacking conspiracy over in England. Who knows, after your conversation with Palmeter, maybe they're monitoring your cell phone?"

"Don't be ridiculous," Blaine snapped, but immediately turned her phone over and carefully examined the back cover. "Getting a bit paranoid in your old age? What about this call, aren't you concerned that maybe they're monitoring you right now?"

"I doubt it. Star Trek Guy put a defragger chip on my phone that scrambles all signals, re-routes each call to an offshore site, then back to the States through a number of local cell phone towers and finally connects to my phone. It's a modification installed on all club member phones, Star Trek Guy said he would give you a modified phone when he returns your photos."

"Club, what club," Blaine questioned with a curious tone of anticipation and a spoonful of doubt in her voice.

"Oh it's just a computer club I belong to, a harmless group of computer geeks that get together once a week and do computer things, that's all. Blaine, I have to go, remember take only pictures. Be careful."

Blaine closed her phone, stared at the shiny black device in her hand, and wondered.

Chapter Sixty-Nine

Sometimes the most obvious is the least noticed. The red, white, and blue truck pulled up to the front of the Brickyard Plaza and parked. The bright red lettering, **Clean Sweep**, embossed on both sides of the truck stood out and a large commercial push broom painted a metallic yellow under the name pushed out a phone number: 800 484 1111. Three cleaners dressed in freshly starched khaki uniforms stepped out of the truck and maneuvered their cleaning carts towards the service elevator behind the frame store at the corner of the building. The Mexican and Greek restaurants packed with patrons spilled out onto the plaza with people anxious to get a table. Lively Mexican music filled the courtyard, while adults drank Margaritas and watched children run around the fountain or in and out of the gazebo at the far end of the plaza.

The night's spirited activities continued with no notice of the three cleaning carts that slowly worked their way along the second floor balcony. Tony led, pushed his cart around to the opposite side of the plaza and entered office # 200. Hubba Bubba stopped in the center and entered office #208. Lou Bravo stopped his cart at office # 223, punched in the security code and opened the door to the double suite. The bottom door of the cleaning cart slid open and a fourth cleaning person with long blonde hair scrambled out and duck-walked into the unlit room. With a vacuum cleaner in one hand and a bucket full of cleaning supplies in the other, Lou Bravo walked into suite# 223 and closed the door.

"Don't move, I'll get the light," Lou Bravo whispered in a low mischievous tone, "are you ready?" A white dusty globe light in the center of the ceiling cast a shadowy glow about the small waiting room and heightened the suspense of the clandestine evening. The walls were painted a hideous grass green with a jungle motif. The place appeared tired and in need of a fresh coat of paint, but most disturbing were a handful of animal drawings missing body parts, worn away by time, impatient clients or both. A lion that stood atop a rock with a missing nose appeared comical and extremely un-regal. Green cafeteria-style plastic chairs ringed the room, separated by an occasional green bamboo table that held out-dated magazines for visitors to peruse. A forest green shag carpet, worn down from years of traffic, led a noticeable trail to a small receptionist window and office door across from the entrance.

"Who is their interior decorator?" Blaine laughed and stood amazed. "Remind me never to use them for any home improvements."

"I don't think you have anything to worry about. By the looks of things, I don't think any improvements have been made in the past twenty years. Who has shag carpet? Anyway, we need to get to the file room, follow me." Lou Bravo pulled open the door and walked down the short corridor. On the left, they passed a small conference room, on the right two private offices and at the end of the corridor a gray steel door. Lou Bravo punched in a combination on the key pad, turned around and said, "Ready," and switched on the lights.

The light was blinding. Six rows of industrial florescent light panels, three deep, lit up the entire file room, the size of a two-car garage, like an airport runway on busy Thanksgiving Day. On the white tiled floor, rows and rows of gunmetal gray file cabinets stood with only about three feet of walking space between each stanchion. Chin high and two-feet-deep, each commercial-grade file cabinet with its four legal size drawers, were numbered and locked.

"There must be a hundred four-drawer file cabinets, each drawer containing at least ten, maybe fifteen files, that's roughly 6,000 files per cabinet, times one hundred. How can I possibly find Troy's file in one night," Blaine sighed and pulled out a blue folder from the first cabinet Lou Bravo just unlocked.

"Tony told me he counted one hundred and eighty-five, that would make over 11,000 files. Better get a move on," Lou Bravo laughed and unlocked the second cabinet with two little pieces of wire from a small black case in his left hand.

The first drawer packed with more than twenty thick, manila, yellow and blue folders alphabetically catalogued by date and color-coded by completion, yellow stamped in progress, blue resolved and manila rejected. Each folder contained a plastic bag of papers, notes and cards neatly arranged in chronological order. The first drawer filled mostly with blue folders were dated 1972, the date the Trace Foundation was founded.

Blaine stuffed the file back into the cabinet, slammed the drawer shut and called out to Lou Bravo who was down at the end of the first row of cabinets, "I can't possibly go through all these files; there are too many. Unlock the cabinets at the end of the room and work your way back to the first file cabinet next to the door. Palmeter said they stopped issuing medallions ten years ago, that would be 2001-2002, I'll start there and work backwards."

As they walked towards the last file cabinet, Blaine began to do the math. Troy was twenty-three when he threw his medallion off the pier eight years ago, that would make him twenty-one in 2002, and the last year Trace issued medallions. He may have had the coin as a teenager, but it was unlikely Trace Foundation would contract with a minor. It had to be 2002 or 2001, Blaine reassured herself.

"Bad news Blaine, Trace has added more file cabinets, now there are two hundred cabinets, see the tiny number in black on the lock, I'll inform Tony later, he might like to request a fee change."

"It's not bad news for me; its bad news for Tony, Trace Foundation is closing this office next year, and moving everything back to Portland. One less office to clean, the Osborne Group may want to renegotiate with Tony for a lower rate. Here we go, January 2002-ground zero. Okay Troy Sterling where are you?" Blaine whispered and opened the drawer.

"Poor bastard, wait until I give him the bad news, he'll be one unhappy sweeper, can't wait to rub it in!" Lou Bravo chuckled and continued to open the locks with just one jiggle of the lock picks.

"I found it! Here it is in the last cabinet marked 2001. A blue folder with the name Troy Sterling and it is stamped Resolved." Blaine waved the folder in the air as she raced to the document table next to the file room door.

Blaine collapsed in the silver folding chair at the end of the table. Cold metal pressed against her back and a numbing chill rushed down her spine. She sat motionless and stared at the blue folder, hands at her side; she was unwilling to move.

"Go ahead and open it," Lou Bravo barked. "That's why we're here."

"What if it's empty? A hoax, like you said?"

"You won't know if you don't open it, it's getting late and we're running out of time," and pushed the folder up against the edge of the table. "Please Blaine, open it."

Slowly she reached up, with trembling hands grabbed the corners of the blue folder, and pulled. There, stapled to a clear plastic folder in bold black print, was the Trace Foundation Birth Parent Search Contract dated July 12, 2001. Quickly she flipped through the four-page document and on the last page were the signatures of Troy M. Sterling, and Jackson S. Palmeter. Tears of joy ran down Blaine's cheeks as she carefully opened the plastic folder and pulled out a photocopy of a Certificate of Birth. At the top read: full name of child, Brandon, James Connelly, male, white, place of birth Venice, name of hospital Venice General Hospital, date of birth May 19, 1980. Blaine's eyes scanned down to birth parents: Father, Dillon Thomas Connelly, age 19, student; Mother, Erin Haley O'Brien, age 18, student.

"His birth name is Brandon James Connelly. Take a look," Blaine called to Lou Bravo, handed him the photocopy and feverishly pulled out the rest of the papers from the folder. The first document was the Adoption Application dated August 6, 1979 and highlighted in yellow were the names of the adoptive parents Mathew J. Sterling and Carol M. Sterling followed by the names of the natural parents, Dillon Thomas Connelly and Erin Haley O'Brien. Then the Adoption Certificate, dated May 19, 1980 with named adoptive parents Mathew J. Sterling and Carol M. Sterling, a Venice Hospital statement paid by Mathew J. Sterling, and from the State of Florida Department of Heath Bureau of Vital Records and Statistics the Birth Certificate for Troy M. Sterling, May 19, 1980. The final paper was a narrative on the natural parents and at the bottom circled in the black ink, Mr. and Mrs. Dillon Connelly 615 Old Oak Knoll Place Bradenton, FL 34212 (941) 741-3028. Blaine could not believe her good fortune.

Lou Bravo pulled his chair alongside Blaine and checked his watch. "Blaine, we don't have all night, you can't sit there and read all the papers, Tony and Hubba Bubba are just about finished with the cleaning. We have to go."

"Two more minutes, I've lined up all the documents, please hold down the corners while I photograph each one." Two minutes later, Blaine e-mailed the pictures, closed her phone and walked out the door.

Just beyond the bridge tender's office, a small black object flew out the window of a passing white truck and disappeared without a sound into the dark waters of the Intracoastal.

Chapter Seventy

The Saturday morning paper felt heavier than usual and the royal blue insert wrapped around the paper with a strange upside down V stamped on the corner appeared out of the ordinary. Blaine waved to a neighbor as he rode by on his early morning bicycle tour de Venice. She walked back into the house, grabbed a cup of coffee, sat down at the kitchen table, removed the plastic sleeve and opened the paper. To her surprise a new red smart phone covered in bubble wrap rested on a stack of papers, the top page titled Trace Foundation Birth Parent Search Contract, July 12, 2001. She picked up the blue insert and read:

Dear Blaine,

I believe these documents belong to you. I hope they find you peace and resolution in your quest to find your husband. Your new phone is equipped with unique security firewalls to protect against any monitoring, hacking, or illicit invasions, so call away, young neophyte. If you need assistance with the new device call MB, she knows how all the bells and whistles work.

Welcome to the club,

Star Trek Guy

P.S. Unfortunately, your regular newspaper delivery person crash-landed back on earth. Sadly, he fell asleep at the wheel and drove his car into the Intracoastal, but you wouldn't know anything about that. In the interim, I will be delivering your paper, minus the Loud Music.

For the next hour, Blaine painstakingly read each word, each phase on every page. A plethora of facts, dates, places and heartaches jumped out from every page. Apparently, Troy's young parents could not afford to raise a baby; the father couldn't find work, enlisted in the army, was sent to Texas for basic training and then stationed at Camp Mannheim, Germany outside of Heidelberg for three years. The

281

mother attended a high school for pregnant girls, after the birth, and graduation, transferred to Florida State College and studied art. They married when Dillon Connelly returned from Germany and moved to Bradenton in 1984 where they still reside. The mother is an artist; works out of the house and the husband is a wood carver and has a small shop in the old barn behind their home on Old Oak Place. They never had children. Blaine paused at the final sentence, held her finger on the telephone number, 941-741-3028 and froze.

"Good morning, Mommy," Brooke called out as she flung open the refrigerator door and stared. "Where are the blueberries you bought yesterday from Publix? I know they're here somewhere. I think I'll have blueberries with my cereal. Where are they?"

"In the bottom drawer with the rest of the fruits and vegetables, dear," Blaine added and went back to the documents.

"What's that you're reading, Mommy, looks important," Brooke giggled and swallowed a heaping spoonful of Rice Krispies and blueberries.

"They're daddy's papers and yes they are very important," Blaine added and picked up the documents. "Brooke, I need to talk to you about these papers."

Over a bowl of cereal, one muffin, a large glass of orange juice for Brooke and a hot cup of coffee, Blaine painstakingly explained in words and phrases an eight-year-old child would understand about her father's adoption, and that she had grandparents living in Florida. Slowly Blaine chronicled how Grandma and Grandpa Sterling while on a vacation to New York City, died in a big explosion on September 11, 2001, when the building they were in collapsed. She showed Brooke an old, yellowed hand-written letter her father found after he cleaned out his stepparents' house. The letter stated that he was adopted and his last name was Connelly. Blaine revealed how her father hired the Trace Foundation to search for his birth parents and that the papers on the table are from that company. Carefully Blaine pushed across the table the last page from the report, Brooke looked down and read:

"Mr. and Mrs. Dillon Connelly, 615 Old Oak Knoll Place, Manatee, Florida 34212, phone number-941-741-3028."

"Call them, Mommy; tell them we're looking for Daddy. Maybe he's with them? Please Mommy, please call," Brooke pleaded and reached out and grabbed her mother's hand. Blaine slowly dialed the number.

"Hello, Mr. Connelly, this is Blaine Sterling and I'm married to your son, Brandon."

Chapter Seventy-One

The solitary ring of an incoming phone call shattered the measured hum of early morning work at 1350 Ridgewood Blvd. By the third ring a hand reached over, picked up the receiver and in an authoritative tone, "Venice Police Department, Detective Beale speaking."

Beale arrived early Saturday to finish the report on his current arrest, bail bondsman Ivan "The Bear" Chernoff. Chernoff looked and in most instances acted like a wild Russian bear, with a big bushy brown head of hair, an unkempt beard, and at six-foot-four, his physical presence was menacing, equal only to his ugly disposition. *How does this man have any clients*, Beale thought as he booted up his computer.

Chernoff's current predicament with law enforcement began Friday afternoon shortly before 5:00 P.M. on Columbine Road in South Venice when *The Bear* attempted to arrest Kyle Coffin for failure to appear in court. Coffin resisted and fled in his girlfriend's red Toyota Tacoma with Chernoff in close pursuit. Along Shamrock Road, Chernoff shot out the right rear tire of the Tacoma, the vehicle limped to the corner of Shamrock and Tamiami Trail where it slammed into a utility pole, and snarled traffic for more than an hour. Coffin, a career criminal, abandoned the vehicle, ran down Shamrock and was still at large. Chernoff on the other hand had to be maced, placed in handcuffs and transported to the Venice Police Station for arraignment Monday morning. In addition to resisting arrest, Chernoff faced a shopping list of misdemeanor and felony charges, the most serious, assault with a deadly weapon, discharging a firearm in public, reckless endangerment and contributing to the destruction of public property. Most likely, any one of the felony charges would revoke the bail bondsman's license. A slight smirk crossed Beale's face as he hit the save key.

"Detective Beale, this is Lieutenant Doug Godwin of the Florida Highway Patrol, good morning, sir. Presently we are investigating a fatal accident involving an automobile and tractor-trailer at State Road 64 and County Road 674 in East Manatee. The reason for the call, a news helicopter covering the accident spotted an overturned car and a human skeleton hidden in the woods a few hundred feet from the accident scene. We ran the plates through DMV and the 2000 black Mustang GT convertible was registered to Troy Sterling of Venice, reported missing by his wife back in 2004. Your name came up as the lead investigating detective. Not much was left of the body; we sent everything to the Manatee County Medical Examiner's Office, just waiting for DNA substantiation, but it looks like it is your missing person."

"I don't believe it. That case has haunted me for eight years, couldn't catch a break. The man just disappeared. So how did Sterling's car end up in the woods?" Beale asked, "And what was he doing around Lake Manatee?"

"That intersection is tricky, especially in the rain; we get about ten calls a year about cars losing control and skidding off the road or causing an accident. Plus, a Mustang has rear-wheel-drive, may have been going too fast for the turn, lost traction and ended up in the woods. I have no idea why he was here, nothing in the car suggested work or vacation. I guess you'll have to figure that one out yourself, detective," Goodwin remarked with a slight hint of envy in his tone.

"Lieutenant, I'd like to be the official to notify Mrs. Sterling about her loss, I believe it would be less of a shock coming from me."

"No problem, it will make my job a hell of a lot easier. Good luck."

Beale hung up and went back to his computer, but he couldn't concentrate on the Chernoff report. With every key stroke, images of Blaine Sterling and her daughter pounded around in his head. How was he, after she waited eight years for her husband's safe return, could he possibly tell her that he was dead and never coming home? Beale knew the answer and he was the best person to tell her.

Chapter Seventy-Two

A misty drizzle fell as Blaine backed the car out of the garage. She looked out at the beautiful yellow Allamanda bushes planted alongside of the driveway soaking up the rain and smiled. She spent most of the morning deciding on an appropriate outfit to wear to meet Troy's parents, something not too flashy or revealing, nor dowdy or matronly-looking. Finally, she selected a blue-and-white checkerboard print dress with matching blue flip-flops. Brooke decided to wear denim shorts and her favorite polo shirt with a horse emblem embroidered over the breast pocket. A box of homemade brownies, photo album, and a jumping stallion drawing sat in the back seat, gifts for her new family.

"Mommy, the car smells like Willy Wonka's Chocolate Factory, it must be your brownies," Brooke said. "Do you think I could have one?"

"Of course not, they're for the brunch at the Connelly's. How would it look if you showed up with confectionery sugar spots all over your pretty red shirt," Blaine quipped and entered the roundabout.

Maybe it was the rain or Sunday morning church traffic, but Jacaranda Blvd. was deserted, even the MacDonald's before the Interstate had only a handful of cars parked out front. Blaine traversed the roundabout without a stop, entered I-75, set the cruise control on 65 mph, and eased into the right hand lane. The GPS programmed for Old Oak Knoll Road estimated an arrival time of 12:45 P.M., fifteen minutes prior to brunch, time to spare if she got lost or somehow Sunday traffic backed up along the interstate.

"Mommy, how long will it take to get there?" Brooke asked and turned on her MP3 player. Blaine could hear Britney Spears singing in the background before Brooke put in the ear buds and cringed.

"About forty minutes, but if it continues to rain maybe an hour, just sit back and enjoy the ride sweetie."

"Oh look, the Ellenton Mall seven miles, do you think we could stop for a minute? I need a new pair of jeans."

"Sorry, honey, we turn off the highway before the Outlet Stores. Maybe another time," Blaine replied and glanced up at the GPS for the turn.

"Exit 220 1.4 miles, turn right onto State Route 64 east," chirped the GPS. Six minutes later Blaine clicked off the cruise control and eased onto Route 64. The expanse of I-75 soon was lost and the confinement of the two-lane country road buffeted on both sides by thick woods or farmland was a little nerve-wracking with each approaching car. An occasional cow wandered out into the open to munch on grass along the wire fence that bordered the road.

Five miles down the wet slicked road, they passed the Desoto Speedway. Open on weekends, weather permitting, the stock car track loomed deserted in the rain. A favorite pastime for locals the bleacher seats on both sides of the quarter-mile straight track, cupped in puddles waited for the sun to shine through the clouds and welcome the fans.

"Country Road 675 one half mile, turn left onto Rutland Road," announced the voice from the GPS.

Blaine glanced down at the clock, 12:35, *plenty of time;* she thought as she slowed down and approached Rutland Road. "Look, Mommy, canoes for rent," Brooke blurted out. "Can we stop and look?"

"Why not, we have time; maybe they have a brochure on their canoe rentals." Blaine turned into the parking lot of the Old Myakka Fish Camp. Surrounded by a forest of ancient oak trees the fish camp and general store was a welcoming breath of old Florida hospitality. The rustic cedar shake building with its screened porch along the front looked like an illustration of a restored pioneer Cracker House from Brooke's history book.

Behind the counter was Boaty Johnson, owner and angler extraordinaire. Boaty was born and raised along Lake Manatee; he fished the Gulf, every stream, river, lake, and bay along the Florida Coast. People joked that his 20-foot ProLine logged in more fishing hours than Carter had liver pills. If Boaty wasn't repairing a boat, building a boat, talking about a boat, then he was fishing from a boat; hence the nickname *Boaty*. At seventy-two, Boaty had slowed down a bit and spent most of his time stationed at the fish camp chatting amiably with whoever walked through the front door. Blessed with a quick sense of humor, his pale blue eyes twinkled as the congenial host greeted each customer with a broad smile and big hello.

"Good morning ladies," Boaty called out as the screen door slammed shut behind Blaine and Brooke.

"Good morning. We'd like a brochure on your canoe rentals please," Blaine requested and walked up to the old weathered wooden counter at the back of the room.

"Well missy, we don't have a brochure, but the rental is $7.00 dollars an hour, $12.00 dollars for a half day or $18.00 dollars for a whole day. The canoes are right out back, fiberglass, lightweight, and the stream right out back leads directly into Lake Manatee. Fishing is good, I was out yesterday morning and caught two legal sized bass right off the point, we can rent you all the gear you'll need if you want to fish or you can just paddle around and enjoy the lake," Boaty proclaimed.

"Thank you, maybe next time we visit we'll rent a canoe and do a little fishing. By the way do you know the Connelly's? They live on Old Oak Knoll Place." Blaine asked as she punched the prices into her smart phone.

"Yes, she was an artist and he's a woodcarver or furniture maker, I believe. They have a studio just up the road about two miles away," Boaty stopped mid-sentence after noticing an alarmed expression on the face of the young woman as she and the girl walked out.

The rain stopped as Blaine pulled away from the fish camp and back onto Route 675. Brooke rolled down her window. "The air smells so fresh, take a whiff."

Blaine lowered her window and inhaled. The air tasted delicious; clean with a sweet odor of fruit, but something the old man said pushed back at her in an uncomfortable way. Was it the syntax or the inference she placed upon the words that provoked concern. *Must the artist be deceased not to be an artist or can an artist stop painting and remain an artist?*

"You're right sweetie; it has an orangey aroma, look." Ahead acres of orange trees crowded against both sides of the road. Row after row of citrus bursting with hundreds of oranges stood in straight lines like soldiers at attention. Every tree cradled hundreds of magnificent shiny orange fruit each one more appealing than the other and waiting for harvest.

"Right now, I'd love to have a tall glass of fresh squeezed orange juice, from that tree over there, how about you?" Blaine joked and gulped down an imaginary glass of juice.

The crackling of the GPS, "Old Oak Knoll Place next right," interrupted Brooke's response. Blaine made a sharp right onto a muddy dirt road and twenty feet from the cut-off observed a large wooden sign with carved forest green letters, *Connelly's Art Studio and Furniture*. A narrow gravel driveway wound to a parking lot, which fronted the entire length of the studio house. Blaine parked next to the brick walkway that lead to a small one-and-half story white farmhouse and back barn.

"Here we are, get the gifts and let's meet your new grandparents," Blaine announced with a hint of trepidation in her voice as they climbed the steps to the front door. "Look Brooke, what a magnificent wrap-around porch with a swing, white wicker chairs and tables, hanging plants and look a big pitcher of ice cold lemonade and three. . .glasses."

"Mommy, look a little green tree frog doorbell, so cool," Brooke drooled. "Can I ring it?" She steadied her finger over the button and waited.

"Of course, sweetie, be my guest."

The weathered oak door opened and there stood Troy Sterling. Blaine gasped, grabbed hold of the doorframe and stared at the tall, good-looking man. He had a linebacker's physique, piercing brown eyes, thinning blonde hair and a smile that lit up his face as he held a tray of sandwiches. She closed her eyes and began to cry.

Chapter Seventy-Three

"Hi, I'm Dillon Connelly; I see you found the house." Blaine blinked as the shock of seeing her husband waned and the realization that the person standing in front of her was not Troy, but an older man. She composed herself.

"I'm sorry you look so much like my husband Troy, that I lost my perspective for a minute. I'm Blaine Sterling and this is my daughter Brooke." She extended her hand.

"Pleased to meet you and you too, Brooke," Connelly remarked and shook both their hands. "Why don't we sit on the porch and have lunch. I made some chicken salad sandwiches, homemade potato salad, fresh squeezed lemonade, and I see you brought dessert."

No sooner had they sat, Brooke in her ever-childlike manner serendipitously sang out, "Isn't Grandma Connelly going to eat lunch?" Blaine held her breath in anticipation of the worst.

"I was going to wait 'til after lunch to tell you, but I'm sad to say she passed away six months ago—cancer. She fought a brave fight. Every month, for the past three years we drove to Moffitt in Tampa for treatment. She was in remission and we were so hopeful, but the cancer returned and last year, her tired body just gave out." Connelly murmured and looked sorrowfully into Blaine's teary eyes.

"Brooke and I are sorry for your loss we were so looking forward to meeting you both and becoming friends." Blaine reached out and touched his hand.

Slowly Mr. Connelly stood, raised his glass of lemonade and said in a cheerful voice, "No more sadness. Today we celebrate a new beginning, the start of a journey that will heal our broken hearts and unite a family once again. This joyous day will be remembered as the first of many occasions we will spend together, so let us start. *Bon Appetite!*" Three glasses touched, three hearts beat and three faces smiled as one, it was a glorious beginning.

Lunch was delicious. Blaine ate two sandwiches; a very unusual undertaking for a calorie conscience eater, but the day was unusual, maybe she was nervous or just extra hungry, either way she ate everything on her plate. Brooke, the fussiest eater in the family, even had a second helping of potato salad.

The piece de résistance was Blaine's chocolate brownies. They were devoured in minutes, and by the end of dessert, confectionery sugar spots dotted everyone's shirts. Blaine gave her daughter a wink as she brushed off the sugar. Brooke smiled and everyone in a cloud of white powder, burst out laughing and in unison brushed away the last remnants of sugar from their clothing.

After lunch, Blaine pulled out the photo album and together the three of them talked for hours. Blaine showed pictures of their wedding, Brooke growing up, vacation pictures, pictures at the beach, photos from Troy's job, pictures from her job, an eight year timeline of family pictures and finally all the documents from Trace Foundation. Tears rolled down Mr. Connelly's face because it was all true, Troy Sterling was his son and the little girl sitting across from him, his granddaughter, and the young woman holding his trembling hand was his daughter-in-law.

"We were so young; Erin and I didn't know what else to do. When I finished my tour in Germany we tried to find our baby, but everywhere we turned, no answers. We were married, moved to this farm, tried to have another child, but could not, maybe we were being punished for abandoning our little Brandon. I just don't know."

"Has Troy contacted you in the past eight years?" Blaine asked as Brooke reached in front of her and picked up the last brownie.

"No we've never heard from him. I thought you said you were his wife, don't you know where he is. . . ." and gave Blaine a quizzical glance before he gulped down the last of his lemonade.

"I don't know, he disappeared eight years ago and we haven't heard from him since," Blaine whispered, "I prayed he was visiting you, but I guess not. I'm not sure what to believe now."

"Ladies, today is not a day to be melancholy. Today is a glorious day because I have gained a lovely granddaughter and a charming daughter-in-law and you have gained a very grateful grandfather. We will find my Brandon or should I say your dear Troy; you found me didn't you? It is just a matter of time until the puzzle is completed.

Now let me show you around and Brooke, I have a very special surprise to show you. Are you ready?"

"Oh yes, I love surprises," Brooke called out and grabbed her grandfather's outstretched hand, adding, "where are we going first?"

"First stop, Grandma's studio," Connelly exclaimed as they walked into the house.

The entire right side of the home was devoted to Erin Connelly's art gallery and studio. Beautiful oil paintings of all sizes and shapes hung on the walls, rested against stands or sat on top of tables. Colorful pictures of landscapes, water fowl, sunsets, sunrises, streams and rivers, beaches, boats, a wonderful collection of rural homes and farms, historic buildings, old bridges, new bridges, and abandoned bridges. It was obvious that the artist crisscrossed the state and captured on canvas her heartfelt impression of paradise.

The back room, which was half the size of the gallery, was Erin Connelly's art studio. Filled with paints, brushes, and boxes of open art supplies, a Bohemian sense of order, compacted the small space. A long wooden art table, hand hewn by her husband, in the center of the room held stacks of unfinished drawings and sketches. Two easels on either side of the only window in the room held paintings in various stages of completion and lastly a yellow post-it-note stuck to the corner of a broken picture frame resting on the arm of an old cushioned chair read, *pick up wood glue Friday,* sat waiting for the artist to return.

On the other side of the main hallway was a tiny bathroom, pinched under the wooden staircase that led to second floor bedrooms and bath. Left of the staircase was a small cozy wood paneled sitting room, decorated in an early American motif, which Mr. and Mrs. Connelly designed and built. Colonial style tables, chairs, cabinets, paintings, and a hand carved wooden mantel over a rustic stone fireplace created a warm inviting feeling inside the room.

The final room and most striking on the first floor was the kitchen, a large sun-drenched room with walls of windows and bright light. An oasis of culinary artistry, the room was filled with state of the art appliances, a pro-style Viking range, a Wolf wall oven, Bosch gas cook top with wall-chimney hood, Dacor microwave, Thermador built-in stainless-steel steam oven, stainless-steel refrigerator/freezer, and dishwasher—all perfectly crafted into mahogany custom build cabinets built to the precise dimensions of the room. Antique wood flooring and a 16-foot dining table from reclaimed timber off an old barn complimented the speckled green granite countertops that held a double-bowl country sink and miles and miles of space for the latest cooking gadgets. It was apparent that someone loved to cook and entertain in this room.

"Wow what a kitchen, I could live in this room all day. Who does all the cooking?" Blaine asked and turned around to view the entire room again.

"Me, I was a cook in the army, strictly meat and potatoes, assembly line cooking German style, but over the years I developed a love for the art of cooking and just continued to cultivate my cooking skills. Tell you what; I will prepare you a special meal next time you visit. Have you ever had Chateaubriand?"

"Chatcan. . .what's a call-it, I can't even pronounce it," Brooke blurted out.

"You'll love it, I'll make a tasty Béarnaise sauce, some potatoes au gratin and for vegetables Parmesan-roasted broccoli. Only on one condition," Mr. Connelly announced.

"What's that, grandpa?" Brooke chirped out.

"Your mother must promise to bring the brownies, confectionery sugar, and all." Everyone laughed and gave their shirts one last brushing. "Okay, now for the surprise," Grandpa Connelly added, grabbed Brooke's hand and led them out through the back door towards the old barn.

Chapter Seventy-Four

The red weathered barn at the end of the driveway was a hulk of a building, twice the size of the farmhouse, its rusted tin roof, splintered white wood framed window and a large plank sliding gate door the length of a two-car garage stood as a reminder of a bye-gone agrarian era. From the outside, the old building was a sad sight; it cried out for a fresh coat of paint, or at the very least, a woodcarver to repair the loose and missing planks that supported the structure.

"Brooke can you help me slide open the door," Connelly called out as he unlocked the metal hasp that secured the door, "grab the large handle at the end of the door." Together they walked the door open until it jerked to a stop against a rock at the corner of the barn. Connelly walked inside, switched on the lights and waited as Blaine and Brooke stood in the entrance mesmerized by the magnificent sight before them. The cavernous room painted a fresh coat of white stabled a kaleidoscope of colorful carousel horses in various stages of completion. Bucking horses, jumping, kicking, and horses standing at attention with heads held high stationed around the entire barn waited majestically for the woodcarver to return. There were horses with long flowing manes and short stumpy tails, horses with short-cropped manes and long sweeping tails, glittering horses painted black, brown, white, red, blue, yellow, pink, orange, and green, all adorned with silver bridles, gold buckles, new leather straps, brilliant brown eyes, and fiery red nostrils. Throughout the barn pictures of horses hung from ancient wood honed rafters, along the back wall scale drawings of legs, heads, hooves and other body parts of different breeds dotted bulletin boards in the six separate work stations. Three long wooden tables in the middle of the room held blocks of a half carved hind leg, a head, or front hoof, each project in various stages of completion would eventually transform tired old carousel horses into magical steeds.

"Well what do you think Brooke? I noticed the horse on your shirt and love your beautiful horse drawing, so what do you think of my workshop?" Connelly repeated, but with an impish smile.

"This place is awesome. The horses are so beautiful. They look alive. Can I touch one Grandpa? Please."

"Sure you can and if you like you can even ride *Black Beauty*, he's completed, maybe your mother will take your picture? Follow me." Brooke held on to Connelly's hand and together the three zigzagged through a maze of horses until they came upon a majestic gleaming jumping stallion standing on a platform. With hooves in the air, head held high, eyes blazing in the light, muscles taut and every buckle glistening, *Black Beauty* came alive. In Brooke's eyes, the carousel horse was alive.

"Here he is Brooke, *Black Beauty*, what do you think?" Connelly exclaimed and helped boost her up onto the shinny brown saddle.

"He's magnificent Grandpa. Mommy, take my picture please, I want to e-mail it to Morgan, she loves horses, too."

"Okay sweetie smile. Dillon, these horses are breathtaking. What are you planning to do with them?" Blaine asked and snapped another picture with her smart phone, this time with Grandpa Connelly and immediately e-mailed it to Mb.

"Eight months ago while online searching for a woodworking tool that I needed to help remove paint from an old desk, a pop-up ad from the Town of Greenport, Long Island tweaked my interest. They wanted to contract with a woodcarver to restore their antique carousel horses and make the carousel the centerpiece of their Bay Front promenade. The project looked intriguing and I needed the work, so that day I e-mailed them my application, photographs of my work and the interior of the barn. Two weeks later a congratulatory letter from the Mayor of Greenport, a contract and a check arrived in the mail. The following week, to the chagrin of my neighbors, thirty-nine boxes of carousel horses arrived by truck and as you can see I am now lovingly restoring these splendid creatures to their original glory."

"What a noble undertaking, your craftsmanship is exquisite and appears painstakingly intricate, every little detail on the horse jumps out at you. How long will it take to restore all of them?" Blaine asked and ran her hand along the horse's glossy front leg.

Connelly rubbed his forehead and looked over at Blaine, "The contract stipulates an extremely rigid timeline, nineteen horses completed the first year and the remaining twenty the second year, along with progress reports and photographs every six months. Some horses only need a sanding and a fresh coat of paint, or should I say five coats of paint, other horses need a complete restoration job, but I love working with wood and to see the smiles on the faces of children when they ride on a carousel horse is priceless. Just look at Brooke."

"Oh, look at the time. I think we should be leaving, tomorrow is a school day for Brooke and I have the early shift at the park. Dillon, we had a wonderful time today and I hope this is a new beginning for the family. I believe this is what Troy wanted and I know this is what Brooke and I hope will happen."

"Today was a memorable day, Blaine, I also hope this is the start of a new family," Connelly gushed as he lifted Brooke off the horse. "Brooke you must come back and help paint these horses. How about in two weeks?"

"Can we mommy, can we?" Brooke pleaded and grabbed her mother's hand.

"I don't see why not, sweetie," Blaine replied as Brooke threw her arms around her mother and gave her a big hug.

"Well, I guess we have a date. That gives me plenty of time to prepare a meal fit for a king, or should I say fit for a queen and my little princess." Connelly walked them to their car.

Chapter Seventy-Five

Saturday was cleaning day at the Sterling house, after an early morning breakfast the two began their chores. Brooke dusted, emptied trash baskets, and cleaned her own room. Blaine vacuumed, did laundry, and cleaned her room. Brooke had just finished dusting the dining room blinds when a white Crown Victoria pulled into the driveway. Two men stepped out and walked towards the front door. "Mommy two men are at the door, I think one of them is Detective Beale," Brooke called out and lowered the blinds.

"Don't answer the door, I'll be there in a minute," Blaine said, turning on the washing machine.

Blaine pulled open the door. "Hello, Ms. Sterling, I don't know if you remember me, but I'm Detective Justin Beale and this is my partner Stan Hordowski. May we come in?"

"Hello Detective Beale, it's good to see you again. Hello Detective Hordowski, please come in," Blaine replied and led them into the living room. "Have a seat." She motioned to the two chairs opposite the couch, "Can I get you gentlemen a cup of coffee? I just brewed a fresh pot."

"That would be appreciated," Beale remarked, "I take mine black, thanks."

"Nothing for me thanks," Hordowski said, "I'm trying to cut down on caffeine, makes me jumpy."

"Oh yes, the last thing we need is a jumpy police detective jumping around Venice all day, makes for a very jumpy public," Blaine quipped and disappeared into the kitchen.

Hordowski shook his head "Where did that come from?" He gave Beale a quick look.

"I warned you about her," Beale whispered and stood.

Blaine returned with two cups, handed one to Beale, sat down on the couch next to Brooke and took a careful sip from her steaming hot cup of java. She felt a bit uncomfortable; Beale's customary swagger was missing, replaced with an awkward silence and a sympathetic stare.

Hordowski on the other hand fidgeted with the manila envelope on his lap and attempted to soothe the situation with an occasional smile.

Beale cleared his throat, leaned forward and said in a faraway voice, "Blaine may we speak to you alone? We have some information that may be too graphic for your daughter to hear. It's regarding your husband."

Blaine almost dropped her coffee cup when she heard the word *husband,* but quickly recovered and answered, "No, I want her to hear what you have to say. It's been eight long years; she has a right to hear what you have to say."

"If you insist; I'll try to be as sensitive as I can," he said, and opened the envelope. Slowly Beale explained that last week he received a call from Florida Highway Patrol, that while investigating a fatal accident at the intersection of State Road 64 and County Road 674 in East Manatee, a news helicopter spotted an upside down car in the woods a few hundred feet from the accident scene. Upon investigation, authorities concluded that the vehicle, a 2000 black Mustang, belonged to her husband.

They also found the skeletal remains of a human body, which they sent to the Manatee Medical Examiner's office for identification and DNA results determined that the remains belonged to Troy Sterling. "A copy of the final report is in the envelope." Beale handed Blaine the envelope.

"Oh my God, he was going to meet his birth parents; they live on Old Oak Knoll Place, right past that intersection. That was the message eight years ago, his parents name and address. Brooke, I'm so sorry." The two hugged and rocked back and forth on the couch as tears rolled down their faces.

"We are so sorry for your loss. Your husband's remains were sent to Farley's Funeral home in Venice, the coroner's report and impound location on your husband's car are all in the folder. If I can help in any way, please call, I left my card and cell phone number in the folder." The two detectives let themselves out.

Chapter Seventy-Six

There had never been a funeral service held in the park, unless you count the one for Squeaky, the long-time resident Gopher Tortoise. Squeaky died five years ago, old age, a Friends worker and retired zoologist Dale Smith reported. Squeaky's burrow was alongside the Nature Center and every morning the tortoise ambled over to the front porch and made squeaking sounds until some benevolent camper left a piece of lettuce or fruit for his morning meal. A taxidermist from Nokomis preserved Squeaky; she estimated the tortoise was about sixty years old. A small gathering of campers, Friends of the Park, and park employees dedicated a display to Squeaky, a memorial to their beloved reptile. Now park employees and visitors can view Squeaky leaving his burrow, no doubt in search of a tasty morsel, from one of the Nature Center's wildlife display cases.

For two days, an endless procession of trucks, cars and vans drove in and out of the park in preparation for the memorial service for Troy. Blaine selected the site, the Campfire Circle, a secluded amphitheatre surrounded by towering old oaks and lush palm trees, a place she and Troy often visited. The funeral home orchestrated all the arrangements, which included a brilliant array of flowers, wreaths, and plants circling the entire amphitheater with startling color. White torch lanterns lit the pathway down to the Campfire Circle and tiny white lights adorned the trees along the perimeter of the amphitheater. Pictures of Troy, Blaine, Brooke, his birth, and adoptive family adorned a natural wood altar along the back of the Circle and in the center of the stage, a small wooden table beautifully carved by Dillon Connelly from a single log held the silver urn with Troy Sterling's remains.

Friends and co-workers filled all the log seats, even campers and day guests stood in the back to listen and pay their respects. The prayers, eulogy, and speeches spoke of Troy's work ethic, his kindness, and devotion to Blaine. Most narratives were upbeat, even humorous at times, but most importantly, the outpouring of emotion for her husband helped Blaine endure the grief. Towards the end of the

Service, Brooke leaned over and whispered in her grandfather's ear, "Grandpa, please don't leave mommy and me."

Dillon held her hand and whispered back, "No honey, I'll never leave you or your mother. Anyway I need you to help paint the horses." They smiled and held hands throughout the speeches.

After the service, the guests walked back to the waiting park tram for the ride back to the Nature Center and a small reception. Blaine was last to leave, a final visit with her husband alone in their favorite place allowed her a private time to say good-bye and hold him close to her heart. Walking up the torch lit pathway to the tram Blaine's thoughts were of the day. She was in a euphoric dream-state as she stepped out into the road. Suddenly, a black truck raced out from behind the waste disposal area and drove straight towards her, missing her by inches. The SUV jerked to the right kicking up gravel and sped down road into the campground. Instinctively Blaine jumped back and tumbled to the ground. It was a miracle she was not hit. Screams rang out at the fleeing truck as a crowd rushed across the road to help Blaine

"Are you hurt?" Mrs. Travers asked as Lou Bravo picked Blaine off the ground and held her steady.

"I'm fine, was that guy blind?" Blaine answered and brushed herself off. "Never saw it coming; did anyone get a license plate number?"

"I got a partial number, V463, a black Hummer, and it had some kind of gold wiggly line along the side of the truck," Ken Brecht called out.

"It was a gold lightning bolt and it ran down the entire side of the car. Shouldn't be too hard for the cops to find that truck," another guest remarked.

As they rode back to the Nature Center, Blaine closed her eyes. There was something familiar about a black Hummer with lightning bolts. She tried to recall where she saw that truck before. *Then she remembered and cringed!*

Made in the USA
Charleston, SC
01 November 2013